"This is the kind of truth you can only tell in fiction, otherwise lives would be lost . . . It's a must-read if you want to know how we'll be fighting our next war."

Robert Baer, veteran CIA case officer
and author of *See No Evil* and *Sleeping with the Devil*

"Better than Clancy at his best. It's like getting on a galloping horse and just letting him run. SOAR shows how the face of war is changing."

Lt. Gen. Sam Wilson, USA (Ret.),
former director of DIA
and a godfather of Delta Force

"[Weisman] knows that future wars will be nothing like the past. No one will put this down. If you have a seat belt, fasten it."

Richard Perle, former chairman of the
Defense Policy Board and former
U.S. Asst. Secretary of Defense

"In an age when you can watch war up close on television 24/7, it still takes John Weisman to bring you deep inside the black op."

Sherry Sontag, coauthor of *Blind Man's Bluff*

SOAR

A BLACK OPS MISSION

JOHN WEISMAN

AVON BOOKS
An Imprint of HarperCollinsPublishers

This is a work of fiction. Names, characters, places, and incidents are products of the author's imagination or are used fictitiously and are not to be construed as real. Any resemblance to actual events, locales, organizations, or persons, living or dead, is entirely coincidental.

AVON BOOKS
An Imprint of HarperCollins*Publishers*
10 East 53rd Street
New York, New York 10022-5299

Copyright © 2003 by John Weisman
Excerpt from *Jack in the Box* copyright © 2004 by John Weisman
The first two chapters of *Jack in the Box* appeared in the August 2002 *Playboy* magazine in a slightly different form, under the title "A Day in the Country."
Map by David Lindroth
ISBN: 0-06-052410-3
www.avonbooks.com

First Avon Books paperback printing: June 2004
First William Morrow hardcover printing: August 2003

Avon Trademark Reg. U.S. Pat. Off. and in Other Countries, Marca Registrada, Hecho en U.S.A.
HarperCollins® is a registered trademark of HarperCollins Publishers Inc.

Printed in the U.S.A.

10 9 8 7 6 5 4 3 2 1

To the memory of
Colonel Charlie A. Beckwith, USA (Ret.),
Soldier, Man o' Warsman, and Patriot

and

To "Rowdy" and "Loner"
Warriors
who are still fighting to keep
Americans safe

He who will not risk cannot win.
—Admiral John Paul Jones, 1791

Contents

SOAR

A BLACK OPS
MISSION

The First Forty Hours
SNAFU

1

West of Yengisu, Xinjiang Autonomous Region, China.
1030 Hours Local Time.

SAM PHILLIPS LOOKED BACK across the tussocky desert
landscape toward the tan speck that was the antique Toyota
land cruiser, making sure for the sixth time in just under
two hours that it still sat concealed behind a ragged row of
poplar trees, far enough off the sparsely traveled two-lane
highway to render it invisible to any traffic. He raised a pair
of lightweight field glasses that hung on a soft nylon strap
around his neck and rotated the knurled center knob until
the boxy 4×4's driver, whose name was Shoazim, came into
focus. For a quarter of a minute or so, Sam spied on the
bony Uighur.

He had rented Shoazim and his vehicle in Ürümqi, the
autonomous region's capital city. Like all official guides,
Shoazim reported at the very least to the local police, or
even more likely, to some department of MSS, the Chinese
Ministry of State Security. And so Sam had kept the man at
arm's length. If there was something sensitive to discuss, he
did it in private, or in French. Still, the guide had been helpful, negotiating their way onto a number of sites Sam's
three-man crew videoed for the travelogue he was ostensi-
bly making.

Sam was pleased to see Shoazim leaning up against the near side of the vehicle, omnipresent cigarette between his lips, his right knee cocked against a tire, his right hand twirling the end of his long, stringy mustache—all body language that indicated boredom. Though compact, the glasses were powerful enough so that Sam could watch Shoazim exhale a plume of smoke from one of the strong black tobacco cigarettes whose nasty stench permeated the Toyota, even though they always drove with all the windows open, even at night when the temperature dropped below freezing.

It was in the low sixties now. Despite the mild weather, Sam was sweating. Between the unremittingly blue sky and the warm morning sun, both his shirt and the rucksack he carried were wet clear through, and the dampness had spread to the waistband of his cargo pants. They were all sweating, the four of them, struggling under the weight of the video gear, which was made all the heavier because of the nuclear sensors concealed within the camera's bulky tripod legs.

The sensors were state-of-the-art, developed by a joint Department of Energy–No Such Agency task force. There were three, and they had to be positioned in a gentle, precise curve at two-hundred-meter intervals to do the job for which they'd been designed. They'd been fabricated out of a space-age nonmagnetic titanium-scandium compound that was harder and lighter than steel and more durable than carbon fiber. They were self-powered, and could operate for years without recharging. And they were programmed to send their readings in secure, coded microbursts to a trio of National Reconnaissance Office SPARROW HAWK stealth satellites launched covertly during one of NASA's shuttle missions in 2000. The three invisible NRO birds sat in geosynchronous orbit twenty-two thousand miles above the earth. They were already receiving signals from other covert sensor pods, although Sam wasn't cleared high enough to know how many had been inserted, or where they might be located.

Sam dropped the glasses back onto his chest, crested the scrub grass of the dune, and made his way along the far side. The soft padded canvas case holding the video camera banged against his right side as he lurched precariously down a steep embankment of packed sand, rocks, and brushwood to catch up to the other three. At the bottom, he took a long hard look at the next series of dunes, which were taller, rockier, and more heavily brambled than the ones they'd just crossed, listened to the protestations coming from his body, and held up his hand to call a momentary halt. "Time to check our position."

"What's wrong, Pops, you need another break?" The sensor tech, whose real name was Marty Kaszeta, even though his Irish passport identified him as Martin Charles Quinn, was a mere twenty-six. He flaunted his youth, Sam thought, quite unmercifully, including the maddening way he insisted on wearing his long-billed Tottenham Hotspurs cap backward. Kaz's right shoulder was wet under the tripod case strap. But he'd set the pace for the whole group, even though his load was almost thirty-five pounds heavier than anyone else's.

So Sam chose to ignore the dig. Instead, he untied the blue-and-white kerchief from around his neck, exhaled loudly, and wiped at his face with the salty wet cotton triangle. He'd always considered himself in pretty good physical shape. But five kliks of packed sand and scrub had just proved otherwise, hadn't it? God, he was bushed. He reached around and dug into his rucksack for one of the three half-liter bottles of water he carried, took a long, welcome pull of the warm liquid, and consoled himself with the fact that he was so wiped because he was the Team Elder. The official CIA geezer.

The communicator, Dick Campbell, a sheep-dipped Marine captain who'd been TDY'd[1] from Langley's paramilitary division (looking far too Semper Fi, which gave Sam some anxiety), had just turned thirty-one. Sam liked to tell him *he* couldn't remember being thirty-one. At least the lanky, team security officer—his name was Chris Wyman but he liked to be called X-Man—was approaching adulthood: Wyman was thirty-five—three years Sam's junior. He had the low-key approach to life you'd expect from a kid who'd grown up in Aspen, spending more time on the slopes than in the classroom. But Wyman was sharp, and thorough, and didn't miss much. He'd done time in enough hardship posts—a countersurveillance assignment against the Iranians in Baku and a black program against al-Qaeda in Pakistan among them—for Sam to know he was good at his job.

Of course, it didn't help Sam's mental state to see X-Man wasn't even breathing hard as he paused to scan the dunes for surveillance, then lifted his field glasses to make sure they weren't being tracked by a UAV.[2] He finally caught Wyman's eye, which was hard to do given the Oakleys. "I hate people like you, y'know."

The security officer's long, tanned face cracked a smile. "When we get home, I'll wangle you an AARP membership at my gym, Sam."

"When we get home," said Sam, double-checking to make sure the screw top was tight then dropping the water bottle back into the rucksack, "I'm hanging up my spurs. Gonna put in for a desk job. I'm getting way too old for this crap."

---

1. Military acronym for temporary duty.
2. Unmanned Aerial Vehicle. A pilotless drone surveillance aircraft.

Kaz snorted derisively. "You, Pops? Never. You're a gumshoe. You just ain't the desk-jockey type."

The kid was correct. At thirty-eight, Sam had been a CIA case officer for just over thirteen years—and served overseas for all but twenty months of that time. He'd begun his career with sixteen months of Pashto language training followed by a two-year posting under consular cover in Islamabad. From there, he'd volunteered for an eight-month immersion course in Kazakh, after which he'd taken on a three-year assignment no other case officer wanted: running the one-man station in Almaty.

Later, there had been tours in Paris, where he'd worked as the Central Asia branch chief, followed by two and a half years in Dushanbe, the Tajik capital. There, he'd managed to pick up some Dari, as well as conversational Russian, bits of Uighur, and enough of what he called kitchen Mandarin to listen to Radio Beijing and understand about a quarter of it. He'd also recruited a productive network of Tajiks and a rare Russian—a lieutenant colonel assigned to the 201st Mechanized Infantry Division.

Sam Phillips had natural people skills and learned and retained languages the way others quickly absorb music or art. His low-key approach to life, wry sense of humor, and the instinctive ability to read nuance and adapt to culturally unfamiliar surroundings made him a shrewd, capable operative. Indeed, Sam preferred working alone in back alleys from Bishkek to Berlin regardless of the potential for risk. It was preferable to what he knew from experience to be a more hostile environment than any denied area overseas: the political minefield at the George Bush Center for Intelligence at Langley, Virginia.

Which is why it was absolutely true he'd never willingly leave the streets for a desk. Not that he'd ever be asked to. In fact, if you looked at the situation coldly, at the relatively

young age of thirty-eight Sam Phillips was considered
something of a dinosaur at the digitized, computerized,
techno-dependent Central Intelligence Agency of the early
twenty-first century. He was seen as a throwback, a foot soldier slogging willingly through the Wilderness of Mirrors.
In the flexi-time culture of latte drinkers and retirement-
portfolio builders, Sam was the odd man out: the sort of
old-fashioned case officer who was professionally indiffer-
ent to creature comforts, identifiable food, and other
niceties. Sam Phillips existed completely, entirely, totally,
to spot, assess, and recruit spies. And if it required that his
living conditions be less than no-star, and his backup nonexistent, well then, so be it. He'd get the job done anyway.

Sam's corridor file back at Langley pegged him negatively as a risk taker, a cowboy who too often pushed the
edge of the operational envelope. Still, he had a reputation
for success in the field. In Langley's op-resistant culture,
which had persisted even after the 9/11 intelligence debacle,
the loss of agents through carelessness, neglect, or simple
inattention to detail all seemed to be grounds for promotion
instead of termination. But Sam Phillips could say—and
did, with considerable pride—that over his decade plus of
street work, he'd never lost a single one of *his* agents.

That kind of rep carried some weight. If not with the present crop of technocrat panjandrums occupying the seventh-
floor executive suites, at least with the small remaining cadre
of streetwise geezers who, like Sam, believed that satellites
capable of reading a license plate from two hundred miles up
were the solution to intelligence gathering only if you were
prone to being attacked by license plates. Uncovering your
adversary's capabilities and intentions, Sam Phillips was
unshakably convinced, required human-sourced intelligence. That meant putting your body on the line.

But Sam had also realized early in his career that risk

taking did not mean the same as foolishness. A history and language major at Berkeley, he'd first read about Alexander Suvorov, the eighteenth-century Russian military tactician and philosopher, as a sophomore. Later, as a greenhorn case officer in his late twenties, he'd reread Suvorov, so as to better understand the intricacies of the Russian military mind.

Sam's reading may have begun as an intellectual exercise to help him in making recruitments. It ended, however, with his enthusiastic acceptance of Suvorov's strategic doctrine as the basis for his own intelligence-gathering operations. He took many of the field marshal's dictums ("Speed is essential; haste harmful" and "Train hard, fight easy" were two of his favorites) to heart, and consciously employed them in the field. And so, what his deskbound superiors often thought to be impetuous, seat-of-the-pants decisions were in point of fact meticulously designed, boldly executed operations that resulted in the obtaining of valuable intelligence for the United States.

Sam's capacity for audaciousness coupled with careful planning was a critical factor in his current role as team leader—at least so far as the three volunteers traveling with him were concerned. That was because SIE-1, which was Langley's bureaucratic acronym for the four-man Sino Insertion Element No. 1 Sam led, was composed of NOCs.[3]

That meant Sam and his team entered China using real but nonetheless bogus British, Irish, and Canadian passports issued under aliases. They'd posed as a four-man independent TV crew shooting an "Outward Bound Trekking along the Silk Road" video for a London-based travel company that wanted to expand its "extreme sports" tour packages. Yes, their travel documents had survived the

---

3. Non-Official Cover intelligence officers.

scrutiny of Turkish, Azeri, Uzbek, Kazakh, and Chinese border guards and other officials. And yes, if anyone had called the accommodation addresses and telephone numbers in London, Dublin, or Toronto that were printed on their business cards, drivers' licenses, credit cards, and other miscellaneous wallet detritus and pocket litter, all of which had been provided by Langley's document wizards, the team's bona fides would have been authenticated beyond a doubt. But all of that didn't lessen the knowledge that in plain English, nonofficial cover meant they were working without a net.

Their objective, precisely expressed in National Security Directive 16226, which had been signed by the president of the United States nine weeks previously, was, quote: *"For officers of the Central Intelligence Agency and/or other officials of the United States government to covertly insert and position at a specific location inside the People's Republic of China a technical means for ensuring that all the conditions of the current-draft nuclear weapons agreement between the United States and the People's Republic of China will be met."*

The word *covertly* meant that for Sam Phillips and his team there was no diplomatic immunity. There was no Geneva convention. If they got caught, it was prison or summary execution. Full stop. End of story. Like the characters in the *Mission: Impossible* movies, the administration would deny any responsibility, etc., etc. Except what Sam and his crew were doing wasn't Hollywood. It was real—and the consequences could prove fatal.

The operation was also complicated by the fact that there were four of them. Typically, case officers are solitary workers, meeting their agents only after taking exhaustive steps to ensure they have not been compromised by the opposition. NOCs generally work singly. Not always: sometimes, a pair of Honeymooners—DO[4] slang for husband-and-wife NOC teams—were assigned if the mission required it. A four-man covert infiltration crew was a rarity these days, especially a team like SIE-1, which had been assembled for this one critical mission. The fact that he, Kaz, X-Man, and Dick hadn't worked together before made Sam a little nervous.

But the four of them gelled remarkably well during the two weeks of mission prep they'd been allowed before assembling in London to pick up their equipment and commence their odyssey through Ankara, Baku, Bishkek, and points east. And Sam had watched with a critical eye as they made their way from Almaty, aggressively bargained themselves through the organized thievery that is Kazakh passport control, and crossed into the free trade zone just outside the ramshackle Chinese border post east of Khorgos. For kids who hadn't had his years of training or street experience, the trio had handled themselves like real pros.

They had been diligent about their tradecraft. China is what is known in the intelligence business as a denied area. For SIE-1 it meant that even in Western China, two time zones from Beijing,[5] the *Guojia Anquan Bu,* or Ministry of State Security, still maintained aggressive technical surveillance on foreign visitors. So, Sam and his security officer, Chris Wyman, took it for granted that any hotel room they were given contained listening devices and even perhaps video. That meant they had to be careful about how they spoke and acted, even in private.

---

4. Directorate of Operations, the CIA's clandestine spy service.
5. All China runs officially on Beijing time. But most of the provinces operate on their own local schedules, which reflect their geographic position vis-à-vis Universal (Greenwich Mean) Time. Xinjiang's "unofficial" clocks run two hours behind Beijing's.

They'd been observant, too, noting the augmented military activity in the cities. Sam had been briefed on that before he'd left Washington. It was an additional operational wrinkle to fret over—that they might be compromised not because of Chinese suspicion about covert American operations but because of a recent increase of separatist violence in Xinjiang, to which Sam coyly referred in a cartoon Boston accent as *terra irredenta*. The past few months had seen an increase in ambushes, kidnappings, and even the occasional car bomb.

Indeed, Sam's preinsertion research showed that Chinese-based Islamists were currently giving refuge and support to a panoply of terrorist organizations that ran the gamut from the complex and sophisticated, like al-Qaeda, to smaller, hit-and-run splinter groups such as ETIM—the Eastern Turkistan Islamic Movement—or the Islamic Movement of Uzbekistan.

ETIM was an unknown quantity. But Sam had worked against the IMU in Dushanbe. Despite the specificity of its name, IMU guerrillas had once ranged over a region that spread from Chechnya to the Mongolian border; and from Afghanistan through all the old Soviet "Stan" republics. In the 1990s the IMU had been well financed, supported by funding and weapons from Iran, and overt support from the Taliban. CIA's counterterrorism analysts estimated that it had made millions more through smuggling, drug dealing, and kidnapping operations. But since 2002, the IMU had gone into a decline. Many of the group's leaders, including its military chief, a former Soviet paratrooper named Juma Namangani, had been killed during America's campaign in Afghanistan.

According to the CIA analysis Sam read in London, the IMU "currently presents no credible threat." But Sam knew from experience how flawed Langley's research could be

these days. And so he did his own—and unearthed among
other documents a broadside issued by a Tajik Islamist
group in North London, hinting that a nucleus of IMU
hard-liners had recently forged an alliance with the Uighur
separatists of Xinjiang Autonomous Region. If true, that
meant another bunch of no-goodniks to worry about during
SIE-1's insertion. At least, Sam rationalized, the IMU's
current numbers would be in the hundreds, not thousands.

"**LET'S SEE** where the hell we are." Sam unlatched the Velcro flap of his deep thigh pocket and fumbled past the pock-
etknife and the spare change until his hand closed around
the Visor Handspring with its attached GPS module. He
pulled the PDA out, snapped the cover off, switched it on,
and watched as the screen came to life.

The Visor was indicative of how cavalier Langley was
these days when it came to supporting operations that put
human beings on the ground in denied areas. The damn
thing had been handed to him in London with dead batteries. If he hadn't taken the time to test it before stowing it,
they'd be sitting out here with no way of knowing where the
hell they were.

It was lucky they had the GPS, because the Agency's clas-
sified maps certainly hadn't helped get them where they had
to be. The Western China branch chief in London—a white-
haired former executive secretary from the moribund Division of Administration whose London posting was her first
overseas assignment—had actually demanded that Sam sign
a security document before handing over six three-foot-by-
four-foot tactical charts stamped SECRET, on which Sam
would plot the team's infiltration and exfil, as well as contingency plans in case they were discovered in flagrante delicto.

Except, after Sam had spent seven precious hours working with the highly detailed 1:100,000-scale documents

(and been amazed at how primitive the road system appeared, given the escalating number of tourist buses working their way along the Silk Road these days), he happened to look at the fine print on the bottom left-hand corner of one of them. It was dated 1985. Then he checked the others. None was more current than 1992. The bloody things were a decade-plus old. Obsolete, outdated, and useless. So he'd summoned the branch chief to the safe house, returned the maps, and shredded his release form. Then he checked the phone book, located a travel-book store on Long Acre, and hiked the mile and a half from his hotel to Covent Garden.

Sixty pounds sterling later, Sam had purchased half a dozen commercial road maps and Lonely Planet guidebooks that showed all the new highways. (Like, for example, the very one they'd used this morning, which had originally been built in 1998 as a north-south military conduit and was nowhere to be found on the CIA's oh-so-secret chart.)

SAM CHECKED the handheld's screen. They were within a half mile of the coordinates he'd programmed into the GPS unit.

He took a reading, showed the screen to Kaz, who, fist clenched, pumped the warm air with his right arm. "Right on course, Pops."

"That's the good news." Sam swung the camera off the ground and onto his shoulder. "The bad news is that we've got to head southeast," he said, his jaw thrust toward the intimidating dunes towering over them like tsunami. Then his voice took on a forcedly optimistic tone. "What the hell, it shouldn't take us more than an hour."

The White House Residence.
2331 Hours Local Time.

PRESIDENT PETER DEWITT FORREST set his mug of de-caf down on a coaster emblazoned with the presidential seal and turned to face his national security adviser as she came into the residence's sitting room.

"Johnny, give us a minute, will you?" He waved the Secret Service agent out, waiting until the door closed behind the young man's broad back. Then he rolled his shoulders and cracked his left-hand pinkie knuckle joint. "What have we heard from the team, Monica?"

Monica Wirth, who'd gone on to Georgetown law school after eight years as a Ph.D. CIA analyst, had worked on national security issues for Pete Forrest since he'd been elected governor of Virginia back in the mid-1990s. So she read his body language well enough to know that whenever the Leader of the Free World tried to mask tension, he cracked the finger joints on his left hand.

"Nothing, Mr. President. We've heard nothing because they're maintaining radio silence until the job's completed."

"But they've been sending progress reports all along, haven't they?"

"Yes, sir."

"So why can't they update us now?"

"They've been using steganography to throw the Chinese off-track, Mr. President."

Pete Forrest blinked. "Steganography?"

"The communications officer has been sending digital pictures to an accommodation address in London on a daily basis," Wirth explained. "A sort of visual 'progress report' on the travelogue they're supposed to be making. The team's reports are embedded in the images. That's steganography."

"Hmm." Pete Forrest pulled on his left thumb until the joint popped. "But when they're in the clear, Monica . . ."

"When they get to Yutian they'll telephone the accommodation address in London and acknowledge."

The knuckle joint of the president's middle finger popped audibly. "But they do have a phone, don't they?"

"Yes, Mr. President, they're carrying a cell phone. But the team leader doesn't want to use it until they're in the clear."

"So we won't get word until they're where? Yuti-something, wasn't it you just said?"

The National Security Council staff had, as always, made sure she was as prepared as he. "Yu*tian*, Mr. President." She took a quick peek at the three-by-five card in her left palm then slipped it into the pocket of her black pantsuit jacket. "It's an old caravan way station on the Silk Road."

Craack. "How long before they get there?"

His apprehension was contagious, and she began to pace behind one of the two facing Empire couches—four nervous steps followed by a quick reverse of course. "Tomorrow, sometime. They're scheduled to implant the devices today. Then it's a three-hundred-kilometer trip south on that new connector road, followed by another hundred on the main east-west road. And of course they have to stop and shoot video from time to time."

"Video," he repeated absently, and cracked the ring finger on his left hand.

The president had been anxious about this operation from the very start. Not that he'd ever wavered. The mission was critical to the nation's immediate national security interests. *Immediate* because in just over six weeks he was scheduled to sign a nuclear treaty at a summit in Beijing. But there was no way Pete Forrest was going to affix his signature to the document unless there was a way to verify beyond a shadow of a doubt that the Chinese weren't cheating by setting off ultra-low-level tests deep within the hundreds of miles of tunnels they'd dug over the last half century in the sandy flats around the Lop Nur test site's prehistoric dry lake bed.

For maddening reasons Pete Forrest couldn't begin to fathom, none of the National Reconnaissance Office's current generation of satellites had the capability to distinguish an explosion that measured less than half a kiloton from a seismic anomaly. The president had a hard time with that, because a half-kiloton explosion is the equivalent of blowing a million pounds of TNT all at once. Which, as he had complained loudly to the director of central intelligence, who'd presented him with the bad news, makes for one hell of a seismic anomaly.

Worse, he'd been told there was no way NRO would be able to get an ultra-low-range-capable bird launched in less than three years. The existing ground sensors, which were located on the high mountain ranges of the Kazakh-Chinese border, had been designed to record the twenty- to eighty-kiloton underground tests the Chinese had performed in the mid- and late 1990s—tests that all measured 4.5 or above on the Richter seismic scale.

But according to the latest analysis, the current Chinese nuclear program was being directed more toward mini-yield tactical weapons than multi-megaton warheads. Which meant that the United States was essentially blind if Beijing decided to secretly test tactical nukes of a half kiloton or less. The president had concluded the only way to guarantee the Chinese weren't cheating was to insert new ground sensors close enough to the tunnels to pick up the faintest of seismic readings emanating from the Lop Nur test site.

Which required a human element to infiltrate across

China's border and place the devices covertly. And so, a little over two months ago, he'd signed the finding that set the operation in motion, even though he knew he'd be risking a confrontation with the Chinese, as well as putting American lives in danger. It was his job as commander in chief, and he didn't have to like it—he just had to order it done.

Still, commonsense, straight-ahead grit was characteristic of the man. Unlike the great majority of future politicians of his generation, Peter DeWitt Forrest had volunteered straight out of Yale to serve in the Army—one of only eight from his class who would serve in the military. He'd qualified for jump wings and seen combat as a platoon commander in Vietnam, where he earned a Bronze Star and a Purple Heart. And he had returned from that mishandled war with deeply rooted beliefs about the use of force, and—just as important—about the quality of leadership.

Pete Forrest came away from Vietnam convinced the only difference between good leadership and poor leadership is whether the lives that leadership spends are well spent or squandered. In Vietnam, he saw too many squandered lives. It was those ghosts that shaped, tempered, and focused his modus vivendi.

As a banker and credit-card entrepreneur who'd once ranked sixty-seventh in the Forbes 500, he'd always demanded that those who worked for him be tough but fair. The hallways of Pete Forrest's corporate headquarters were filled with posters promoting character and integrity. He demonstrated loyalty to his employees just as he demanded loyalty from them by sharing the company's considerable wealth based on their performance, just as his remuneration was based on his own. Later, as governor of Virginia, he'd always tried (and most of the time succeeded) to be guided by a moral compass, as opposed to the amoral political pragmatism fashionable in the 1990s.

Perhaps most important, he never forgot the lessons he'd learned from his brothers-in-arms on the battlefield. Which was why Pete Forrest had taken a silent vow in the same breath with which he'd boldly affirmed the presidential oath. His hand on the family Bible, he swore to himself that as the nation's commander in chief he would try never to squander a single American life.

And so, before putting Americans in harm's way, Pete Forrest always took the time to consider the hard question of whether he was about to spend lives or squander them. If he determined it was going to be the latter, he found an alternative solution, no matter that it might be politically unpopular. But if it was the former, he never hesitated. Which was why, if the four CIA officers he'd put in jeopardy didn't return from China, he'd be able to live with the fact that he had ordered them to their deaths. Their lives would not have been squandered, but spent in the pursuit of Duty, Honor, Country, just as so many other lives, snuffed out on Omaha Beach and Pointe du Hoc, on Mt. Suribachi, at A Shau and Plei Me and Mazār-e Sharīf, had been spent, in the pursuit of Duty, Honor, Country.

PETE FORREST dropped onto one of the drawing room's couches and stretched out his long legs, watching as his national security adviser did the caged-tiger thing. "Grab a seat, Monica, you're making me itchy."

Immediately, she dropped onto the couch opposite his. "I'm sorry, Mr. President."

He eased up a bit. "One of the perks of this job is that people tend to do things when you ask 'em to." Then his face grew serious. "So, bottom line: we won't know anything concrete until tomorrow."

The national security adviser's hands formed a steeple. "Well," she said, "we'll know when the sensors have been activated, because they've been programmed to transmit a baseline reading."

"I want to be notified as soon as that happens."

"I've already had the word passed to the operations center at Langley," she said. "The duty officer knows she's to give you a call immediately."

"Good." The president cracked another knuckle. "She knows not to be shy—no matter what time?"

"I made that abundantly clear, sir."

He nodded affirmatively. "Good." The president stood up and stretched. "Then get out of here, Monica. It's past midnight. Go home. Get some rest. Like you said, nothing's going to break until tomorrow."

"I think I'll just grab a combat nap in my office, sir. If you need me for anything—"

"I know the extension, Monica." He gave her shoulder a gentle nudge toward the hallway. "Go."

2

IT WAS FINALLY SHOW TIME. Using what appeared to be two audio cables, Kaz ganged the video camera's spare batteries together. Then he uncoiled a ten-foot-long, double-male-ended video cable and plugged one end of it into the batteries.

As he did this, X-Man was pulling the zoom lens out of its case. He handed it gingerly to Dick Campbell: "Hold this." Then he turned the two-foot case upside down, reached inside, released the false bottom, and withdrew a small, cylindrical motor about the size of a soup can.

He handed the motor to Sam, who cradled it in his arms as gently as if it were spun glass. Next, as the communicator replaced the zoom lens, X-Man slipped the tripod out of its case. Using a pair of Allen wrenches, he disassembled the tops of the three legs from their hinges, removed the three support straps from the bottom leg collets, and snapped the pieces together, forming a four-foot six-inch drill shaft. He tipped one of the tripod legs over and unscrewed its spiked foot, which he reversed, revealing a drill bit. The bit snapped into the bottom of the shaft and locked into place with an audible click.

With Sam holding the power unit, the shaft was quickly attached by using a second spiked foot and locked tight with a pair of Allen bolts. As X-Man completed the drill shaft, Kaz was unscrewing the angled pan and slide-tilt head locking handles from the camera platform head. These he screwed into tapped receivers on either side of the power unit.

Sam checked his watch. The drill had taken less than five minutes to assemble. He looked over Kaz and X-Man's handiwork. It sure was ugly, looking like the illegitimate offspring of a Dremel tool on steroids and the core-sample drills used by NASA's Apollo lunar landing teams back in the 1970s. But it was also cannily, intricately, wonderfully ingenious. Designed, no doubt, by an engineer who'd been well inculcated in Goldbergian rubric.

Kaz hefted the drill, tested to make sure the connections were secure, and then pronounced it acceptable. "Let's test it."

The communicator handed the male end of the video cable to Kaz. "Insert Tab A into Slot B," Kaz said as he screwed the connector home. He manipulated the switch on the motor's top side, and the drill began to turn. "All *right!*" Kaz gave a thumbs-up to the rest of them and looked in Sam's direction. "If Pops here will be so good as to verify our position, we'll set the first of these babies so we can start getting home."

Reflexively, Sam checked the digital watch on his left wrist again. It was well past midday. They'd been out for more than four hours now. They probably had more than an hour's work to do setting the sensors, then burying the drill, followed by a two-and-a-half- to three-hour trek back to the Toyota. That would mean they'd be traveling at night. He didn't like the idea. The Chinese increased their patrols at night.

The White House Residence.
0448 Hours Local Time.

A LIGHT SLEEPER, Pete Forrest heard the start of the distinctive ring, rolled to his right, and reached for the secure phone before the instrument completed its first cycle. "Yes?"

"Mr. President?"

"Yes." He sat up, hooking the phone receiver between his neck and shoulder and squinting at the red numerals of the digital clock, which read 04:49.

"This is Carrie at the Operations Center, Mr. President."

"What's the news, Carrie?"

"Signal received, Mr. President. Loud and clear."

Pete Forrest exhaled audibly. "Good. Anything else to report?"

"No, sir, nothing else."

"Okay, then. Thank you."

"Good night, Mr. President."

"Good night, Carrie." He replaced the receiver in its cradle, then reconfigured the pillows on his side of the bed into bolsters. Forrest sat upright, his head touching the headboard rail, and stared into the darkness.

Next to him, his wife, Jennifer, stirred, semiawake. "Anything urgent?" she murmured.

"Just an update on something, sweetie," he said. "Nothing critical. Go back to sleep."

She purred and rolled over. Idly, he stroked her shoulder. Then he cracked all the finger joints on his left hand, clasped both hands behind his head, and stared into the darkness. They'd done the job. God bless them. He'd have the team to the residence when they got back. Get to know them a little bit. Ask them about China. Listen to their stories. Let them know how much he appreciated what they'd done for the country.

But first, they had to get out. And exfiltration, Pete Forrest knew from his own combat experience, was the most dangerous part of every mission.

14 Kilometers north of Tazhong, Xinjiang Autonomous Region, China. 2245 Hours Local Time.

SAM SAW THE BIG TRUCK blocking the highway only because he was playing with his night-vision monocular. They were driving, as was the habit in this part of the world, with running lights. So his device hadn't been blinded by the Toyota's headlamps.

They came over a gentle rise in the road, and there it was—straight ahead, maybe a mile away. "Shoazim— *sür'ätni astiliting, sür'ätni astiliting*—slow down, slow down," he ordered. The Toyota eased to a crawl on the darkened highway. They drifted off the rise, and the truck disappeared from Sam's view.

"Pull over. Stop."

The driver steered onto the narrow shoulder. Sam reached across the Uighur's body and turned the running lights off. "There's something ahead—a truck's sitting in the middle of the highway," he said by way of explanation.

Shoazim squinted into the darkness. "A truck? Where?" he asked.

Sam pointed. "Maybe a couple of kilometers down the road."

The driver flicked his cigarette into the darkness. "This is most unusual," he said. "It is not my fault."

"I know it isn't," Sam said.

He reached up and turned off the Toyota's interior light switch. Then he opened his door and clambered down onto the sandy shoulder. "I'm going to take a look," he said.

Kaz opened the rear door. "I'll keep you company."

"Sure." Sam trudged ahead, his eyes growing accustomed to the dark, Kaz's footsteps scrunching the loose sand a few steps behind his right shoulder.

"Think we have a problem?" Kaz whispered when they were out of earshot.

It was Kaz's first overseas assignment, and Sam could sense the kid's apprehension. That was to be expected. Kaz was one of the Agency's new generation of post-9/11 hires: an IT guy, whose degrees included a B.S. in physics from the University of Maryland and an M.S. in computer science from Duke. He wasn't the case-officer type but a techno-wonk. He'd been talked into this little jaunt because he understood precisely how the sensors worked, and—more important—exactly how they'd have to be inserted to do their job.

"Don't know," Sam said, trying to sound reassuring. "But I want to see what's going on."

The two of them walked another hundred yards or so in silence. When Sam felt the grade increase, he slowed down and put the monocular up to his eye. It was a cheap, first-generation Russian device that Sam had bought in Turkey. But cheap or no, it was still amazing how bright things were through the lens. After another twenty yards, Sam dropped to his knees and silent-signaled Kaz to do the same. "I don't want us silhouetted against the crest of the hill."

Then he stopped. Dead in the water. Sam closed his left eye and refocused the night-vision scope. It had only two-

power magnification. But that was quite sufficient for Sam
to be able to make out the truck, its hood raised, straddling
the two-lane highway at about a forty-five-degree angle, ef-
fectively blocking the road. Half a dozen uniformed figures, some of them carrying weapons, stood shuffling in the
chill night air around the huge vehicle while one man,
perched precariously on the front bumper, shone a flashlight on the engine with one hand and tinkered with the
other.

Kaz's hand touched Sam's shoulder. "Can I have a
look?"

Wordlessly, Sam passed Kaz the monocular. The tech
peered through it for some seconds, then handed it back.
"Army."

"Yup, PLA," Sam confirmed. "They're in uniform—I
could make out their hats clearly. Could you see any markings on the truck? I couldn't."

"Negatory." Kaz shook his head.

The two of them backed off the crown of the rise. There
was nothing wrong. At least nothing Sam could put his finger on. But the situation still made him uneasy. "I don't
like it."

Kaz shrugged. "So what do you want to do?"

Sam was already heading toward the Toyota. "Let's talk
it over."

The X-Man was leaning up against the open front door
when they got back. He pointed at Sam's night-vision
monocular. "Who are they?"

Sam said, "Let's take a stroll."

The four of them ambled past the Toyota's rear bumper
and turned west, into the desert. Their footfalls scrunching
the sand, they walked about fifty yards. Sam hunkered
down and drew a diagram in the sand with his index finger.
"It looks like a PLA truck broke down."

Kaz said, "Or, it could be a roadblock."

"I disagree." Sam wagged his head. "They don't look like they're set up to make a traffic stop. I think they broke down and they're waiting for help." He saw the disappointment on Kaz's face. "Okay, Kaz has a point. Could also be they're some kind of security unit checking road traffic."

Kaz said, "Hell, Sam, this is the only north-south connector in three hundred miles."

"So, what if it is a roadblock?" Dick Campbell asked.

"It means we'll probably be shaken down," Kaz said. "Remember the traffic stop in Dabancheng?"

"Traffic stop? It was more like highway robbery," X-Man said. "They shook us down for two hundred bucks."

"And three hours, while they went through every single piece of our equipment," Sam said.

Dick Campbell folded his arms. "Hell, so what if we lose a few hours, Sam? It's not as if we're on a tight schedule."

"You're right," Sam said. "It's probably nothing. I'm being overly sensitive."

"Oh, yeah," Kaz said. "Sam, you've turned into a real Mr. Touchy-Feely."

Sam smacked Kaz on the upper arm. But he wasn't sanguine about this turn of events. He'd survived for more than a decade by trusting his instincts. And now his instincts were telling him something about the truck just . . . wasn't . . . right.

"So?" X-Man hooked his thumbs through his belt loops. "What's the plan?"

"I'll think of something. Let's get back before Shoazim gets suspicious."

Sam mulled the possibilities as they walked back to the 4×4. Then he walked up to the Toyota on the passenger side. "Shoazim, back up. We're turning around. I don't want to drive through the Army checkpoint tonight."

The driver crossed his arms. "No, Mr. Sam," he said. "We cannot."

Sam wasn't in the mood to be contradicted. "Shoazim—" he began.

The Uighur tapped the fuel gauge. "Two hundred kilometers at least to where we can get fuel if we go back," he said. "But fourteen kilometers straight ahead in Tazhong is gasoline. Turn around is impossible."

"How much fuel do we have, Shoazim?"

"Just a little."

Sam walked around to the driver's window. "Let me see."

The Uighur twisted the ignition key and Sam checked the gauge. It showed just under a quarter of a tank—maybe three, three and a half gallons. He did the math in his head and came up about a hundred kliks short. "Okay," Sam said, improvising, "what we'll do is, we'll go around."

Shoazim's eyes widened. "Around? But it is the *Army,* Mr. Sam. They will not like it."

"They won't ever know." Sam tapped the Toyota's roof. "Four-wheel drive," he said. "No problem."

The Uighur's expression showed he didn't like Sam's decision at all.

Sam said, "Hold on." He reached into his pocket for the Visor, turned it on, then held it toward the sky. "Let's see what Mr. GPS says about where we are and where we can go."

Half a minute later, Sam shut the PDA down. "Dammit—I can pull map coordinates, but nothing topographical." He took a deep breath. "Okay. Let's just do it."

"Wait a sec." Dick Campbell pulled the cell phone from his pocket and turned the power switch on. "Just in case we get stuck in the sand and have to call the office in London for a tow," he said.

Sam nodded in agreement. "Good idea." He climbed into

the cab, pulled the door shut, turned on the interior light, and unfolded the road map. "Okay, here's the plan." His finger tapped the yellow line showing the road they were on. "We're about here. We roll forward about half a kilometer. We're still out of sight because of the rise in the road . . ." Sam's finger strayed off the yellow line. "We go west, across the basin."

Sam saw the dubious look on the driver's face. "Shoazim, there are no big dunes this far south. We'll be just fine."

"We are too heavy for the desert," the driver said. "Too much weight. Soft sand."

"I just tested the sand, Shoazim," Sam bluffed. "We'll be just fine." Sam's finger went back to the map and drew a half circle. "All we have to do is give 'em a wide berth, then swing back onto the road."

Kaz said, in French, "What if they see us?"

"If they see us," Sam answered in the same language, "we'll deal with it." Then he swiveled in the front seat until his eyes settled on the X-Man. "Everybody's documents in order, Mr. Chris?"

Chris patted the upper left side of his photographer's vest, where he kept the group's passports and visas in a zipped interior pocket. "Ready for inspection, Mr. Boss Man."

Sam grinned. But it wasn't because he was happy. "Mr. Chris" was the private emergency signal he and X-Man had worked out in advance to indicate trouble. "Mr. Boss Man" was the confirmation. Which also meant that as they drove, X-Man's left hand would be in his jacket pocket, wrapped around the emergency transponder sewn inside the lining. If the situation went south, he'd let Langley know they were in trouble—and more important, where they were.

"Okay," Sam said. He extinguished the interior light, folded the map, then took one deep breath. His lips were dry. He could feel his pulse racing. But he fought for control so no one would notice his anxiety. "Let's roll."

He was specific with Shoazim. "Go slowly," he instructed the Uighur, "until we reach the dip in the road half a kilometer ahead."

He waited until the driver nodded in agreement.

"Then turn west, straight into the desert."

"Chataq yoq," Shoazim said. "No problem."

"Then go two kilometers and turn south. After two more kilometers, head east until we hit the road again."

The driver may have nodded obediently after listening to each sequence. But he obviously had no intention of following Sam's directions. Because Shoazim drove straight through the dip in the road at forty kilometers an hour, crested the rise, and continued down the far side.

He finally stopped in full sight of the truck and its occupants. "Turn now, Mr. Sam?" he said facetiously.

Sam thought seriously about throttling the driver. "No—go straight," he said through gritted teeth, resigned to an hour's delay—probably more.

Shoazim grunted, put the Toyota in gear, and moved ahead.

They were less than fifty yards from the truck when Sam realized how badly he'd misjudged things. He and Kaz had spied half a dozen uniformed men. Now, even in the dark, he realized they weren't wearing PLA uniforms, just PLA uniform parts.

He'd spotted the easily identifiable Chinese Army hats and jackets through the night vision. But up close, it was obvious they didn't fit the people wearing 'em. Not even remotely.

Sam glanced at the driver. Shoazim had obviously seen what Sam had seen, because there was a look of sheer panic on his face. The Uighur screamed something unidentifiable and slammed his foot on the brake pedal without taking the truck out of gear. The Toyota stalled out.

Sam yelled, "Dick—"

He hadn't needed to say anything. The communicator had already slapped the cell phone to his ear.

But it was too late. There was sudden motion on their flanks. A tide of armed men came out of concealed positions on either side of the road. They ran, screaming, at the 4×4.

Their hands were already on the vehicle when Sam saw—holy Christ—that these were Uzbeks, Tajiks, Afghans, Kazakhs.

The first to reach the Toyota wore a red-and-white kaffiyeh wrapped around his head like a Hizballah guerrilla. He stuck the butt of his pistol through the driver's-side window and hammered at Shoazim's head as the Uighur screamed and tried to twist away from the blows. Sam's peripheral vision caught a beetle-browed youngster in a striped Russian uniform undershirt coming at him. Instinctively, he raised his arms to protect his face. The kid grabbed both his wrists, yanked hard, pulled Sam straightaway through the Toyota's open window frame, leaving a fair amount of skin behind in the process. He punched Sam in the face. He kneed him in the gut. Then he bodyslammed the American roughly onto the highway and kicked him savagely.

Sam was frozen by the sudden intensity of the violence. He regained his senses barely in time to see a heavy jackboot coming at his face. He rolled away but still took a steel-toed kick that sent a shock wave of pain up his spine. The butt of a rifle glanced off his shoulder. He tried to tuck into a fetal position and got a breath-stopping kick in the balls for it.

There was a lot of noise—yelling, cursing, and shouting—in a language Sam didn't understand. There was shooting: quick, deafening bursts of automatic weapons fire and the raw smell of cordite mixed with dust. He thought he heard Kaz scream and then the kid's voice cut off, abruptly.

Sam tried to crawl away from the barrage of boots and gun butts. But his attempts grew pitifully futile and he finally collapsed in a bloody heap, mercifully unconscious.

3

MIKE RITZIK NEVER FELT completely comfortable in business attire. And so, the normal anxiety over where he was right now—the cozy hideaway office of the secretary of defense—was compounded by the fact that he was wearing his only dress suit: ten years old, navy-blue worsted, and very seldom worn. Oh, you didn't have to look very hard to see the hanger marks imprinted just above the trouser knees, or get up close and personal before you caught the faint yet unmistakable cedar-tinged perfume of mothballs issuing from the jacket.

The suit still fit him well enough. That was to be expected. At the age of thirty-nine Mike Ritzik hadn't put more than six pounds on his five-foot eight-inch frame since he'd graduated sixth in his class at West Point eighteen years before. He worked out daily: a constant but varying routine of distance running, weight-pile sessions, and the once-a-week torture of the obstacle course. He knew that sooner or later his body would betray him—lose the agility and elasticity that allowed him to trounce men half his age on the basketball court they'd built behind the razor wire of the CAG.

CAG, which stood for Combat Applications Group, was the Army's neutral-sounding designator for the never-acknowledged First Special Forces Operational Detachment–Delta, otherwise known as Delta Force. Delta's compound was buried well inside Fort Bragg, the huge, sprawling post that was home to the 82nd Airborne Division, as well as the Joint Special Forces Command, and which sat a dozen or so miles northwest of Fayetteville, North Carolina.

But his body hadn't betrayed him yet. And it wouldn't—not for a while, anyway.

Ritzik unclipped the yellow plastic ID with its bold blue *V* for visitor from the lapel of his suit and examined the fine print. It told him that the badge—number 120342—was the property of the United States government, and its return was guaranteed if it was dropped into any postal box. If he'd been in uniform, he wouldn't have had to wear it. His Special Forces photo ID with its smart chip would have gotten him through the thumbprint card readers and into the building. But at nine-twenty last night, the secretary's chief of staff had called the Old Man, who passed the word down the chain of command. SECDEF himself wanted Major Michael Anton Ritzik in Washington. Posthaste. Forthwith. Chop-chop. Zero seven hundred in SECDEF's office. And in mufti, please.

They'd sent a plane—a C-12—that had him on the ground at Andrews Air Force Base one hour and six minutes after departing Pope. From there it had been a twenty-six-minute ride in an anonymous black Chevy with red and blue flashing lights, driven by an anonymous driver who wore an anonymous Sig Sauer 228 in a shoulder holster under his blue blazer. The ride was followed by a six-minute walk escorted by a pair of DOD rent-a-cops that entailed jogging up one escalator, marching through four separate metal detectors, and showing his North Carolina driver's license to three huge Marines and a prissy Air Force colonel, the secretary's deputy military assistant.

The colonel, relatively satisfied about Ritzik's identity, had ushered him reverentially into SECDEF's ceremonial office, which was (Ritzik knew this because he'd seen it once before) about the size of a soccer field. There, the four-striper recounted, as if speaking from a TelePrompTer, the history of the secretary's desk: "Made from the wood and hardware of a twin-masted British privateer bravely captured during the Revolutionary War." He dragged a manicured finger languidly across the "Four Top" table, where, he said, SECDEF and his deputy had a twice-weekly lunch with the chairman and vice-chairman of the Joint Chiefs of Staff. And, in an unctuous tone, he pointed out his personal favorites from the secretary's Me Wall—that unvarying Washington political custom of displaying political relics, warmly inscribed photographs, editorial cartoons, and newspaper headlines relating to the VIP—for all to see.

The photos and headlines Ritzik could understand. But it had always baffled him to see the cruel caricatures so willingly displayed by the very butts of the cartoonists' derision. It was, he thought, kind of like walking down the street wearing a huge sign that said KICK ME! Go figure.

From there, Ritzik was led down a short, private corridor to the holy of holies. Actually, he found the secretary's hideaway office to be comfortable, even inviting. There were no VIP pictures or ego-boosting tributes on the walls. Instead, the cherrywood bookshelves bore framed family snapshots of the secretary's wife, children, and grandkids. A fire crackled in the fireplace. An afghan, which bore the huge likeness of a black Labrador retriever, had been flung over the arm of a well-used leather wing chair, in front of which sat an equally well-used leather footstool.

"Sit, Major," the four-striped major domo instructed, pointing schoolmarmlike toward a rail-backed wooden armchair placed at an oblique angle to a small, burlwood writing desk.

He complied. The colonel's nose actually twitched as Ritzik passed downwind to drop into the chair, and the man's face momentarily betrayed the fact that he'd caught a whiff of the detested *eau de mothball.* But he wasn't a Pentagon staff puke military assistant for nothing. This guy was a *pro.* His expression quickly returned to neutral. Then he turned on his mirror-shined heel. "The secretary will be with you shortly," he said to the hideaway office door, and left without waiting for a response.

Ritzik sat where he'd been ordered, his eyes scanning the small office. He played with his ID badge and was still looking at it when the thick wood door eased open and Secretary of Defense Robert W. Rockman, carrying a well-worn brown document folder tucked under his arm like a football, entered the room.

Ritzik snapped to his feet and turned toward the doorway. "Mr. Secretary."

"Major Ritzik. How good to see you again." Rockman gave him such a genuine, wide smile Ritzik could make out the gold crowns in the back of the man's mouth. "Let me just toss—" He dropped the folder onto the wing-chair cushion, advanced to Ritzik, and pumped the younger man's hand. "Thank you so much for coming on such short notice."

As if he'd had a choice. "Good to see you again, too, sir."

It wasn't the first time they'd met. Back in 2001, Ritzik—then a captain—had been a part of Task Force 555, a joint Special Operations unit that had put Delta operators, CIA paramilitary personnel, and British SAS shooters inside Afghanistan weeks before the announced start of the ground and air campaign against al-Qaeda and the Taliban.

Triple Five's mission had been both clandestine and critical. First, to organize and synchronize the ethnic Tajiks and Uzbeks who formed the core of the anti-Taliban Northern Alliance. Second, to serve as "force multipliers," providing weapons and training for the indigenous Pashtuns in the south. And third, once the campaign started in earnest, to use their SpecOps abilities for sneaking and peeking—getting close to the enemy without being seen—to provide real-time targeting information for American pilots and "light up" al-Qaeda and Taliban troops and equipment with their self-contained, handheld, state-of-the-art laser target designators.

Ritzik's twelve-man First SFOD-D Troop Hotel—four three-man squads—had been inserted into northern Afghanistan by Task Force 160 chopper on September 21, ten days after the terrorist attacks on the World Trade Center and the Pentagon. By chance, Ritzik and two of his Delta troopers had been ten miles outside Almaty, the Kazakh capital, on September 11, assigned to a JCET—Joint Combined Exchange Training—mission, schooling the Kazakh Special Forces in counterterrorist tactics to be used against the IMU and other extremist groups. Within twenty-four hours, they'd been joined by nine of their colleagues, and just over a week after that, they'd fast-roped out of an MH-53E Pave Low Special Operations chopper onto the lunar landscape of the Panjshir Valley.

Ritzik and his group had finally been extracted—under protest, let the record show—in March 2002. Twelve days later, after he'd been cleaned up and allowed to decompress a little, Ritzik was flown to Washington, where Rockman, the no-nonsense SECDEF, had offered him a newly created position on his staff: special assistant to the secretary for counterterrorism.

Respectfully but unequivocally, Ritzik declined. Not because he wouldn't be able to make a difference as a staff officer, but because he honestly believed he'd be of greater benefit to the nation back at Bragg. Mike Ritzik understood his duty to be the business of making war, not making policy. And passing on the lessons he and his men had learned through six months of hard combat—their defeats as well as victories—would make his Army all the more effective in achieving its fundamental goals on the battlefield. So, despite Rockman's entreaties and the promise of rapid advancement, Ritzik stood his ground, convinced he was better off returning to Bragg than taking an E-Ring office at the Pentagon.

That had been more than two years ago. He'd spent the intervening time commuting between the CAG and Fort Campbell, Kentucky, headquarters of the Special Operations Air Regiment's Task Force 160, known as the Nightstalkers. It had been Ritzik's assignment to fuse the SOAR pilots and crews seamlessly with Delta, to make sure that the multiple snafus that had taken place in Afghanistan did not repeat themselves elsewhere.

Now he'd been summoned to see SECDEF once more—without the faintest idea why.

"We have a serious problem," Rockman said by way of terse explanation.

"Sir?"

"In Western China. A lousy situation with huge political consequences and unreal time constraints. When I was asked to fix it, you're the one I thought of first." Rockman's lined face grew dead serious. "Take a seat, son, and I'll explain. We're due at the White House in an hour and a half."

Robert Rockman had served as both White House chief of staff and secretary of defense long before Mike Ritzik had entered West Point. Rocky, as he was called in the press, was now in his mid-seventies. He'd been brought back from a successful business career by Pete Forrest to revitalize a military that had been both demoralized and marginalized during the 1990s. Rockman had been low-profile for the first few months of the administration, working the way he preferred: quietly, without publicity. But after 9/11, Rocky had become the reluctant but highly effective public face of America's worldwide war against terrorism.

The long hours and seven-day weeks had taken their toll. Ritzik saw weariness in the secretary's bearing. But he understood enough not to mistake fatigue for apathy. Rocky was a tough old bird, as insightful, astute, and shrewd a political operator as he'd been during his younger days. After four and a half minutes of the SECDEF's monologue, Ritzik also had to admit that the man knew how to brief. There were no wasted words, no hyperbole, no polysyllabic bureaucratese.

The way Rockman laid it out, the national security adviser had pushed for the sensor-planting operation to ensure that the Chinese weren't going to cheat. Rockman had agreed it was crucial. But then the mission had been assigned to the CIA over his objections. And, as with most Agency ops these days, the numbskulls at Langley hadn't factored in Mr. Murphy. Yesterday, after successfully planting the sensors, things went sour. The team had been captured by terrorists—Uighur separatists, perhaps, no one was certain. The Agency panicked—no one notified the White House for six whole hours while they attempted to cover their butts. The president went ballistic when he found out the CIA had no contingency plan to get its people back, and he'd dumped the problem on Rockman at about five o'clock.

It got sticky, SECDEF continued, because the Joint Chiefs of Staff tried to take things over, and he'd wasted valuable time derailing what he called their Machiavellian plottings—which is why he hadn't been able to get hold of Ritzik until zero-dark-hundred.

And to make matters worse, the director of central intelligence was being stingy with intelligence. The secretary retrieved his leather document case from the wing chair. He opened it, revealing a red-tabbed folder. "I was only able to get these from Langley an hour ago—although they've been sitting on the DCI's desk since last midnight." Rockman opened the folder. It contained a dozen satellite photographs. "This'll give you some idea of what you're up against."

"Do you have a magnifying glass?"

Without a word, the secretary reached in his desk drawer and withdrew one. He handed it to Ritzik, who used it to study the eight-by-tens. He counted trucks and people. "Looks like a force of about fifty—maybe sixty." He shuffled the images. "Do we know where they're going? Are the Chinese in pursuit?"

"We can track them by satellite," the secretary said. "And so far as I know, the Chinese don't know what's going on—their satellite capabilities don't allow them to shift their birds as quickly as we can move ours." Rockman's face hardened. "Of course, they may be privy by now. But since they're playing this pretty close to the vest at Langley, I haven't been told."

"That's SOP[6] for the Agency." Ritzik knew from bitter experience that the CIA did not like to share its wealth. They held on to intelligence like misers and doled it out the way John D. Rockefeller used to hand out dimes to street urchins.

But real-time intelligence was the key to victory in Spe-

---

6. Standard Operating Procedure.

cial Operations. The essence of Special Operations, as Ritzik knew, was using small, well-trained units to achieve operational success in denied areas. The mission might be direct action, or it might be political, economic, or even psychological in nature. But no matter what the nature of the mission, Ritzik understood that without a constant flow of detailed, up-to-the-minute intelligence, any small and lightly armed force would be doomed. SpecOps Warriors cannot fight blind.

Rockman's clear gray eyes met Ritzik's. "I want you to go out and clean up the Agency's mess—extract those four men covertly and bring 'em home before the Chinese find out we've violated their territory."

It wasn't a question.

Ritzik's index finger tapped the satellite pictures. "I'll need real-time intelligence to get the job done, Mr. Secretary—information I can download onto my tactical laptops and handhelds."

"Everything you need, you will receive," Rockman said. He watched as Ritzik perused the pictures. "Now, before we leave for the White House, I want to hear from you a rough idea of how you're going to bring those four men home."

"I'd feint in the Pacific first, Mr. Secretary," Ritzik said coolly. "Use the Navy to draw China's attention away from Xinjiang. Once they were diverted, I'd go in by air and get positioned ahead of the sons of bitches. I'd employ speed, surprise, and violence of action. I'd hit when they least expect it. I'd kill them all, so there's no one left to come back and bite us on the rear end later. I'd grab our people and run like hell to a predetermined, secure extraction point. And then I'd link up with some of our air assets and get across a safe border."

"Can you be any more specific, Major? The president is going to want to hear more than high concept from you."

"Sir," Ritzik said candidly, "I'm going to need a secure phone so I can talk to my sergeant major before I go any further."

"Why is that, Major?"

"Because Sergeant Major Yates and his cadre of senior NCOs will be the ones doing most of the planning for this mission, not me. They've forgotten a lot more about the specifics of putting these sorts of ops together than I'll ever know."

"What?" Rockman's unflappable composure dissolved.

Ritzik understood immediately what he'd done. Rockman, after all, was SECDEF. Meaning that he was treated like some sort of god. He was "handled." He was "guided." He was "shielded" from certain . . . realities.

The shocked look on Rockman's face told Ritzik that no general, no military assistant or SpecWar adviser had ever told him that Delta's operations were developed and planned not by the guys with the scrambled eggs on their hats and the stars on their collars, but by the unit in question's senior enlisted personnel.

At Delta the mission tasking might come down the chain of command from the president or secretary of defense to SOCOM—the U.S. Special Operations Command at McDill Air Force Base in Tampa, Florida—or through JSOC, the Joint Special Operations Command at Fort Bragg. But once the tasking—which boiled down to the overall goal to be achieved—had been issued, all the hands-on mission planning was done by the unit's senior non-coms. It was a system that Delta's creator, Colonel Charlie A. Beckwith, had brought from his days as an exchange officer with the 22nd Regiment Special Air Service. "Bottom-up planning," Beckwith called it. At Delta, in fact, senior NCOs had more than once told JSOC or SOCOM staff

puke colonels to shove it after said staff pukes had tried to
impose mission-specific orders.

It made perfect sense, too. Ritzik had been at Delta for
two tours totaling five years. Of that time, twenty-three
months had been spent in language training inside the
Delta compound—he spoke Uzbek, Kazakh, and some
Dari, as well as a little Russian—and a series of specialized
courses where he'd been taught such esoteric skills as
breaking and entering (by a career criminal at the medium-
security federal prison in Petersburg, Virginia) and guerrilla driving at West Virginia's Bill Scott Raceway, just
outside Charles Town.

But Ritzik was the exception to the rule. Most junior officers spent only two years with Delta, using their tour as a
ticket-punching way station on their way to a colonel's
command, followed by a general's stars.

NCOs, however, could spend a dozen years or more at
the unit, participating in hundreds of operations, drills, re-
hearsals, and call-outs, and more important, the hot-
washes, those no-holds-barred, rank-has-no-privilege
debriefing sessions that followed every op or full mission
profile exercise. Sergeants were the ones who ran the ops at
Delta Force. Junior officers like Ritzik were—as the senior
NCOs liked to say—no more than overpaid RTOs (radio
telephone operators).

"Mr. Secretary, it's the truth. When we were in
Afghanistan, I was the nominal troop leader. Sure, I worked
on developing the unit's mission concepts and fine-tuning
its goals. But once we were tasked I deferred the operational planning to the master sergeant, Fred Yates, who was
my team leader back then."

Rockman hooked a thumb toward a heavy black telephone sitting on his desk. "Then get this sergeant major of

yours—Yates, you say—on the line, Major, and do whatever head-shedding you have to do to come up with something workable. I need to hear specifics before we leave for the White House."

14 Kilometers north of Tazhong, Xinjiang Autonomous Region, China. 2045 Hours Local Time.

SAM PHILLIPS opened his right eye—which took considerable effort and caused him a fair amount of pain—and tried to figure out just where he was. He concluded, after some woozy seconds, that he was in a dark void, lying on his side, his head drooping into a puddle of something nasty. He thought, *That road we were on must have been paved with good intentions, because I have obviously gone to hell.*

He wriggled slightly—which caused a sharp twinge in his rib cage—and learned that his arms were bound tightly behind his back. He tried to straighten his legs, which were tied at the ankles tightly enough to hurt, and bent at the knees. But when he moved, a noose around his throat tightened, and he eased up quickly so as not to choke himself. The mothers had hog-tied him.

There was foul-smelling wetness under his face. He tried to open his left eye, but it was fused shut. So he lay there for some seconds, hoping that he'd get some degree—any degree—of vision back in his blurry right eye, and listening desperately for any clue that might indicate where he was. He heard snippets of muffled speech coming as if from a distance. But it was impossible to decipher what was being said.

How long had he been awake? Three minutes? Four? However long it had been, his eye wasn't getting any better.

And so he lay quietly, working hard not to panic, trying to regulate his breathing so he wouldn't choke on the tape gag, letting his body and his brain recover by counting silently back from two hundred; a Zen exercise to steady himself.

By the time he'd reached zero, the sight in his right eye had finally unblurred enough for him to be able to make out worn floorboards below his nose.

Okay—that meant he'd been stashed in a vehicle or a house. There were no houses anywhere close by, unless they'd been driven into Tazhong. Which from the lack of ambient sounds was improbable. So, most likely, he'd been tossed into the bed of the truck that had been sitting astride the road. Or some other truck. After what had taken place earlier, Sam Phillips was not about to assume anything. Sam rolled right so he could look up. He was rewarded with a fuzzy image of canvas and metal. He raised his head, sniffed, and caught the faint but clear odor of diesel fuel.

A truck it was, then. Sam squirmed to his left, and made contact against something. He had to roll completely over now, scraping his nose across the wet floorboard. But finally his eye settled on X-Man's photographer's vest. He fought his way onto his shoulder—Whoa, *that* hurt—so he could see his teammate's back. He watched, for a minute or so, and was hugely relieved to see that X-Man was taking shallow but regular breaths.

Then he forced his legs as far up as he could so he could see the security man's legs without choking himself. X-Man was hog-tied, too.

Forcing his legs to comply, he scrunched forward until his forehead touched X-Man's back. He tapped the security man's back twice, *knock-knock*.

There was no one home.

He prodded the back of the photographer's vest once more, grunting through gagged lips as he did.

Still nothing.

He squeezed up against the photographer's vest and smacked his whole body against X-Man until he heard a short, muffled groan from his colleague. Sam moved back, until he'd put a foot or so between them. "Chris, try and roll over," he said. "But be careful not to rock the truck and attract attention." Of course, given the tape gag, it didn't quite come out that way. But X-Man's body told Sam he'd gotten the message.

It took perhaps five or six minutes, but they were finally face-to-face. Sam wriggled close and examined the cut over X-man's eye and the bruises on his cheeks. Christ, he was a mess.

X-Man started to blink rapidly. Sam thought he was having a seizure, until he realized that the security man was transmitting Morse code.

Oh, Christ, Sam thought. He'd learned Morse back at the Farm during his initial training. They'd taught it so case officers could mark dead drops, or leave signals for their agents, or—the instructor had actually once joked—"Just in case two of you are tossed into adjoining cells and you want to communicate with each other."

Sam remembered how the whole class had rolled their eyes at that one. Which was when the instructor said, "Well, smart-asses, that's how we did it at the Hanoi Hilton."

But Sam hadn't used Morse for years.

He closed his eye and counted to ten, racking his befogged mind as he tried to remember the twenty-six dit-dah long-short combinations. It was useless. His brain was mush. All he could come up with was *SOS*—three short, followed by three long, followed by three short.

Which jogged his mind a little. *Wait a second. H* was four short. *S* was three short. *I* was two short. And *E* was one short. That was all the shorts. There was no four long. *O* was three long—he knew that. What the hell was one long? *T. T. T* was one long. And *M; M* was two long.

He opened his eye and waited until it focused on X-Man's face. He blinked three short, four short, two short, and one long, then waited for X-Man's reaction.

Three long, followed by long-short-long. *O* something. *OK-OK-OK.*

Sam opened his eye as far as he could and nodded.

X-Man was transmitting again. Short-short. Long-long. Short-short-long.

I-M-short-short-long.

Sam shook his head. Negatory.

X-Man cocked his head toward the outside of wherever they were being held. Then he transmitted again. *I-M*-something.

U. Short-short-long was *U*. It was the IMU out there. He was telling Sam they'd been snatched by the IMU.

The IMU. That figured. Langley said the IMU was seriously weakened these days. Well, these guys didn't appear very weak. Sam blinked *T*, then *E*, then *I-S-T-S*, because he couldn't think of what the hell *R* was.

X-Man gave him an affirmative nod. Then he started blinking again. "I-s-i-t," he said.

Thank God he was keeping it simple. But sitting? What if the truck moved? What if one of *them* outside saw it move?

X-Man didn't give him a chance to object. He slithered backward to give himself some clearance. Then, knees bent, the security officer rolled onto his belly. And then somehow, incredibly, without garroting himself, he levitated and jerked himself upright, into a kneeling position. The move actually slackened the hog-tie cord between X-Man's neck and his ankles.

Sam was still holding his breath. Jeezus. It was okay: the truck hadn't moved. Not a millimeter.

X-Man's eyes told Sam what to do next. Sam complied, squiggling forward until he'd put his face close up against X-Man's butt and the soles of his feet. X-Man's fingers found the back edge of the tape across Sam's mouth and pried it loose.

The instant it came off his lips, Sam breathed so rapidly he began to hyperventilate.

Quickly, he fought to bring his body under control. "I'll be okay, I'll be okay," he whispered, the sound of his own hoarse voice both reassuring him and giving him back some blessed degree of control over the situation, even though he was still bound hand and foot.

Sam swallowed hard. "X, do you know where Kaz and Dick are?"

Instead of answering, X-Man wriggled his butt and his shoulders at Sam.

Who finally got the message—and got with the program. He buried his face between X-Man's shoes and worked with his teeth at the hog-tie knot just above the ankles.

They'd used cheap plastic line to do the job, and Sam was able to pull the frayed end out and release the knot in a few minutes without chipping any teeth. Then he attacked the thick roll of dark tape that pinioned X-Man's wrists and forearms behind his back. He had managed to gnaw through two of the perhaps half-dozen layers of foul-tasting tape when the shooting started and the truck was rocked by nearby explosions.

4

NATIONAL SECURITY ADVISER Monica Wirth glanced at
the legal pad in her left hand. Then her eyes flicked in the
president's direction. A barely noticeable movement by Pete
Forrest's eyebrow told her exactly what he wanted her to do.

Wirth dropped the pad to her side, crossed the rug with
its Great Seal of the United States, and moved behind the
president, where she could focus on Ritzik. "I like your
overall plan, Major. It's simple and direct. But there is one
huge flaw."

"Ma'am?" Ritzik was shaken. He thought he'd covered
all the bases.

"As proposed by you, there is only one service branch
employed on the actual rescue—the Army. The other
branches are used in support roles, or not included at all."
She dropped the pad out of sight. "The Navy wants a sub-
stantial piece of this, Major Ritzik. So does the Air Force.
So does the Central Intelligence Agency. The Joint Chiefs
chairman is strongly recommending—his staff has already
drawn up a mission profile and detailed operation plan, I
might add—that we assemble a company-sized unit made
up of Army, Navy, and Air Force Special Operations per-

sonnel to do the job, as opposed to your twelve-man Army element with Air Force support." Wirth paused. "So, Major, how do we deal with the chairman's objections?"

Mike Ritzik glanced at the dark circles under the national security adviser's eyes as she stood behind the president's wing chair, and realized she'd probably been up all night. The president didn't look too good, either. Neither did the SECDEF. "I don't believe a company-sized force is a good idea for this mission, Dr. Wirth."

"Why?"

"First of all, the size alone is cause for failure. Moving a hundred-plus people attracts attention. Second, I totally reject the chairman's concept of a unit assembled specifically for this operation. Jointness is a concept that Congress first forced on the military for political reasons. Unlike most of the dumb ideas they come up with on Capitol Hill, this one actually worked—like when the Navy carriers served as forward basing for Special Forces during the Afghan campaign. But when it comes to the sorts of small-unit operations I do, jointness for jointness's sake can be dangerous."

"Dangerous, Major?"

"Dangerous, ma'am. I'm not talking about being able to communicate on the same radio frequencies—that's a good idea. But so far as I'm concerned, unless you've trained with someone for a long time, it's impossible to operate with that man successfully on a high-risk op. You don't know what the other guy is thinking, how he works, or what he's good at."

"But we're talking about our most elite forces, Major," Wirth said. "You're all professionals. Certainly that counts for something."

"It does, ma'am," Ritzik said. He paused just long enough to sneak a look at the president, who was staring at him intently. Strange that the man hadn't said anything. Ritzik's eyes shifted back to the national security adviser.

"Working with strangers increases the chance of failure— increases them exponentially. Sure, symbiosis and integration—and those are a couple of the buzzwords you hear from the Joint Chiefs these days—can be achieved. 'Integration' is precisely what I've been doing for the past two years with the SOAR. But fluidity in combat takes months of work. The schedule the secretary outlined to me doesn't allow any time for that kind of mission prep."

"I'm still skeptical," Monica Wirth said. "Admiral Buckley makes a strong argument that a joint strike force would be effective and successful."

"The admiral would say that." Ritzik almost had to laugh. Phil Buckley, the current JCS chairman, was a Navy sea systems manpower specialist who had spent twenty-eight of his thirty-one-year career behind a desk as a staff officer. According to the RUMINT[7] at Bragg, he'd been selected for chairman in the last months of the previous administration because he'd been the safe choice, a bureaucrat who wouldn't rock the boat. Phil Buckley had spent the past decade and a half not commanding or leading, but writing legislative memos.

The role suited him, too. Buckley was precisely the sort of individual who looked good marching down the marble corridors of the Hart or Cannon office buildings. He was tall and lean and had the eagle-eyed stare of a Warrior. But in point of fact, the man had never seen a shot fired in anger. He was a manager, an apparatchik, one of the Pentagon's detested professional paper pushers.

Ritzik knew the suggestion Chairman Buckley was putting forward was a recipe for disaster. *But they all had to know it, too, didn't they?* He started to speak again. But the

---

7. *RUMor INTelligence* is military slang for "urinal gossip."

words caught in his throat, because Ritzik, openmouthed, caught something he hadn't been supposed to see: an imperceptible signal, passing like electricity, between the other three.

That was when Ritzik realized what was going on. The president was testing him. Challenging him to prove he could succeed. This was all about will. Resolve. Tenacity. Determination.

Ritzik viewed Pete Forrest with fresh respect. And as a sign of that esteem, he'd give his commander in chief the unvarnished truth. At Delta, you always spoke your mind during the hot-wash sessions, no matter how much it might wire-brush the senior officers. Because as Ritzik saw it, the Warrior's ultimate goal wasn't getting promoted, but to prevail over your enemy and bring all your people home.

So Ritzik focused on the president and hot-washed. "Units like the one the chairman is suggesting do work out just fine—in Hollywood movies, sir. But in the real world, they get people killed. That's why at CAG, our senior noncoms insist on doing the mission planning. Because every time some staff puke colonel or dumb-as-a-brick general comes up with a bright idea—we pretty much know it's going to get our people killed."

Pete Forrest looked intently at Ritzik. "I was a staff puke, Major."

"Yes, sir, you were," Ritzik said, his tone unyielding. "But before that, you were Airborne. You led a platoon in combat. You know I'm right."

The shocked look Ritzik got from the national security adviser told him he'd probably just put an end to his career.

But he wasn't about to back down. "The way I see it, sir, junior officers like you and me often end up sending good men home in body bags because somebody with stars on his collar wants a piece of the glory for his service, or his unit."

Ritzik focused on President Forrest's face. "Remember that Navy SEAL who fell out of the chopper in Afghanistan a couple of years back, sir?"

"At the start of Operation Anaconda," the president said. "Chief Petty Officer Jackson."

"Yes, *sir.*" Ritzik was impressed the man remembered. "Well, I was in the AO, sir. I *knew* that assault element hadn't ever worked together before. It was thrown to-gether—Rangers, Special Forces, and SEALs, with SOAR pilots and aircrews. All strangers. But you know how it was: we had all those alleged instant communications setups in operation, and so instead of letting some junior officer or master sergeant on the ground run things, all the staff pukes—excuse me, ma'am, the 'joint operations advisory staff' officers—a hundred miles away at Bagram Air Base, and the middle-manager pukes seven thousand miles away at Central Command in Tampa, they all put *their* two cents in on how things should be done."

The national security adviser stroked her chin. "I never looked at it that way before—DOD never put it in those terms when they briefed us."

"They wouldn't," Ritzik said. "But it's the truth, ma'am. Bottom line is that the Navy micromanagers at CENTCOM wanted their service to grab a piece of the glory, and so did the Marines, and the Air Force, and my boss's boss's boss, and the rest of 'em. So the mission was hobbled from the get-go. Worse, COMCENT[8] didn't have the, the"—Ritzik caught himself up—"the guts to tell the paper pushers to

---

8. Commander CENTral Command.

butt the hell out. And then Mr. Murphy got himself added to the manifest."

Monica Wirth said, confused, "CIA?"

"Of Murphy's Law fame, ma'am. Of course, your briefers tend not to use that term. They prefer to talk about 'the fog of war,' or what Clausewitz called *la friction*. But it all boils down to what can go wrong usually does. At Takhur Ghar—that was the objective—first, the chopper, it was an MH-47E, developed mechanical problems, which delayed takeoff until very close to dawn. So the team lost one of its key assets, its ability to attack at night, when the enemy couldn't see them coming. Then the weather changed—for the worse, naturally. But they kept going. The comms got spotty, because they were using line-of-sight radios, and the ridges got in the way. So they couldn't stay in touch. The altitude presented new challenges, too. Takhur Ghar is twenty-one hundred meters high—that's almost seven thousand feet. But the pilots hadn't trained to fly combat missions at that altitude and under similar weather conditions, so they had virtually no idea how the choppers would react in the thin air, zero visibility, and turbulence. Then the intel turned out to be bad. The satellites and the Predators and the billion-dollar photo recon systems all missed the bad guys because al-Qaeda had done a good job of camouflaging themselves and their bunkers. And we didn't have any HUMINT. So no one warned the assault element they'd be facing Chechens. No one told them the LZ was going to be hot. That's why the pilot brought the chopper in a little flat, flying an admin approach, because it was easier to control in thin air. But he caught ground fire. The chopper was hit. The hydraulic systems went out, and the pilot panicked."

"Panicked?" Wirth said. "That's strong language, Major."

"Yes, ma'am. And it wasn't what the official reports about

Takhur Ghar said. But that's what happened. I was there." He paused. "If you train the way you fight, your instincts will kick in when things go bad. You'll be able to overcome the obstacles. You'll outthink and outfight the enemy. And you'll get the job done. On Takhur Ghar, the mission hadn't been bottom-up planned by shooters, but top-down planned by staff pukes. On Takhur Ghar, no one had trained the way they were going to have to fight. So the pilot reacted badly. Instead of putting his people on the ground to suppress the fire and counterambush the hostiles, he retreated. He hauled butt. And I guess he thought he'd done an okay job getting everyone out of there. Except he hadn't. Jackson had fallen out." Ritzik paused, his eyes scanning the room. *"And no one noticed Jackson was missing."*

He was pretty worked up by now. "Why was that? I'll tell you something: *why* doesn't matter. What matters is that somebody with stars on his collar back in Tampa wanted Navy SpecWar to get a piece of the glory that night, and so this patchwork-quilt unit that had never trained or operated together before was sent out to do a job. And when the you-know-what hit the fan, things went bad. Bottom line: seven men died. Seven. If you ask me, they were squandered, because no matter how good each of them might have been individually, the group didn't have any unit integrity." Ritzik caught his breath. "Mr. President, let me tell you about unit integrity—"

"Major," Pete Forrest broke in, his tone rebuking, "I know all about unit integrity." He didn't need a lecture on the subject from this young pup, and the peeved expression on his face displayed it.

Ritzik realized he'd gone too far. "I apologize, sir, but I lost men in Afghanistan because . . . idiots back here made decisions based on political considerations, or pure ignorance about what was taking place on the ground."

"Sometimes that's the reality," the president said.

"Yes, sir, it may be reality—but I don't have to like it. The problem is that when screwups like that happen, the politicians and generals who caused the problems in the first place never pay for their mistakes. They get promoted. Me, sir, I'm the one stuck with the job of filling body bags. So if you don't mind, I'll take a pass on the politics. The way I see it, my only job is to make sure the mission succeeds, and my men come home."

"And you say those two goals are impossible if we assemble a joint force."

"Yes, sir." He took a few seconds to consider what he was about to say, then continued. "Mr. President, if you think the Navy, or the Marines, or whoever, should take this job on, that's up to you. You're the CINC. My only recommendation is that no matter who you assign, please deploy a single unit—a group of operators who have worked together so long they can finish one another's sentences and read one another's body language—to do the job. Otherwise, you're going to squander those men's lives just the way they were squandered on Takhur Ghar."

The president took his time before responding. He liked this compact, muscular young man. Liked the fact that he spoke his mind. Liked even more that he obviously put the welfare and safety of his people ahead of his own career. Loyalty *down* the chain of command, Pete Forrest knew, was a rare, even uncommon virtue in today's military culture. "Point taken, Major."

"Thank you, sir."

After some seconds, the president said, "Outspoken youngster, isn't he, Rocky?"

"I told you he was," the secretary said, a Cheshire-cat smile on his face.

Pete Forrest leaned forward. "The only question *I* have

remaining, Major Ritzik, is whether, as an operator, you really believe this is doable."

"Mr. President, in almost twenty years in the military I've learned that nothing is impossible, given the right resources and, more important, the political will to get the job done."

Pete Forrest stared across the low butler's table separating him from the young officer, his eyes probing the man's demeanor for any sign of weakness, indecision, or hesitation. So far, he'd sensed none. "Don't worry about resources, Major," the president finally said. "Or politics. Do *you* have the will to get the job done?"

Mike Ritzik's response was instantaneous. He looked the president in the eye. "Sir, I will not fail. I will bring those four men home."

After a quarter of a minute, the president's gaze shifted to his secretary of defense, who was now sitting next to Ritzik on the couch. "Monica."

"Mr. President?"

"This comes under the 'Special Activity' rule, doesn't it?"

"I believe so, Mr. President."

"Then draft a Finding. I want this done by the numbers."

"Yes, sir."

"And let's keep it close hold: that means you, me, and the general counsel." The president looked back at Rockman. "Rocky," he said, "give this op a compartment.[9] Give the major whatever he needs to get the job done." The president paused. "And both of you"—he swiveled in the chair until he caught Monica Wirth's eye again—"both of you, you take whatever heat is necessary to protect this boy's back."

---

9. Security level above top secret known as SCI, or Sensitive Compartmented Information, which requires code-word clearance.

Sword Squadron, Fort Bragg, Fayetteville, North Carolina.
1134 Hours Local Time.

SERGEANT MAJOR FRED YATES tucked the handset between his bull neck and rippled shoulder, swung his boon-
dockered feet up onto the coffee-stained gray steel desktop,
and shouted into the mouthpiece, "Talgat, you Kazakh su-
perman, *assalamu alaykim.*"

Yates paused, a wide grin spreading across his sun-
reddened face. "Yeah, it's me, Rowdy Yates. *Salemetsiz be,*
Colonel—you okay?" He nodded his head up and down.
"*Jaqsë*—I'm just fine, thanks. No"—he laughed—"my
Kazakh is still lousy as ever. So how are *you?*" Yates waited
for an answer. "She did? A boy? What's his name?" Yates
flipped to a clean page of the legal pad that sat on his lap,
took a felt marker out of his BDU breast pocket, and wrote
A-I-B-E-K in capital letters on the page. "Three-point-three
kilos? That's *huge,* Talgat, huge," he boomed. "You gotta be
very, very proud, buddy."

"Uh-huh, uh-huh." Yates covered the phone's mouthpiece, ripped the page from the pad, and waved it at the first
sergeant whose desk sat opposite his. "Yo, Shep—he had a
kid. We'll get one of those pint-sized BDU shirts made up.
This is the name that goes on the pocket strip."

Gene Shepard looked up from his to-do list, flashed a
toothy smile, and ran his fingers through curly dark hair.
"Great idea, man. How is the colonel these days?"

"Like I said, he's a new papa and proud as hell. Gonna
raise himself a little soldier, just like his daddy."

"Tell him *assalamu* from me, will you? And that I'm
looking forward to seeing him again."

Yates gave the first sergeant an upturned thumb. "Will do."

Then-captain Talgat Umarov had been Ritzik's initial

contact in Kazakhstan's small, underfunded Special Forces counterterrorist unit, back in 1988. That year, a four-man Delta element led by Mike Ritzik went to Almaty to cross-train with the Kazakhs and teach them cutting-edge tactics. Over the ninety-day deployment, the four Americans and their twenty Kazakh counterparts bonded the way soldiers who share similar passions, missions, and dedication so often do.

Over the ensuing six years, Ritzik and Rowdy Yates stayed in touch with Umarov, who had been the counterterrorist team's OIC, or officer-in-charge. He'd been friendly, helpful, and outspokenly pro-American. In fact, Umarov impressed Ritzik so much that in the spring of 2000 they'd wangled a trip to Fort Bragg for the Kazakh and three of his senior NCOs, and sent them home after two exhausting but exhilarating weeks of blowing things up, jumping out of perfectly good aircraft, and long, beer-soaked nights in Fayetteville's better barbecue joints, with three cases of premium sourmash bourbon and two sets of fourth-generation night-vision goggles—equipment that was impossible to come by in Talgat's part of the world. In January of the following year, Ritzik had arranged another visit for Umarov, which included a month of English language training.

The rapport between the Kazakh officer, Ritzik, and Yates had, in fact, been crucial during the first days after 9/11, when it became imperative for the United States to insert huge numbers of Special Forces troops into Central Asia as part of its military buildup in the region. The Kazakh military had quickly agreed to support the American request in no small measure because of the tight personal relationship between Mike Ritzik, Rowdy Yates, and their close friend Talgat Umarov, who, in 2001, was a lieutenant colonel, a battalion commander, and most important, a trusted officer who had the ear of the chief of staff. And the COS was the cousin and confidant of Kazakhstan's all-powerful president.

Yates shouted, "Gene Shepard says hello." There was five seconds of silence. Then Yates bellowed, "Yes, Colonel, he still likes that awful Guinness Stout. Sometimes he likes it too much."

Shepard gestured to the sergeant major, who cupped his hand over the mouthpiece again. *"What?"*

"Why the hell are you shouting like that, Sergeant Major?"

"Because it's long distance, putz." Yates uncupped his hand from the mouthpiece and said, "Uh-huh. Great, buddy. Yes, we accept. We're honored. We're all very honored."

The first sergeant said, "Honored?"

"Affirmative. He wants us to be godfathers." Yates extended a thick arm, snagged a huge mug of steaming, sweet black coffee, and sipped it gingerly. "How's Kadisha doing? That's just super." He listened for about half a minute, his grin crescendoing all the while. "Sounds absolutely effing great, Talgat. I wish we could have been there with you."

Yates plucked a pair of Wal-Mart reading magnifiers, set them on the ridge of his nose, and checked the scribbled list on the top page of the notepad on his lap. "Listen, Colonel, I'm actually planning to be in your neck of the woods soon, and I'm gonna need a little help." He took another gulp. "Day after tomorrow, actually.

"Day after tomorrow," Yates repeated, fighting for the Kazakh word. *"Erteng,* old buddy, day after *erteng.* That's right." The sergeant major swept his feet off the desk. "Yeah, it came as a surprise to me, too. But you know how these things are—they never tell us anything." He juggled mug, notepad, and phone as he scrunched his chair up to the desk. "A bunch of us. The old crowd plus a few new faces."

The sergeant major paused and listened. "Naw—nothing special. Talgat—Talgat, no!" Yates cupped his hand over the handset. "Jeezus, the son of a bitch wants to give us a big welcome party." He exposed the mouthpiece. "Talgat, we gotta keep this quiet. So maintain OPSEC. Remember OPSEC? Yeah—good. That's right." Yates wriggled his eyebrows at the first sergeant and mouthed, "He finally got it."

Shepard gave the sergeant major an upturned thumb.

"Naw," Yates bellowed. "We're just dropping in to see some old friends on the way to Afghanistan. That would be great, Colonel—absolutely terrific." He tapped his pen on the legal pad. "Well, actually, I do. You got a pencil?" Yates paused. "You still have any of that Iranian 5.45-X-39 ammo left from our last trip? Yeah—about five thousand rounds should do." He listened. "Uh-huh. Great. And can you have one of your people hit the bazaar? We need some of those Tajik shirts and hats we found last time. And maybe a bunch of Russkie cammo anoraks and those striped Russkie undershirts, too. All extra-large, Talgat. As big as you can find 'em.

"Right—put 'em all in that warehouse at the airport we used as our HQ last time we TDY'd." Yates's basso profundo suddenly dropped by twenty decibels. "And I'll need to borrow a plane, too. Nope—not Army. Commercial. Remember your cousin Shingis from Air Kazakhstan who we worked with on jump exercises when we were over last year? Well, if you can make your usual subtle approach to him, let him know we'd make it worth his while if we could borrow one of Kazakh Air's Yak-42s for a day or so." He paused. "Yeah—a Yak-42. Nothing else will do. But it's got to be done very, very quiet since we're just visiting on an unofficial basis. Like no ripples anywhere, if you catch my drift. Use lots of OPSEC, Colonel. We have to keep this one in the family."

Yates listened, then grinned. "No problem you say? Oh, I

do like that, Colonel. I like that very much, sir." There was another pause. Then Yates roared, "Anything you need from the States, old buddy? Don't forget: I'm traveling at government expense—weight is no problem." He laughed. "That's easy," he said. "You got it." He rubbed a big paw over the top of his shaved head and looked at the wall clock he'd already set to Almaty local time. "I'd say by zero five hundred hours your time." He paused. "Okay. Yeah. Yeah. Day *after* tomorrow, Colonel, see you. *Sau bol, sau bol,* Talgat—b'bye, b'bye."

Yates slapped the receiver down. "Shep," he said, "see how the system works? We don't need to go to Congress and beg for no stinking foreign aid. We don't need any damn striped-suit diplo-dinks negotiating for us. We don't got to hijack anything, either. We got ourselves a plane, a pilot, some ammo, local duds, and all it's gonna cost us is a kid's shirt, a couple of cases of great bourbon, and a pallet load of Pampers."

"Not to mention the suitcase full of cash."

"Hell, yes. The well-known suitcase full of cash. The *expediter. Hoo-ah!*" Yates stood up, extended his big hand, and high-fived the first sergeant. "Is this a great friggin' country or what?"

"*Hoo-ah,* a great friggin' country, Sergeant Major. God Bless America." Shepard gave Yates a quizzical look. "But why did you ask for the Russian uniforms. And how come you didn't tell him about the Rangers?"

Yates plucked a tiny, well-worn copy of Sun-Tzu's *The Art of War* from the breast pocket of his BDU shirt and brandished it in Shepard's direction like a talisman. "The Master says, 'Use deception to throw your enemy into confusion,' Grasshopper. We were on an open line, Shep. People listen in on open lines. And I want anybody listening to believe we're headed for Afghanistan. Besides, if Talgat knew we were bringing a security force, he'd realize we had something serious going on."

"Talgat's no dummy, Rowdy. The minute he sees that C-5, he's gonna know."

"By then," Yates said, stowing the book, "the Big Suit at the White House will have put the fix in at the Kazakh presidential palace and we'll be slicker than deer guts in a pine forest. Besides, we'll have all them young pecker-wood Rangers making a cordon sanitaire around us, so who's gonna complain?" He stood up and rapped his scarred knuckles on the desk. "Remember the holy trinity, Shep: speed, surprise, and violence of action." The sergeant major unsheathed his marker, flourished it like a sword, and thrust at the legal pad, drawing a quick *Z* through a trio of items. He scanned the remainder of his to-do list. "That leaves sixteen for Zorro. How you coming, Sancho Panza?"

"I think you're mixing your characters." Shepard flipped through half a dozen sheets of paper. "Okay: I finally located the chutes, masks, and O-two prebreather units," he said. "There are two dozen RAPS[10] out at Marana the CIA was saving for some black op. Two tandems, sixteen masks, and sixteen double-bottle units. The Air Force bitched and moaned, but SECDEF has the juice, and they're already on the way. ETA is about fifteen hundred. Then we have to get the chutes out to the rigger's shed and go over 'em before we repack and stow."

Yates's head bobbed up and down once. "Get Curtis, Goose, Marko, Tuzz, and Dodger on it. They're gonna be

---

10. Ram Air Parachute Systems.

jumping the damn things; they might as well make sure they're sound."

"Wilco, Sergeant Major."

"Equipment?"

"Good to go equipment-wise: Russian Kirasa-5 tactical vests. Everybody already has GSG-9[11] boots. I've got French Nomex coveralls, Russian web gear, and Bulgarian AKs. We can't use MBITRs,[12] so I found fourteen secure CipherTac satellite-compatible radios. They were made for a Kraut contract. They'll work with our duplex system and the satcom chips, so the comms are good to go. And the Chinese claymores are up at Dam Neck—they'll be here by close of business today."

"Hey, asshole," Yates growled, "we never close. Remember that." He swallowed the last of the sweet coffee. Departure was scheduled for twenty hundred hours—not enough time, he worried, to get everything done.

At least, Rowdy thought, they'd be comfortable on the trip over. The big C-5 was one of the Air Force's SOLL-II, or Special Operations Low Level II aircraft, capable of landing, unloading, and taking off under complete blackout conditions. It was coming in from the 436th Airlift Wing at Dover, Delaware. The plane's upper deck had reclining seats for seventy-three, as well as a galley and real heads. That beat the canvas strap benches, piss tubes, and chemical buckets on the C-130s they usually flew.

Plus, the C-5's cargo bay was huge. If they had to, they could check and repack all the chutes in the belly of the Galaxy. It might be awkward working around the pallets, but it could be done. Rowdy shook himself out of his stupor.

---

11. Assault boots specially designed by Adidas for *Grenzchutzgruppe* 9, Germany's primary counterterrorist unit.
12. Handheld multiband inter/intra team radios.

What the hell had Shep said about Chinese claymores? "Shep?"

The first sergeant said, "Yo?"

"Chinese claymores?"

"Coming from Dam Neck."

"Good. Pack three or four blocks of Semtex, too." Semtex was the old Soviet-bloc equivalent of C-4 plastic explosive. Originally made during the Cold War in Czechoslovakia (for which reason Rowdy liked to say it was great for canceling Czechs), it was durable, malleable, and stable. And forensically, it would leave behind no indications that those who'd employed it were Americans.

Shepard made a note. "Roger that."

Rowdy glanced up at the clock, thinking again how there's never enough effing time. He had to scramble one of Delta's six-man IST—intelligence support teams—to run the tactical operations center at Almaty. And he still had his research to do. The unit kept case study files on operations running all the way back to World War II. Colonel Beckwith had insisted on maintaining the case studies—and they'd always proved valuable in the past. Rowdy wanted to look at some thirty-year-old SAS operations in Oman. The geography was roughly similar to the Tarim Basin—except for the huge Tian mountain range ringing the Western Chinese desert. He pulled the reading magnifiers off his nose and stuck them in his pocket. "Be back in about half an hour."

"Gotcha. I'm just about finished with the comms."

"Good. You get hold of any RPGs?"

"Not yet. I sent Bill Sandman to dig 'em up. All he could find was LAWs."

"Crap." Yates scratched a large spider bite just below his sunburned ear. "I'll take care of it. I think I know where I can lay my hands on a dozen or so." He chicken-scratched the acronym on his legal pad. "What about IR strobes?"

"Got 'em." Shepard gave the sergeant major a wicked grin. "One less item on my list."

"And one more on mine. Now, if the sons of bitches at Langley ever give us some of their precious intelligence, we might be able to get this show on the road."

"Knowledge is power, Sergeant Major."

"If we don't know where to look we're going to be running around that desert in circles with our dicks in our hands—and right now the latest poop is eight hours old."

"Loner said he's got it covered." Shepard used Ritzik's call sign.

"Loner's dealing with all those sharks in Washington," Yates growled. "I'll believe it when I've got real-time satellite images downloading on my laptop, and no assholes from Langley deciding what I can receive and what I can't."

"Amen to that."

"When's Mickey D supposed to arrive?"

Gene Shepard scratched his head and consulted his note pad. "Mick? Fourteen hundred at the latest. He's bringing the strobes."

"Primo." Chief Warrant Officer Michael Dunne was a chopper pilot who worked out of the SOAR at Fort Campbell. For the past six months he'd been working closely with Ritzik's Sword Squadron to help merge the Delta shooters and the Task Force 160 aircrews into a seamless, unified operation. He'd been brought in by Ritzik, who had first worked with the young warrant officer during cold-weather combat-readiness exercises in the Sierra Nevada, three weeks after Ritzik had been pulled out of Afghanistan in March of 2002.

Because the ops had been so rough in Afghanistan, Ritzik had pushed hard to change the SOAR's training parameters. The 160th had gone to Afghanistan using by-the-book training guidelines: pilots were not required to fly in visibility of less than two miles and a ceiling of less than five hundred feet. But combat had forced the SOAR to deliver SpecOps troops in zero-zero conditions: zero visibility and zero ceiling (not to mention unpredictable downdrafts, crosswinds, and wind shears).

Back at CAG, Ritzik argued that unless a unit trained the way it would fight, the training was essentially useless. Delta trained that way. So did most SEAL units. Ritzik maintained that SOAR's pilots wanted to push the training envelope, but that a cabal of play-it-safe desk jockeys in the Army chief of staff's office was holding them back, afraid of losing one of SOAR's multimillion-dollar MH-53E aircraft. Ritzik took his case to the three-star who ran JSOC—the Joint Special Operations Command—at Fort Bragg. The result was an experimental, three-week, balls-to-the-wall, high-altitude training session under brutal weather conditions, sleep deprivation, and scores of zero-zero landings in rough terrain. It was during those twenty-one days that Ritzik and Rowdy Yates concluded WO-2 Michael Dunne was the best damn chopper pilot they'd ever seen.

Which was why within a minute and a half after he'd spoken with Ritzik from Rockman's office, Yates put in a call to the SOAR and had Dunne TDY'd to Bragg on a SECDEF Priority One.

Yates's draft op plan called for Mickey D to accompany the main contingent to Turkey. That way he could be briefed on the operation's problems and add his input to the solution. At Diyarbakir, the CIA's air base in southeastern Turkey, Ritzik and his people would pick up the last of their supplies, then fly on to Almaty, Kazakhstan.

In Turkey, Mickey D would rendezvous with an unmarked, unscheduled transport from Fort Campbell, which he'd ride to Dushanbe, the Tajik capital. From there, he and a four-man Task Force 160 aircrew would fly the radar-defeating covert-ops Black Hawk chopper that was co-cooned in the transport to an old Soviet paratroop-battalion command post at Tokhtamysh, within twenty-five miles of the Chinese border. There, they'd install fuel bladders that would triple the chopper's range, and wait for the signal to exfiltrate Ritzik's unit. The two dozen battery-powered infrared strobes Dunn was bringing with him would allow Ritzik to guide him to the LZ without using conventional lights.

Yates started for the door. "I gotta get out of here." Halfway, he stopped cold. "Oh, crap—I forgot the RPGs." Yates plucked up the handset and punched a series of numbers into it. "Keep me posted." He looked up at the twenty-four-hour clock above the door. "Christ Almighty, we're running out of time, Gino. I wish Loner's ass was here with us, not up in D.C. playing with the suits. I don't like working in a vacuum."

5

SECDEF LOOKED UP from his meeting notes and switched off the limo's right-rear reading light. He scribbled a telephone number on a Post-it, swiveled toward Ritzik, and handed it to him. "That's my cell-phone number—the one my wife uses." Rockman cracked a self-conscious grin. "She calls it my electronic leash. I pick it up—no one else."

"Yes, sir."

"Now you have it. It's not a secure line, so be careful what you say. But you call me with an inventory—everything you need—within two hours, and I'll see that it gets to Fort Bragg, or wherever else you want it sent, by the end of the day."

"Roger, Mr. Secretary." Ritzik memorized the number then rolled the Post-it into a ball and swallowed it. His head was spinning. The logistics were overwhelming—and there were already strictures on what he could and could not do. Before they'd left the White House, the president arranged for saturation satellite surveillance of the Xinjiang Autonomous Region, which would be up and on-line within sixteen hours. The pictures would provide Ritzik real-time intelligence about how the CIA people were being held, and where they were being taken.

That was the GN—the good news. The bad-news list was much longer.

BN-1 was the fact that there'd be no time for rehearsal. Whether it was hitting the Modelo prison compound in Panama to free an American national who'd operated an anti-Noriega TV station at the behest of the CIA, or going after terrorists holed up in Iranian-built barracks in Lebanon's Bekáa Valley, Delta would work with the techno-wizards from CIA's National Photographic Interpretation Center (NPIC) to build a full-scale model of the target and practice assaulting it until the operational wrinkles were ironed out. There'd be no rehearsal time for Xinjiang, which would increase the chances that Mr. Murphy of Murphy's Law fame would insinuate himself into the proceedings from the get-go.

BN-2 was that they'd be going in sterile. That meant no U.S. equipment. From bulletproof vests to boots to web gear, to the very weapons and ordnance they carried—none of it could be traceable back to the United States. There was some sterile equipment at Fort Bragg. But most of it was going to have to come from CIA, which maintained a warehouse full of non-American gear for its paramilitary units. From previous experience, Ritzik knew that CIA didn't like to share its wealth—whether it was information or gear. Even when the poor sons of bitches who'd been snatched were Agency people.

Which brought up BN-3: secure comms were going to be a problem. Delta had several tactical multichannel systems that allowed Ritzik to communicate with a forward base, as well as Washington if necessary, no matter where in the world he might be. But since they'd be operating with sanitized equipment, most American-made systems were out of the question.

Christ, what a mess. Ritzik hoped Rowdy Yates was making progress, because he obviously wasn't.

He looked up. They were crossing the Memorial Bridge. Ahead, Arlington National Cemetery lay spread out in front of the limo. Ritzik could see up, past the rows of white grave markers, to where the Lee House stood. He never failed to stop at Arlington when he passed through Washington. But there would be no time on this trip.

His thoughts were interrupted by the shrill, distinctive double ring of the red telephone mounted between the jump seats of the armored vehicle.

Rockman snatched the phone from its cradle. "This is the secretary," he said. Rockman clapped his free hand to his left ear to drown out the road noise. He listened carefully for about half a minute. Then he said, "Yes, sir. Will do. I'm on my way."

The SECDEF slapped the phone onto its cradle, reached forward, and slid the glass divider open. "Danny," he said to the security man riding shotgun, "we've been called back to the White House." He slid the divider closed and settled back in his seat as the big car negotiated the traffic circle and headed back across the Memorial Bridge.

Ritzik said, "Is there any way I can take a pass, Mr. Secretary? We're on an incredibly tight schedule. It's critical I get my people forward-based so we have some operational flexibility during the next thirty-six hours. I also need to see whatever satellite photos are available—right now—and I'll need to create secure uplinks to track the Tangos on a full-time." Ritzik checked his watch. "And I need your office to pull the military attachés in Ankara and Dushanbe into their offices so I can talk to 'em on a secure line."

"You can move your people anywhere you want. And I'll get you the intelligence that you need. But there's been some kind of development that affects the situation over there. So like it or not, son, you're coming with me."

The irritation in Ritzik's voice was unmistakable. "I guess I am, sir."

A cloud came across the secretary's face. He removed his gold-rimmed aviator-frame glasses, extracted a handkerchief from his trouser pocket, and cleaned the lenses. "You're a very outspoken fellow, Major. I might even say uncomfortably blunt on occasion. I don't mind that—it's been said that bluntness is one of my signature traits, too. But when I say you're coming with me, that's the way it is. One more thing: where we're going right now I don't want you uttering so much as a single syllable unless *I* ask you to say something first." Rockman folded the handkerchief and shoved it back into his pocket. He slipped his glasses back on, then cocked his head, hawklike, to look Ritzik in the eye. "Am I understood, Major?"

"Understood, Mr. Secretary."

68 Kilometers west of Tazhong, Xinjiang Autonomous Region, China.
0118 Hours Local Time.

SAM PHILLIPS FINALLY MANAGED to open his left eye. It hurt like hell and the vision was blurred. But at least he could see. He'd passed out again. For how long he had no idea. But it was night again. He guesstimated the truck was moving at about twenty miles an hour. From the way his kidneys and ribs were being punished, they were driving on an unpaved road, or caravan track, or through a wadi. He and X-Man were finally free of the hog-tie nooses that had bound them, although they kept the cords around their necks and the ends buried between their feet.

They'd hunkered down on the truck bed during the fighting, flinching as rounds tore through the wood and canvas. He resumed chewing at the tape around Chris's wrists only after the truck began rolling. Sam figured it had taken him an hour and a half, maybe more. After that, it was a matter of minutes until they'd loosened their remaining bonds. But they'd been careful to resecure a single strand of the thick tape around their wrists and ankles so they appeared to still be trussed.

As soon as Chris had freed him, Sam had asked the security man about Dick and Kaz.

X-Man's bloodied face was grim. "No idea," he whispered. "I never saw what happened to them. I hit the panic switch—God knows whether it transmitted or not—and then three guys yanked me out of the truck and beat the bejesus out of me. I passed out. Next thing I knew, you were trying to hump me awake."

The two of them had gone over what they did know. And it wasn't much.

First, the gunfight at dawn had been intense, even though it had lasted only a matter of minutes. Sam knew it had been intense because in the morning light he could make out dozens of bullet holes in the canvas over their heads. After the shooting stopped, there'd been a lot of shouting. Some of it had been in Uzbek, and so Sam had understood enough of it to grasp that whoever was in charge wanted everybody to haul butt quickly before the army showed up.

Within a short period of time—he didn't know how much because the crystal display of Sam's digital wristwatch was smashed, and someone had taken X-Man's—the truck they were in was slammed into gear, and they began bouncing across what Sam took to be the desert basin.

From the way the dawn had broken, he'd decided they were heading west. Sam listened to the sounds of the convoy as it ground through the high desert. If he was correct, he thought he'd identified the sounds of three trucks, maybe four. X-Man concurred. But they couldn't be sure—and in any case however many trucks there were didn't matter. Moreover, there was no way either of them was going to risk a peek through the canvas to find out.

He'd spent a long time as he lay there trying to reconstruct a map of the region in his mind's eye. He was reasonably certain the bad guys would ultimately move northwest, heading for Afghanistan or Tajikistan. His reasoning was twofold. First, because the Afghan and Tajik borders were more porous than the Kazakh or Kyrgyz ones. Second, the mountain passes to Tajikistan had scores of unmarked, narrow roads that had been used by smugglers for decades. During his tour in Dushanbe, Sam had even been taken across into China—for a kilometer or so of bragging rights—on a precarious, rutted, cliffside smuggler's road by Halil Abdullaev, the *muktar* of a small village on the Chinese border and one of Sam's most productive Tajik agents.

He'd been certain they wouldn't head south. The southern border—with India—was heavily fortified because of an ongoing Sino-Indian boundary dispute. And the Hindu Kush region that led to Pakistan was not hospitable to the IMU.

But Tajikistan was in a state of political flux, and the IMU, although weakened, still enjoyed support among the Muslim population. And northeast Afghanistan was still in a relative state of war. Remnants of al-Qaeda and the Taliban roamed more or less unhindered, shielded by the local tribes.

"Chris, Chris . . ." Sam used his knees to shake the X-Man until he stirred.

The security man finally responded. "Christ, how long have we been passed out?"

"I don't know. Hours." Sam grunted as the truck bounced. "We can't just stay here like this."

X-Man whispered, "Sam, I don't want to do anything precipitous until we know where Kaz and Dick are."

"Agreed." Sam swallowed hard. "God, I wish we had some water." The two of them lay there for some minutes in silence. Then Sam said, "Thank God at least they don't know who they got their hands on," he whispered.

X-Man rolled over. "What do you mean, Sam?"

"Jeezus, X, think how much the IMU could get for us if they sold us to al-Qaeda. Or the Iranians."

"Don't even say that as a joke."

Sam forced a wry expression. "Hell, at least the people who have us are moving in the right direction."

X-Man snorted. "I was taught by the nuns always to be grateful for small blessings."

Sam whispered, "Let's hope they get across whatever border they're heading for before the Chinese catch up with 'em. I—" He started to say something else. But the truck braked to an abrupt stop.

Fifteen seconds later, Sam heard movement outside. And then the rear flap was lifted, and he was rendered blind by a sudden shaft of incredibly bright light.

Sword Squadron, Fort Bragg, Fayetteville, North Carolina.
1254 Hours Local Time.

"GODDAMMIT, Loner, if that's the way it's gotta be, then that's the way it is. But I tell you, this sucks. And if you won't tell those suits to go screw themselves and let you get back where you belong, then put me on the friggin' phone with 'em and I will—and that includes the goddamn secretary of defense." On the Long List of People Rowdy Yates Does Not Like, *suits* was his comprehensive term for all self-important, limp-dicked, spineless, backstabbing, politically motivated individuals including (but not limited to) most flag-rank officers and virtually all politicians, attorneys, and CEOs of Fortune 500 corporations. In fact, the only two categories of humanity Rowdy Yates detested more than suits were traitors and cowards.

The bad news, which Ritzik was relaying from the secretary's car, was that he was probably going to miss his connections because they were being called back to the White House and the secretary had just indicated that he wasn't going to be leaving Washington until the evening. And so he'd just told Rowdy to unlock his cage and grab his gear while he met with whomever. With the secretary's help he'd catch a commercial flight out of Dulles to Frankfurt. There, he'd catch the Lufthansa flight direct to Almaty. If all the planes were on time, he'd beat Rowdy and the C-5 by two and a half hours.

The sergeant major was not convinced. "This op has already turned into a huge Charlie Foxtrot, Mike, and I'm still sitting behind my friggin' desk." Yates balanced the reading magnifiers on the tip of his nose and scribbled on a notepad. "I know you've already been promised coordination, but maybe you'd like to know anyway that I haven't heard friggin' word one from Langley. Not that it would make a bit of difference. Those self-important pencil-pushing sons of bitches wouldn't know real intelligence if it walked up and bit 'em on the ass." He paused. "Yes, sir, Major, sir, you can put me on the speakerphone and I'll say the same thing to SECDEF."

Yates paused and listened. "Yes, Mike. Okay. Will do. We'll pack each Fire Team One laptop, and every man gets a handheld and GPS module. I'll make sure Talgat has clothes for us, too." Yates made another series of notations on the legal pad, then cradled the telephone. The effing suits in Washington were going to get them all killed. There was no doubt about that whatsoever.

6

MIKE RITZIK followed Robert Rockman as they descended a narrow, carpeted stairway, turned right, then left, past a warren of offices. The secretary led Ritzik down a short corridor lined with framed photographs of the president and first lady on their overseas trips. At the end of the hallway, Rockman waited as a Secret Service agent opened the unmarked Situation Room door and stood aside so they could enter.

Rockman's palm thrust Ritzik forward. The room was smaller and narrower than he had expected. He'd envisioned high-backed, hand-tooled leather judge's chairs, lots of telephones and laptop computers, and high-definition flat screens displaying real-time satellite images. What he saw was a long, narrow, wood-paneled space dominated by a basic table with a dozen spartan leather armchairs around it. A single judge's chair sat below the wall-mounted presidential seal at the head of the table. In front of each chair a notepad and a blue ballpoint pen, both bearing the presidential seal, had been carefully positioned. In front of the president's place sat a black leather legal-pad holder, imprinted with the Great Seal of the United States, as well as a large universal TV remote-control unit.

There were two multiline telephone consoles—one at each end of the table. At the head, there was also a single secure telephone. Two wall clocks were hung high on the walls at opposite ends of the room. There were three small TV sets jammed into a utilitarian cabinet at the rear, opposite the doorway. The screens displayed the Fox News Channel, CNN, and Sky News, but there was no sound coming from any of them. Stacked against the wood-paneled walls were perhaps two dozen plastic chairs, randomly scattered in stacks of two or three.

There were already a few officials sitting at the long table. The national security adviser was there, half glasses perched on the end of her nose, engrossed in a red-tabbed document as she sat at what Ritzik assumed to be the president's right hand. She said, "Mr. Secretary," but didn't acknowledge Ritzik's presence. Next to Wirth sat Nick Pappas, the rumpled, chubby former congressional staffer who was now director of central intelligence. Next to him sat a middle-aged, slightly overweight woman with a severe haircut and thick, retro eyeglasses. Three chairs down from the DCI, Admiral Phil Buckley, chairman of the Joint Chiefs, scratched an itch just above the starched collar of his uniform shirt and stared at the wall, pointedly ignoring the SECDEF. At the far end of the table, an attractive young Chinese-American woman was listening to a middle-aged man whose face Ritzik had seen on the evening news but couldn't identify. As he whispered, the woman's head bobbed up and down as she made notes on a yellow legal pad.

Rockman nodded at the man at the far end of the table, then commandeered the armchair closest to the head of the table, directly opposite the NSC adviser. Ritzik started to sit next to him, but the secretary's quick shake of head and abrupt hand signal indicated that he "park it" on one of the black plastic chairs up against the wall instead.

He did as ordered, sitting silently, idly fingering the visitor's pass clipped to his lapel and scanning the faces, absorbing the surroundings. The young woman conferred with her colleague, then scribbled even more feverishly. Monica Wirth passed the red-tabbed document to Rockman, who flipped it open and read its contents, his expression devolving into a hound-dog frown.

Then the door opened. Without fanfare or announcement, the president strode in. Twenty-eight casters rumbled across the linoleum tile in unison as everyone in the warm room scrambled to their feet.

"Everybody sit, sit, please." Pete Forrest pulled the high-backed swivel chair away from the table and dropped into it.

Over the sound of chairs being settled into, the president said, "Give us the latest news, Nick."

Pappas opened a leather folder and glanced down at the file inside. "The locator signal activated by the Sino Insertion Element is still transmitting strongly. The team is being moved in a northwesterly direction across the Tarim Basin." The DCI paused long enough to run a stubby finger inside the collar of his white button-down shirt. "We believe the kidnappers to be from the Islamic Movement of Uzbekistan, or IMU. Our assessment was that SIE-1 was being taken toward the Tajik border."

"We knew most of that eight hours ago, Nick," Robert Rockman growled.

The DCI's dark eyes flashed in SECDEF's direction. But his neutral tone never changed. "Here's the latest news, Rocky. Three hours after SIE-1 was snatched up, the guerrilla contingent that took them ambushed a small, lightly armed PLA convoy that was clandestinely transporting an obsolete weapons package to the underground nuclear storage facility located southeast of the Lop Nur test site. We believe the operation is part of an effort by the IMU to reconstitute itself after years of decline. And we have revised our assessment. We now believe that the IMU plans to detonate the weapon inside China.

"Jeezus H. Kee-rist, Nick," Rockman exploded. " 'Three hours after' is five hours ago. How the hell can you keep that kind of information to yourself? You know what we're trying to do."

"We had to verify the information," Pappas said. "There is a formal process that has to be followed, Mr. Secretary, before raw information can become intelligence."

"Screw the process, Nick—just get the damn information disseminated."

"That's enough, Rocky." The president's voice betrayed irritation. "Go on, Nick."

The DCI reached into the center of the table for a black-and-silver plastic thermos pitcher that sat on a salver surrounded by a half-dozen empty glasses. He poured himself a glass of water, sipped, then continued. "Anyhow, because of its ambient nuclear activity, the convoy was being dual tracked. From overhead by a FORTAE[13] satellite operated jointly with the British, and from our unilateral monitoring station in Sumbe Tekes, Kazakhstan. Shortly after the PLA convoy was intercepted, gradient effluvium readings from both satellite and unilateral monitors intensified exponentially, indicating to us that the package had been—"

"Nick," the president said, "use English, will you?"

"The terrorists broke the seals on the protective container, Mr. President. They are currently in possession of a first-generation nuclear weapon—from the looks of it, it's a

---

13. Fast Onboard Recognition of Transient Atomic Experiments.

fifteen-kiloton MADM, or medium atomic demolition munition, from the late 1970s or early 1980s. From our other unilateral overhead assets in the region, we know for sure they have already been playing with it."

Rockman said, "Playing with it?"

"Fiddling with the dials, or whatever's on the damn thing," Pappas said. "At least that's what it looks like on the photos I've seen."

President Forrest massaged his forehead. "Okay, Nick, now give us the good news."

The DCI didn't miss a beat. "That *was* the good news, Mr. President."

The president peered down toward the end of the table. "Roger," he said, "you're my well-paid secretary of energy. You do nuclear. What's your department's take on this mess?"

"I've brought Tracy Wei-Liu with me to shed some light on that, Mr. President."

Pete Forrest said, "Welcome, Miss Wei-Liu. What do you do for a living?"

The young woman stammered, "I'm deputy assistant secretary of energy for national security policy, Mr. President."

"That's a hundred-dollar title, young lady. What does it mean in buck-and-a-half words?"

"I keep track of nuclear weapons, Mr. President."

"Ours or theirs?"

"Everybody's, sir."

"Okay," Pete Forrest said. "What can you tell us about this alleged fifteen-kiloton medium atomic demolition device Nick just told us about?"

"I'd like to see a picture of the device, if I could."

Pete Forrest shot an angry glance at the DCI. "Didn't you messenger the photos to Energy?"

"I couldn't verify that Miss Wei-Liu had the appropriate clearances," Pappas said.

"Goddammit, Nick—"

The DCI passed the folder to the Joint Chiefs chairman, who slid it below the salt to where Wei-Liu sat. The young woman took a magnifying glass out of a briefcase at her feet and examined the photos. "This device is a J-12—the largest of the Chinese MADM series, with an explosive power of fifteen kilotons. The J-12 was developed in the late 1970s. It was known as the Icebox, because it looked like one of those old-fashioned refrigerators with the compressors on the top." Wei-Liu paused long enough to draw a deep breath. "The J-12 was intended as a tactical weapon to be used against India and Taiwan. It is based on an early Soviet design."

Rockman waved a hand at the young woman. "When I was secretary back in 1974, I decommissioned all of our MADMs because they were obsolete. You mean the Chinese only began to use them after that?"

"Mr. Secretary, you have to understand that until the Chinese intensified their technical espionage programs in the 1980s and 90s, they'd always been fifteen to twenty years behind both the U.S. and the Soviet Union in nuclear weapons development. Both we and the Soviets discarded the MADM by the mid-1970s because we'd moved on to smaller, lighter, and more precise tactical devices. The Chinese kept their MADMs operational until 1988. That year, one of the smaller J-series weapons detonated as it was being taken from a bunker on the Indian border during a military exercise. Shortly after that, all thirty MADMs were abruptly removed from China's tactical inventory."

The president asked, "What caused the 1988 incident?"

"Our best guess," Wei-Liu said, "was the weapon's primitive detonation system."

The president said, "How primitive are we talking here?"

"Somewhere between Cretaceous and Jurassic, Mr. President," Wei-Liu said. "Today, sir, we achieve detonation through highly precise electronic means. In the 1970s, the Chinese were still technically unable to accomplish this. And so they made do—until relatively recently—with what might be called an IED, or improvised explosive device. The Chinese inserted a series of thin wires into an eighty-five-pound core of an explosive that's similar to our military Pentolite, which is a fifty-fifty mixture of pentaerythritol tetranitrate, or PETN plastic explosive, and TNT. The Chinese use a slightly different formula, which makes theirs more volatile. The Pentolite we use has an explosive power of one and a quarter times TNT. The Chinese version is two and a half times more powerful than TNT, which was what they needed to achieve an explosion generating critical mass. They initiated the Pentolite by vaporizing the wires in a precise sequence, using a huge surge of electrical current generated by a series of powerful capacitors."

"What's the problem with that?" Monica Wirth asked.

"First," Wei-Liu said, "it was technically efficient but unwieldy—similar in many ways to the detonation system on the atomic weapons in the Manhattan Project. If you look at the photograph—" She slid the magnifying glass and one of the prints down the table to the chairman, who slid it to Monica Wirth, who passed it to the president. "See, sir, that boxlike attachment bolted onto the top of the device—it's roughly two feet by three feet."

Pete Forrest moved the glass back and forth across the photo. "Yes," he said. "I see it. Cumbersome."

"That's the electrical component for the detonation package, sir."

"Uh-huh," the president said.

"So, as I said, it's unwieldy. Second, under certain conditions the Chinese version of Pentolite can degenerate and become unstable, similar to the way mishandled dynamite sweats nitroglycerine. Third, there are the capacitors. They require a bank of storage batteries to keep them fully charged. And despite insulation, batteries can still generate both volatile fumes and static electricity under certain conditions. Static combined with fumes can result in a spark, which in turn can set off the Pentolite if the explosive has begun to deteriorate."

"Give us the situation in a nutshell," Rockman said.

"We're basically talking about your terrorists driving around Western China with the equivalent of a thirty-million-pound mason jar of nitroglycerine in the back of their truck," Wei-Liu said, matter-of-factly.

The president said, "Well, Miss Wei-Liu, thank you for putting all this in such unambiguous terms." He paused. "Thank you for coming. And thank you, too, Roger."

The energy secretary rose and slid the photos back toward Nick Pappas. "You're welcome, Mr. President."

The room remained silent as the two of them made their way out. As Wei-Liu passed Monica Wirth, the NSC adviser handed the young woman a note, which Wei-Liu read, folded, and dropped into the pocket of her jacket.

After the door clicked closed behind them, the DCI raised his hand. "Mr. President—" The CIA director was churning his legs and squirming uncomfortably in the chair, reminding Ritzik of the poor guy in the Preparation H commercials.

"Yes, Nick."

"I can also report that NSA's technical capabilities have confirmed Beijing has activated its rapid reaction forces and assigned them the task of hunting the terrorists down and retrieving the weapon."

"Jeezus H. Kee-rist." Robert Rockman's palm slapped

the table surface. "What made you wait until now to give us *that* piece of intelligence? What's next, Nick?"

"Just hold on, Mr. Secretary," Pappas interrupted. "There also happen to be two pieces of hugely positive intelligence."

The SECDEF crossed his arms and hunched his shoulders—body language that told Ritzik Rockman didn't believe a word of it. Rockman rolled his chair across the floor. "And they are?"

"First, the Chinese are incapable of tracking the guerrillas by satellite because their birds take up to a week to be shifted."

The secretary's hand slapped the table. "I know that, Nick."

"Last night, Chinese intelligence used its front companies to call every commercial satellite operation in the world in order to secure one-meter imagery of Xinjiang Autonomous Region. They tried the French. They called the Belgians, the Finns, the Germans, the Canadians, the Japanese, and finally all our own American companies." Pappas tapped his pen on the table. "But CIA anticipated the move and successfully preempted Beijing. Last week, through half a dozen cover firms, CIA bought up exclusive rights to every bit of commercial European and Asian satellite imagery with a resolution of twenty-five meters or less, covering the western Xinjiang Autonomous Region. Then I had NSA exercise shutter control over all the American-owned commercial birds in the same target area. So the Chinese are blind."

The president visibly perked up. "Good work, Nick."

"Thank you, sir. And now . . ." Pappas flicked through the papers in his leather binder until he came to a white-covered folder that had a single, thick, diagonal blue line running from top left to bottom right. He opened the dossier. Inside sat a thin stack of National Security Agency paperwork. "Second, NSA transmitted these Zulu-grade intercepts to me not half an hour ago. China's Central Military Command has just assigned the task of interdiction and retrieval to its Army Aviation Unit." The DCI's stubby fingers played air piano on the NSA documents. "And that, ladies and gentlemen, is very good news."

SECDEF's eyes narrowed belligerently. "What's so good about it?"

Pappas said, "I will let Margaret Nylos explain." He paused to acknowledge the middle-aged woman sitting next to him. "Margaret is the national intelligence officer for China. She is responsible for keeping me up-to-date on all of China's internal politics."

The president said, "Miss Nylos?"

"Mr. President, this is hugely positive news because we believe it demonstrates irrefutable evidence of the growing rift within the PLA, a schism my people have been predicting for more than a year now. That split—between the elders who lead China's conventional forces and the young generals who control its Special Operations units—has long-term strategic and tactical implications for us. It is a situation the United States can exploit to great advantage as we enter the next stage of our relationship with Beijing."

Pappas noted the look of impatience on the president's face, sipped at his water, and cleared his throat. "Thank you, Margaret. Of more immediate interest to us this morning, the assigning of AAU as the retrieval force is noteworthy because, unlike our American special operations units, the Chinese have never fully integrated their air and ground special operations forces. The AAU's operations are highly centralized. They are headquartered in the Beijing Military District. Every one of the unit's assets lie within sixty miles of the Chinese capital. And not one AAU aircraft has the capability of reaching the Xinjiang Autonomous Region without multiple refueling stops."

Rockman interrupted: "Can't they refuel in the air?"

Margaret Nylos said, "No, sir. The Chinese lag far behind the West in helicopter technology. In fact, most of the current operational Chinese helicopter designs have been adapted from Soviet or French models. As you will also recall, the United States sold China a squadron of MH-60 Black Hawk helicopters in 1991, in return for Beijing's allowing NSA to establish six Russian listening posts in the Tian mountain range. But those helicopters lack spare parts, and our statistical models indicate that today, the majority of them are inoperable. I also think—"

"*Thank* you, Margaret." The DCI squirmed awkwardly. "The bottom line is that this development buys us the time we need to extract our people," he said.

"Nick." Rockman cupped his chin in his hand. "Refueling a squadron of aircraft can be accomplished in a matter of minutes. It seems to me we're not going to gain but a few hours."

The DCI's head wagged negatively. He tapped the NSA intercepts with his middle finger. "Mr. Secretary, what we have here proves otherwise. The commanding officer of the Army Aviation Unit is China's youngest major general. His name is Zhou Yi. Zhou just turned forty—a real up-and-comer. He has been pressing the political leadership to allocate more resources to such areas as Special Operations, information warfare, and other unconventional methods and tactics. He has many supporters within the CCP, and it's expected that within the next six to eight months he will be put forward as the next chairman of the PLA's Central Military Command."

The DCI sipped his water. Margaret Nylos picked up the

narrative. "Zhou's strongest rival for that post is the commanding general of the Beijing Military District, an army four-star named Yin Zhong Liang. Yin is sixty-eight, married for forty-one years. He's very old guard and tied closely to President Wu Min. Now, General Yin stumbled a few years ago when he lied to the political cadre about who was responsible after that Chinese F-8 fighter hit our EP-3 reconnaissance plane, and Beijing held twenty-three of our Navy personnel for eleven days. But since then, his position has been strengthened because he's kept dissent in the capital under control, and he's mended his fences with the leadership. In fact, Yin has single-handedly built such a cult of personality around the president that I can now state we believe Wu will remain in power for the foreseeable future—more significantly, he will not, as previously thought, relinquish his chairmanship of the committee that oversees the military. Equally significant, Yin has made strong political alliances with the generals in charge of the Nanjing, Jinan, Guangzhou, Shenyang, and Lanzhou military districts. All these commands stand to lose massive funding if the budget reallocations young Major General Zhou Yi is advocating go through."

"Miss Nylos, stop right there," the president interrupted. "I think I already heard a lot of what you're saying on CNN last week." The president glared at the DCI. "Nick—can you people please get to the point."

"Of course, Mr. President." The DCI's voice took on a pedantic tone, and he tapped the tabletop with his pen for emphasis. "Point: General Yin believes he is vulnerable to a challenge from Zhou. Point: Yin's political allies control every military installation and every liter of aviation fuel between Beijing and Xinjiang. Point: There is no way they will make things easy for the young upstart Zhou."

Rockman's eyes went wide. "Even though there's a loose nuke, Nick?"

"Yes," the DCI said confidently. "Even so."

Pete Forrest rapped his knuckles on the table edge. "Enough political theory. There are lives on the line. How much time do we have? How much time?"

Margaret Nylos said: "A minimum of four days, Mr. President, from the sample of message traffic we managed to skim this morning. Possibly as many as five days. I'll know more after the intercepts are translated."

The president's jaw dropped. "Miss Nylos, aren't you the national intelligence officer for China?"

"Yes, sir, I am."

"And yet you can't read Chinese."

"Mr. President," Nick Pappas interjected, "I promoted Margaret for her analytical skills, not her language capability."

Rockman raised his hand. "Nick," he said.

"Yes?" The DCI shifted his gaze.

Rockman pulled at his earlobe. "I don't want to sound like a doom-and-gloom kind of guy, but how do you know that the Chinese aren't putting out false message traffic?"

Pappas said, "False message traffic?"

Monica Wirth cocked her head in the DCI's direction. "Disinformation, Nick."

Ritzik watched as Rockman's right hand slipped into his inside jacket pocket and retrieved a thin paperback. The secretary flipped to a page that he'd marked with a yellow Post-it, slipped a pair of half glasses out of his breast pocket, perched them on his nose, and read: " 'When strong, appear weak. When brave, appear fearful. When orderly, appear chaotic. Draw your enemy in with the promise of gain, and overcome him through confusion.' "

The secretary dropped the paperback on the table. "That, ladies and gentleman, is Sun-Tzu—the granddaddy of all Chinese generals, including General Zhou and General Yin."

Nick Pappas's cheeks grew red. "What's your point, Rocky?" he asked.

"I guess," Rockman said dryly, "my point, Nick . . . and Margaret, is that everything the two of you have told us so far appears to be the result of technical intelligence gathering. But what if Beijing is playing with us—sending out false message traffic in order to deceive us and suck us into a situation that will embarrass the United States? There's a summit in six weeks, and the Chinese are good at mind games. What's the hard evidence that your intercepts are genuine? I've seen reports from our military attachés in Beijing that describe a possible schism—and I underline the word *possible*—within the PLA. But the mere appearance of a rift between factions isn't good enough for me. I'd like to know if you have reports from agents on the ground in China who have verified the situation you've just described."

"Jesus Christ, Rocky," the DCI exploded. "What the hell are you doing here? You're tossing a wrench is what. Goddammit, you've been trying to undermine me from the get-go, and I—"

"Gentlemen, that's enough." Pete Forrest's voice took command of the room. "What has been decided has been decided." The president stood. He glanced quickly in Mike Ritzik's direction. "I think we all have a lot of work to do."

Rockman was first on his feet. "Yes, Mr. President."

The president focused on Nick Pappas. "Nick, I want you to deliver any information Rocky wants—anything he asks for—without delay."

"There are certain procedures—" the DCI began.

"I don't give a damn about procedures," the president interrupted. "These are your people we're talking about. If Rocky wants something from you, he gets it. Immediately. No questions. No waiting. No bureaucratic delays for 'procedures.'" He paused. "Have I made myself crystal clear, Nick?"

Pappas glanced around the room. "Yes, Mr. President."

"Good." Pete Forrest wheeled and left the room.

There was about a quarter minute of dead air. Rockman caught Monica Wirth's eye. "Can you spare me a few minutes, Monica?"

"I was about to ask you the same question, Mr. Secretary." The NSC adviser closed the document folder in front of her. "Mr. Director?"

"Monica?"

She held her hand out, palm side up. "I'm going to need those photographs and whatever else you have in that folder."

The DCI started to object but then thought the better of it. Without a word, he handed the folder to Wirth.

"Thank you, Nick." The national security adviser turned toward the doorway. "Mr. Secretary, let's adjourn to my office, shall we?"

7

68 Kilometers west of Tazhong, Xinjiang Autonomous Region, China.
0239 Hours Local Time.

AT LEAST KAZ AND DICK CAMPBELL were alive. Sam Phillips thanked God for that. They looked like hell. But then, he and X-Man looked worse.

Sam and X-Man were yanked out of the truck, tossed onto the rocky, cold desert floor, and kicked and beaten for having freed themselves. Then they were dragged over to their commandeered 4×4—where Kaz and the Marine stood, still bound and gagged.

All the camera equipment as well as their luggage had been dumped onto the ground, illuminated by headlights from four big trucks with numerals and Chinese characters on the doors. Sam took a fast reading of the situation. The video equipment was still in its cases, sitting on the ground.

Sam gave his team a quick glance and saw in their eyes that they were ready to follow his lead. He wished he had one.

Shoazim. The guide was nowhere to be seen. Sam realized he was probably dead. Brutal as it might sound, that made sense. These people had to know that guides reported to the police. That made Shoazim a collaborator. Also,

Shoazim was of no material value—in fact, he was a drain on whatever rations and supplies the terrorists might have. But they were passing as Brits, Irish, and Canadians— Westerners who could be ransomed.

He smelled cigarettes. Sam's eyes swept a hundred and eighty degrees, trying not to make direct contact with any of the bad guys, but able to see half a dozen red spots in the darkness as they pulled on their smokes. No one spoke. The four of them were on display. The boss man, whoever he was, was probably trying to figure out how to deal with them. Sam hoped boss man wasn't a Chechen. Brutality was a way of life in this part of the world, but the Chechens were the worst. In Afghanistan, al-Qaeda's Chechen fighters had tortured and mutilated every American they'd gotten their hands on. According to one report Sam had read at the time, the Chechens at Takhur Ghar had cut the ears and privates off a Navy SEAL they'd captured before finally putting him out of his misery with a bullet to the brain. Even the Russian light colonel he'd recruited in Tajikistan had warned him to steer clear, "Sam, out here is what we call *dikiy-dikiy vostok*—the Wild, Wild East. Out here, the Tajiks, Turkmen, or Uzbeks, they take no prisoners. But compared to Chechens, Tajiks and Uzbeks—they are nice guys."

Sam's mind was racing. His most important job was to keep everyone alive. To do that, he knew that he had, somehow, to establish control. Control was the key. That was the first rule of case-officerdom he'd been taught at the Farm.

No matter how desperate or dicey the situation might be, the instructors told them over and over, you always try to gain control. Just the way you control your agents, your developmentals—everyone you deal with. And even if you're captured, or detained, you work to establish some form of control over the people who grabbed you. You come up with a tactical strategy—and you find a way to execute it.

It's like that old cartoon, one instructor'd said, the one in which two guys are manacled to a wall, hand and foot, suspended twenty feet above a pair of hungry lions. There's no window to their cell, and the lions are between them and the door—which is locked from the outside—and besides, they're chained up. So one guy is saying to the other, "Now, here's my plan . . ."

Sam understood that he had to find a way to establish control over the lions who were holding them hostage. Even though the lions had just beaten the crap out of them. Even though the lions were holding automatic weapons.

And so, he struggled to his feet.

From somewhere, a heavy boot swept his legs out from under him. Sam went crashing face first onto the desert floor.

Scattered laughter erupted from the darkness beyond the truck headlights.

Establish control. Sam fought the pain and the panic that was rising in his throat. He pushed himself off the sand.

A shadow loomed in front of him. Sam looked up. He was a large man, with a Saddam Hussein mustache and a single, prehominid eyebrow. He was dressed in a PLA uniform jacket and what looked like U.S. Army–surplus woodland-camouflage BDU trousers. Even in the nighttime coolness he reeked of sweat, garlic, and tobacco. In his left hand was an AK-47, its barrel pointed at the ground.

Slowly, Mustache Man brought the weapon up, up, up, until its muzzle was even with Sam's clavicle. *"Tökhtang—stop."*

Sam raised himself farther off the ground.

The AK's front sight jabbed against his chest. *"Tökhtang!"*

Sam fought to keep his eyes steady and his voice even. "*Siz Inglizcha gaplashasizmi?* Do you speak English?"

In response, he received another shove with the AK's muzzle.

He took the risk of getting shot by pushing back. "*Siz Inglizcha gaplashasizmi?*"

After what seemed to him like a decade, the pressure of the AK barrel on his chest was reduced slightly. "*Inglizcha?*"

Sam pushed himself on to his knees, and then stood up as straight as he could, looking directly into Mustache Man's black eyes. He anticipated the boot coming at his legs again, but nothing happened. "*Kha,*" he said. "Yes, *Inglizcha.*"

"*Men Inglizcha. Uzbekchada, Ruscha, Tojik.*"

Mustache Man's accent was Uzbek, not Chechen. A huge surge of relief washed over Sam. But outwardly, he showed nothing.

The Uzbek's eyes bore into him. Sam realized he had to speak—the team's lives depended on what he'd say, and how he'd say it. But he didn't trust his Tajik or Uzbek. "We are English," he said in halting Russian. "Journalists. Media. We work for a television company in London. We do not understand why you have taken us"—he tugged at his brain for the right word—"prisoner," he finally said. He paused, translating in his head before he spoke. "Please free my friends. Please give us all some water, or tea, and some rice. It has been a long time since we have had anything to eat or drink."

Mustache Man said nothing. But he stepped back three paces and lowered the AK's barrel. Sam was relieved until he realized the muzzle was pointed directly at his crotch and Muzzle Man's finger was still wrapped around the trigger.

There followed what could only be described as a long, unnatural pause. And then Mustache Man lowered the muzzle of the AK until it pointed into the desert floor. He looked at Sam and said in Russian, "Journalists?"

"Television journalists," Sam said.

"Television. BBC?"

"Yes, just like BBC," Sam said.

Mustache Man said, "You make television of us?"

"Of course," Sam said. "We can make a video of you. An interview. And then, after we leave, we can show it on television. The whole world will see and hear you."

Mustache Man said, "Show me."

Sam looked at his three companions. "Free them. Give us water and rice. And then we will be happy to show you."

"You show me *now*." Mustache Man swept the AK's muzzle across Sam's body. One-handed, he fired a long burst into Dick Campbell's chest. The Marine was blown two yards backward, dead by the time Sam screamed, "*No!*"

"I said you show me now." Mustache Man butt-stroked Sam with the AK, knocking him onto his face. He reached down, grabbed Sam by the collar of his shirt, and started dragging him toward the video equipment.

Sam twisted free of Mustache Man's grip. He rolled onto his hands and knees, crawled to get away. But the Uzbek followed. Sam tried to struggle to his feet. He got a roundhouse kick that sent pain from his hip into his eye sockets.

Mustache Man stood over him. The AK started to come up. Sam's palms went up. "Please," he said. "I'll show you. But I'm going to need help." Sam's brain wasn't being helpful. Suddenly he'd lost every bit of Russian he'd ever known. He fought to remember the vocabulary, then, like some kind of demented child, spoke slowly, in a monotone. "They have to help me."

There was a pause. Sam chanced a quick look up at Mustache Man, wincing in anticipation of a rifle butt—or a bullet. Mustache Man's face told him the guerrilla was debating whether or not to shoot them all.

Finally, the Uzbek said, "*Da*. Show me." He flicked a glance into the darkness. Kaz's gag was pulled off, and his arms freed. Sam looked into the kid's eyes and knew he was in shock. Well, Kaz wasn't the only one. Sam had never lost an agent. But now he'd just killed a colleague. Dick was dead because of him. Because of his stupidity. His game playing. Stupid goddamn game playing.

Sam's eyes lost focus. He started to hyperventilate. It was X-Man who brought him back. Chris took him by the shoulders and shook him. "Sam," he said. "Sam, we have to get to work. The man's waiting."

Sam blinked a few times. "Get to work." He looked over at the Marine's bound, gagged corpse. There'd been no time for anything. Not even a good-bye glance. Now Dick was dead. Murdered. The rage started to build inside Sam now. His eyes grew wide. His fists clenched. And then Sam's training took over and he shut down the partition inside him that hurt more than he'd ever realized anybody could hurt, and he nodded his head and said, numbly, "Okay, Chris."

Revenge would come. But later. The shock of seeing his teammate murdered would hit him hard. But not now. Sam couldn't let anything touch him now. His only job was to keep himself, Kaz, and X-Man alive.

As quickly as they could, the three of them set to work. They pulled the camera out of its padded case and checked the battery. It was weak—drained from the earlier drilling.

Sam's hip throbbed painfully. "How much time do we have on the battery?"

"Don't know," Kaz said. "Maybe eight, ten minutes." He gave Sam a grim look. "The spare's dead."

Sam gritted his teeth. "Maybe they have a generator."

"If not, I can recharge using the cigarette lighter in the Toyota."

"Good." Sam watched as Chris set up the tripod. Kaz placed the camera on the tripod head and secured it. Sam unpacked the zoom lens and twisted the bayonet mount until it clicked. Chris screwed the audio cable into the back of the camera.

Kaz found the hand mike and attached it to the cable. "Good to go."

Chris positioned himself behind the camera and took a quick squint through the eyepiece. He nodded at Sam. "Ready when you are."

Sam beckoned to Mustache Man. "We are ready." He took the mike out of Kaz's hands and waved it in the guerrilla's direction. "What would you like to say?"

"Not here." Mustache Man shouted something in a dialect Sam did not understand. Someone climbed into one of the PLA trucks, turned it around, and backed it in a half circle until the headlights of the truck in which Sam and X-Man had been held lit up the canvas covering the tailgate.

Mustache Man's boots scrunched across the sand and stone. He stood twenty feet from the truck. "Put the camera here."

Sam limped over to where Mustache Man stood. "C'mon, chaps, let's do it."

Mustache Man gave more orders. The canvas was pushed aside and the tailgate dropped. Half a dozen men slung their weapons and clambered aboard. Another four stood below.

Sam waited as the camera was brought up and set where Mustache Man wanted it. He got behind the tripod, sidled up to the eyepiece, and squinted through the viewfinder. He adjusted the focus, then zoomed in on the knot of bodies struggling to wrestle a large, rectangular object that looked somewhat like one of those 1930s refrigerators—the ones with the compressors on the top—out of a cumbersome storage container.

They pushed and pulled for perhaps half a minute. Sam was about to shut the power off when the cluster of men separated long enough for him to catch a fleeting glimpse of the yellow-and-black nuclear radiation symbol stenciled on the storage container. He said, "Oh, my God," and involuntarily took a big step backward.

X-Man said, "What's up?"

Sam rubbed his face. "I don't bloody believe this." He watched as they wrestled the fridge out of the truck and lowered it onto the ground.

"Now," Mustache Man said. "*Now* you give me the microphone."

It was at that instant that Sam Phillips understood that he was a dead man, too. That they were all dead men. Dick Campbell wasn't going to be SIE-1's only casualty.

The West Wing of the White House.
1355 Hours Local Time.

RITZIK WAS SURPRISED to find the young woman who'd briefed in the Situation Room waiting for them in the national security adviser's inner office. Monica Wirth said, "Mr. Secretary, Major Ritzik, this is Deputy Assistant Secretary of Energy Tracy Wei-Liu."

Ritzik said, "Michael Ritzik. Nice to meet you." He extended his arm and got a cool, firm handshake in return. She certainly was attractive, Ritzik thought. She had almond eyes and the well-conditioned body of an athlete under her well-tailored black pantsuit. Wei-Liu was probably, he decided, in her early thirties. Ritzik caught himself staring and self-consciously shifted his gaze toward SECDEF, who was looking at him quizzically.

Rockman said, "Major Ritzik will be leading the unit that's going to bring the CIA sensor team back from China."

Wei-Liu's expression didn't change a whit. "Not an easy job, Major, given the latest developments."

"No, it's not. But it can be done."

"I certainly hope so. They're brave men. We should do everything we can to bring them home."

"I feel the same way."

Monica Wirth's heels tapped the wood floor as she crossed her office and dropped into a high-backed upholstered leather wing chair that faced away from the tall, narrow windows. "Why don't we all sit down where it's comfortable." Wirth indicated the upholstered couch in front of which was a coffee table piled with foreign-policy journals.

"Thank you, Monica. My old bones could use a comfortable chair." The secretary eased into the wing chair facing Wirth. Ritzik and Wei-Liu stepped over his knees and settled somewhat self-consciously into the soft sofa cushions.

"So, Major," the NSC chairman asked, "what did you think of our RIG?"

"Rig, ma'am?"

"Restricted interagency group."

"I was wondering," Ritzik said, "whether Admiral Buckley is always that quiet at meetings."

A single, acidic cackle broke from the back of the national security adviser's throat. "We call him the stealth chairman," she finally said. Then her expression changed. "Major," Wirth asked, "is there anyone in your unit who has experience in dealing with medium atomic demolition devices and the disarming of nuclear weapons under tactical situations?"

Ritzik didn't have to think very long about that one. "We have trained with the Department of Energy's counterterror NEST teams, ma'am. We have also worked counterterrorist scenarios in which nuclear warheads were tactical factors, and so we are familiar in a general way with the arming and disarming of such devices. But the weapons we've been exposed to are current generation—not thirty-plus-year-old MADMs."

The national security adviser shot a quick glance in Rockman's direction. "I see," Monica Wirth said.

"So defusing the stolen weapon could present a problem."

"It might," Ritzik said. "But I'm confident that if Miss Wei-Liu draws a detailed diagram and explains the problem to me thoroughly, we'll be able to deal with the situation efficiently."

Wei-Liu swiveled toward Ritzik. "It's somewhat more complex than just drawing a diagram, Major."

"An IED is an IED," Ritzik said. "A detonator is a detonator. An ignition wire is an ignition wire."

Wei-Liu said, "Major, I may defer to you in all things military. But I have been dealing with these sorts of devices for more than fifteen years now. I have demilitarized Soviet ICBM warheads, dissected their cruise missiles, and examined the innards of the second-generation MADMs they left in bunkers in Poland, Czechoslovakia, and Hungary. I have even worked on the ignition sequencing for our own current generation of weapons. And believe me, this is not a matter of 'Do I cut the red wire first or the blue wire first?' Because there are no colored wires, Major. Not on the J-12. Moreover, as I started to explain in the Situation Room, capacitors can be very unstable. And the battery packs emit both acid and static, which can result in sparks and explosions. The J-12 is tricky and problematic. It is complex in its simplicity, if you know what I'm saying. You have to un-

derstand the gestalt of the J-12—be totally comfortable in
its instability—or it is altogether likely that in the course of
rendering it safe, you will cause an unintended detonation."

Ritzik's expression told Wei-Liu he wasn't convinced.

"I'm telling you the truth, Major. I'll draw you anything
you want—and more. But believe me: you've got your work
cut out for you."

"Yes, you do, Major," Monica Wirth said. "Because the
implications of an unintended detonation are extremely far-
reaching." The national security adviser shot a glance at
Rockman. "Mr. Secretary, don't you agree?"

"I do," Rockman said. "And I think I know where we're
headed now—and I concur."

"Thank you, Mr. Secretary." Monica Wirth smiled in
Ritzik's general direction and noted that the major had no
idea at all where she was headed.

So she told him. "Major, Miss Wei-Liu has just joined
your insertion element."

Mike Ritzik didn't have to think too long about *that* one
either. "No, ma'am, she has not."

Monica Wirth gave Ritzik a hard look. "You don't get a
vote here, Major."

Wei-Liu pushed herself to the edge of the cushion.
"What about me, Dr. Wirth? Do I get a vote?"

"You're the only one who does," the national security adviser said. "You get the option of volunteering."

"Ma'am," Ritzik began.

"Shush, Major. You don't know the full story."

"Frankly, ma'am, I don't give a damn what the full story
is. I'm wasting my time here. I should be back at the compound, with my men, trying to anticipate everything that
might go wrong so that we can deal with it. This device is
just another problem. It can be overcome."

"No, Major, this is different."

Ritzik set his jaw. "I don't think so. Let me be brutally honest, Dr. Wirth. Let's say we get as far as the convoy, and we rescue our people, but we screw up with the MADM and it goes off. So what if it does?"

"So what? *Ka-boom.* Mushroom cloud, Major. And then—"

Ritzik cut her off. "Exactly, ma'am. *Ka-boom.* And when we vaporize, all the evidence that Americans were ever on Chinese territory goes with us. So far as the Chinese are concerned, it's another nuclear accident caused by a bad detonator—just like the one in 1988." He paused when he saw Wirth's shocked expression. "Nobody here wants to die, ma'am. That's not the point. The point is—"

Monica Wirth's tone turned frosty. "You have no idea what *the point* is, Major. The *point* is way above your pay grade."

Condescension was a quality Ritzik didn't like. "Since I'm the one putting his men's lives on the line, perhaps you'd be kind enough to fill me in, then . . . ma'am."

Wirth didn't give an inch. "I'll let Miss Wei-Liu 'fill you in,' Major. She's the nuclear expert in the room." Wirth said, "Please, Miss Wei-Liu—give him a thumbnail."

The young woman shook her head self-consciously, cascading longish, black hair around her shoulders. "I'll certainly try, Dr. Wirth." She turned to Ritzik, her hands folded on her lap. "Major, five years ago I had a small part in a program that designed the prototypes for the low-yield sensors the CIA team just inserted."

"Congratulations." Ritzik's tone indicated he wasn't in the mood for a history lesson.

Wei-Liu continued, undeterred. "In 1996 the Chinese stopped testing weapons with a yield greater than one kiloton."

"In 1996," he repeated, frustration evident in his voice.

"Yes, Major. But they didn't stop testing."

"How did you know?"

"We didn't—for sure. And the previous administration wasn't interested in finding out. So the sensor program languished, until 2001, when it was revived."

Ritzik nodded blankly, wishing she'd get to the point.

"Major, these sensors were designed specifically to identify ultra-low-level nuclear blasts—one kiloton or less."

"So?"

"The MADM I saw in this morning's photograph is a fifteen-kiloton device, Major Ritzik. The sensors were planted two hundred and sixty miles from the tunnel complex where we expect the Chinese to test their low-level nuclear capabilities. I checked the map over there." Wei-Liu pointed at an easel where a thick green atlas sat open. "The distance from where the sensors were placed to the mountain range along the Chinese border is slightly less than four hundred miles. If the MADM explodes anywhere within that radius—whether you do it by accident, or the terrorists do it by design—the seismic shock wave, which will be somewhere in the four-point-six to four-point-eight Richter area, will jolt the sensors' internal readers severely enough so as to render them essentially useless."

The national security adviser broke in. "So your samurailike offer of *seppuku,* Major, is noted and appreciated, but respectfully declined." She gave Ritzik a quick triumphal glance. "Not because it wasn't heartfelt, either, I'm sure. But now you see that if you screwed up, you'd not only throw away your lives and the lives of the men you were sent to rescue, but you would, in fact, be doing the national security interests of the United States a great deal of damage." Wirth paused. "A great deal of damage. And *that,* Major, is the point."

It took Ritzik some seconds to digest what Wirth had said.

Finally, he replied. "I accept your premise, ma'am. And I apologize for jumping the gun."

Wirth gave him an unexpectedly gracious smile. "Accepted, Major."

"But I have to insist that taking a civilian along on such a hazardous mission is never done."

"You're wrong about that, too, son," Rockman broke in. "It has been done—and successfully."

Ritzik was shocked. "When?"

"During the 1962 Cuban Missile Crisis," Rockman said. "A CIA missile analyst was assigned to accompany a Navy SEAL infiltration to Cuba."

Rockman's eyes crinkled. "The SEAL component commander, by the way, didn't argue about it. He gritted his teeth and said, 'Aye-aye, sir.' "

Ritzik winced internally. "Point taken, sir."

"It was no cakewalk, either," Rockman went on. "Two SEALs and the CIA officer were transported by the submarine *Sea Lion* to within two miles of the Cuban coastline. Then they locked out of one of the hatches and surfaced. Then the SEALs swam in—towing the analyst, by the way, because the fella couldn't swim himself. Finally, they made their way ashore past the Cuban patrol vessels, right into Havana Harbor. The SEAL mission was to identify the warehouses used by the Soviets to store the missiles out of sight of our U-2 overflights so they could be attacked by aircraft without causing collateral damage to the civilians nearby. The SEALs did their job. Then they broke into the warehouses, which allowed the spook to get detailed photos of the missile components and warheads. Those pictures gave President Kennedy an accurate assessment of how far the Soviets had been able to develop their guidance systems and other design elements relating to ICBMs."

The secretary paused to draw a breath. "So you won't be the first to do this sort of thing, Major. Nor the last."

Maybe not. But the original plan was out the window. They'd be dodging the Chinese now—and they couldn't risk a chopper extraction. Not with Deputy Assistant Secretary of Energy Tracy Wei-Liu in tow. Ritzik cursed silently. Now, because of Wei-Liu, every step of the op was going to have to be viewed through a political prism. Every move now had to be seen as a potential headline in *The Washington Post*.

SECRET U.S. UNIT CAUGHT,
DISPLAYED AS SPIES, BY CHINESE

UNITED NATIONS SECRETARY GENERAL
DEPLORES U.S. SPY INCURSION

PRESIDENT TO FACE SPECIAL PROSECUTOR
IN CHINAGATE SPY SCANDAL

The political aspects meant Ritzik would now be doing a lot of improvising. Which made him extremely nervous. Improvisation got people killed.

But Ritzik didn't say any of that. Instead, he said, "Except we won't be doing any swimming, Mr. Secretary."

He turned to Wei-Liu. "We'll be using parachutes during the course of our mission, Miss Wei-Liu." Ritzik paused, then flat-out lied: "I hope that doesn't trouble you, ma'am."

Unfortunately, it didn't trouble her at all. "That's all right, Major. I've jumped out of a plane."

He was astonished. "You *have*?"

"Yes." She smiled at his obvious discomfort, and a tinge of pride crept into her voice.

In spite of himself, Ritzik noted for the record that it was a lovely smile. "How many jumps do you have under your belt, ma'am?"

"One, Major. On my thirtieth birthday. From five thousand feet. Floating down from a mile in the sky was the thrill of a lifetime."

"I'm glad you thought so," Ritzik said coldly, "because I'm about to increase your thrill factor by about five."

She looked at him quizzically. "Five what, Major?"

"Five miles, Miss Wei-Liu, five long, freezing, windy, oxygen-deprived, dangerous miles."

Ritzik's words were followed by a long silence. Wei-Liu panned slowly, noting Rockman's impassive face and Wirth's tacitly encouraging expression. "It would seem the major's made me an offer I can't refuse," she finally said.

The Second Forty Hours
TARFU

8

20 Kilometers Northeast of Almaty, Kazakhstan.
0210 Hours Local Time.

"*ASSALAMU ALAYKIM,* my brother." Talgat Umarov wrapped Mike Ritzik in a tight bear hug and kissed him thrice on the cheek, heedless that he was blocking the bottom of the Lufthansa stairway and unmindful of the scant dozen disembarking passengers and the knot of ground personnel waiting to service the aircraft.

"*Assalamu uluykim,* Talgat." Ritzik replied, happy to be breathing the cool, jet-fuel-tinged air after the nine-hour flight. "It's great to see you again."

"No—the pleasure is mine, I assure you." The Kazakh officer beamed.

Ritzik stepped aside. "Allow me to introduce Miss Tracy Wei-Liu. Miss Wei-Liu is traveling with me."

Umarov cocked his head at Ritzik's obscure introduction. Then he bent slightly at the waist, pressed Wei-Liu's right hand between his own two hands, and pumped it once, up and down, formally. "*Assalamu alaykim,* honorable Miss Wei-Liu. I welcome you to Almaty in the name of Kazakhstan Republikasy."

"Thank you, Colonel."

The back of Umarov's palm slapped air. "It is nothing."

He was an uncommonly big man for a Kazakh, barrel-chested, round-faced, and sloe-eyed, with a wispy, drooping mustache, an obvious direct descendant of Genghis Khan's Mongol warriors. He towered over the two Americans in his starched Russian camouflage fatigues, scuffed jump boots, and pistol belt and Tokarev in its flapped holster.

Umarov snatched Wei-Liu's carry-on out of her grasp and tucked it securely under his arm. "You have your baggage receipts?" he asked her.

"I do." Wei-Liu pulled a ticket folder from her handbag.

Umarov took the document, turned, handed it off to a jug-eared teenager of a soldier, and machine-gunned five seconds of rapid-fire Kazakh. "Taken care of," he said. "Now you will follow me, my friends." Without waiting for a reply, the Kazakh led the way across the flood-lit apron toward a squat, dented olive-drab 4×4 with Cyrillic military markings.

Wei-Liu followed self-consciously, thinking she probably looked like some tourist. Which she wasn't. In fact, she was a veteran. She'd been a member of more than a dozen U.S. delegations. She'd visited Moscow and Beijing, Paris, London, and Brussels in her capacity as a top-ranking American nuclear nonproliferation official. Before that, as a senior fellow at the RAND Corporation, she had attended more than two dozen scientific conferences in places as varied as Budapest, Kiev, Oslo, and Tel Aviv. In the winter of 1998, as a consultant to CBS's *60 Minutes II* news magazine, she'd been the first American scientist allowed inside Krasnoyarsk-26, the former Soviet Union's gargantuan secret underground nuclear city. There, buried deep beneath central Siberia, Moscow had, from 1950 on, manufactured tons of weapons-grade plutonium.

But from her undergraduate days at Princeton to her graduate work at MIT, her tenure at the Lawrence Livermore laboratory, RAND, and even DOE, all of Wei-Liu's work had been . . . abstract. Until now.

That was the difference. Until twenty-six hours ago, she'd always lived in an academic universe, examining galaxies of conjecturals, theoreticals, and hypotheticals. But twenty-six hours ago, she'd been dropped into a frightening parallel universe, where all the what-ifs became jarringly, terrifyingly, real. People would die. She might, too. She'd always been able to deal intellectually with the consequences of thermonuclear war because the scenarios were abstract and the numbers surreal. She could calculate radiation exposure and ground-blast effects coolly on a spreadsheet because that's what they were: numbers on a spreadsheet.

This was different. She was about to experience warfare on an intensely personal basis, and she wondered whether or not she could handle it, and how it would affect the rest of her life. She was already experiencing the consequences. Time, suddenly, had become a blur. Memory had become selective. Wei-Liu had gotten drunk—once—as a teenager. Over the past twenty-six hours she felt as if she'd experienced many of the same symptoms. She didn't remember being driven to her home so she could pack a few items. But Talgat Umarov had her baggage-claim check, so she must have packed. She didn't remember being photographed for a new passport, either. But there it was, in her purse, with visas for Germany, Turkey, Kazakhstan, Tajikistan, and Kyrgyzstan stamped in it.

She'd sat on the flight to Frankfurt in a stupor. She had hardly spoken to Ritzik. Well, there was a reason for that: he was remote, withdrawn, distant. Zoning, she'd felt, in his own thoughts. She was uneasy with him, too, and had trouble making small talk. It didn't help that he had been very specific that he wasn't going to talk about his job, her job, the past few hours' events, or their impending business in public. So, in the first few minutes of the flight she tried broaching one or two safe subjects, like the weather, and Washington's perpetual gridlock, and the problems of traveling in the post-9/11 security milieu. But after a few seconds of inane monologue she lapsed into embarrassed silence in much the way she did on the infrequent but always uncomfortable blind dates well-meaning friends arranged for her.

In any case it hadn't mattered: within half an hour after they'd departed Dulles, Ritzik was asleep. And he didn't wake up until they were on the ground in Frankfurt. He'd pulled the same damn routine on their flight to Almaty, while she'd sat wide-awake, unable to get any rest.

It was, she thought, bizarre how crises brought disparate personalities together. No one in her household spoke Chinese. She'd grown up in Westwood, a fashionable, upper-class Los Angeles neighborhood that adjoined the UCLA campus. She'd gone to Catholic schools. Her father, Henry, was a third-generation American, a senior partner at Skadden, Arps, Slate, Meagher, & Flom, a huge downtown law firm, where he represented multinational corporations. Her mother, Sybil, was a Shaker Heights aristocrat with a Harvard Ph.D. who taught art history at Marymount College. Not a single one of Wei-Liu's friends or classmates had entered the military. For young men and women of her upper-class background, it wasn't seen as a viable option.

Ritzik was from a different planet—West Point. She had no idea how to read the man. He was bright—that was obvious—and attractive, in a compact sort of way. But who he was and what he did were totally foreign to her. Because, when you came right down to it, he killed people for a living. Equally astonishing, he spoke about his vocation without apology or euphemisms. Ritzik didn't talk about "neutralizing," or "getting rid of the bad guys," or any other politically correct term. Back in the national security adviser's office he'd said point-blank he was going to kill the terrorists—kill every one of them—in order to give her the opportunity to do her job and render the MADM safe.

Later, on the plane, watching him sleep, she realized that what had shocked her most was that she'd found his bluntness reassuring.

"WE WILL WAIT for the others on the military side of the field." Talgat Umarov's thick accent interrupted Wei-Liu's thoughts. The Kazakh said, "I have shashlik and fresh cucumber for you and good hot sweet tea that will drain the pain of your long trip away."

"Frankly," Ritzik said, "before you feed us, Talgat, I figure Miss Wei-Liu would like to freshen up a bit. I know I'd like to get out of these clothes." He fingered his blue suit and wrinkled shirt as if they were contaminated. "I've been in them for two days now and I'm beginning to get pretty ripe."

The Kazakh's face fell as he turned to Wei-Liu. "I am apologetic for my behavior, Miss Wei-Liu. You have been traveling long and hard. I am pleased to offer you my meager hospitality."

"I am sure it is anything but meager, Colonel," Wei-Liu said.

"This Miss Wei-Liu is a seasoned diplomat, I see." The Kazakh roared with laughter. "So she must work for your State Department." When he did not receive a direct answer, he punched Ritzik's upper arm hard enough to make it numb. "No matter. We have uniforms that will suit you—and even hot water, too. You will look good as a Kazakh officer, my brother. Maybe it will fit so well, you will decide to stay, God willing."

"Are you asking me to defect, Talgat?"

"There is always that hope, God willing." The Kazakh laughed. "My brother-in-law has a cousin who has an unmarried sister-in-law who is a beautiful gem of a woman. I have seen her and can vouch for it. She would bear you many sons, Michael. You would make a good life here."

Ritzik's face flushed. "I am grateful for the offer," he said. "But I am married to my job."

"As am I," Umarov said. "As are all soldiers. Still, if there is time perhaps we will pay my brother-in-law's cousin's sister-in-law's parents a visit anyway." Umarov opened the front passenger door of the vehicle and held it for Wei-Liu. "*Marhamet*—please, miss."

Wei-Liu climbed in. "Thank you, Colonel."

"It is nothing." He slapped the door shut behind her, walked around the flat hood, and slid behind the wheel. He waited until Ritzik climbed in, then stepped on the starter button.

Ritzik said, "How's the baby?" He glanced toward Wei-Liu. "Talgat and his wife, Kadisha, just had a son."

"Congratulations. What's his name?"

"Thank you. He is fine. His name is Aibek. And I hope that you will see him, God willing."

"I do, too—if there's time."

"I understand." The Kazakh twisted in his seat. "Rowdy Yates told me on the phone you will be just passing through, Mike."

"Sort of."

"If there is anything I can do . . ."

"Believe me, Talgat, I'll let you know."

"Rowdy said you will need a civilian aircraft to practice on."

"A Yak-42. I do—it is critical. For a day or two."

"Critical. So." The Kazakh licked his lower lip. "Ah,

yes—I understand now—to rehearse takedowns." His tone turned eager. "Is there an incident? I have heard nothing, Mike. If there is an incident, I would like to be able to come and observe."

"There's no incident," Ritzik said quickly. "Something else. It's complicated." He looked toward the glass front of the terminal building three hundred feet away. "Let's drive, Talgat. I don't want to be talking where anybody can see us."

"I understand." The Kazakh rubbed his palms together, put the vehicle in gear, popped the clutch, and sped off across the concrete apron and turned onto a taxiway running parallel to the long, single runway. "Security first— what you and Rowdy call SEC-OP."

"OPSEC, Talgat." Ritzik corrected. "OPSEC. Operational security."

"OPSEC." The Kazakh steered precariously off the taxiway, heading away from the terminal on rough concrete, until he pulled around the far side of a huge hangar, then came to a screeching stop in the dark space between two floodlit areas. "Now we cannot be seen or heard, Mike," he said. He turned in his seat. "I gather you are traveling with this beautiful woman for a reason?"

Ritzik chose to ignore the question completely. "Talgat, Rowdy didn't fill you in completely about our visit."

The colonel's face clouded over. "Ah?"

"He couldn't, Talgat. He was on an open line."

"OPSEC." The Kazakh's sunny expression returned. "I understand, Mike."

"So here's what's going to happen: we're bringing in a C-5—a big transporter—tonight, not the Hercules we've been using on our other visits. The plane will arrive at zero three fifty-five, two and a half hours before the first commercial flight departs; three hours before the first incoming flight. I'll need the airport lights shut down between zero three-fifty and zero four forty-five, because we'll be working under total blackout conditions. We're bringing our own security force, because we're going to have to cordon off that warehouse of yours."

The Kazakh's face darkened. "Mike, this is no drop-by visit. You are arriving in force. If the ministry had known about this . . ."

Ritzik's hand fell onto Umarov's shoulder. "I know we're bending the rules, Talgat."

"Bending the rules? You have shredded the rules." Umarov shook free of the American's hand. "I will have to inform the minister."

"Talgat." Ritzik's voice was insistent. "You can't."

"I must."

"Believe me, Talgat, this has been cleared at the highest level. But you can't call the Defense Ministry." Ritzik paused. "You're going to have to trust me."

The Kazakh turned. Eyes narrowed, he took Ritzik's chin in his huge paw and manipulated the American's face up, down, and sideways, looking deeply. "Mike—"

"This is no drill, Talgat. My president has spoken personally to your president about what is going on. My president has received your president's promise of complete cooperation. And has promised another American aid package as a way of saying thanks. But it's crucial that we maintain OPSEC—absolutely critical. People's lives depend on it. Your defense minister is a good man—an honorable man. I know that. But you know as well as I do that the Ministry of Defense is a sieve. You yourself have said to me that just about every op you've ever advised the ministry about in advance has gone sour."

Umarov frowned and said, "I cannot deny that."

Ritzik read the Kazakh's eyes and knew he'd broken through. "So, you know the ministry has been penetrated:

by the Chinese, by the Russians, by al-Qaeda, and even by the IMU. I trust *you*, Talgat. I trust *you* to do the right thing. But I couldn't put my people at risk by giving you the whole story until we were face-to-face."

"But a *C-5*, Mike."

"It is flying completely blacked out."

"They can do that?"

"There are squadrons specially trained. It will be here for less than an hour." Ritzik waited to see what effect his words were having. "I can promise you that what we're here to do will not in any way infringe on Kazakh internal affairs, or affect Kazakhstan's current relationship with the Russian Federation."

"So the president knows."

"Yes."

"Does Moscow know what you are doing?"

"That's way above my pay grade, Talgat, but my guess would be no."

The Kazakh nodded. "But what you just said—is that on your honor, Mike?"

Ritzik nodded. "On my honor, Talgat. On my *life*."

Umarov bit his lips. "Less than an hour on the ground?"

Ritzik said, "Forty-five minutes."

"And the Rangers?"

"At first light they can wear Kazakh anoraks over their uniforms, if you wish."

Umarov nodded. "I do." He exhaled deeply. "This is truly something big?"

"Yes." Ritzik looked at the big Kazakh. "And I will need your help if I am going to be successful."

"My help?"

"Your participation."

The Kazakh's eyes widened. "I can do more than observe?"

"Absolutely." Ritzik was happy with the effect his words were having. "But first things first, Talgat. Will you black out the airport for me?"

Umarov fingered the end of his mustache. Finally, he said, "It will be done."

"Good. Zero three-fifty to zero four forty-five. No runway lights. No taxiway lights. No apron floodlights."

"Agreed."

The Kazakh pulled a tin of cigarettes out of his pocket, tapped one on his watch crystal, and stuck it between his lips. "When this is all over, you and I will share a bottle and talk things over."

Ritzik watched as the Kazakh lit the cigarette and exhaled pungent smoke through his nostrils. "Yes," he said, "we will, Talgat, I promise." Then he reached inside his soft briefcase and withdrew a small radio receiver. He switched the device on, then checked the signal-strength indicator. He pressed the transmit button. "Cocoa Flight, this is Urchin."

There was a four- to five-second pause. Then a female voice answered, "Urchin, Cocoa Flight."

"Confirm arrive-arrive."

"Roger. Arrive-arrive zero three fifty-five SOL-Two confirmed."

"Roger your message." Ritzik paused. "Urchin out."

"Cocoa Flight out."

"It's done." Ritzik clapped the Kazakh on the shoulder. "You're going to be a busy man tonight."

"More than I expected, my brother," Umarov said. He stomped the accelerator and the 4×4 lurched forward.

"Whoa, Talgat," Ritzik continued. "There are other things to discuss before we go anywhere."

The Kazakh sighed and held the cigarette between his thumb and index finger. "Such as?"

"What about the aircraft? You told Rowdy it would be no problem."

"It is not such an impossible problem as you would think. But it is still—how you say?—delicate."

This demurral Ritzik understood. He'd seen it before. In Central Asia, just as in many other places in the world, it was considered impolite to say no directly. And so you told people what they wanted to hear. It wasn't considered lying, simply being polite. The problem was, from Cairo to Bishkek, you seldom got the unvarnished truth when you asked for a sit-rep. Ritzik had learned from bitter experience in the region never to assume anything. He also understood that direct confrontation was not the way to get results.

And so he followed Umarov's lead. "Delicate, Talgat? How so?"

"Kazakhstan Airlines has six Yak-42s," Umarov said, twisting the end of his mustache. "Two are used on the Al-maty–Ürümqi route during the high season—the rest of the year, only one. The others are on—how you say it?—haul shorts. To Kiev, to Astana, and Ashgabat. Normally, taking one Yak for two days would not be a problem. Shingis Al-tynbayev—he is my cousin, the pilot you met when we did the jump training last year—will pilot the aircraft, because he will take time off from his normal routes."

"Where does he usually fly?"

"Ürümqi, Astana, and Ashgabat. But listen, my brother: when I asked after Rowdy spoke to me, Shingis checked—quietly, just as Rowdy asked—and then reported to me two of the Yaks are this week suddenly out of service, and the spare-parts inventory is very low. So the remaining planes are heavily scheduled. The chief mechanic says if he gets one of the out-of-service planes air ready there will be no spare-parts inventory." The Kazakh paused. "I believe it is a question of money."

"You do."

"Shingis agrees. He believes that if some"—the Kazakh fought for the word—"accommodation could be found, it would all be easier. And would guarantee OPSEC, too."

"OPSEC from the chief mechanic."

"And his people," Umarov said. "So, if there is some way to . . . you know . . ."

Ritzik didn't waste any time dancing around the bribery issue. In fact, he'd anticipated it and brought a briefcase full of greenbacks. "You tell Shingis to pass the word to the chief mechanic that his spare parts will be covered—payment in American dollars—as well as his overtime and his people's overtime," Ritzik said quickly. "But I need the plane this afternoon, Talgat. Ready to go. Full tanks. No excuses."

Umarov's face displayed relief. "Then it can be done, God willing."

Ritzik was relieved to discover it had only been a question of money. His initial fear had been that Talgat had promised something that couldn't be delivered.

"*Masele joq,* my brother. No problem."

"Good." Ritzik slapped the Kazakh on the shoulder. "C'mon, Talgat—Miss Wei-Liu and I are both tired and hungry. You have to deal with the control tower. And I'd like to see how well this uniform of yours is going to fit me before my troops land."

160 Kilometers Northwest of Mazartag, Xinjiang Autonomous Region, China. 0420 Hours Local Time.

EVEN IN SHOCK, Sam Phillips always preferred to look at the bright side of things. So he counted his blessings. First, at least the three of them were together—and still alive.

They were tied securely. But they weren't gagged, and they'd discovered that if they kept their voices down, the guards in the cab of the truck wouldn't squeeze through the small window and beat on them. They'd been fed and watered, too. Minimally, to be sure. But enough to keep them going for a while. That, too, was definitely a step in the right direction. X-Man had another piece of good news: the bad guys had missed the composite boot knife he kept in his sock, so they had a weapon. The bad news—there is always bad news along with the good news—was that they'd all probably glow in the dark for the rest of their lives. That was because Mustache Man had put them in the same truck he was using to transport the nuclear device.

Sam had never seen anything like it before. His written Chinese was practically nonexistent, and so he couldn't decipher any of the markings on its crate, except for the big yellow-and-black decal on the outer container that was the international sign for DANGER—*Radioactive Material.* But it didn't take much imagination to figure out that it was some sort of bomb. It was much bigger and more complex than the suitcase nukes Sam had seen mock-ups of at Langley's CTC—the huge and ever-expanding CounterTerrorist Center that took up much of the sixth floor these days.

The Agency's suitcase bombs were full-size copies of Soviet weapons known as special atomic demolition devices, or SADMs. They had an explosive power of about half a kiloton. This was much bigger than a SADM. And potentially, therefore, a lot more powerful.

The question was what to do about it. For the immediate future, the answer was nothing. Sam had taken the Agency's rudimentary three-day course in explosives. He could, for example, wire up a basic, Hizballah-style car bomb, or set a shaped charge where it would do a bridge or a highway overpass the most damage. But he'd never been taught anything about disabling suitcase nukes or rendering atomic devices harmless. X had gone one step further and taken longer, more intensive explosives instruction. But neither had any experience with nukes.

Even so, he had to formulate a plan to deal with the damned thing. There had to be a course of action—or a series of scenarios—that they could put into effect if the opportunity arose. And most important, he and his two colleagues had to escape.

The trucks were heading in a northwesterly direction, which convinced Sam his initial instincts had been correct. Mustache Man was still heading for one of the old smuggling routes into Tajikistan or Kazakhstan. But escape wouldn't be easy. They also understood the clock was ticking—and time worked against them. Indeed, since Mustache Man had stolen a bomb, the Chinese would be coming after him.

X-Man's guess was they'd send at least a battalion. "Guess how the U.S. would react if some Mexican guerrilla group hijacked a nuclear convoy in Texas. Tons of shit would have hit the fan is how. I'm surprised they haven't smacked us by now."

But the U.S. had NEST teams, Department of Energy search units equipped with sensitive nuclear sniffing devices that could locate radioactive material with relative ease. Maybe the Chinese lacked similar equipment. It was impossible to know.

Another factor that gave them hope was that the guerrillas hadn't ever discovered the transponder sewn inside X-Man's vest. If it was still working—which was uncertain given the beating he'd taken—their location could be pinpointed. Kaz thought Langley might send people after them. Sam insisted they couldn't count on it. After all, he'd been told they'd be on their own. No—they'd have to deal with the situation themselves.

"The sooner we escape, the better," Kaz said. "And frankly, the farther away we are from the damn bomb, the healthier it's going to be for us."

"You got that right," Sam said. "Holy shit, if the Chinese catch up and Mustache Man decides to make a BPS—"

Kaz asked, "A BPS?"

"Yeah—a big political statement. If he does, we could all end up as cinders."

"Don't talk like an ash-hole," Kaz said.

"Kaz is right," X-Man said. "You're being ash-enine."

X-Man leaned over and crooked his neck in Sam's direction. "You have anything to add to this abuse?"

Sam remained mute.

"What's your problem—tongue-tied?" X-Man finally asked.

"No, but I think I've got a cinder block," Sam finally deadpanned.

The laughter did them some good. But then Sam got serious. "Look," he stage-whispered, "Kaz is right. We'd better come up with an escape plan. Mustache Man had no compunction about killing Dick. That means we're all expendable to him. And then there's the bomb. I don't want to be anywhere in the neighborhood when the PLA hits these guys." He paused. "Agreed?"

X-Man nodded. "I think we're all on the same page, Sam."

Sam thrust his chin in the nuke's direction. "Well, since none of us are going to play with the bomb, we can devote all our time to working on E and E. And we'd better think of something in the next few hours."

9

20 Kilometers Northeast of Almaty, Kazakhstan.
0352 Hours Local Time.

THE MOST INCREDIBLE ASPECT of it all, Tracy Wei-Liu thought, was how quiet the C-5 was. The plane was longer than a football field and almost seven stories high. And yet she'd never heard it until it was on the ground. And she never would have even seen it if she hadn't been looking through the night-vision monocular Ritzik had given her.

Ritzik was pleased. The weather was perfect for a black op. It was overcast, with low clouds and a seventeen-hundred-foot ceiling. There was some minimal ambient light from the terminal building. But the runway and taxiway lighting and the orange sodium floodlights that illuminated the aprons and the tower had all been extinguished, plunging the airport into darkness. There'd been some complaining by the airport apparatchiki, but Talgat and a platoon of his Special Forces soldiers had smothered it within moments: "*On the orders of the president . . .*" They'd even blocked the phone lines.

She'd waited for the plane, standing between Ritzik and Umarov. The three of them peered blindly into the gloom, the dark warehouse at their backs. And then the radio in Ritzik's hand had come to life: "Cocoa Flight. Signal arrive-arrive." Then Ritzik handed her the night-vision device, pointed to the northwest, past the end of the runway farthest from the terminal, and said, "They're a mile out."

Wei-Liu put the monocular to her eye and swept the horizon. "Where?" She could see no aircraft.

"Wait."

She peered intently through the monocular. She saw the end of the runway clearly. And the fence line beyond it, and then nothing but darkness. "I can't see anything."

"You will."

Wei-Liu refocused the night-vision device and pressed her eye against the rubber lens cup. And then she saw it. She was mesmerized.

It was awesome. Huge. Silent. Menacing. A behemoth. And completely blacked out. It materialized out of the void and was on the ground, its huge tires scuffing the runway, before she'd even heard the whine of its engines. She lowered her arm and looked over at Ritzik. *"How did they do that?"*

Umarov said, "Give me the glass, please, miss." Wei-Liu handed it to him. He squinted through the lens. "They know where to go, Mike?"

"Yes," Ritzik said. "They have a photograph. And Rowdy's in the cockpit." He brandished a small pair of flashlights and twisted the caps to turn them on. "I'm the ground crew tonight."

Wei-Liu said, "Your batteries are dead."

"No—these are infrared. Look through the NV."[14]

Wei-Liu took the monocular back from Umarov and stared at the ground. "Whoa—that's bright."

Ritzik dropped the radio into the pocket of his ill-fitting

---

14. Night-Vision.

Kazakh blouse and headed for the warehouse. "You guys wait here until they shut down and chock the wheels."

0357. The only reason Wei-Liu saw anything at all was because she'd kept the monocular. She stood to the side, fascinated by the complexity of it all—and the ability of these people to work at breakneck speed in complete darkness, without any talking. That wasn't her only surprise, either. Her vision of Special Operations—what there was of it— had been formed by the snippets she'd seen on television and in movies. So she'd expected to find a bunch of profanity-spouting, trigger-happy rogues pile out of the darkened C-5 aircraft, not the quiet, disciplined group of men who'd arrived just before four.

Even their equipment was different than she'd anticipated. She'd thought they'd all be in camouflage, carrying huge machine guns, wearing flak jackets, and strapped into harnesses dripping with grenades, like the photos of Special Forces teams she'd seen in Afghanistan.

She'd been partially correct. Certainly, the Rangers, who'd come through the troop doors, jumped off the plane, and set up a defense perimeter even before the engines had shut down, were dressed that way. They all had night-vision goggles attached to their helmets. They wore camouflage uniforms, flak jackets, and combat harnesses or load-bearing vests hung with equipment. The Rangers carried short carbines with electronic red-dot sights and sported side arms in thigh holsters. They wore dark knee and elbow pads over their uniforms, and Wei-Liu could make out black earpieces and small microphones under their Kevlar helmets, with wires running to the radios Velcro'd to their vests.

But the Delta people? Well, except for the Buck Rogers devices strapped to their foreheads, they looked like a senior-league rugby team. Their hair was longer. Some had mustaches—a couple even sported beards. And they all wore civilian clothes—jeans or khakis, polo shirts, anoraks, and running shoes—and almost every one of them carried a soft-sided briefcase that looked as if it held a laptop computer.

0402. One of Ritzik's Delta people, a barrel-chested man with a shaved head and short, light-colored mustache wearing a black polo shirt and black cargo pants, dropped out of the forward port-side troop door and jogged over to where Wei-Liu stood with Umarov.

He flipped up his night-vision goggles, grabbed the big Kazakh, hugged him, and lifted him clean off the ground. "*Assalamu alaykim,* Colonel, it's great to see you again."

Umarov beamed. "And upon you, Rowdy, *waghalaykim assalam.*" He stepped back. "You look good—ready to fight."

"So do you."

Umarov wagged his index finger under the American's nose. "But you didn't tell me everything, did you?"

Yates shrugged. "I couldn't."

Umarov shrugged, too. "It is all right," he said. "I understand. OPSEC."

The American bear-hugged him again. "We'll make it right for you, Talgat. I promise." Then he turned toward Wei-Liu. "Miss Wei-Liu?"

"Yes?"

"Please call me Rowdy. The major wants me to look after you. So, anything you want or need, just come and find me, and I'll try to help you out."

"Thank you." She looked up at him and, flustered, blurted, "Major Ritzik always refers to you as his best shooter. So, where are your guns?"

"Pistol's in my briefcase." Rowdy tapped his padded black nylon attaché on its shoulder strap. He pointed toward the C-5's cavernous fuselage. "We stow our long guns when we travel, ma'am," he growled amiably. He turned, flipping the night-vision down over his eyes. "If you'll excuse me, ma'am."

0407. Wei-Liu watched as a pair of Rangers leaned an extension ladder against the side of the two-story warehouse. Then, long, bulky cases slung over their shoulders, they clambered up onto the roof. She saw them pass down a length of rope. Other Rangers carried a series of good-sized bundles of painted plywood from the plane. These were quickly pulled up onto the roof one after the other. Then four more Rangers carrying cases made the assent, and the half-dozen men quickly assembled what appeared to Wei-Liu to be three large, dark rectangular boxes. The rigid boxes, perhaps three and a half feet high, eight feet long, and four feet wide, were then set slightly back from the edge of the flat warehouse roof.

She broke off, found Rowdy, and pointed to the warehouse. "What's going on, Sergeant?"

"They're constructing sniper hides," he explained.

"Huh?"

"What would you think if you were a tourist, or a business flier, and you happened to catch a glance at some building, say, at Washington Dulles Airport, and you saw a bunch of men in uniforms, with binoculars and big sniper rifles, lying on the roof scanning the area with their weapons and field glasses?"

"I'd probably be scared out of my wits," she answered.

"Exactly. So now what do you see?"

Wei-Liu peered upward through the night-vision device. "My God, the boxes look just like air-conditioning units.

They've even got exhaust fans on top." She turned back to Yates. "And the snipers are inside."

"Give yourself an A." He paused, uncomfortable. "Look—Miss Wei-Liu, I'd love to talk, but I've got—"

"Things to do. I understand. But thanks for the info." She turned back toward the aircraft. In just a few seconds, the entire back end of the humongous dark-painted fuselage had split into clamshell doors. Now the rear deck was dropping so as to form a ramp.

0410. Wei-Liu walked the hundred and fifty feet to the aircraft and peered inside. It was too dark to see anything. She brought the night-vision up. There, secured by straps to cargo hooks in the flooring, were a dozen pallets, their contents hidden beneath thick, black plastic sheeting.

A forklift, driven by a man wearing night-vision goggles, was backing rapidly toward her. "Make a hole. Make a hole—"

"Sorry!" Wei-Liu jumped off the edge of the ramp as the forklift and its speared pallet bounced onto the apron, wheeled sharply, and careened toward the warehouse. She retreated, embarrassed, not wanting to get in anyone's way.

0419. Two four-man groups hefted a pair of generators out of the Galaxy's forward troop door and lugged them to the side of the warehouse. There, the devices were fueled and fired up. From a black trunk, one of the Delta people pulled a pair of industrial-size surge protectors. He attached them to the generator outlets, then plugged light-colored junction boxes to the surge protectors. He pulled a dozen coiled electrical lines from the trunk, attached them to the junction boxes, and began to run them into the building. Thirty seconds later, a puddle of light seeped under the warehouse doors.

0426. Wei-Liu made her way back to the C-5 and peered inside the Galaxy's cavernous fuselage. It was virtually empty. Night-vision to her eye, she made her way up the ramp and took a dozen tentative paces inside. The interior smelled of hydraulic fluid and jet fuel. Her back to the bulkhead, she watched as the flight crew, in their overalls and long gloves, stowed cargo straps and checked hose connections. Up by the forward troop door the sergeant called Rowdy, along with two others, was stacking bulky canvas carryalls on a lonely pallet. Wei-Liu walked forward and prodded a bag with her foot. "What are these?"

He looked up at her. She almost laughed because the night-vision goggles attached to his shaved head gave him a sort of alien-creature bug-eyed appearance.

"Our parachutes, ma'am." Rowdy put two fingers to his mouth, turned toward the port-side doorway, and gave a shrill whistle. He slipped a cargo net over the pallet and secured it.

As he bent over, his polo shirt rode up and Wei-Liu saw the butt of a pistol protruding just above the thick leather belt of his cargo trousers.

Rowdy looked toward the rear ramp, frowning, and whistled again. "Goddammit." He jerked his thumb toward the warehouse. "Doc, get Curtis and the effing forklift back, will you? They have to close this thing up in three minutes so they can get the hell outta Dodge."

"Yes, Sergeant Major."

Wei-Liu blinked. It was the most dialogue she'd heard anyone speak since the C-5 arrived.

* * *

0429. Wei-Liu stood under the C-5's massive wing looking up at the huge turbofan engines through her NV. Each one had to be almost thirty feet long.

"Impressive, aren't they?"

She turned toward the sound of the voice. A woman in a dark flight suit appeared out of the darkness. She wore a flight helmet with night-vision goggles attached, and she carried an infrared flashlight. Wei-Liu said, "Are you part of the crew?"

"I'm the pilot." She thrust the flashlight into the thigh pocket of her flight suit and extended her right hand "Captain Jodi Wright."

Wei-Liu took her hand and shook it. "Tracy Wei-Liu. You were on the radio with the major. 'Cocoa Flight.' "

"Yup."

"That was incredible, the way you brought this . . . thing in."

"I didn't believe my eyes the first time I saw somebody do it, either. But with practice . . ."

"A lot of practice, I'll bet," Wei-Liu said. "What are you doing now?"

"A walk-around," Wright said. "Visual inspection. I gotta be out of here in eleven minutes and I don't want anything falling off."

Wei-Liu nodded. "I won't keep you." She offered her hand. "Good luck."

"Thanks." The pilot smiled. "Good luck to you, too."

0440. Holding her ears against the whine of the massive turbofans, Wei-Liu walked across the dark apron and pushed through the warehouse door. The curtain of brightness made her squint. Inside, lit by half a dozen generator-powered work lights, men were stringing cables that connected secure telephones, laptops, and servers. Others had opened the weapons cases and were checking over the short, wood-stocked carbines. Still others sat on the floor, scores of curved metal magazines in front of them, loading round after round of ammunition. One man was taking grenade bodies out of a small wood crate and screwing handles with pins and rings stuck through them into the baseball-sized explosives. A length of curved metal that resembled a half-column mold leaned incongruously against the wall behind the ammo loaders.

Ritzik was on his back, under a long folding table that held three large flat computer screens. A trio of video cables trailed behind him. Wei-Liu said, "Major?"

Ritzik looked up at her. "Hey."

"I'm feeling useless. Isn't there any way I can help?"

"You could grab some sleep. You're going to need it."

"Frankly, Major, I'm too wired to sleep."

"Too bad for you." He pulled himself off the floor. "I should introduce you." He put two fingers to his lips and whistled shrilly. "Hey, people."

The men stopped what they were doing and looked up. Ritzik said, "This is Deputy Assistant Secretary of Energy Wei-Liu, who's volunteered to come with us." He paused as Wei-Liu looked around the room self-consciously, then he started pointing people out. "You already know Sergeant Major Yates. That tall prematurely gray fella hiding behind him is Doc Masland—you can probably guess what he does by his name."

Rowdy said, "Yeah—he gives second opinions."

Masland tapped Yates on the shoulder. "You want a second opinion, Rowdy?"

"Sure."

"Okay—you're ugly."

Ritzik barked, "Hey, can it for a couple of seconds, will you?" He continued moving counterclockwise. "The slightly built guy standing next to Doc—the one who thinks that's a mustache on his upper lip—is Curtis Hansen. Next to him is Shep—Gene Shepard. The two people on the floor loading magazines—Ty Weaver, one of our snipers on the left; and Alex Guzman—we call him Goose—on the right." Ritzik frowned momentarily when he spied a young, red-haired Soldier peeking over the top of a flight navigation chart. "The surfer hiding from me in the corner is Michael Dunne—Mickey D. He's a chopper jockey from the SOAR. I think he's lost."

Dunne self-consciously wiggled his fingers in Wei-Liu's direction and ducked behind his map.

Ritzik continued: "The squinty-eyed fella working on the computer over there, he's William Sandman," Ritzik paused. "Know what we call him?"

"Sand Man?"

"Close but no cigar, Miss Assistant Secretary," Ritzik said. "We call him Bill." His index finger kept moving. "That's Roger Brian next to Bill—Roger the Dodger—and Todd Sweeney next to Brian. Todd's our other sniperman, call sign Barber—"

"Like Sweeney Todd, the demon barber of Fleet Street?"

"You got it." Ritzik peered at the far side of the warehouse. "Finally, back in the corner there, working on the explosives, are Joey Tuzzolino—the Tuzz—and Mark Owen, call sign Marko." He paused. "Say hi, guys—and be nice. She outranks all of us put together."

0444. "Okay," Wei-Liu said, "I've been introduced. If you don't mind, I'm going to do some homework."

Ritzik shrugged. "Be my guest."

Wei-Liu slipped the canvas briefcase off her shoulder, unzipped it, extracted a sheaf of handwritten wiring diagrams, and flipped through them until she found the one she wanted. She paused, then looked up at Ritzik. "What's going on in here?"

"We're setting up a TOC—a tactical operations center."

"Which is?"

He raised his voice to carry over the whine of the C-5's engine, then decreased his intensity as the sound grew fainter. "Something like a command post. We'll coordinate the mission from here. All the real-time intelligence— satellite imagery, signals intercepts, target intelligence, weather conditions, everything—will funnel into this building from the U.S. The crew manning the TOC will be in constant touch with Bragg, with Washington—and with us, too—all on a secure basis. They'll pass us what we need as we need it."

Wei-Liu peered at the racks of electronics. "This looks like one of my research labs, Major. But when you say 'command post' all I can think about is sandbags and crank telephones."

"That was *The Dirty Dozen*." Ritzik grinned. "Welcome to Net-Centric warfare[15] and the twenty-first century."

"Touché." She settled onto a crate and focused on her diagram. When she looked up some minutes later, he'd disappeared into the night.

0512. The satellite images were finally feeding in. Ritzik looked at the streaming infrared video of the IMU's six trucks and three 4×4s as they made their way across the desert. On another screen, he saw overhead imagery of the single runway at the Changii military airfield, forty-five

---

15. Net-Centric warfare makes real-time data and information available on demand across the entire battlefield spectrum, both horizontally and vertically.

kilometers northwest of Ürümqi. The fact that there was no activity was reassuring. A third screen showed a two-hundred-square-mile picture of the Tarim Basin. The terrorist convoy, displayed as a flashing star, was right in the middle of the screen. Two other screens displayed weather patterns for the region.

Tracy Wei-Liu tapped Ritzik on the shoulder. "Pretty incredible stuff."

"It's helpful."

"That seems like an understatement. How did anybody deal with warfare before this kind of information was available? It must have made things awfully difficult."

Ritzik said, "It may have been harder in the old days, sure. But not impossible."

AS A CADET at West Point, Ritzik had read several studies of Ranger operations during World War II. The one that had stuck most deeply in his mind was Colonel Henry A. Mucci's January 30, 1945, rescue of the Bataan Death March survivors from the Pangatian Japanese POW camp, five miles east of the Philippine city of Cabanatuan.

In 1944, Mucci was a thirty-three-year-old West Point graduate who, through force of character, motivation, training, and example, had transformed the 98th Field Artillery Battalion, a moribund rear-echelon unit that had never seen any combat, into the Sixth Ranger Battalion, one of the finest fighting machines of World War II.

Short, muscular, and almost never pictured without a trademark pipe clenched in his teeth, Colonel Mucci had quickly become one of Ritzik's heroes. He was, Ritzik soon discovered, one of those rare, instinctive Warriors who led from the front, like Arthur "Bull" Simon, who'd led the 1970 raid on the Son Tay prison camp in North Vietnam, or

Jonathan Netanyahu, the hero—and the only IDF fatality—
of the Israeli hostage rescue at Entebbe in 1976.

Whether in training or in battle, Mucci never asked his
men to do anything he hadn't done first. He trained his men
the way they'd fight: twenty-mile forced marches at night;
ten-mile runs in the mud and rain; two-hundred-and-fifty-
yard swims with fifty-pound combat packs under live fire.
Those who failed, or quit, were sent down—no exceptions.
Mucci wanted no one who didn't have the heart, the will,
and the guts to overcome all obstacles.

And like officers in the very best unconventional units,
Mucci didn't stand on ceremony, either. He thought—and
acted—outside the box. He'd once been faced with a serious discipline problem: one of his NCOs made highly dis-
paraging public comments about him. Mucci sought the
man out. In front of the Rangers, he tossed the sergeant an
unsheathed bayonet and taunted the man to kill him if he
felt so strongly. The sergeant took Mucci up on his challenge. It took Mucci mere seconds to disarm the malcon-
tent—and win his total loyalty.

In combat, Mucci's Sixth Rangers wore no insignia. In
fact, he ordered his men not to recognize rank in the field.
His reasoning was keep-it-simple-stupid battlefield logic:
insignia made the NCOs and officers easier targets for
Japanese snipers. "If you're stupid enough to call me
colonel, I'll salute and call you general," he reportedly once
told one of his junior officers. "We'll see which one of us
the Japs shoot first."

On January 27, 1945, Mucci was given the go-ahead to
hit Pangatian. His mission: truck 120 enlisted men and
eight officers seventy-five miles through Japanese-occupied
territory to a town called Guimba. There, Mucci and his
Rangers would link up with roughly 250 indigenous Philip-

pine forces. The combined group would then work its way past villages and Japanese garrisons, ford the Talavera River, then work its way south, bypassing the large Japanese garrison at Cabu. The march would take them more than twenty miles behind enemy lines. Just southwest of Cabu, the Rangers would attack the Japanese camp and liberate the Americans (and any other prisoners they might find) before the Japanese could slaughter them. Then, with the help of fighter aircraft cover, they'd exfiltrate everyone to safety.

Mucci assembled his intelligence from sparse aerial photographs, as well as from local resistance fighters and reports from an American unit known as the Alamo Scouts. But it was sketchy at best—which hadn't allowed the Rangers to practice their assault. And so, on-scene and behind enemy lines, Mucci made a tough call: he would delay the attack by one day in order to gather more intelligence and gauge the enemy's strength.

That decision, Ritzik believed, proved to be the deciding factor. In the ensuing twenty-four hours, Mucci's forces initiated multiple (and successful) reconnaissance missions of the camp and its guards. By January 29, Colonel Mucci had made detailed sketches of the Japanese compound, allowing the Rangers to rehearse their moves.

The attack on Pangatian was executed at dusk. Twenty-four hours later, Mucci had rescued 512 Bataan death-march survivors and evacuated them safely through hostile territory to the American lines. And while he and his Soldiers killed more than five hundred of the enemy, the operation cost him only two of his Rangers: Captain James C. Fisher, the Ranger doctor, and Corporal Roy Sweezy. More: he accomplished it all with nothing more than basic aerial photographs, good orienteering, and labor-intensive, eyes-on, sneak-and-peek ground reconnaissance—no GPS units; no satellites; no computer technology.

These days, a cow can hardly break wind anywhere in the world without a satellite, or a sensor, or a UAV analyzing the methane content. But there is a downside to this information avalanche: there is so much data coming in that timely analysis and distribution often becomes impossible. This results in the unfortunate situation known as garbage in, garbage *in*.

Ritzik first came to this judgment in Afghanistan. There were so many satellites, so many Predator and Global Hawk UAVs, so many U-2 and Aurora[16] stealth flights, and other SIGINT, TECHINT, PHOTINT, and ELINT vacuums sweeping up information, that the bosses back in Tampa were rendered incapable of making simple yes/no, or go/no-go decisions.

Very early on in the campaign, for example, one of the CIA's Hellfire missile–carrying Predator UAVs actually spotted the Taliban leader, Mullah Omar, himself. But by the time this info-bit was filtered through the multiple management layers of CENTCOM's captains, majors, lieutenant colonels, colonels, generals, and the all-important Judge Advocate General (JAG) legal cadre, it was too late to do anything about it. And so, Omar-baby escaped to fight another day.

It was, Ritzik therefore concluded, just as dangerous to be presented with too *many* options as too *few*. Both were limiting.

Ritzik knew that good intelligence, like a dependable

---

16. Aurora is the stealth-technology successor to the SR-71 "Blackbird" spy plane. It was first flown tactically over Afghanistan. Its existence has not yet been disclosed.

weapon, was one of the better tools he had at his disposal. But it was just that: another tool. It wasn't a crutch, or a panacea.

The essence of unconventional warfare would always boil down to one fundamental element: *Warriordom,* the deeply ingrained will and fierce determination of Soldiers to use the holy trinity of speed, surprise, and violence of action to prevail against great odds. Full stop. End of story.

And that's the way it would play out in Xinjiang. If he and his people were able to overcome their initial vulnerabilities and achieve what the SpecWar historians called "relative superiority" over the larger guerrilla force, then in all likelihood they'd be able to complete the mission successfully. No sophisticated, complex op plans, either. Just basic, no-frills, straight-ahead, in-your-face Soldiering.

Warriordom was the heart of Ranger School, and the even tougher Delta Selection course. The weeks of physical and mental anguish were a crucible of pain in which SpecWarriors were forged. The hardship and the severe crescendo of challenges were deliberate. Their goal was to make the Soldier-candidates demonstrate to themselves that they could put out 200 percent more exertion, concentration, and tenacity than they ever thought they could.

Ritzik had entered Delta's Selection with 159 other men. When it was over, a mere three were accepted into the Unit. The process, which was designed by Delta's founder, Colonel Charlie Beckwith, and based closely on the British SAS Selection process, has not been altered since the very first volunteers showed up at Fort Bragg back in the late 1970s. Delta Selection proved conclusively to Ritzik that no physical or mental obstacle—not cold, or fatigue, or stress; not topography, or water, or even a determined and dedicated enemy—could ever keep him from completing, and prevailing, in his mission.

That fundamental truth about himself and the Soldiers he worked with was what kept Ritzik on track. He knew that to succeed, at some point he'd have to suck up the pain, overcome the crises, and *Drive On,* just the way he'd done during Selection, or Colonel Henry Mucci had done during the assault on Cabanatuan. And if Mr. Murphy showed up and the going got rough? Then he and his Soldiers would grit their teeth, say FI*DO*—Fuck It, Drive On—and grind it out. *FIDO:* surmount any physical obstacles in their way. *FIDO:* get close without being seen. *FIDO:* sneak and peek to ascertain the enemy's strengths and weaknesses. *FIDO:* attack with utter ferocity and kill as many of the enemy as they could. *FIDO:* disable the MADM and get the hell out with the American prisoners.

10

ROBERT ROCKMAN pulled the heavy secure telephone across the top of the desk in his hideaway office and dialed a similar instrument on a desk at the Navy Command Center, a bustling warren of windowless, interconnected offices on the fourth floor's D-ring. Once the phone rang with its unique monotone, he pushed the button that enabled the encryption and voice-distortion devices. And didn't begin to speak until the red light on the phone receiver had turned green. When it did, Rockman barked, "This is Mr. Rogers at OSD.[17] Get me O'Neill."

Captain Hugh O'Neill, USNA '86, was one of eight "sweat hogs," or action officers, at the Command Center, working twelve-hour shifts to track naval movements and crises worldwide. At zero eight hundred, just over twelve hours ago, he'd been abruptly seconded to the secretary's personal staff on a temporary additional duty, or TAD, assignment. At 0805 O'Neill had been ushered into the secretary's hideaway, where he was presented with a file folder

17. Office of the Secretary of Defense.

diagonally striped in orange, on top of which sat an SCI—sensitive compartmented information—secrecy form and a Parker ball pen with the seal of the secretary of defense engraved on its gold-plated cap.

The secretary said, "Sign the form, Captain. Then read the file. You can keep the pen."

O'Neill didn't have to be asked twice.

The compartment was called SKYHORSE-PUSHPIN. O'Neill's assignment was to track the Chinese military's reaction to a provocative wave of unscheduled American reconnaissance flights and naval ship movements, and report as necessary to the secretary. He was to work his network of fellow sweat hogs and his contacts in the other uniformed services and intelligence agencies to elicit information without advising his sources as to its ultimate destination. He would act with absolute discretion. He would write nothing down. And he would deliver his findings only after he had asked for and received the Skyhorse recognition signal from the secretary.

Rockman waited out a fifteen-second delay. Then he heard: "This is Captain O'Neill."

"This is OSD—Mr. Rogers."

O'Neill said: "Signal?"

Rockman said, "Skyhorse-Pushpin." He paused. "What do we know, Hugo?"

"They're pinging us, sir, no doubt about it."

"Good." That meant the Chinese had taken the bait. "What's the evidence?"

"I'll call you back from the SCIF in two minutes with that information, sir." The NCC's SCIF—the acronym stood for sensitive compartmented information facility—was a small, bug-proof room with a thick door and a cipher lock at the very end of the maze of Command Center offices.

Rockman replaced the receiver in its cradle and waited.

Thirty seconds later the phone squalled once. He picked the receiver up and repeated both the encryption process and the code-word recognition signal. "Sit-rep, Hugo."

"Naval Air confirms six close-quarters intercepts of our routine surveillance aircraft in the past eight hours. A message from COMPAC details two Chinese ELINT trawlers moving in the straits of Taiwan. My colleagues at DIA are reporting huge military message traffic surges. And Rear Admiral Taylor, our naval attaché in Beijing, has just been summoned to the Defense Ministry at ten hundred hours Beijing time—that's about an hour from now, sir—to explain what the Chinese are calling our 'highly provocative moves in Chinese territorial waters.' "

"I love it." Rockman slapped his palms together then rubbed them. "Anything else?"

"The Air Force's Command Center is tracking unanticipated PLA flights out of the Beijing and Guangzhou military districts."

Rockman said, "Hmm."

"Sir?"

"Any details?"

"Nothing out of the ordinary, sir. A flight of three HIP-H transport choppers and two HIND-D gunships flying cover moved out of Beijing early this morning."

"Transport choppers with gunship cover. Are you sure?"

"Yes, sir."

The hair on the back of Rockman's head stood up. But he didn't betray his concern. "You're positive?"

"Yes, Mr. Secretary. There was also a flight of eight J-7D Fishbed fighters that flew out of Guangzhou, heading south."

Rockman kept his voice neutral. "Keep me posted if there are any further developments from the Navy. You might as well keep tracking the Air Force, too." He made a quick note. "I'll be here at least until midnight, Hugo—which means you will, too."

Rockman slapped the receiver down without waiting for a response. He paused five seconds, then dialed a second number, repeating the encryption process before speaking. When he saw the green light, he said, "Nick—this is Rocky. Give me the latest on what the Chinese are up to—and don't try to hand me a load of your usual smoke-and-mirrors political analysis or hand me any horse-puckey about what sensitive information you can and can't talk to me about."

20 Kilometers Northeast of Almaty, Kazakhstan. 0900 Hours Local Time.

MIKE RITZIK was pissed. That was an understatement. Mike Ritzik was royally pissed. Royally pissed at Rowdy Yates because the sergeant major hadn't filled him in. And even more royally pissed at himself because he hadn't even noticed until he was introducing the men to Wei-Liu.

What had escaped his attention was the presence of a lanky, red-haired warrant officer named Michael Dunne. Dunne had no business being in Kazakhstan. He was the chopper pilot from Task Force 160 at Fort Campbell, Kentucky, whom Ritzik had selected to extract the Delta element from China. But Dunne's mission had been scrubbed. Given the PLA's involvement, there was no way Ritzik was going to use a helicopter to extract his people and the CIA officers. Odds were, the Chinese would provide their troops tactical air support. Against fighter aircraft, the slow-flying MH-60 would be a sitting duck. And yet Dunne was in Almaty. And it was Fred Yates who had brought him.

Ritzik finally found the time to pull Rowdy aside. "Rowdy, we gotta talk." He'd learned a long time ago never to wire-brush a man in front of the troops.

The pair of them walked to the far end of the warehouse. When they were out of earshot, Ritzik jerked his thumb toward Dunne. "Why the hell is he here?"

"Who?"

"Goddammit, Rowdy—"

"Mickey D? He's here because I want him here, Loner."

Ritzik crossed his arms. "I scrubbed him, Sergeant Major," he said, the use of Yates's rank a sign of displeasure. "You agreed."

Yates reached into the left thigh pocket of his cargo pants and withdrew a tin container of snuff. He took a pinch, stuffed it between his cheek and his lower jaw, wiped his fingers off on his trouser leg, then closed the container and replaced it. "That was how we left it, Major," Rowdy said. "But, I got to thinking after your last call."

"I love you like a brother, Rowdy, but you're pissing me off."

"Hear me out, boss. We train differently than most units. We cross-train, just like Special Forces. But we add a lot more esoteric specialties. We learn to pick locks and bypass alarm systems. We can hot-wire everything from cars to locomotives. I brought ten men—we have twelve with you and me, thirteen with the lady. Between us, there's nothing we can't do. You want to stage our exfil using a combine harvester? Shep can drive one—and he can also perform a minor operation, because he's cross-trained with Doc Masland. And Doc's not just a dicksmith, he's a sniper, because he's cross-trained with Ty Weaver. And Ty can handle just about any heavy machinery we come across." Yates spat into the polystyrene cup in his right hand. "Are you receiving yet?"

"Not really."

"So what happens if we need to steal a plane instead of a combine harvester, boss?" He spat again. "When I went up to Dam Neck last month, I found out there are four enlisted men at Dev Group who have pilots' licenses. They told me they paid for their own training, by the way, because Navy SpecWar officers don't believe enlisted men should be allowed to touch aircraft controls. That's neither here nor there. What is, is that Sword Squadron currently doesn't have a single pilot—officer or enlisted."

"And you concluded we need one out here."

"Frankly, yes," Rowdy said. "We used to have half a dozen people with pilots' licenses, and guys were always going to flight school in their spare time. That guy Dean Williams who retired last year was qualified to fly multi-engine jet aircraft. But lately we've been so busy no one's had the time to take the courses, and no pilots have come through Selection." Yates spat into his plastic cup. "Mickey D brought it up when I told him he was scrubbed. He's got a pilot's license. What if the shit hits the fan and we have to get out using an aircraft, Major? Bottom line is, the more I thought about what Mickey D said, the more it made sense."

Ritzik said: "Does he have the quals?"

"I don't know if he'd make it through Selection," Yates said.

"Well . . ."

"That's not the point. Doing this particular job is the point. Look—he's a runner. He completed the Marine marathon last year. And he took the MFF HALO–HAHO[18] parachute course at Marana four months ago."

---

18. Military Free Fall High Altitude Low Opening–High Altitude High Opening.

"All eight jumps?"

"Roger that. He has the quals."

"That's fourteen people, Rowdy—plus the four spooks. Eighteen is a lot to move around."

"I know, Loner." Yates used his improvised spittoon. "I'm just thinking about flexibility in the field. I want us to have as many options as possible."

"You probably brought everything he'd need, didn't you?"

" 'Be Prepared,' isn't that the Boy Scouts' marching song?" Yates growled. "You let me take care of the details."

1020. "Loner—call for you. Some guy claiming to be secretary of defense." Bill Sandman wasn't a big man, but he had an aggressive edge to him and a raspy, gravel-toned voice that came from two packs of Marlboros a day for more than twenty-five years. He swiveled Ritzik's chair away from the computer screen, pointed it toward the STU-III satellite phone, and gave a gentle shove.

Ritzik rolled to the phone and picked it up. "Ritzik."

"Major." The satellite connection mildly distorted Robert Rockman's distinctive voice.

"Sir."

"How's it going?"

"So far so good."

"Glad to hear it. The president wants an update, so sit-rep me."

"We are on schedule, sir. I'm planning our departure at seventeen-thirty local time."

"Any chance you can go earlier?"

"Not really, sir. Any reason why we should?" Ritzik's question was greeted by silence. "Mr. Secretary?"

Rockman hesitated. "I just got off the phone with Nick Pappas. Major General Zhou Yi's air unit departed Beijing at zero eight hundred this morning."

Ritzik hadn't known, which disturbed the hell out of him, because he was supposed to be getting real-time intelligence dumps from Langley. Christ, the CIA was still stovepiping its precious information. "That's a full day ahead of schedule."

"I know, Major."

"What's their ETA at Changii?"

"Langley says the earliest would be about eighteen hundred tomorrow, local time."

"How did they arrive at that?"

"Major?"

"Is Langley tracking them? Because if they are, we're getting none of it."

"You're breaking up," Rockman said.

Ritzik said, "If Langley's tracking them, sir, we need the info out here now."

There was static on the line. Then the secretary's voice, sounding metallic, said, "I don't think they are, Major."

Ritzik found Rockman's reply troubling. "Mr. Secretary?"

"I asked Nick. The son of a bitch said there's some sort of problem with cloud cover between Beijing and Taiyuan. He said his analysts are working off statistical models."

"Jeezus." Ritzik didn't like that at all. The problem was basic: *statistical model* was a fancy way of saying "simulation." Intelligence analysts liked statistical models because they were neat and easy to put together on the computer. But no matter what you called them, simulations were *simulated,* not real, events. They were simply educated guesses. More than that, statistical models didn't take any part of the human element of operations into consideration. Nor did they factor in Mr. Murphy of Murphy's Law fame.

Nor, for that matter, could a statistical model predict a ground commander's reactions or leadership qualities or lack of them. Interpreting those issues required real-time intelligence. "What's the worst-case scenario, Mr. Secretary?"

"Arrival at Changii in twenty-six hours—that would be about noon tomorrow local time."

Which, Ritzik understood only too well, would give the Chinese six hours of daylight in which to go hunting. And those hours were precisely the same time frame Ritzik had planned to use to begin his exfil. Events had progressed well beyond the SNAFU range. They were now in the TARFU zone, where things are *really* messy.

"Mr. Secretary."

"Major?"

"Any news about whether or not we'll be vulnerable during the infiltration stage?"

"I don't get you."

"Are the Chinese capable of intercepting our launch aircraft?"

"Let me look at my notes." There was a pause on the line. Then Rockman said, "Nick said there are three bases in the region with fighter aircraft."

"Hell, Mr. Secretary, I can see that much on my imagery. I need to know whether or not they're going to scramble when we break out of our scheduled flight plan."

There was another pause. "Nick's people can't say one way or the other."

"Can't or won't, sir?"

The irritation in Rockman's voice was palpable. "Does it really make a difference, Major?"

There were five seconds of silence while Rockman waited for Ritzik to reply. When he didn't, the secretary said, "You keep me posted, son." Then the phone went dead.

11

20 Kilometers Northeast of Almaty, Kazakhstan.
1230 Hours Local Time.

TWO OF RITZIK'S RANGERS dressed in Kazakh Special Forces uniforms towed the big white Yak up to the warehouse. Umarov himself directed the tug to position the plane so the fuselage would block any view of what was being loaded. Then he waved the Rangers off with a flourish and a wink. As they cleared the aircraft, Doc Masland, Ty Weaver, Gene Shepard, and Rowdy Yates, all dressed in airport worker's overalls, emerged from the warehouse to muscle an auxiliary power unit under the nose of the plane. Weaver uncoiled the thick rubber electrical cable and attached the business end to the power pod just fore of the plane's nosewheel assembly.

Yates said, "Contact," and hit the APU generator switch.

Masland and Weaver pushed a wheeled stairway up to the side of the aircraft. Shepard climbed the steel treads, opened the forward hatch, and disappeared inside. Fifteen seconds later, the plane's interior lights came on.

Ritzik scampered up the stairway. "Shep—let's get the shades drawn, and then you start removing seats and install the prebreathers." He looked down the long, narrow single aisle. "I think two rows on each side will do it. You agree?"

The first sergeant squinted aft. "Should be enough. If not, I'll pull a third." He made his way rearward, racked the exit door lock to his left, and dropped the aft stairway, testing it after he heard it *thwock* onto the apron.

A welcome stream of cool air wafted through the stuffy aircraft. Shepard came forward. "Amazing how strange yet familiar this thing is," he said. "Like one of those tofu entrées they say tastes just like chicken."

"Chicken Kiev, maybe." Ritzik tapped an overhead luggage bin. "The Yak-42's a doppelgänger of the Boeing 727. It was built during the height of the Cold War when we weren't selling planes to the Soviets. So one of their most senior aircraft designers—a guy named Alexander Yakovlev—managed to get his hands on a 727 for a few weeks. He reverse-engineered the design, and built his own version."

"No shit."

"No shit." Ritzik heard noise forward. He watched as Talgat hulked through the doorway, blocking the light.

The Kazakh said, "The Yakovlev is a beautiful design, is it not?" He stood aside as Shepard eased past him, smiling.

"Just what the doctor ordered." Ritzik settled onto an armrest. "When is Shingis due?"

"My cousin? I told him thirteen hundred."

"Good."

Umarov said, "So, Mike, what is the story?"

"I'm going to need you to crew the plane," Ritzik said.

"Crew?"

"Shingis will fly. You'll crew."

"Just the two of us?"

Ritzik said, "Talgat, sometimes less is more."

The Kazakh scratched his head. "I do not understand. How can less be more?"

"It's a figure of speech," Ritzik said. "It means I want to keep it in the family."

"Ah—idiom." Umarov took his cigarettes out of his breast pocket, tamped one on his watch, and lit up. "Sometimes fewer personnel is more efficient than many. 'Less is more—keep it all in the family.' Now I understand."

Curtis Hansen and Gene Shepard pushed onto the aircraft, holding a small metal toolbox. Umarov brightened at the sight of Shepard's face. "Sergeant Shepard," he exclaimed. He grabbed the trooper in a tight embrace and kissed him on each cheek. *"Assalamu alaykim."*

"Waghalaykim assalam—and upon you, Colonel." Shepard extracted himself from Umarov's grip. "This is Staff Sergeant Hansen."

The slightly built Soldier ran a hand through his thinning blondish hair and said, very carefully, *"Assa-lamu alaykim,* Colonel," then reddened self-consciously at Umarov's delighted expression.

Shepard hefted the toolbox. "Excuse us, Colonel." The pair headed aft, retrieved a pair of socket wrenches, and began to unbolt the rows of seats over the aircraft's wings.

The Kazakh watched them. "Less is more," he said. "Right?"

"Colonel Umarov," Shepard said, "in this case, sir, less is actually less." He looked at the puzzled Kazakh and grinned.

1332. Ritzik was squatting beside the pair of six-man portable oxygen prebreathers, which were secured against the aircraft's midbulkhead, as Ty Weaver and Bill Sandman wrestled the ten-foot-long metal mold up the rear stairway. He looked up. "Set it on the starboard side."

"Nautical today, ain't we, Loner?" Sandman's voice reverberated in the narrow fuselage.

The two men walked the smooth pan forward until it cleared the rear bulkhead. Then they flipped it over and jammed it between the windows and the innermost seats.

"Where are the tie-downs?"

Weaver said, "I'll get 'em."

"Do it now—I don't want to be airborne and find we've left 'em behind."

"Wilco."

1337. Rowdy Yates climbed the rear stairway to find Ritzik, a checklist in his hand, inspecting the prebreather. "You beat me to it," the sergeant major said.

"I was bored." Ritzik watched as Yates rummaged through the forwardmost luggage bins until he found the aircraft's safety-display items, took both lengths of demonstration seat belt, clipped them together, and stuffed them in his left cargo pocket.

"Collecting souvenirs?"

"I'm gonna need these later and I don't want to have to go looking for 'em."

"If you say so." Ritzik tapped the prebreather consoles. "Looks as if they survived the flight over. No visual flaws. The valve stems are all straight. None of the screws are backed out. And the gauge is showing eighteen hundred psi." He paused. "How's the lady?"

"Asleep, finally," Yates said. "Out like a light."

"Good. The less time she has to worry, the better."

Yates said, "Loner, I'm worried about her."

"We don't get no vote, Rowdy. Our job is to take her in so she can do her job."

"*Hoo-ah,* boss. But do us all a favor."

"What's that?"

"Get a friggin' diagram out of her before we wheels up.

Just in case she croaks at some point, I want to be able to at least take a crack at disarming the sucker if we have to."

"Makes sense to me." Ritzik turned the shutoff valve five and a half turns counterclockwise, then squinted at the second gauge on the prebreather faceplate. "Reducer gauge is holding at forty psi."

"On the money."

"Yup." Ritzik stood up. "Get the third unit and secure it as close to the cockpit as you can."

"What third unit?"

"Don't shit me, Rowdy."

"Major, we brought two six-man prebreathers. Twelve people—twelve hoses, twelve couplers."

Ritzik said, "Then we're screwed. You've read the tables. Each of us needs a full hour on O-two before we depressurize the aircraft and switch to the portable units."

"So?"

"Count, Rowdy, count."

Yates looked up toward the aircraft ceiling. "Oh, Kee rist. Fourteen, Major."

"That's not including Talgat and Shingis. We need sixteen hookups."

"Oh, Christ. I must have had a major brain fart yesterday." Yates rubbed his scalp. "I really screwed this up."

"How many O-two sets do we have?"

"Sixteen sanitized units—and two walk-around bottles for Talgat. I got sixteen double tanks from Marana, Major. I brought 'em all, because I knew I'd need O-two for the lady and Mickey D—prebreathing and descent." Yates spat into his plastic cup. "We can rig something for Talgat by using the plane's internal O-two system."

"Maybe." Ritzik glanced toward the nose of the plane.

"Wait here." He rose and headed toward the cockpit. "Shingis—"

He emerged sixty seconds later, his face grim. "They don't have oxygen." He anticipated Yates's question: "The units are shipped from Germany. They're on back order. And this particular aircraft is used on short-haul flights— they stay below ten thousand feet. So they don't bother to keep the system charged."

Yates cocked his head, incredulous.

"Hey, this is Kazakhstan. The flight safety regs are a little more flexible here."

"I guess they are."

"Bottom line," Ritzik said. "We cut two people."

"Loner—"

"Do you have a better idea?"

"No, sir, I do not." Yates spat into his cup. "But having two less jumpers creates its own set of problems."

"I know, I know." Ritzik's mind was racing. The situation was already edge-of-the-envelope dangerous. Offset HAHO jumps—high-altitude, high-opening operations in which the aircraft does not overfly the drop zone—were incredibly risky maneuvers. At altitudes above twenty-five thousand feet, ice can actually form on the parachute canopy, affecting its performance and response. Weather data is essential—the wind's direction and velocity are critical in determining the infiltration route.

In training, every element of a HAHO jump was broken down and double-checked. Safety was paramount. And even when all the bases were covered, jumpers still died. Twenty-seven thousand five hundred feet was almost six miles up. The temperature was well below freezing. The air was thin. Hypoxia—lack of oxygen—could cause a jumper to become careless, or even pass out. The "stick" could leave the aircraft imprecisely and the jumpers could get tangled up. Chutes might foul, reserves misdeploy. Communications could go bad. Wind shears, crosscurrents, and thermals might scatter the jumpers over a hundred square miles, or run them into the ground at forty miles an hour. And that was under optimum conditions: well-supervised jumps in clear, mild weather, with red or purple smoke grenades to indicate wind direction, and safety officers to scrub the jump if the ground wind speed exceeded eighteen knots.

Tonight, they'd be jumping blind.

Intelligence was virtually nonexistent. Ritzik still had no idea whether or not fighter aircraft were capable of intercepting the Yak from the three air bases in his target area because the CIA hadn't told him what the Chinese tactical capabilities were. He was unsure about the current location of the PLA's Special Operations troops. Worse, he had no idea how big a force General Zhou Yi was bringing.

Then there were the physical hurdles. Wind currents and speed: uncertain. Obstacles: unidentified. Amount and origin of potential air turbulence: unknown. LZ: hostile. Friendlies on the ground: none. Charlie Foxtrot potential: very high.

Finally, there were the immutable laws of physics to contend with. The maximum sustainable load for a Ram Air parachute is 360 pounds. If a chute is subjected to excess weight, the cells can stress and the canopy may begin to disintegrate. So, every round of ammunition, every piece of equipment has to be tallied: the chute, the reserve, and all the accompanying web gear; the weapons and ammunition; the combat pack; the body armor, load-bearing vest, and two canteens of water; the uniform; the cold-weather gear; the helmet, oxygen mask, and boots; the O_2 bottles, hoses, and regulator, as well as the GPS navigation, night-vision, chest-pack computers, and communications equipment. All of it, when combined with the jumper's weight, couldn't total more than 360 pounds.

The loss of two jumpers meant less total weight on the ground. The part of the equation that bothered Ritzik most was that they'd be carrying fewer rounds of ammunition and a reduced amount of ordnance. Which weakened one-third of the SpecWar trinity. Any degradation of firepower would result in diminished violence of action, which in turn would shrink Ritzik's chances of success.

It was time to recalibrate.

1447. Ritzik, Bill Sandman, and Ty Weaver were gathered in a knot, staring at the streaming satellite video of the convoy. Rowdy Yates joined them and poked his finger at the screen. "See how they're stopped?"

He squinted over the top of the magnifiers perched on his nose. "The third truck—number 4866—that's the one with the prisoners and the device. Look how they've got it surrounded." His finger tapped the plastic screen surface. "Three tangos with weapons on each side. And the driver—he's standing just ahead of the cab; his weapon's pointed down, but the sumbitch has his hands on it. And they've got another five people at the rear."

Ty Weaver looked at the column of vehicles. There were six heavy trucks and three boxy SUVs. He tapped the image of the Toyota 4×4 that was parked fifty yards out in front of the ragged column. "That Toyota's consistently been the point vehicle since the satpix started coming in. The big enchilada's riding in it, too."

Sandman stared at the tiny figures on the screen. "Which one is he?"

Weaver's finger found a small figure pacing between the

second and third trucks. "From the way he's moving I think he's making a phone call."

"Bullshit." Rowdy Yates laughed. "How the hell can you tell he's making a call by how he moves?"

"Don't believe him," Sandman said. "We saw the asshole take a phone out of his pocket and punch a number into the keypad."

"Get the number, too, did you, Bill?"

"It was a 1-900 sex line, Sergeant Major. Same one you always call."

Yates spat into his cup. "Bite me, First Sergeant Sandman."

Ty Weaver said, "Do you believe they have coverage out there—cell towers and everything?"

"Why not? Anything's possible these days," Ritzik said. "Hey—look."

He turned his attention to the screen. Two guerrillas were dropping the rear gate. Three others stood, muzzles pointed toward the rear of the truck. The two who'd dropped the gate climbed inside the covered truck bed.

As the Soldiers watched, they saw three figures thrown out onto the hard sand. The trio caromed between the guards like pinballs as they were punched, butt-stroked, and kicked mercilessly.

Ty Weaver said, "I thought you said there were four prisoners."

Ritzik's eyes narrowed. "There are." He paused. "Or, there were." He cast a quick glance at Rowdy Yates. The sergeant major's somber face reflected the same nasty conclusion Ritzik had come to. The tangos were killing Americans—and the rescue element was still on the ground in Almaty.

Ritzik's voice took on an urgent tone as he wrenched his

eyes away from the sight of the prisoners being beaten. "Clock's ticking, guys. What's the plan?"

Rowdy Yates looked past Ritzik and stared at the screen. All he felt was fury. White-hot and murderous. But he'd learned over the years to temper his anger and channel his rage; to use those searing emotions constructively in order to give himself a psychological and tactical edge over his enemy. Which is what he did now. Coolly, Rowdy shifted focus and scanned a screen on which flickered an infrared image of the north end of the lake. His voice was dispassionate. "Can't really know for sure until we're on the ground, Loner. Too many unanswered questions about the site. How high's the causeway wall? How deep's the water? How close together will the vehicles be? Right now it's one of those generic keep-it-simple-stupid ops."

He reached past Sandman, swiped a legal pad off the folding table, and drew a rough diagram. "They're coming north. They turn west over this bridge"—he brought his marking pen up—"and we're set up on the far side of the causeway." Rowdy paused. "Snipers execute— suppressed—and bring the column to a stop before they can react. We claymore wherever we can. Hopefully kill a bunch of 'em before they're able to get out of the trucks. Those we don't claymore, we create a fatal funnel, and we hit 'em." His expression hardened as he drew overlapping fields of fire. "Hit 'em hard. Kill 'em all."

Weaver tapped the 4×4 on the screen. "If I take out the big enchilada's driver first, it'll stop 'em dead in their tracks."

Sandman wagged his head. "Negatory, Ty. You're not listening. They'll just be coming over a bridge—moving slow because they've just had to negotiate a tight left-hand turn. You and Barber take out that back truck first, just as it hits the west end of the bridge—that way they don't have an es-

cape to the rear. You guys wax both the driver and whoever's riding shotgun so there's nobody alive in the cab."

"Good catch, Bill," Weaver said. "Makes sense."

Rowdy agreed. "You let the 4×4 with Mr. Big go past."
He looked at Sandman. "You and Tuzz deal with Mr. Big
from the flank, okay? And disable but don't destroy."

"La big enchilada or the 4×4?"

"Don't be a wiseass," Rowdy snorted. He dribbled tobacco juice into his plastic cup and wiped his lower lip.
"You snipers will take out the front truck right after you've
hit the rearmost vehicle. That'll bring 'em all to a stop—
they're on a narrow causeway with marsh on both sides
here." He drew his marker across the page. "Then, as soon
as the trucks are stopped, Goose and Doc, Shep, and
Mickey D and Loner and me, we'll deal with anybody in
trucks one, two, and three. And we'll claymore wherever
we can."

"If they're polite enough to stop where you want them to
stop," Ritzik said.

"The column will stop right where we want it to if Ty and
Barber do their jobs," Rowdy said. "Because the friggin'
drivers will all be dead."

"Gotcha," Ritzik said. "But don't forget: leave two trucks
undamaged."

Ty Weaver nodded. "Understood, boss."

"And all the 4×4s."

"Loner's beginning to repeat himself," Ty said. "Hey,
Rowdy, isn't reiteration one of the first signs of dementia?"
The sniper tapped Ritzik's chest. "Maybe the dicksmith
should look at you before we wheels up just to make sure
you're mission-eligible."

Ritzik started to respond but Sandman broke in. "Hey,"
he said, "they threw the prisoners back onto the truck and
locked it down. Mr. Big Enchilada just climbed into the

4×4." He stared at the screen. "They're pulling out—moving north."

245 Kilometers Northwest of Mazartag, Xinjiang Autonomous Region, China. 1644 Hours Local Time.

SAM PHILLIPS SAID, "We should go tonight. Agreed?"

"I don't think we have any other option—except making a run for it right now." X-Man's voice was tense. Half an hour ago he'd maneuvered himself and Sam to one of the bullet holes and he'd sneaked a look through the canvas. There were mountains out there in the distance, he reported. Big, jagged snowcapped peaks. God, how he'd love to ski them. But not now. There'd be no skiing in X-Man's life for the foreseeable future.

How far are the mountains? Kaz wanted to know. Good question. Maybe a hundred miles; maybe fifty miles; maybe thirty miles. It was difficult to tell.

The convoy had jolted to a halt some quarter of an hour earlier. The Americans waited, trying to listen in on the terrorists' conversation. But it was nigh on impossible to hear anything over the growl of idling diesel. After no one looked in on them after about ten minutes, X-Man and Sam rolled to their right again, up against the frame supporting the canvas where a round had punctured both wood and canvas. Sam ended up with a splinter in his cheek. But he was able to grab a quick peek. The pair of them crabbed back and leaned up against Kaz. "We're on a slope leading down to the bank of a huge river," Sam said. "Or maybe it's a lake. From what I can tell, the water's at least a mile wide."

Kaz asked: "Swimmable?"

"I didn't see any rapids," Sam said. "But there's no way

to tell the strength of the current—or even if there is a current." He paused. "Look—we can't go now. It's still light. We'd be caught."

"I think if we could make it to the water, we'd have a chance—even now," X-Man said. "Frankly, Sam, we're better off in the water than we would be trying to get away on foot tonight—harder to track, and better concealment than the scrub and dunes we've been traveling through."

"You've got a point, X. But only if we can stay warm." Sam worried about hypothermia. The temperature at night dropped to close to freezing, and he didn't like the idea of being wet, cold, and out in the open. "I want to take a better look at that water."

"Let's do it, then." The pair of them made their way back to the canvas and Sam pressed his cheek against the rough material.

"Hey," X-Man whispered urgently, "watch—"

And then the rear gate of the truck was dropped with a violent clang. Two IMU goons saw what Sam and X-Man were up to. They vaulted inside, grabbed the three Americans, and threw them off the truck onto the hard desert floor.

12

THE DROP ELEMENT began to suit up. The first layer was clothing: lightweight, German thermal underwear, French green, windproof Gore-Tex coveralls, Russian body armor, thick socks, and Adidas GSG-9 boots. Over the coveralls, each man wore a wide, nylon web belt around his waist. Suspended from it on the right side was a flapped and taped pistol holster, which was secured by two elastic straps fastened tightly around the thigh. On each man's left thigh, another flapped, taped pouch held three AK-74 magazines.

The chutes came next. The flight would take less than an hour, so they'd enter the aircraft fully geared up. The ten men worked in pairs. The chutes were final-checked for visible defects. Then the harnesses were let out and the chute assemblies laid out on the floor, pack trays facing downward.

Rowdy Yates picked up Gene Shepard's chute by the lift webs attached to the canopy release assembly. "Okay, Shep—let's see if this sucker fits like it's supposed to."

Shepard bent his knees and leaned forward, assuming a mock-high-jump position. Yates settled the chute on Shepard's back. Shepard threaded the chest strap, cinched it tight, and fastened it securely. As he finished, he called, "Right leg strap, Sergeant Major."

Yates passed him the strap. Shepard ran his fingers over the webbing, making sure it wasn't kinked. Then he inserted it through one of the kit-bag handles, cinched it tight through the turnbuckle, and fastened it. Shepard repeated the process with the left leg strap. Then he stood erect.

Yates said: "Check your canopy release assemblies."

Shepard tapped the hollows of his shoulders. "They're good, Rowdy. You can snug up the horizontal adjustment straps."

"Wilco." Yates fiddled with the webbing. Then Shepard threaded the long, flat waistband through its turnbuckle and snugged it tight. Finally, he took half a dozen elastic "keepers" from Rowdy Yates and used them to secure all the loose ends of the webbing. The sergeant major rapped Shepard on the back. "Feel okay?"

The tall, lanky first sergeant bounced up and down on the balls of his feet and tried to roll his shoulders to shake the parachute loose. He couldn't. "Great. Now let's get you dressed."

"Gimme a minute." Yates looked over at Wei-Liu, who'd been observing the two men. "I think you need a tad of tailoring, ma'am."

"Do you, Rowdy?" Wei-Liu had brought her own boots, long underwear, and socks. "At least a few things fit," she said ruefully as Rowdy used olive-drab duct tape to bind the baggy coveralls around her wrists and ankles. He also taped two liquid-filled plastic cylinders, each about eight inches long, to the outsides of her calves.

"What're these?"

"Chem-light sticks, ma'am. So we can keep track of you." She reached down to squeeze them, but Rowdy caught her hand. "Not yet, ma'am. Please don't fuss with 'em until we're ready to go."

"You're the boss, Sergeant Major." She pointed toward Shepard in his chute. "Am I going to wear one of those?"

"No, ma'am. You're going to travel in tandem with the major." Yates retrieved a harness set from the floor and helped Wei-Liu into it. He fitted the shoulder and chest straps first, then the leg straps. He cinched the waistband—but discovered something in the way. He poked at Wei-Liu's ribs. "What the hell have you got on under there?"

"My tools. They're in a shoulder pouch. I thought they'd be more secure that way."

"Let's adjust them." Rowdy waited until she'd fitted the sack under her arm. Then he cinched the waistband once more, tugging until he was satisfied it was snug enough. He brought half a dozen more elastic keepers out of his pocket and secured all her loose webbing. Then he signaled for Wei-Liu to turn completely around for a visual inspection.

He was satisfied. "How does that feel, ma'am?"

She imitated Gene Shepard's jumping motion. "Okay, I guess."

"And now?" Yates grabbed the rear support straps of her harness in both hands, jerked Wei-Liu three feet off the ground, and shook her.

If he expected her to scream, she disappointed him. He set her down. "Anything feel loose, ma'am?"

"No—it's all snugged up."

1645. Ritzik peered over Marko's shoulder at the flashing point of light on the computer screen. "Their progress still constant?" He wanted to be on the ground before any more Americans were killed, and his voice betrayed the anxiety.

"Has been for the last two hours, Loner. They're heading

north." The Soldier tapped a series of numbers into his laptop and checked the screen. "About seven and a half, maybe eight hours from the bridge at the rate they're going."

"Finally—some good news." Ritzik clapped his shoulder. "I'm going to suit up. If there's any change, let me know."

"You got it, boss."

1655. They all looked, Wei-Liu decided, like alien Kung Fu artists in spacesuits. The men appeared to be practicing martial arts, moving their arms in slow, ritualistic motions, adjusting their stance, arching their backs. When she'd asked, Rowdy explained that they were miming their free-fall and HAHO emergency procedures: cutaways in case of partial or total malfunctions; corrective maneuvers in case of spins; reactive moves for premature brake release, or closed end cells on the chutes.

She watched, impressed with the men's ability to move smoothly, given all they were carrying. The night-vision goggles attached to their helmets were taped down for the jump, giving their profiles a decidedly reptilian appearance. Then there were the oxygen masks, which were also held firmly to the helmets by bayonetlike lugs. From the end of the masks, a dovetail fitting led to an AIROX-VIII regulator assembly attached to a short oxygen delivery tube that descended to the dual oxygen bottles strapped just above the right hip.

Wrapped around the thick tube was the send/receive communications cable. One end of the cable was connected to the mike inside the O_2 mask and the helmet's integrated headset. The other looped around to a pouch attached just above the O_2 package and plugged into the duplex miniature communications system that would allow them to talk to one another and the TOC simultaneously. A second, backup duplex system rode in a pouch on the right shoulder.

Around each man's left wrist, a thick Velcro strap held an illuminated, German-made QA2-30/G free-fall altimeter. On their right forearms, another pair of Velcro straps held a wide double unit: a secure wireless PDA with a GPS positioning module, which would help to guide them and also keep them updated on their target's position.

Weapons were slung over the left shoulder, muzzles pointed downward, with loaded magazines inserted in the receivers and taped securely. More tape was used to wrap padding around the muzzle and the sights. Then the slings were tightened so that the butt of the weapon was safely above and behind the jumper's armpit. If the gun shifted and ended up shoved into the armpit, a jumper's shoulder could be dislocated, or even broken, by the sudden force exerted by the parachute's opening shock. Todd Sweeney and Ty Weaver, the two snipers, carried Heckler & Koch MSG90 7.62mm sniper rifles in padded scabbards that rode behind their left shoulders. The rifles' ten-power scopes, attached to their prezeroed quick-mount systems, were insulated from shock inside the fifty-pound, front-riding combat packs. Maybe.

1705. Rowdy Yates sliced open a black-and-gold case of nine-volt French-manufactured alkaline batteries. He snapped them onto the connector buttons of the small, infrared strobe flashers that Michael Dunne had brought from Fort Campbell, and taped one strobe to the rear of each jumper's helmet. When he finished, he called over to Gene Shepard. "I'm ready to suit up now, Shep."

"And about damn time, too."

1711. Ritzik ran his own checklist. He was visibly weighed down by the large tandem chute assembly, plus his equipment, weapons, and navigation devices. Under normal circumstances, the jumpers wouldn't attach their combat packs and sling weapons until twenty minutes before insertion. But tonight wasn't normal, and they'd completed their preparations before entering the aircraft. The only prep they'd do aboard the Yak would be to arm their automatic rip-cord releases, which had to be done after they'd climbed above 2,500 feet. Checklist complete, he put a radio transceiver to his ear. "Talgat?"

He waited for a response, finally nodding. "Good. Okay. See you in three minutes." He looked around until he focused on Rowdy Yates. "Talgat's just done his part." The Kazakh had used his clout to delay the scheduled Air Kazakhstan flight to Ürümqi because of "mechanical difficulties." Today, Ritzik's plane would assume the commercial flight's place. "Time to saddle up, Sergeant Major. Let's get this show on the road."

1722. They were crowded together, kept on short tethers by the prebreather hookups. Wei-Liu's goggles began to fog up. Yates pulled them off her head, reached past the big bowie knife secured on his combat harness into a zippered pocket on his left sleeve, brought out a silicon cloth, and wiped them clear. "They should be okay now."

"Thanks."

He looked at her face. "Nervous?"

"You better believe it."

"Good. I'd be worried if you weren't."

"What about you?"

"Funny thing is," Rowdy said, "I bet I've jumped out of planes more times than I've actually landed in 'em. So I'm nervous every time I go out the door—but I'm a lot more nervous when we land." He took her by the shoulders. "Don't worry, ma'am, you'll do just fine. Just sit back and enjoy the ride."

The Yak's engines caught and whined into life. Talgat Umarov climbed aboard. He waited until the rolling stairway was cleared, then reached around and pulled the front door closed. He swung the thick locking arm, tested the door, then gave the Americans an upturned thumb, swung around, and disappeared into the cockpit.

Ritzik waddled after him. "Talgat."

The Kazakh turned.

"We okay?"

"Everything has been cleared for takeoff, my brother."

Ritzik handed the big Kazakh a harness. "Get into this once we're off the ground."

"*Masele joq*—no problem." Umarov dropped the harness on the copilot's seat and sat on top of it.

Ritzik leaned forward, squeezing as much of himself as he could into the cockpit. Shingis Altynbayev stowed his checklist. His right hand moved the throttles forward slightly and the plane began to move. As it did, the pilot flicked a toggle switch on the control panel and spoke into his mike.

Ritzik glanced out the small side window. It was growing dark, the reddish evening sky turning purple in the west. The aircraft swung completely around now, its engines gaining power as Shingis pulled off the wide apron and onto the taxiway. He spoke to the tower once more as he navigated between the blue lights.

Ritzik swung his right arm up so he could make out the backlit screens on his GPS and handheld. They were working properly. He pressed the transmit button on the secure radio. "TOC, Skyhorse Element."

Dodger's voice came back into his ear five by five. "Skyhorse, TOC."

"Sit-rep?"

"No changes."

"Target progress?"

"Constant—we are transmitting. You should be receiving."

Instinctively, Ritzik glanced at the handheld strapped to his wrist once more. "Affirmative. Hostiles?"

"No news."

The effing CIA again. "Roger that. See what you can do to shake things up. You know who to call."

"Wilco."

"Skyhorse out." At least the comms were working the way they should. Of course, he and Dodger were less than a thousand feet apart. How the system would work when he was sitting in the desert, with twenty-thousand-foot mountains, and hostile weather conditions, he wasn't sure. After the screwups caused by line-of-sight communications equipment in Afghanistan, Delta had gone to redundant systems of satellite comms. But they weren't foolproof either: satellites could be affected by weather as well as by solar thermodynamics. Nothing was perfect.

Ritzik peered down at his wrist to confirm the target's attitude. The convoy was moving north at a constant sixteen miles an hour along the eastern bank of a lake called Yarkant Köl. The lake was ninety-six miles long. It ranged from eight hundred to a thousand yards wide, and was three hundred feet deep for most of its length—far too dangerous for the terrorists to ford. At its southern tip, a two-lane highway headed west, toward the region's largest commercial center, Yengisar. There was a large PLA garrison at Yengisar, which was precisely why the convoy was going in the opposite direction.

At Yarkant Köl's northern end, where it was fed by a system of mountain streams, the satellite imagery had displayed vast, impassable marshlands. The only route the big trucks could take without bogging down in the soft ground was to stay on the lakeside road until it intersected with an old, one-lane causeway that crossed the marsh. On the far side of the causeway, a paved road led north toward a Uighur town called Jiashi. More significantly, there was also an unpaved, partially washed-out road that, according to the satellite images, threaded across sixty miles of sand dunes and scrubby desert. That road, Ritzik realized, was a smuggling route that fed into the foothills of the Kunlún Mountains. And across the Kunlún lay Tajikistan—and sanctuary for the terrorists.

What worried Ritzik was that the Chinese had to know that fact, too. What worried him most right now was that they'd still had no input from Langley about how far Major General Zhou Yi's assault force had progressed.

1728. The Yak lined up for takeoff with its nose facing northeast. Shingis Altynbayev rattled through the takeoff checklist, both asking and answering the questions. He flipped switches and tapped dials. He set and reset the radio frequencies to Almaty and Ürümqi. He peered at the small radar screen. He set and double-checked the flaps. He growled at the control tower, his prominent Adam's apple bobbing up and down as he spoke. He checked the runway for obstacles.

And then he took his right hand off the wheel and pushed the throttles forward until he got the thrust he was looking for. His left hand firm on the wheel, he released the brakes and the plane catapulted down the runway. Shingis checked his airspeed, made a quick adjustment to the throttles, and then eased the wheel back and the Yak climbed into the darkening sky.

Quickly, the pilot reached for the upper right side of the control panel and pushed the landing-gear lever up. Ritzik felt a slight rumble as the wheels retracted. Then Shingis added flaps. He banked the plane to the left, gave it more power, and increased his angle of attack. Then he banked right, brought the aircraft into a more horizontal position, and eased off slightly on his throttles and flaps. He pulled back on the wheel and the Yak gained more altitude.

Altynbayev turned so he could see Ritzik's face. "Good takeoff, huh, for a solo guy?"

Ritzik gave the pilot an upturned thumb. "First-class, Shingis."

The pilot beamed. Looking at his face, Ritzik realized how fortunate he had been to trust his instincts about Altynbayev.

On Ritzik's previous deployment in Kazakhstan, he had required an aircraft on which to train Umarov's counterterrorist unit in low-level parachute insertions. There were no American planes available, and so the military attaché at the embassy instructed him to make a formal request through the Kazakh Ministry of Defense.

Ritzik did as ordered. But the ministry, which was institutionally hostile to the elite unit Ritzik was helping to train, informed him that the request would take at least two weeks to process. By that time, the Kazakh apparatchiks knew, Ritzik and his people would be out of the country, and the training—which might come in handy if the CT unit ever participated in a coup—would not take place.

Talgat, however, suggested that his cousin Shingis might handle the matter quickly and discreetly. Ritzik, frustrated with the bureaucracy, agreed. Eight hours later, Altynbayev dropped out of the sky in the cockpit of a decrepit Antonov An-2, a short, stubby Soviet-era biplane with a small, single rear wheel that gave it the same 1930s, Art Deco, nose-in-the-air look as a DC-3. The Antonov, which was far older than any of the people who would be jumping from it, had faded CCCP Air Force markings and was configured as a parachute trainer, with space for fourteen jumpers. When Ritzik checked the plane out, he'd found crumpled packs of

Russian cigarettes on the deck and empty vodka bottles jammed behind the crude canvas benches. He'd asked where Shingis had come up with the aircraft, but Altyn-bayev deflected the question with a sly smile and a slight bow, and said, "It was my pleasure to be of service, Major."

The exercise had gone exceptionally well. Ritzik offered Shingis an extravagant "consulting fee" for his assistance—and for obtaining the aircraft.

The pilot had turned him down cold. "You have helped my cousin Talgat," he explained. "You brought him to the United States. You provided him training, and materials. You treat him as more than your ally. You are loyal to him. You are his *friend*. And therefore, I am loyal to you, Major. I am *your* friend."

And from that point on, whenever Ritzik needed anything to do with an aircraft, Talgat would get hold of cousin Shingis—and whatever equipment Ritzik was looking for would suddenly appear.

It was Rowdy, who had become an avid student of Central Asian society, who explained things to Ritzik after they returned to Bragg. "In that part of the world, boss, you don't just recruit an individual. You recruit the whole *clan*. In Central Asia the society is totally family-oriented. It's friggin' tribal. By trusting Talgat's cousin, you demonstrated to Talgat that you trusted *him*. And they both respect you for it."

"The old friend-of-my-friend-is-my-friend way of life," Ritzik said.

"You got it, boss."

"But you and I know that wasn't why it happened. It was just easier to go through Talgat than it was to do all the stupid paperwork."

"I understand," Rowdy'd spat Copenhagen into his omnipresent plastic foam cup. "But this was one of those times when all you should do is thank the God of War for serendipity and take yes for an answer."

1731. Ritzik looked at his watch and was horrified to realize that he wasn't on oxygen yet. He backed out of the cockpit and waddled to seat 3-Б, where he grabbed one of the three walk-around bottles seat-belted down. He coupled the spring-loaded bayonet connector from his mask into the regulator, turned the knurled knob until he sensed the O_2 flowing into his mask, and hung the bottle over his shoulder. Then he one-handed the other two walk-around bottles, careful not to damage the attached mask units, and made his way back to the cockpit.

He handed one of the walk-around bottles to Umarov. "Strap this on, then make sure Shingis gets his mask secure and his O-two turned on as soon as we've leveled off."

The Kazakh pressed the mask to his face, hooked the straps, pulled them tight, and gave an upturned thumb to Ritzik's back. But the American was already shuffling aft.

13

12,000 Feet Above the Shilik River, Kazakhstan.
1738 Hours Local Time.

RITZIK DISCONNECTED the walk-around bottle and plugged his O_2 rig into the prebreather unit. Then he plucked the pilot's map out of Rowdy's hand.

"Point of contact still make sense to you?"

The sergeant major's head bobbed up and down once. "Target's moving at a more or less constant twenty kliks an hour." Rowdy tapped the handheld screen on his right wrist. "That puts them at the northern end of Yarkant Köl in six hours thirty minutes—just after midnight. We'll have a workable margin of error if Shingis gets us to here"—Yates tapped a spot on the big map slightly northeast of Kashgar—"and we exit the plane. It's a fifty-mile glide, almost due southeast. A little long—and a bumpy ride for the first half hour. But the winds will be behind us and we'll make it in plenty of time to position ourselves."

"Are you sure about the winds?"

Yates tapped the map. "It's a law of nature, Mike. Winds flow upslope on warm days in mountainous terrain—it's called a 'valley breeze.' In the evenings, the air masses cool, and the flow reverses downward, into a 'mountain breeze.' The weather has been constant: warm days and cold nights.

The satellites don't show any anomalies. So if Shingis turns south, running along this ridge . . ." Yates's finger traced a rough route. ". . . it's just over seventeen thousand feet here, and the ridge where we'll be exiting is nine thousand feet above sea level . . . we should be in good shape when we jump."

"You're the jumpmeister. I'm the overpaid RTO." Ritzik folded the map, disconnected from the prebreather console, plugged his hose into the walk-around bottle, and waddled forward to the cockpit. "Shingis—"

The pilot was speaking on the radio. He raised his hand and Ritzik waited. The Kazakh completed his transmission and banked the plane slightly to the south, still in a gentle climb.

"It is okay now," he finally said, his voice muffled by the oxygen mask. He swiveled his head toward Ritzik. "What is up?"

Ritzik handed him the map. "Here's how it works." The tip of his index finger tapped the runway at Almaty. "We came out of here, then turned west, correct?"

Shingis's head bobbed up and down once.

Ritzik's finger moved in a big circle across the map. "We're coming around now, and we'll head east, parallel to the Kyrgyz border."

"Affirmative."

"That takes us between the mountain ranges."

The pilot's head bobbed up and down. "Yes."

"And we finally cross into China just north of Tekes, right?"

"Affirmative." Altynbayev tapped a wristwatch hanging next to his vent window. "Do not forget—the time changes by two hours."

Ritzik noted that the digital readout was two hours later than the watch on his own wrist. He cursed silently because he hadn't remembered the detail. "Thank you, Shingis. Okay—your normal route overflies Kuqa and Korla, then north to Yanqi and into Ürümqi, right?"

The pilot's attention was momentarily diverted by someone speaking on his headset. He raised an index finger and Ritzik halted.

Finally, Altynbayev spoke. "I am sorry. That was Almaty control talking to another flight. I wanted to listen."

"It's okay." Ritzik tapped the map. "So far everything is normal. But right here—" Ritzik retrieved a marking pen from his sleeve and put a dot on the map. "Right here, you turn southwest."

"Yes?"

"Ürümqi control will want to know what's happening."

"Of course."

"Let them try to contact you once or twice before you respond. Then, you declare an emergency. Tell 'em you can't make Ürümqi. You have to divert and take an alternate route back to Almaty." He paused. "Can you do that?"

"Yes," Altynbayev said. "That can be done."

Ritzik put a second black spot on the map. "From here, you give me every bit of speed you can muster, for sixteen minutes, bitching all the time to Ürümqi that the plane is unmanageable—lost pressure, engine-oil leak, hydraulic failure—whatever you can get away with. After twelve minutes, we should be . . . *here,* right?" Ritzik put another dot on the map.

The pilot thought about it for a few seconds. "Yes, more or less."

"I hope it's more rather than less."

"So do I, Major."

"You'll drop to twenty-seven thousand feet. We'll open the door and depressurize. After we do, you'll swing due east, along the mountain ridge, drop airspeed to two hundred and twenty knots, and maintain a constant twenty-seven thousand feet for ninety seconds."

The pilot pulled his mask off. "The airspeed is cutting the cloth close a little bit, Major."

"I know. But you can do it."

Altynbayev bit his lower lip while he performed a mental calculation. "I think I can." He looked at the chart. "Ninety seconds at two hundred twenty-five knots would put us about here." He tapped the paper.

"Right on the money," Ritzik said. "As soon as you make the turn east, you'll switch off all the interior lights so we don't give ourselves away."

"I will do it."

"You signal when you're right on target—flash all the exit and seat-belt lights—and we'll exit the aircraft." Ritzik examined Altynbayev's face, but the pilot remained impassive.

"It should take less than a minute and a half. Then Talgat will close you up. You'll swing back north, haul ass, and hope the Chinese don't scramble fighters and shoot you down before you cross the border."

"That will not happen," Shingis said.

"Why?"

The pilot pulled the map onto his armrest. "There are small airports at Aksu and Kashgar," he said, pointing to the chart. "But the closest fighter aircraft is Yining. It is too far north to intercept us when we go off course. And besides, the planes at Yining are not on standby since the end of the Soviet Union, so they will not be scrambled because it would take too long."

"How do you know, Shingis?"

Altynbayev reached into his pilot's briefcase and displayed a pair of binoculars. "Because Ürümqi control allows us to fly routes that used to be forbidden—and we can see that the planes are not ready."

Ritzik listened—and marveled. The CIA's budget was well into the scores of billions. Shingis Altynbayev made perhaps $20,000 a year as a pilot for Air Kazakhstan. But his intelligence was more current than Langley's. And it didn't rely on statistical models either, but old-fashioned, eyes-on reconnaissance.

"I hope you're right," Ritzik said. He reached over Altynbayev's shoulder and pointed to the dot he'd made on the map where he wanted the pilot to change course. "How long until we get to this point, Shingis?"

The Kazakh returned the binoculars to his case. He sat back in the heavy chair, scratched his cheek, and checked his instruments. "Twenty-one minutes," he said. Altynbayev slipped the O_2 mask back over his nose, secured the strap, and placed both hands on the wheel. "Twenty-one minutes."

31,500 Feet Above Wushi, China.
1808 Hours Kazakhstan Time.

THE PLANE BANKED SHARPLY to the right. The sequence had begun.

Ritzik slapped Rowdy Yates on the arm, and the sergeant major hand-signaled Doc Masland and Curtis Hansen to wrestle the length of half conduit down the aisle. When they'd set it on the floor by the rear bulkhead, they attached ten-foot lengths of webbed strap securely to their belts, then cinched the loose end of the straps around the rearmost pair of aisle seat belts.

Yates waited until the pair came forward as far as their leashes allowed and gave him "go" signals before his hands instructed the rest of the element to stand. Then he faced the right side of the aircraft and put his left hand on his left hip, paused, then extended the arm out at a forty-five-degree angle.

The troops pulled the arming pins from their ARR assemblies, performed buddy checks, then signaled Yates with upturned thumbs.

"PRICE check," the sergeant major growled into his mike.

Wei-Liu turned to find Ritzik and shrugged when she caught his eye.

Ritzik reached around and brought them face-to-face. "It's an acronym we use to examine our O-two systems: *p*ressure, *r*egulator, *i*ndicator, *c*onnections, and *e*mergency equipment." He tapped each element on her gear as he spoke the word. "You're good to go, ma'am."

31,500 Feet Above Kumblun, China.
1810 Hours Kazakhstan Time (2010 Hours Local Time).

RITZIK CHECKED the global-positioning-unit readout on his PDA, then shifted screens to make sure the convoy was more or less where it should have been. It was. He pressed his transmit button and said, "TOC, Skyhorse Element."

"Skyhorse, TOC." Roger Brian's voice was five-by-five.

"Sit-rep, Dodger."

"No news. Are you getting picture?"

"Affirmative. Anything from home base?" Ritzik would have liked to hear that Langley was finally doing its share of the work.

"Nothing new."

So much for interagency cooperation. "What's the imagery?"

Dodger said, "No changes. Changii is quiet. No other developments."

"Roger that. Skyhorse out."

Ritzik changed frequencies so he was on the insertion element's net. He looked up the aisle. Talgat emerged from the cockpit, his arm extended, his thumb upraised.

There were less than sixteen minutes to go.

He looked at his men as they ran their hands over one another's web gear, weapons, and combat packs, checking and double-checking. Until now, they'd been quiet, each one lost in his own thoughts. That was SOP. They'd been preparing themselves mentally for the challenges: working out emergency scenarios, running flight sequences, dealing with the absolute certainty of the uncertainties that make up the practice of warfare.

Now they'd become decidedly animated: their eyes were wide, their respiration shallow but accelerated. It was the body's way of dealing with the imminent physical dangers: depressurization, the shock of subfreezing air, the blackness of the void outside the aircraft's hull, the total aloneness of HAHO insertion.

Like them, Ritzik's breath was thin. There was a knot in his gut, too, and his sphincter was tight—all normal reactions prior to the stress of combat. He could feel the beat of his heart, rushing, and he fought to control it. There'd be enough time for a huge adrenaline surge once they'd exited the plane.

29,500 Feet Above Subexi, China.
2019 Hours Local Time.

TALGAT CAME AFT, his O_2 bottle dangling from the waist strap of his harness. He threaded his way past the Soldiers and made his way to the rear door of the aircraft. He straddled the curved metal sluice. "Time to depressurize," he called out, and reached for the door handle.

From the middle of the aircraft, Rowdy shouted, "Talgat. *Tokhta*—stop. *Qozghama*—don't move!"

The Kazakh froze.

Quickly, Yates unplugged from the prebreather, thrust his O_2 hose connector into the jump bottle's regulator, and pushed aft. He withdrew the demonstrator seat belts, looped one of them around the back strap of Talgat's harness, then pulled it tight. Then he buckled the male end of the second belt to the buckle end of the loop and ran the loose end to the closest seat, where he snapped it into a seat-belt buckle. He slammed Umarov on the chest. "Now," he shouted. "Now you're safe." He motioned to the Kazakh, instructing him where to stand. "Stay there—and open the door when I give you the signal, okay?"

Umarov saw that Yates had taken him out of the door's path and gave the American a thumbs-up. "*Maqul*—okay."

27,500 Feet Above Tashik Tash, China.
2023 Hours Local Time.

NOW YATES'S EYES turned to Ritzik. The major had attached his harness to Wei-Liu's, and he had to contort his body so that he could be seen clearly. Yates shouted, "We're ready, Loner."

They heard the change in turbine pitch as Shingis throttled back to slow the aircraft down. Ritzik took a quick glance at his GPS. He focused on the coordinates, calculated, raised his arms above his head, and held all ten gloved fingers up where everyone could see them. Then he folded one finger, and then another, and then another, and another. When his left hand displayed only four, Rowdy turned, pointed toward the rear as if he were leading a cavalry charge, and screamed, "Talgat—*go!*"

The Kazakh threw the thick handle to the left. The door blew inward, smashing into the rear bulkhead. The loss of heat and pressure was immediate, palpable. Wei-Liu's ears popped painfully. She saw Rowdy, Gene Shepard, and the one they called Goose wince, too. The plane vibrated violently from the stress to its airframe. It bucked and twisted left, then right, before regaining level flight. The noise from the three rear-mounted engines was overwhelming.

The interior lights went out, plunging the cabin into darkness. From his position in the aisle, Curtis Hansen produced two pairs of chem-lights. He twisted them, then shoved them between seat backs and cushions, providing the aisle with a path of glowing red light.

Doc Masland, who stood just forward of Umarov, snared the door handle and secured it with a long Velcro strap to the closest seat arm. He stepped in front of the Kazakh and, leaning into the darkness, peered out to make sure that the rear stairway had extended properly.

Masland shouted something, but his voice was lost in the roar of wind and turbine scream inside the plane. The vibration increased now, keeping them all off balance, as if the plane were driving on cobblestones. Masland reached back, waved at his comrade, then reached for the leading edge of the metal sluice and pulled it aft. As Masland pulled, Curtis Hansen pushed. The pair of them muscled the sluice onto the top end of the extended folding stairway. Then, with the Kazakh's help, they forced the concave sheet into the blackness, covering the treads of the descending stairway with a smooth slide. Only the wide flanged end of the slide prevented the whole apparatus from slipping past the top banister of the stairway railing and falling.

The Yak shuddered once more as Shingis banked the plane ninety degrees to the left, turning from south to east.

The unsecured metal slide shifted by twenty-five degrees

and rolled in the same direction as the plane. Doc Masland lurched aft and grabbed the top-end flange. For a few seconds he seemed to have lost his grip, but he finally managed to regain control of the unwieldy slide. Without waiting for the aircraft to recover, the American ripped a Velcro strap from his coveralls, slid it through a handle welded just below the flange, turned the slide straight, wrapped the strap twice around the top banister of the stairway, and attached it to itself. Then he stepped across the aisle, knelt, and repeated the action on the opposite side.

Masland crossed back to the plane's starboard side. He tapped Talgat's chest with a gloved index finger, as if to say, *You . . .*

The Kazakh tapped him back, then pointed at himself.

"*Iye*—yes." Masland mimed ripping the Velcro off.

Umarov gave him an "okay."

Then Masland showed the Kazakh how to twist the slide so the flange wasn't restrained by the banisters, and when Umarov indicated he'd got what the medic was trying to show him, Masland aimed a mock kick at the upper end of the slide and pantomimed the slide tumbling down.

The Kazakh indicated he understood.

Masland pointed at the exit door, swung his arm as if he were pushing it closed, and mimed securing the lock.

Umarov's hand made a fist. His thumb stuck straight up.

Doc returned the gesture, steadying himself as Shingis deployed the flaps to slow the aircraft down.

Rowdy Yates made his way up to the rearmost row of seats. His right arm extended fully straight out from the shoulder, then bent smartly, his fingers touching his helmet as if he were saluting—the silent signal for "Move to the rear."

The medic unhooked his safety strap, swiveled, and faced forward. Curtis Hansen waddled up directly behind him and squeezed Masland's right shoulder. Gene Shepard followed, squeezing Hansen's right shoulder when he'd reached his position. He was followed by Mickey D, Ty Weaver, Goose Guzman, and Bill Sandman. Ritzik and Wei-Liu came next. Ritzik nudged Wei-Liu, bent down, and crushed the chem-sticks on her legs. Then he stood, reached around her, and squeezed Sandman's shoulder. Wei-Liu squirmed out of Ritzik's grasp and craned her neck. Joey Tuzzolino stood in back of them; Barber Sweeney brought up the rear. Tuzz grinned behind his O_2 mask and wriggled his eyebrows at Wei-Liu. She tried to smile back.

From his position, Rowdy Yates exaggeratedly tapped his ears. One by one the Soldiers mimicked him, then turned thumbs up, signing that their comms were tuned to the insertion element's secure net and signaling to confirm they were working.

2024. "Stand by." Rowdy Yates held his right arm high above his head. Wei-Liu peered forward and stretched onto her toes so she could see what was happening. She watched as Doc Masland quickly lowered his legs over the edge of the slide and grabbed the exit-stairway banisters. Then she was shoved against Bill Sandman's parachute as the jumpers scrunched together as tightly as they could, and she lost sight of Masland altogether.

The no-smoking, seat-belt, and exit lights flashed on and off three times. Rowdy's right hand swung downward, pointing toward the exit. And then the jumpers began to move up the aisle. The stick's progress was far faster than Wei-Liu had thought it would be. In fact, the constant movement gave her very little time to think about what she was about to do, because it was enough of a challenge simply to put one boot in front of the other without tripping over all the gear. She tried to remember all the things Ritzik had told her, all the things Rowdy had told her, but her mind had suddenly turned to mush.

And then Ritzik's voice burst into her brain. "Goggles secure?"

Her head bobbed up and down. There was a red chemlight jammed into the seat on her right.

"Gloves on?"

She wiggled her fingers at him. She saw a second chemlight jammed into a left-hand seat cushion.

"Remember—I'll control us immediately after we exit the aircraft. As soon as we're facedown, extend into the Frog position."

She raised her right thumb.

"Do what I do."

And then Bill Sandman vaulted feetfirst onto the slide, shoved himself forward, grabbed the two thin aluminum banister rails at the top of the stairway, launched himself down the slide, and vanished into the darkness. And there was nothing between her and the void but the open doorway.

All of a sudden Wei-Liu felt an enormous measure of fear; a visceral, instinctive, primeval animal terror she had never before experienced.

She pulled up short like a horse refusing a jump. "Michael, don't let me die."

Ritzik's voice exploded inside her brain. "Tracy—sit."

She did as she was told. She felt Ritzik's body up against hers; felt his legs on her hips, her back against his chest. Well, okay, against his reserve chute. He wouldn't let her die.

"Tracy, let go of the banisters."

She hadn't realized she was holding on to them; holding on for dear life. She tried to let go, but her hands wouldn't budge.

Ritzik's gloved hands pried her fingers open one by one. "Make fists," he commanded.

She obeyed the voice in her brain, cursing her damnable instinctive compliance. And then his hands grasped the banister, and he was tight against her and he was pushing and pushing and all the while her legs were pumping, too, except she was trying to go backward, not forward. And then his arms were wrapped around her so tight she couldn't budge and all of a sudden they were traveling down the slide going faster and faster and even though there was a huge amount of noise in her ears she could hear her heart pounding even louder than the wind and it was freezing cold and the mask lens began to fog and she started to see spots in front of her eyes and then and then and then *Oh . . . My . . . God* she shot off the end of the slide into the abyss.

14

27,220 Feet Above Artu, China.
2024 Hours Local Time.

"**DON'T HYPERVENTILATE.**" That was Mike Ritzik's voice in her head. He was still there. She was, too.

"Okay, okay, okay." She struggled to keep her breathing under control.

"Frog position, Tracy—Frog. Help me. Help me."

Wei-Liu's scrambled brain searched for input and finally achieved a rough synapsis. She arched her back, extended her arms, bent her knees, and tried to hold her legs apart.

"Good girl."

Above her, Ritzik's head turned slightly left so he could read the altimeter dial. He was delighted with how she'd performed, although he wasn't about to say anything right now. She hadn't panicked, causing the pair of them to tumble, or worse, go into a flat spin. And although he could feel her trembling under him, she was performing like a trouper—or more to the point, like a trooper. Even in the freezing air he could sense the warmth of her body pressed close up against him.

He felt Wei-Liu shift slightly. He used his thighs to keep her exactly where she was. Movement was dangerous. They were still well above terminal velocity—the maximum constant miles-per-hour rate for a falling object—because the plane's forward speed had thrust them into the sky at more than 200 miles an hour. They would have to fall more than 2,500 feet before their airspeed would drop to 125 miles per hour—180 feet per second—at which point it would be safe to deploy the parachute.

They'd left the plane at twenty-seven thousand five and would open at twenty-five thousand. That gave them about twelve seconds of total free fall.

Trying to maintain the arched, Frog stable-flight position, Wei-Liu wasn't sure she'd live that long.

Ritzik took a look at his compass. They were still heading due east. "I'm going to turn us to the south."

No one had told her how to make turns in free fall. "What do I do?"

"Hold your position. Don't change a thing."

Above her, Ritzik bent his torso and head to the right, brought his left arm six inches closer to his body, and extended his right arm out by six inches.

The pair of them glided laterally and to the right for two seconds, and sixty degrees, then Ritzik straightened his body and arms out, resuming the stable free-fall position. "Good."

He checked the altimeter again. Twenty-five thousand eight hundred feet. Four seconds until deployment.

"Steady—we're ready to deploy."

His right arm moved toward the rip-cord handle. Simultaneously, he extended his left arm over his head and drew his legs up farther, in order to keep them from toppling into a head-down position or barrel-rolling to the right. Ritzik peered down to where the main rip-cord handle sat in its pocket, making visual contact. Then he extended his left arm forward, simultaneously reaching his right hand down toward the handle, careful to stay away from the oxygen hose. On Ritzik's first HAHO night-combat-training jump—from 17,500 feet—he'd been so pumped up he'd reached down without looking, grabbed his O_2 hose instead of the rip-cord handle, and yanked the frigging thing right out of its socket. By the time he'd cleared 10,000 feet, he'd damn near had a case of hypoxia.

His gloved hand closed around the handle, and in one fluid motion he unseated it and pulled it from the rip-cord pocket. Now both his arms were fully extended in a forward position, and he glanced upward, over his right shoulder, to make sure his canopy was deploying.

When Ritzik pulled the rip cord, it yanked a pin on the chute assembly, releasing a pilot chute bridle, which opened its flaps and launched upward. The bridle's release extracted the deployment bag from the main container, which in turn unstowed the suspension lines from their retainer bands. When the suspension lines were fully extended, they pulled the main chute from the deployment bag, the sail slider was driven downward toward the risers, and the big Ram Air cells began to inflate.

This, Wei-Liu thought as the harness cut into her and she jerked upward, *must be what a head-on collision feels like.* Her downward speed went from terminal velocity—125 miles an hour—to 18 miles an hour in less than four seconds. The G-force was incredible—it was like being dropped through the trapdoor of a gallows. Her head was yanked backward. Her arms flailed helplessly. She closed her eyes tight and screamed into her mask.

And then, as quickly as it had all happened, it was over. She felt herself dangling, pendulumlike, in the air, the soles of her boots parallel to the ground. Tentatively, she opened her eyes and dared to breathe. She actually pinched herself to make sure she was still alive. Wei-Liu looked up past Ritzik and saw the huge rectangle of the Ram Air chute, its cells filled with air, above her head. "We made it," she said. "We actually made it."

RITZIK'S BODY ACHED in every joint from the big chute's opening shock. But there was no time to think about pain. He pulled the extended steering toggles from the brake loops and released the control lines. He raised his head and looked at the big canopy above them again, double-checking to ensure it was fully inflated.

Wei-Liu's voice was hyperexcited. "Oh, Mike—"

"Quiet." Ritzik didn't want to talk right then. There was too much to do. He was already scanning a three-sixty, as well as up and down, while straining to listen for canopy chatter just in case they'd deployed dangerously close to another jumper.

It was unlikely. The Yak had been flying at just over two hundred miles an hour. That speed translated to three and a half miles per minute. In a normal HAHO insertion, jumpers would either leave the plane at one-second intervals, or jump as a group, depending on the aircraft type. Tonight, they'd had to use a slide for the covert operation. Moving as quickly as they could, they'd still taken five to six seconds each to jump. It was easy—and depressing—to do the numbers. Twelve jumpers times six seconds exit time per jumper equaled seventy-two seconds. At 210 miles an hour, the Yak was traveling 3.5 miles every sixty seconds, 308 feet per second. A six-second interval would separate each jumper by 1,848 feet. Multiply that by twelve jumpers, and Ritzik's crew was separated by more than four miles of dark, uncharted sky. Even forming up was going to make for problems.

He reached up and removed the tape from his night-vision device, flipped it down, and turned it on so he could pick out the infrared flashers on his men's helmets. He scanned—and saw nothing.

Ritzik switched the secure radio to the predetermined in-flight frequency. "Skyhorse leader. Respond-respond."

He listened—and heard nothing but white sound. Not only were they separated by distance and altitude—now the goddamn multimillion-dollar satellite radio system wasn't working. He cursed silently at the crackling circuitry.

Then he heard Rowdy's familiar growl, stepped on by Bill Sandman's.

Ritzik used his upwind toggle to turn the canopy in a tight circle. He would repeat this maneuver until the rest of his team assembled around him. As he pulled on the handle, he heard a partial transmission. "Sk—c."

Ritzik held steady and broadcast again. "Skyhorse leader—repeat."

"Shep confirms."

"Goose confirms."

"—z confirms."

"Skyhorse leader. Repeat-repeat."

"Skyhorse leader—Doc confirms."

Followed by white sound. Then: "Tuzz confirms."

And right on top of that, "Mickey D confirms."

That was seven.

"Curt confirms."

Eight.

The altimeter on Ritzik's wrist read 25,300 feet. He was moving in a slight updraft. He adjusted his toggles to increase his speed and descend.

"Ty confirms."

Nine.

One to go. "Skyhorse leader—Barber-Barber."

* * *

SUSPENDED BELOW RITZIK, Wei-Liu saw one, then two other chutes, even though she wasn't wearing night-vision. They, like she and Ritzik, were circling. And then she felt Ritzik adjust the toggles, and the big sail above their heads swung them around, and she watched as the other parachutes began to adjust their positions.

She strained to look up at Ritzik. She couldn't hear him because her headset was tuned to another frequency.

Ritzik was oblivious to her. "Rowdy—repeat." He was trying to hear Rowdy Yates, but the frigging transmission kept fading out.

"Repeat."

". . . caught u . . ."

Who? What? Where?

"Repeat."

"Stick . . . came . . . Un . . . down."

Dammit. "Repeat-repeat-repeat."

And then, just as inexplicably as the net had decided to stop working, Rowdy's voice suddenly blew five-by-five into his headphones. ". . . went out just ahead of me. The Yak hit an air pocket—real bad buffeting for five, six seconds, boss. He bounced off the slide into the stairway header—slammed him hard—then he was gone."

Ritzik said: "Skyhorse leader. Did you see a chute?"

"Negative-negative. But I was busy fighting the vibration and turbulence trying to get myself out alive."

"You okay?"

"I got smacked pretty good, but I'll live."

Ritzik knew it was altogether possible that Barber's automatic rip-cord release had deployed at twenty-five hundred feet even though the man was unconscious. "Skyhorse leader. Anybody see Barber's chute deploy?" Ritzik waited for answers. But deep inside he knew there would be no responses. And to confirm what he knew, all he heard was white noise.

This was not good. Todd Sweeney was one of the element's two snipers. He also had been carrying two of the five Chinese claymores they'd brought, along with two spools of firing wire and two firing devices. And six hundred precious rounds of ammunition. Yes, the man had left a wife behind. And parents, both still alive. And two gorgeous kids—Ty Weaver was their godfather. But there'd be time to mourn him later. Right now all Ritzik could think about was how to compensate for one less shooter on the ground. One less weapons system. Fifty percent of the sniping team, and—most critical—the suppressed MSG90 sniper's rifle. Doc Masland was every bit the shooter Barber Sweeney was. But Sweeney'd been carrying the big HK rifle. That was the other fatal loss.

In a night ambush, the sniper's role was critical. They'd pick off the drivers before the bad guys even knew they were being attacked. Ritzik had learned this in Kosovo, where he'd used his sniping team to take down a heavily armed convoy belonging to a group of Serb paramilitary goons known as Arkan's Tigers. There were ten trucks in the Tiger column. By the time the Serbs realized what was happening, Ritzik's snipers had already head-shot eight drivers. Two trucks overturned, the Serbs panicked, and Ritzik's fourteen-man element had been able to take an entire company-sized unit out of action and turn it over to NATO.

Tonight, Ritzik needed not only to stop the tango convoy, he would require at least three of its vehicles to make his escape. That was the genius of using two snipers with their silenced weapons, as opposed to claymores. But with only one long gun now available, the situation was going to become far more dicey.

Plus this nasty possibility: given the omnipresence of Mr. Murphy on the op, it was not inconceivable that Barber Sweeney's body would drop right on top of some effing PLA general. The Chinese could very well know they had visitors hours before Ritzik's element was even on the ground. That prospect, Ritzik understood all too well, was not good juju.

"Skyhorse leader." Gene Shepard's voice forced him to focus on the here and now.

"Skyhorse leader sends."

"We are forming on you."

Ritzik illuminated his GPS screen, took a reading, called out his position, and asked for a verbal confirmation that they'd all received it so they could assemble. The infrared chem-sticks on Wei-Liu's legs would help them see him as he circled. He checked his elapsed-time readout and cursed. They hadn't even begun yet, and they were already running behind schedule.

Since it was dark, they'd be flying a trail formation. In daylight, Ritzik preferred a wedge, with the element spread out at seventy-five-foot intervals in a broad spear tip. But at night, a wedge was problematic. Jumpers could miss the wide, echelon turns and go astray. And so they'd form up single file. Since he was the slowest, given the tandem chute, he would take point. They'd be an eleven-car freight train, with Ritzik as the engine, Rowdy as the caboose, and the others in predetermined positions in between.

RITZIK BLINKED TWICE, sucked some O_2, and scanned through his NV, counting the flat Ram Air chutes as they banked into a line behind him. He verified the heading on the GPS unit strapped to his wrist and checked the elapsed-time display. When he was satisfied that everyone was there he called out the element's initial flight heading and asked for verbal confirmation. After he'd received ten wilcos, he used the Ram Air's toggles to adjust his trim and bank gently southeast.

As soon as he'd confirmed his heading, he set the lap timer so the leg could be measured, rolled his shoulders, which were sore as hell given the weight he was carrying, then switched his comms package to the radio frequency Wei-Liu could hear. "This is your pilot, Johnny Cool, speaking from the flight deck. We're expecting smooth sailing all the way to Las Vegas, but please keep your seat belts fastened anyway. The steward will be around with liquid refreshments in just a few minutes. Have a nice day."

Hanging there helpless, suspended five miles above the earth, and still more than an hour away from landing, Wei-Liu wished Ritzik hadn't just used the word *liquid.*

5 Kilometers West of Markit,
Xinjiang Autonomous Region, China.
2035 Hours Local Time.

SAM PHILLIPS GROANED and blinked a puffy right eye. There wasn't a part of him that didn't hurt. He looked over at X-Man and Kaz's inert forms and realized they were screwed. Pure and simple. And they'd done it to themselves. No. That was not correct. *He* was the guilty party. He'd screwed everybody. After all, he was in charge. They should have tried to make their break earlier. He should have had the balls to insist, the audacity to make a decision and act on it. Because he'd just fought his way to the canvas and taken a peek—and what had been a mile-wide lake was now little more than a hundred yards wide. No cover. No concealment. Nothing but sandy marsh. It looked like the southern Virginia bog where he'd taken the CIA's land-navigation course. In which, he remembered ruefully, he hadn't done very well.

At the time he'd rationalized his dismal performance because he was a city boy. He'd grown up in Chicago, where his father was a stockbroker and his mother stayed at home to raise him and his two sisters. He'd never done the Boy Scout thing, or asked to be taken camping, preferring Soldier's Field and skiing trips to Aspen to neckerchiefs, poison ivy, and hobo stoves. But right now, realizing how badly he'd screwed up, he wished he'd paid more attention to the instructors at the Farm when they'd tried to inculcate the Ways of the Wild in him.

The way Sam saw things, they had two alternatives. The first was to make a break for it tonight. The Tarim Basin was basically an egg-shaped oval, 650 miles long and 275 miles wide. They hadn't yet traversed the basin's western border, which was a wide, well-traveled highway that ran from Kashgar, on the western edge, to Yarkant Köl, in the southwest. But they were close—Sam had spent the past hour guesstimating how far and how fast they had come in the past three days. If they could make it to the highway, he was even willing to risk contact with PLA troops. After all, their documents were in order.

Well, that might be a problem. They didn't have any documents—Mustache Man had their passports and wallets. But Sam and his team had been duly vetted when they'd crossed the border. So they were official. They could bluff their way through. Of course, if the Chinese called the British consul general to come and get them, they'd be in the proverbial deep du-du, because Sam was pretty certain that Langley hadn't informed the cousins, as MI-6 was known, of SIE-1's existence.

So Plan One was to make a break for it tonight, try to flag down a PLA unit, and ask for help. But Sam knew the odds of

Plan One working were slim to none. That left Plan Two.
Plan Two would be to wait until they were well along the narrow, rutted trail leading across the mountains to Tajikistan
and then escape. After all, there was nothing so invigorating
as a fifty-mile hike through twenty-thousand-foot-high
mountain passes, with a bunch of well-armed, pissed-off
guerrillas in hot pursuit.

But there was an upside to Plan Two. When Sam had departed Dushanbe two and a half years previously, he'd left a
small but productive agent network in place. One of his
principal agents, Halil Abdullaev, was the *muktar* of
Tokhtamysh, a small Tajik settlement where the Soviets
had once based a parachute battalion.

Tokhtamysh sat astride two barely traversable smugglers' roads, one leading east through the Sarkolsk Mountains sixteen kilometers to the Chinese border, the other
south across the Pamirs to Afghanistan. From its strategic
location Halil—and therefore Sam—had been able to monitor narcotics shipped to the West from Afghanistan, and the
weapons that were smuggled back across the border. From
Tokhtamysh, he tracked Uighur infiltrators coming from
China to join up with their al-Qaeda allies in the Stans, and
IMU terrorists moving in the opposite direction to stage
raids in Xinjiang Autonomous Region.

If they could reach Tokhtamysh and Sam could find
Halil, he'd pay his old agent to smuggle them to the American embassy in Dushanbe. Sam realized Plan Two was also
somewhat far-fetched and prone to lead to disappointment.
But frankly, it was all he could come up with right now.

Whichever option he decided to go with, there was one
constant: before they left, he'd find some way of disabling
or booby-trapping the nuke. And the way Sam felt right
now—which bordered on clinical depression—he wouldn't
give much of a damn if the frigging thing went off, either.

15

21,775 Feet Above Xinjiang Autonomous Region, China.
2029 Hours Local Time.

RITZIK REALIZED that the Universe had shifted, and the laws of nature obviously weren't working anymore. At least, not for him. Yes, it was dark—the moon was in its waning eighth. And it was inhumanly cold—his fingers were numb and he couldn't feel his toes anymore. But, to get to the point, Rowdy had promised nighttime mountain breezes. Tailwinds, to speed them on their way. And yet, according to his lap timer and the GPS unit, he was currently being assailed by daytime valley breezes. Head winds.

This glitch was causing the insertion element a thorny logistical problem. The Ram Air parachute glides at a constant ground speed of thirty miles per hour. With a twenty-mile-an-hour tailwind, the airspeed grows to fifty miles an hour. With a twenty-mile-an-hour head wind, however, ground speed is reduced to a mere ten miles an hour. And that's what Ritzik was currently doing. This meant that instead of reaching the drop zone in an hour and a half, it was going to take almost five hours to cover the same route.

Which would mean they'd arrive at the intercept point an hour after the IMU tangos had passed through it. More bad juju.

And then there were the Chinese. The gate-crashers. Given the way things were progressing, the PLA had already found Barber's body, checked the coordinates programmed into his GPS unit, and were waiting in ambush for Ritzik's element to drop into the LZ.

He inhaled a deep, therapeutic breath of O_2 and switched transmission frequencies. "TOC, Skyhorse."

As if to confirm the complete TARFUness of his mission status, there was no response.

He tried a second time, and a third. Finally, he heard, "Skyhorse, TOC."

"Sit-rep, Dodger."

"No changes."

That was good to hear. "Target?"

"On course. ETA four hours eighteen minutes."

"Gate-crashers?" Ritzik was desperate for another small shred of good news.

He got it: "Imagery is consistent. No movement at Changii."

"Skyhorse out." Ritzik switched to the radio's insertion-element frequency. "Skyhorse back door."

"Skyhorse back door." Rowdy's growl answered in his ear.

"We're not making required speed, back door."

"That's been factored, leader."

Ritzik was dubious and said so.

"Patience, grasshopper. Think sniper. Back door sends."

Ritzik sighed into his mask. He'd always envied the sniper's mental strength, the capacity to wait, immobile, for hours—days, if necessary—observing the target, waiting for the right moment to make the shot. The ability to do so—in more than a rudimentary way—was beyond him. Oh, he could physically make the shot; that was no problem. The physical requirements of slowing your heart rate and learning how to fire between beats, so bullet placement wouldn't be affected by your respiration, were technical elements that could be learned. Marksmanship was a frangible skill that required practice, practice, practice. No, it was the mental aspect of the craft, the snipers' Zen-like ability to get outside their own bodies and look at their environment in a holographic sense, which had always escaped him. And that was what Rowdy'd just been talking about.

His gaze dropped to Wei-Liu, suspended beneath him. He wondered what she was thinking. He tried to speculate how she'd respond when the shooting started, and surprisingly found himself optimistic. If the way she'd come through the jump was any indicator, she'd be all right under fire. He also tried to figure out why she'd agreed to come with them in the first place. It certainly wasn't going to do her career any good.

Still, the willingness to stick her neck out was something Ritzik appreciated. He himself had come to grips with the fact that he'd probably never make O-6—colonel—although it would be a disappointment to his family. Ritzik came from a large North Philadelphia family of émigrés—refugees from the abortive pro-democracy Hungarian uprising of 1956. His father, Andy, had been a beat cop for thirty-five years before he'd pulled the pin and retired to the Gulf Coast of Florida in the mid-nineties. The move was well deserved: Andras Ritzik had raised five children alone after his wife died of a stroke at the age of forty-two. And he'd done well as a single parent: Ritzik's brother Frank was a sergeant on the Philadelphia PD's SWAT team; elder brothers Andy Junior and Joe were Pennsylvania State Police troopers, and his sister, Julianna, worked as an investigator for the City of Brotherly Love's district attorney.

Ritzik's father, who'd never gone above the rank of patrolman, had always wanted to see his firstborn command a battalion or a regiment. But Ritzik knew all too well that promotion these days was based not on the ability to lead, but on the pure Machiavellian cunning to thrive within the backstabbing environment of staff assignments and the willingness to curry favor with paper-warrior generals.

It just wasn't his milieu. Indeed, Ritzik was considered bureaucratically challenged because he preferred stabbing his people in the front—and with a knife, not a memo. Plus, he had a short fuse. He was undiplomatically blunt. And obviously, he was impolitic: he'd turned down the chance of a lifetime to work on SECDEF's staff, after which promotion would have been a gimme. Neither was he particularly anxious to attend the National War College, which was where you went if you were fast-tracked for a command billet and a general's stars. No, Ritzik was a most atypical West Pointer: no eagles or stars in his sights; happy where he was as a junior officer who had the privilege of serving with the finest and most capable Soldiers in the world.

Two years before, when Ritzik told Rowdy he'd just turned SECDEF down, Yates thought over what he'd said for about thirty seconds.

Then the sergeant major spat tobacco juice into his cup, wiped his lower lip, and said, "The way I see it, Loner, the only real difference between a brown nose and a shithead is depth perception—and there are already so many damn officers with depth perception working at the Pentagon they just don't need you and your twenty/twenty vision screwing up their lives."

RITZIK SHOOK HIMSELF out of his reverie. He checked his timer and GPS unit and discovered much to his amazement that they'd picked up a little speed. The winds actually *were* shifting. Maybe. Still, he did a little quick mental math and was happy to see that if everything remained constant, they'd reach the LZ in just under three hours. That wasn't good enough—not by a long shot. But the situation was far better than it had been half an hour ago.

Room 3E880-D, The Pentagon.
0739 Hours Local Time.

THE SECURE PHONE on Robert Rockman's desk was ringing as the secretary came into his hideaway office. He launched himself at the receiver, hit the button, and waited for the green light. "Rockman."

"This is Captain O'Neill, sir. Signal, please?"

"Skyhorse-Pushpin."

"Thank you, sir. You were anxious to hear about PLA aircraft movement yesterday. I just picked up something relating to those HIP-H transports out of Beijing. You asked me twice about the choppers and only once about the fighter aircraft, so I figured you had a special interest in keeping 'eyes on' the choppers."

Perceptive fellow, this O'Neill. "Yes?"

"I made some quiet inquiries. DIA reports SIGINT that the choppers have been diverted from their original destinations."

Rockman wrinkled his brow. "Diverted," he said.

"Langley had plotted them going to Changii," O'Neill said. "I know that because of—" He paused. "Well, sir, I just know it from a good source."

"Go on."

"The flight plan was changed. The transports are going to Kashgar instead."

"Kashgar. Gunship cover as well?"

"Affirmative, Mr. Secretary."

Rockman cursed silently. The shift put the PLA four

hundred miles closer to Ritzik's rescue operation. "Has CIA advised anybody of this?"

"Not that I know of, sir."

"Do you know why they've buttoned up?"

"May I speak with you face-to-face, sir?"

"Come on down."

As O'Neill came through the door, the secretary could see that he hadn't been to sleep. The captain said, "I'm sorry for my appearance . . ."

Rockman waved him off. "Don't apologize, Hugo. You've been crashing. Tell me what's up."

"It's a CIA Charlie Foxtrot, sir, if you'll pardon my French. Late yesterday, NSA scooped up a series of open telephone calls from Beijing to roughly a dozen commercial satellite imaging companies all around the globe."

"Yesterday." That was funny. Rockman remembered Nick Pappas had told the president Beijing had tried to buy one-meter commercial imagery two nights ago. "Are you sure it was yesterday, Hugo—not the day before?"

The captain nodded. "Absolutely, Mr. Secretary."

"And all of the firms that were contacted—do they sell one-meter-resolution digital satellite imagery?"

"They do, sir."

"Go on."

"Beijing asked each company for the precise coordinates in China that had been acquired for exclusive commercial use recently. I'd bet they suspected CIA had purchased a lot of one-meter imagery in the past couple of days in order to keep them blind. I think Beijing—or to be more precise, the *Er Bu,* China's foreign intelligence organization—repolled the companies to discover precisely which areas were out of bounds. My guess is that they washed those coordinates through some kind of matrix. Ultimately, it became a process of elimination. From what I've been able to ascertain from my sources, when CIA bought up the one-meter imagery, the front companies doing the purchasing didn't ask for anything except the one precise area Langley wanted to keep the Chinese from seeing."

Rockman shook his head. "Nick couldn't be that stupid." Then he thought about what he'd just said and slammed his palm on his desk. "Oh, yes he could."

But more to the point, the DCI was covering up his latest gaffe by withholding this critical piece of intelligence. Rockman looked at O'Neill's haggard face. "Good work, Hugo—you showed real initiative. I owe you a big one."

He waited until the officer turned and left. Then he hit his intercom button so violently that he snapped it in two. "Get me the president on a secure line—ASAP."

16

RITZIK NUDGED WEI-LIU with his left leg and pointed a booted foot groundward. There were sparse lights scattered below. He adjusted his NV and peered down, but he could make out no sign of life other than the half-dozen twinkling lights. They were gliding almost due southeast now, at a ground speed of just over thirty-three miles an hour. Distance to the LZ was 21.6 miles—40.6 minutes of flight time given the current tailwind. He checked the time. It had been eight minutes since the last radio check. He pressed his transmit switch, uneasy until he'd received a verbal confirmation from every member of the element. Navigation on night HAHO operations, he was happy to note, was so much simpler with the GPS units—so long as the damn things worked.

Something that hadn't changed was the fatigue of long Ram Air glides. Ritzik's arms were gradually growing sore. Even with the toggle extensions, which allowed him to keep his hands at waist level, maintaining the full-flight position was exhausting after more than half an hour or so. And Ritzik's arms had been virtually frozen in position for almost an hour.

The slow progress also made him nervous. ETA at the drop zone was now close to twenty-two hundred hours. That would give them little more than two and a half hours to bury the chutes and the rest of their jump equipment and proceed to a rear assembly area, which was more commonly called a LUP, or lay up position. From there, well back from the ambush site, Ritzik's troops would begin their recon. Once they'd gone over the ground thoroughly and decided just where to hit the convoy, they'd set the explosives and unobtrusively mark their fields of fire. Then the team would withdraw, leaving no sign that they'd been prowling and growling. Finally, long before the enemy was anywhere nearby, the team would conceal themselves and let the ambush site slip back to its uninterrupted nocturnal rhythms—letting the "critters and shitters," as an old Special Forces master sergeant had once described them to Ritzik, return to normal.

That last element was critical. As a second lieutenant not two years out of West Point, Ritzik had once had occasion to accompany a platoon of General Juan Bustillo's Salvadoran Special Forces on a mission to capture an elusive, deadly, and particularly nettlesome female FMLN[19] *comandante* named Nidia Calderon. The team had choppered from the airfield at Ilopango, northeast, into San Vicente Province. There, they fast-roped down into a rugged landscape of ravines and thick brush, to lie in wait alongside a narrow, twisting trail identified by infrared satellite photography as used by the guerrillas to bypass the local army garrison.

Everything had been thought of. An FMLN defector had given Bustillo up-to-the-minute intelligence about Coman-

---

19. The Farabundo Martí National Liberation Front, an umbrella organization for El Salvador's Marxist-Leninist terrorist groups.

dante Calderon's schedule. OPSEC had been achieved by keeping the entire SF company in isolation at Ilopango for the previous forty-eight hours. The local army commander was not informed that the unit would be in his area of operations. The pilot flying the platoon into San Vicente was a Cuban-American retired CIA veteran using the nom de guerre Maximo Gomez. "Gomez" had volunteered his services to General Bustillo to help defeat the Communist insurgents. Gomez hovered his slick as the platoon dropped into the ambush zone in a matter of seconds. Then he quickly flew off to the north.

The Salvadoran Special Forces quickly deployed into their ambush positions and settled down to wait for the *comandante* and her six escorts. They hadn't been in position more than fifteen minutes when the FMLN point man slowly worked his way down the trail. Ritzik watched through night-vision goggles as the guerrilla came closer. He was moving very slowly—one step in a minute or so—cautiously examining the trail as he went.

Like a bird dog catching a scent, the guerrilla stopped cold, fifty yards from the ambush site. He didn't move a muscle. He stood, statuelike, for two minutes. Ritzik watched transfixed as the man's nostrils actually twitched, his eyes darting as he scanned left, right, and ahead.

And then, the point man slowly, slowly, slowly . . . backed away. The Special Forces platoon leader, a Salvadoran captain named Lopez, sent his men charging after the guerrillas. But to no avail: the trap had been discovered. Nidia Calderon escaped. And no one could figure out why.

It wasn't until months later, while talking to a Vietnam-vet master sergeant at Fort Benning, that Ritzik finally understood why the mission had gone south.

The sergeant asked a single question. "How long before the ambush did you set up, sir?"

"A quarter of an hour, Master Sergeant," Ritzik answered.

"That was it, sir."

"What was?"

"The platoon leader's timing, sir. We learned in Vietnam that you gotta set up at least an hour in front of any ambush—longer is better—because it takes that long for the critters and shitters to get back to normal. Think back, sir. Were the birds chirping? Were the bugs buzzing? Were the tree monkeys whoopin' it up on that trail?"

Ritzik thought long and hard about it. And the answer was no. "But why was the point man's nose twitching?" he asked. "What was that all about?"

"That, Lieutenant"—the master sergeant's eyes crinkled—"is a real-life example of the sociocultural aspect of warfare that very few people ever come to appreciate."

Ritzik was entirely confused, and he said so.

"Think back, Lieutenant. Think hard. What exactly did you smell when you were laying up in that ambush position?"

Ritzik thought for some seconds. "Earth," he finally said. "A kind of vegetal, rootsy, jungle smell."

"And that was all."

"Yup."

"Are you sure, sir?"

"Yes, Master Sergeant, I am sure. Absolutely certain."

"Then let's go back a little further, sir. Back to when you departed Ilopango. Take me through it."

Ritzik described the sequence. He'd taken his gear and walked to the Op Center, where he'd pored over the map with the platoon leader, double-checking the best insertion and exfil routes.

And then it hit him. Like the proverbial ton of bricks. "Oh, goddamn," he said, his face lighting up. "That was it."

"What do you remember, Lieutenant?"

"He was wearing cologne. Lopez—the Special Forces captain. It was sweet, and he wore a lot of it. Most all the Salvadoran officers wore cologne."

He turned to the master sergeant. "That was it, wasn't it? The point man smelled Captain Lopez's aftershave."

"Lieutenant, if you learn two simple lessons about ambushes, you're never gonna get caught with your skivvies down. One: give the critters plenty of time to get back to normal before the opposition shows up. And two: leave the Skin Bracer at home."

7,000 Feet Above Xinjiang Autonomous Region, China. 2146 Hours Local Time.

RITZIK'S ETA was less than twelve minutes. He and Wei-Liu had pulled off their oxygen masks at 8,500 feet, reveling in the cool night air. Then Ritzik replaced the internal communications hookup with an earpiece and throat mike and ran a quick comms check with the rest of the unit. He was astonished to find the radios were all working properly.

The tailwind had picked up. It was strong enough now—eighteen miles an hour—that the team's landing would have to include a downwind leg, basc leg, and final approach. He checked his altimeter and took a reading off the GPS screen. They were right on course, and descending steadily. At one thousand feet of altitude, he would execute the landing pattern. The rest of the element would come in behind him, each offset and well separated from the others so that the turbulence from their parachutes wouldn't affect one another's landings.

Indeed, even now, things could go terribly wrong. A nighttime thermal could lift them willy-nilly thousands of feet above the desert floor. The wind could shift, or increase beyond the twenty-knot maximum for safe landings. Wind shears or microbursts—short-lived downdrafts—could slam the jumpers into the desert floor at fifty miles an hour. A sudden dust devil could corkscrew them into the ground. And then there was ground turbulence. It could be caused by anything from a ragged tree line to a ridge of sand dunes. Ground turbulence was similar in many ways to the roiling air caused by jet aircraft when they take off or land. That powerful vortex behind them can—and sometimes does—cause smaller aircraft following too close behind to invert and crash.

3,500 Feet Above Xinjiang Autonomous Region, China. 2151 Hours Local Time.

RITZIK COULD MAKE OUT the dunes below clearly through his NV. He scanned the area to the southeast. There was scrub brush and more dunes, with an occasional clump of wind-stunted trees. Directly to the south, he picked out an unpaved, rutted road moving almost due east-west. That would be the smugglers' track leading from the bridge. He steered slightly south, then turned eastward, flying parallel to the pathway. He'd pick out a landing zone away from the road, far enough from the bridge and causeway so there was no chance they'd be spotted.

Altitude: 1,800 feet. Ritzik adjusted his trim and went to half brakes, decreasing his airspeed to about ten miles an hour but increasing his descent rate. He steered a wide left-hand turn, his altitude dropping quickly now. Now he was flying crosswind. Ahead and below, he could pick out a series of brush-topped dunes. As he crossed over the top of them he could sense a change in the canopy as he hit the mild ground turbulence. He descended to fifteen hundred, fourteen hundred, thirteen hundred feet. Off to his left, half a kilometer away, he picked out the narrow causeway that stretched from the bridge across the soft marsh leading away from the Yarkant Köl. And then he worked the brakes once more and began a wide, flat right hand turn that would take him on the downwind leg of his approach.

Altitude: 1,000 feet and coming down rapidly. Ritzik released the brakes to slow the descent speed. But, with the wind behind him now, his ground speed accelerated. He dropped his arms and slowed down as he brought the parachute into a second right hand turn. Now he was on the base leg. His altitude was about eight hundred feet. He was concentrating now on picking out the best possible landing zone—didn't want to come down in the marsh, or hit the crest of the dunes. Off to his right, he saw one possibility: a slight depression perhaps two hundred feet across. At its far end was a clump of vegetation; to its left, six hundred feet away, half a dozen ragged, windblown trees.

Altitude: 300 feet. The head wind had picked up. He raised his arms, reducing the brakes. Off to his right was a small row of dunes. The Ram Air canopy reacted, buffeting Ritzik and Wei-Liu.

Altitude: 200 feet. He reached down with his left hand and hit the quick release on his combat pack. It fell away. As it reached the end of its tether, the shock bounced the two of them violently. Then, quickly, he eased both toggles up into the full flight position. Their airspeed quickened, but the rate of descent slowed, giving them a more gentle angle of attack.

* * *

Altitude: 60 feet. One hundred yards straight ahead, Ritzik saw that what had appeared from a thousand feet to be a clump of vegetation was in fact a wall of thornbushes perhaps five feet high that crowned the far rim of the depression. They represented instant pain and suffering. He'd flare well in front of them. Wind speed appeared to be constant from the way it was hitting his face.

Ritzik shifted in the harness, flexing his legs. "Stand by. At about fifteen feet I'm going to flare—bring us to a nice, gentle landing. We'll touch down and walk away as if we were stepping off an escalator."

Wei-Liu's head bobbed up and down. "Way to go."

Altitude: 15 feet. Ritzik eased both of his toggles downward, applying full brakes. The Ram Air slowed to almost a complete stop. Their soles were perhaps ten feet off the ground, when the entire left hand side of the parachute folded in half. "Oh, shit—" Instinctively, Ritzik released the toggles to allow air back into the cells. It didn't happen and they dropped like rocks.

"Uhhhh." Wei-Liu went down hard, Ritzik crumpling on top of her like a linebacker. He hit the quick releases and freed himself, then rolled to his right and released the chute straps. He pulled himself onto his knees, then rolled onto his side, pain shooting from his left ankle up his leg.

He crawled back to Wei-Liu and rolled her onto her back. "You okay?"

All she could do was suck air.

Ritzik pulled her harness off and ran his hands over her coveralls. She didn't wince, so he figured nothing was broken. "Just got the wind knocked out of you," he said.

A second chute descended rapidly. Wei-Liu watched as it flared, stopped dead in the air; the jumper stepped on to the desert floor as the canopy dropped, deflated, behind him. A third chute appeared out of the darkness. Wei-Liu pulled off her helmet. She could hear the canopies fluttering above.

Ritzik snagged Wei-Liu's arms and pulled her to her feet. "C'mon," he said. "We can't stay in the middle of the LZ—we'll get somebody killed."

He pointed at his combat pack. "Grab that, will you?"

He pulled his chute toward him, gathered it up into his arms, and hobbled toward the trees. Fifty feet from the tree line, Ritzik dropped his bundle and sat. Gingerly, he worked his hands around his left ankle. The good news was it wasn't broken, only sprained. He'd work the pain off. He untied the triple knots on his Adidas, pulled the laces as tight as he could get them to support the ankle, retied his boot, and pulled himself to his feet. "Time to get down to work."

"Down to work?" Wei-Liu looked at him incredulously. "Major, so far we've thrown ourselves out of a perfectly good aircraft, paraglided about sixty miles, and just walked away from a rough landing in hostile territory. Sounds like a pretty full day to me."

"Does it, now." Ritzik's eyes hardened. "Well, that's just the commute, ma'am. The easy part. The part we do before breakfast. We haven't begun the real work yet."

17

1.5 Kilometers West of Yarkant Köl.
2214 Hours Local Time.

As soon as the entire element was on the ground, Ritzik tried to check in with the TOC. But the frigging radios weren't send/receiving on any frequency except the close-range, insertion-element comms channel. Curtis Hansen tried to pull a satellite signal from the TOC on his laptop, but all the damn thing pulled in was static. The one piece of satcom gear still operational was the feed of the convoy's position displayed on the tiny screen of Ritzik's Blackberry PDA. It was still moving north alongside the Yarkant Köl.

As the element blacked out their faces with multicolored cammo cream and pulled on the Russian anoraks and dark knit caps, Ritzik did the math on the coordinates. He put the ETA at the bridge in just over two hours—the clock was really ticking now. Ritzik decided he'd worry about the comms later. Right now they had to cover just over a kilometer and a half of road—about a mile—and set the ambush. They'd leave Mickey D and Wei-Liu at the LUP.[20] The

---

20. Lay Up Position.

pair of them could spend their time concealing the jump gear. Maybe the chopper pilot could get the radios to work.

2220. The approach to the road was slow going—slower than Ritzik might have wanted. That was because the sand was soft, and even though the LUP was far removed from the ambush site, Ritzik wasn't about to leave tracks that could be seen after the fact. And so, with Gene Shepard on point, the nine-man element carefully picked its way foot by foot from the LUP across three hundred yards of rolling dunes, camouflaging their boot prints as they moved, then turned east onto the washed-out, rutted smugglers' road leading to the western end of the narrow causeway.

Roads made Ritzik nervous. You were exposed and vulnerable out in the open. Noise discipline was also a problem, especially when the unit was carrying heavy equipment—as this one was. But there was no choice now. Either he used the road, or he spent valuable time trying to cover up all those easily identifiable tracks in the soft sand. He concentrated on moving as quietly as possible, running what-if scenarios through his head as he put one boot in front of the other.

What would they do if the convoy showed up early? What would they do if they came across a shepherd? What would they do if a group of smugglers or an uninvolved civilian drove up the road? That had actually happened during Delta's first mission, the attempted rescue of the American hostages in Tehran, back in April 1980. Within literal seconds of the assault element's arrival on an allegedly isolated stretch of Iranian desert where no one ever went, three vehicles—a busload of civilians, a gasoline tanker, and an old pickup truck—all drove past the site. Result: instant FUBAR—and a compromised mission. The lesson learned? Plan for all contingencies. Never stop rolling those scenarios in your head.

So Ritzik paid careful attention to possible cover positions and ways to reach them as he moved forward. A branch of the scrub to his left, for example, could be used to mask his footprints as he backed off the road to seek cover behind the boulders thirty feet away, or he could hunker down under the thorny bushes to the east. Fifty, maybe sixty yards off the right side of the road stood a patch of knee-high grass that might provide some camouflage.

Complete concealment wasn't necessary, either. At night, the best way to keep a man from being seen was by following what the R&E instructors called the Quadruple-S Rule, the four being *s*ilhouette, *s*hine, *s*hape, and *s*peed. Don't silhouette yourself against the horizon; don't allow any light to shine off you or your equipment; don't allow the rectangular shape of your equipment to give you away, because there are virtually no naturally square shapes in nature; and don't move so fast that your enemy's peripheral vision will pick you up.

The last S-rule was perhaps the most important—and least understood. Without going into the technical elements, the way we see an object at night is different from the way we see that same object during the day. In daylight, light comes into the eye directly, moving from the lens back to the cone cells in the center of the retina. At night, it is our peripheral vision that dominates, because instead of hitting the cone cells of the retina, illumination is picked up by its rod cells, which are grouped around the periphery of the cones. That is why, on night patrol, constant scanning in a figure-eight, as opposed to a straight-on, left/right approach is utilized. At night, by always looking off center, you are much more likely to catch a piece of something than you are by staring straight at it. A quick or jerky motion, therefore, is much more likely to be observed at night because it "reads" more distinctly in a man's peripheral vision.

2224. From the number two position, Ritzik watched as Gene Shepard worked his way up the road. The point man's footfalls were absolutely silent, even though the gravel wasn't being helpful. Sound was a unit's biggest tactical problem at night. In the old days it had been the ability to see. But with miniaturized thermal imagers and fourth-generation NV readily available, darkness was no longer an impediment. In fact, Ritzik preferred fighting at night because he knew that his equipment was lighter, better, and more sensitive than anyone else's. But sound and smell were still dead giveaways. Sound and smell told the enemy where you were—even how many of you there were.

At night, every sound is amplified. You can hear the scrape of metal against metal, the rasp of a man clearing his throat, or the click of a loose rock from two hundred yards away. How much smell can affect an operation was something Ritzik had learned in El Salvador. And one immediate result had been that he made sure none of his men ever used any scented products in the field. But there was more: sweat, food, even web gear could actually give a man's presence away. The odor of a cigarette, for example, can carry as far as a football field if the wind is right.

Eighty yards ahead, Gene Shepard moved slowly, cautiously, deliberately, his suppressed weapon carried in low ready, his trigger finger indexed alongside the receiver, scanning through his NV as he went. He made his way through a slight depression, then inched up the incline on the far side. As he drew closer to the crest, he slowed his pace even more, lowering his body to keep himself from making a silhouette. Finally, he dropped onto the ground and, with his weapon held in both hands, he proceeded at a crawl.

At the ridgeline, the point man froze. After a half minute he clambered slowly backward, below the crown. There, his right arm extended straight from the shoulder, his gloved hand a fist.

The eight others froze where they were. Now Shepard's thumb extended from his fist—thumb up—and his hand quickly inverted, thumb pointed at the ground.

It was the silent signal for "enemy seen or suspected."

Ritzik's hands told the element to deploy to the left side of the road. There was more cover available to the left than to the right. Moreover, splitting the force could prove hazardous if there was any shooting, with the two groups firing directly at each other.

The men moved quickly, camouflaging their footprints with branches as they backed away from the rutted track. Ritzik kept his head up long enough to make sure they'd all cleared. He slid his pistol out of its thigh holster and attached the suppressor to the threaded barrel. Then he settled down behind a clump of bushes perhaps sixty yards off the road and eased the Sig's hammer rearward. Ty Weaver lay next to him, the dull muzzle of the sniper rifle's silencer poking through the thorns.

Ritzik pushed the transmit switch on the radio. "Shep— how many?"

"*Uno.*" Gene Shepard's whispered voice came back in his ear. "Half a klik away and approaching on foot."

"Armed?"

"Affirmative."

They'd have to wait this one out. Ritzik looked at his watch. It was already past the half hour. If they didn't start setting the ambush by twenty-three hundred . . .

He didn't want to think about the consequences.

* * *

2229. The double-clicks in Ritzik's left ear told him the target was getting close. Ritzik couldn't see him, not yet. But Shep could. And he signaled by hitting his radio transmit twice.

And then . . . there he was. A lone figure, cresting the rise. Ritzik focused as he drew closer. He was wearing a PLA uniform top and non-descript pantaloon trousers tucked into some sort of calf-high boots. His head was bare, his face framed by a fierce beard and long, matted, unkempt hair. He strode, oblivious to his surroundings, right in the middle of the road. If he was the point man for the convoy, he wasn't taking the job seriously. His rifle—it looked to be an AK—was slung over his shoulder. The tip of the cigarette dangling in Mr. Oblivious's mouth recorded as a hot spot in Ritzik's NV. A cellular telephone was clutched in his right hand. As he came over the crest, he soccer-kicked a stone. He cursed in Uzbek as the damn thing glanced off his toe and skittered only a couple of feet. Then he took a second shot, which sent it ricocheting past Gene Shepard's nose.

About ten yards over the ridge, Mr. Oblivious stopped long enough to take a huge double drag on his cigarette. He exhaled smoke audibly through his nose, then pulled the butt from between his lips, stared at it quickly, dropped it on the road, and ground it out with the toe of his boot.

Mr. Oblivious walked another twenty-five paces and stopped again. He looked left, then right, as if to make sure there was no traffic coming. Then he strode over the narrow shoulder and marched away from the road, ten yards onto the hard sand of the desert floor, not twenty-five feet from where Ritzik and Ty Weaver lay. He turned his head and checked the road again. And then the son of a bitch set down the AK and the cell phone, unfastened his pantaloons, dropped into a squatting position, and took an Uzbek dump. A noisy Uzbek dump. A smelly Uzbek dump.

He squatted there for about a minute before cleaning himself off. He appeared to be about half clean when the phone rang, and Mr. Oblivious cursed long and loud. Despite the tense situation, Ritzik nevertheless found himself amused that the universal law that governs the timing of unwelcome phone calls worked equally as well in China as it did back Stateside.

Mr. Oblivious snatched the phone off the ground and barked into it.

Ritzik listened. Mr. Oblivious was indeed Uzbek, and he was the convoy's point man. From the one side of the conversation he heard, Ritzik confirmed Mr. Oblivious had been sent ahead to make sure there was nothing untoward in the bridge and causeway areas. Moreover, the man was obviously dealing with a superior, because while he'd let loose a string of deletable expletives when the phone rang, he was now being deferential. Dutifully, the man reported that everything was clear and safe, and yes, he'd wait to be picked up in a couple of hours.

The conversation lasted less than half a minute. And then, Mr. Oblivious snapped the phone shut, slid it into a pocket, called his boss a less-than-polite name, and finished wiping himself. Then he rubbed his left hand in the sand to clean it, brushed the sand off on the uniform jacket, cleared his nose, adjusted his pantaloons, took half a dozen steps toward the road, dropped into a sitting position, reached into his breast pocket, and pulled out a cigarette.

Which is when Ritzik shot him. The suppressed round made a soft *thwock* as it hit Mr. Oblivious square in the back of the head. The Uzbek fell forward without making a sound.

Ritzik scrambled to his feet, covered the fifteen yards between them in less than two seconds, and—careful to select a firing angle from which ricochets wouldn't pose a hazard to his own people—put two more silenced rounds in the man's head.

Killing Mr. Oblivious wasn't something Ritzik had been especially anxious to do. He took no joy in killing. It was an essential part of his job. And he was proficient at it. But the Selection process for Delta was careful to weed out the rogues, the thrill killers, and the sociopaths, who thought that throat-slitting or double-tapping was fun. Still, Ritzik had no hesitation about killing. And he wasn't about to compromise his mission by wasting time waiting for the Uzbek to finish his cigarette and move on.

He knelt, checked the man for a pulse, and found none. He rolled the corpse over onto its back, stood astride it, searched for documents or any other intel, and came up dry. Mr. Oblivious wasn't carrying anything—not even an ID.

Ritzik secured his weapon, extracted the cell phone from the dead man's jacket, switched it off, and dropped it into a pocket. It would be interesting to discover who paid the bills. "Let's get moving."

18

AS THEY REACHED the end of the causeway, Ritzik was pleased to discover that the gap between the concrete surface and the unpaved road was huge—an eight-inch drop from the end of the causeway into an enormous pothole. The literal bump in the road hadn't shown up on the satellite images. But it was going to force the convoy to slow down precipitously.

Rowdy Yates jogged through the light ground fog the slightly less than half a kilometer to the bridge, carefully paced back, and took Ritzik and Ty Weaver aside. "Change of plans. You initiate on 'Two—just like always.' But you hit the lead truck first." Yates looked at Ritzik. "Time your countdown so Ty can shoot just as Truck One comes off the causeway. It'll bottleneck the others. They won't know what's happening in the back of the column until it's too late. I'll set the claymores off and you'll be picking 'em off from the rear like Gary Cooper in the old *Sergeant York* movie."

The sniper snorted. "Promise it'll be that easy, Rowdy?"

"On my word." Yates held up his right hand, palm raised.

"Oh, by the way, I got some lovely waterfront property to sell you right outside Mazār-e Sharīf."

"And you'll respect me in the morning, too, right?" Ty started walking to the rear to search out a shooting position.

Yates gestured toward the causeway. "Setting those claymores is gonna cause us a headache or two, boss."

Ritzik nodded. "I saw." The trouble lay in the narrowness of the causeway. The Chinese claymores had an effective range of roughly two hundred meters. But they were most deadly when the target was within a sixty-meter cone. The problem was that the concrete sides of the causeway were just over three feet high, and the causeway itself was more than ten feet above the marsh. The precise measurements had been impossible to gauge from the satellite images. It was going to be unworkable to position the claymores where he'd wanted to, because the causeway sidewall would mask too much of the blast.

Oh, the situation could be remedied. But it was going to take precious time to camouflage the damn things and hide the firing wire. Ritzik shook his head, disgusted. "Do what you have to. They're critical."

2316. The firing positions were going to be problematic, too. The marsh was soft—and much deeper than expected. That was the trouble with technical intelligence: it could give you just partial information. Nothing was as good as an old-fashioned, eyes-on recon. An old-fashioned, eyes-on recon would have shown what Ritzik and his team discovered in a matter of minutes: there were fewer cover and concealment possibilities than they would have liked.

But the downside came with an upside: there was no easy avenue of escape for the bad guys, either. The ambushed tangos would have to try to flee by jumping off the causeway into the marsh—where they'd be killed quickly. Or, they'd try to push forward onto the roadway, where Ritzik's second element would cut them to pieces. Once the convoy was stopped, it could be decimated. Terrorists seldom practiced vehicular counterambush drills. And at 2340, Ritzik got another piece of good news: Rowdy, Goose, and Shep had solved the claymore situation. They'd camouflaged the devices and set them so the deadly cones of the blasts would broadside directly into the last three trucks in the column, the shaped charges killing most of those inside.

2325. Ritzik called back to the LUP. He'd need Mickey D's firepower. And he wanted Wei-Liu close by, to work on the MADM as soon as the killing zone was safe.

2345. Now came the hard part: the waiting. The ambushers had laid themselves out in a modified letter *L*. Rowdy, Shepard, Masland, Curtis, and Goose were strung out in the marsh shallows by the western end of the causeway, concealed by the patchy fog and clumps of saw grass. The other five were split: Ritzik, Ty Weaver, and Mickey D on the right side of the road; Tuzz and Sandman on the left, to deal with any tangos who tried to flank from behind. The element's fields of fire were marked by IR chem-lights.

Rowdy Yates ran the marsh-side group—and controlled the claymore detonators. Ritzik and Mickey D had the road—positioned close enough to be able to engage the first vehicles close-quarters. Ty Weaver had the high ground. He lay concealed atop a small dune at an oblique angle to the convoy's path. The position would afford the sniper a panoramic view and a protected shooting site that allowed him to engage targets anywhere along the convoy. Well behind him, hidden by a dune, Ritzik stashed Wei-

Liu, with instructions not to show herself until he or Weaver came for her.

0006. The ambushers could hear the tangos coming a long time before they actually saw them—even with the NV. The diesel trucks' rumbling carried a long way in the still night air. Ritzik snorted. No need to worry about critters and shitters tonight, not with all that racket. He glanced skyward and was relieved to see opaque clouds moving from west to east. That was good, too. It cut back on the possibility of ambient light reflecting off the fire teams.

0008. The convoy was turning onto the bridge. Ritzik could listen as the drivers downshifted, transmissions whining, motors growling. And now he made out the lead vehicle—the 4×4—as it started across the bridge, moving herky-jerky, only its yellow running lights illuminated. Truck Number One followed six or seven yards behind—close enough so that he could pick up two human silhouettes behind its windshield. The other trucks followed closely, too. Ritzik bit his upper lip. It was textbook. Absofrigging textbook. He glanced to his right. He sensed Ty Weaver's breathing modulate as the sniper zeroed in on his targets.

0008:24. Now the lead vehicle passed the rear infrared marker. The countdown was starting. There was a sudden, painful twinge in the lower part of Ritzik's gut. This was normal: his customary physical reaction to the vacuum before action. All the planning, all the options, all the scenarios had been sucked out of him. He was dry.

0008:40. The second two 4×4s crossed the bridge. There was nothing more to be done, nothing more to be said, nothing more to be adjusted, fixed, fine-tuned.

* * *

0008:49. The number six truck pulled onto the bridge. Either the plan was going to work, or it wasn't. But since *wasn't* wasn't an option, he would have to make it work. They would *all* have to make it work. This was when everything came down to FIDO. Fuck it—*drive on.*

0009. The first three trucks moved onto the causeway, followed by the two 4×4s. Ritzik could hear the suspensions creak as the vehicles came forward.

0009:38. The rear trio of trucks crossed the narrow bridge, passed the outer infrared marker, and crowded, pachydermlike, trunk to tail, onto the causeway. He pressed his transmit button. *"I have control."* And as quickly as it had come over him, the butterflies, the uncertainties, the doubts all vanished.

Indeed, it was now, during these final instants before he attacked his target, that an extraordinary, ethereal calmness washed over Ritzik. *"Execute in ten . . ."* In the brief hiccup of time before *Execute! Execute!* he became one with all the other Warriors who ever lived. *"Nine . . ."* One with Joshua, waiting to attack Jericho. *"Eight . . ."* One with Odysseus, sitting silent with his Warriors in the huge, hollow wooden horse outside the walls of Troy. *"Seven . . ."* One with Major Robert Roger and his green-clad Rangers in the French and Indian Wars. *"Six . . ."* One with Stonewall Jackson at Manassas. *"Five . . ."* One with the Second Ranger Battalion—the Boys of Pointe du Hoc—on D day. *"Four . . ."* One with Colonel Henry Mucci at Cabanatuan. *"Three . . ."* One with the First Division Marines at Chosin Reservoir. *"Two—sniper shoot . . ."* One with Captain Dick Meadows in Banana One, the lead chopper closing in on Son Tay prison camp. *"One . . ."* One with

Randy Shughart and Gary Gordon in the bloody streets of Mogadishu.

In his split second of *one*ness with history's men o' warsmen, Ritzik understood that tonight he would win, overcome, persevere, and ultimately prevail. *"Execute! Execute!"*

1.5 Kilometers West of Yarkant Köl.
0009 Hours Local Time.

Minus four seconds. Ty Weaver's brain scrolled the sniper's mental checklist. Correct body position—check. Don't cant the weapon—check. Good breathing. Rifle butt tight against shoulder with no straps or web gear in the way. Perfect spot weld. Consistent eye relief. Correct sight picture. Trigger control. Precise point of aim. Follow-up shots planned.

Minus two seconds. Weaver's first shot slapped the truck driver's head back against the rear window of the cab. The man was dead by the time he impacted the glass. The sniper swung the scope to the left. *Damn*—the tango riding shotgun had dropped out of sight. But there was no time to worry about it. Fighting adrenaline, concentrating on keeping his breathing even and his heartbeat steady and slow, he panned the long gun to the right, and found his third target: the driver of the number two truck.

Minus two seconds. Rowdy Yates moved the safety bail on his claymore firing device from the safe to the armed position. The third truck—the one with the prisoners and the device—was almost clear of the mines' conical killing zone.

* * *

Minus one second. Weaver put the HK's crosshairs on the man's upper lip and squeezed the trigger. His ten-power nightscope was sensitive enough that he could make out the fine mist of blood and brain matter as the tango's head dropped out of sight.

Weaver's crosshairs found the second man in the cab. The tango was wild-eyed, confused. He was reaching out to help his buddy when Weaver's third shot in less than two seconds caught him in the left eye. Now the big rifle moved again, Weaver's crosshairs searching for the driver of the number six truck. As they found the point between his eyebrows, the three claymores went off simultaneously. There was no discernible reaction from the sniper as Weaver's index finger tightened around the HK's trigger.

1.5 Kilometers West of Yarkant Köl.
0009 Hours Local Time.

THE HUGE EXPLOSIONS sent them sprawling. Sam Phillips screamed, "Jeezus H. Christ—hit the deck."

The heavy truck shuddered, staggered as if it had been hit by a wrecking ball. It was the whole goddamn Chinese Army—had to be. Automatic weapons opened up—a deafening, freaking barrage of mayhem. He heard the concussive explosions of grenades or mortars. Sam could see the trucks behind them exploding right through the canvas—the yellow flames were that bright. There was screaming everywhere. He rolled onto his right side, yanking X-Man with him. "Kaz—get X's knife—now. We've gotta get the hell out of here before the sons of bitches kill us along with the rest of them or blow up the goddamn bomb."

"Yo, Sam." Kaz snaked across the rough wood. X-Man stretched his leg out. Kaz scrunched around and pulled the small composite blade out from behind the security man's boot top. Quickly, he cut Sam's arms free. Sam grabbed the blade. He cut the bonds that pinioned X-Man's arms.

But then the truck lurched, and the knife fell out of his grasp and skittered across the rough wood of the bed. "Shit. X—"

X-Man dove after the blade as another explosion shook the truck and rounds smacked dangerously close by.

The truck pitched forward, knocking them ass over teakettle as it—*smack*—rear-ended the vehicle in front of them and stalled out.

"Jeezus—*Sam*—"

Sam looked in the direction of Kaz's voice. "Holy shit."

The nuke had broken loose from its moorings. It began to totter. Mindless of the gunfire, the three men struggled to their feet and pressed up against the MADM, trying to hold it steady against the cab end of the truck bed before it fell and crushed them all.

"C'mon, goddammit." Sam thrust his shoulder up against the nuke. Outside, the firing was deafening—long bursts; short bursts; grenades; shouts. Sam could hear rounds *p-p-pinging* off the metal of the vehicles. There were other explosions. And more screams.

They finally wedged the nuke tight against the front bulkhead. Sam could sense the crate was stable. "X," he shouted over the gunfire, "get the knife. We'll hold this thing steady."

1.5 Kilometers West of Yarkant Köl.
0009 Hours Local Time.

RITZIK'S VOICE in Rowdy's earpiece: *"Execute! Execute!"* The sergeant major's hand closed around the firing trigger and pressed down evenly, just as the four men spread out beside him opened up on the convoy.

The mines caught the fourth and fifth trucks and the middle 4×4 in a perfect and deadly broadside. Screams erupted as the steel fragments found their targets through the thin sidewalls and canvas.

Rowdy pulled the pin on the grenade in his left hand, let the spoon fly, and then lobbed the device in a long arc at the rear of the sixth truck. The grenade gone, he shouldered his AK and raked the kill zone.

Goose's RPG caught the third truck dead center. He could see body parts fly as the rocket grenade exploded. The second RPG caught truck number four. Almost immediately, both caught fire. Using AKs and grenades, Rowdy's shooters took down the tangos as they tried to scramble to safety.

Mike Ritzik didn't have time to notice Rowdy's success. He and Mickey D were too busy trying to kill the occupants of the first two vehicles, who were being highly uncooperative.

The 4×4's driver had obviously dropped onto the floor, because Ritzik couldn't see anybody in the vehicle but the Toyota was moving straight forward, jouncing on the rutted roadway. Obviously, the tango inside was steering blind. But he was doing a good job of it. He was almost parallel to Ritzik's position, and gaining speed.

Ritzik came up off the ground to get a better angle, and saw muzzle flash from the vehicle. Bright yelloworange-white death. And then, things slowed down, almost as if time were standing still. He could sense the rounds coming at him in slo-mo. He pancaked. Rolled to his left as sand kicked up all around him. He fired back: one-two-three quick bursts of suppressive fire. Real time resumed. Crawling on hands and knees, he scurried around the berm and put a second series of five-round bursts through the Toyota's door. But the goddamn 4×4 took the licking and kept on ticking. Not good. He yelled at Mickey D: "Shoot at the tires—"

Too late. The 4×4 was out of range. Now the big truck loomed into Ritzik's sight picture, the top of the driver's head visible. Ritzik fired. Glass shattered. But the truck kept going. Ritzik and Mickey D loosed a series of long bursts as the cab drew even. They could see the profile of the driver, head lolling against the broken window.

Ritzik head-shot the man. But he didn't move. He just kept driving. He was a goddamn bullet sponge.

And then Ritzik realized what was happening. The driver was dead. Ty had killed the son of a bitch. The second man in the cab was using the corpse as a shield. Where the hell was an RPG when you needed one? Ritzik's bolt locked back. He dropped the empty mag out, slapped a new one into the mag well, and raked the canvas-covered truck bed.

But the big vehicle kept going forward. Gaining speed. Moving out of range.

"Boss—" Mickey D's voice in his ear.

Ritzik spun around.

"Third truck."

Ritzik saw. A knot of hostiles were crawling, shielded by the causeway sidewall, working their way toward the number three truck. The one with the hostages.

His AK came up, front sight on the leader. He put a three-shot burst into the sumbitch. One down.

From Ritzik's right, Mickey D emptied a full mag at the tangos. The muzzle flash from the AK was blinding. "Fire discipline, Mickey," Ritzik screamed at the pilot. He blinked, trying to regain any semblance of night vision. Jeezus. He aligned the AK's front sight and squeezed off a quartet of three-shot bursts at the advancing tangos.

SOAR245

Two of them managed to crawl to the rear of Truck Three. Ritzik saw a grenade. "Ty—your twelve-thirty."

"Roger." The sniper brought his muzzle up. Found the target. Squeezed the trigger. The grenade rolled under the truck and exploded.

Ritzik spoke coolly into the throat mike. "Rowdy, Shep—one-two-three-four hostiles—rear of truck three."

"Roger, Loner. We'll take the truck and hostages."

19

SAM WAS SCREAMING, "C'mon, c'mon, c'mon—don't let it tip."

And then the corner of the rear flap was pulled aside. A bearded face. An arm. A gun.

"Jeezus—X," Sam yelled.

As the gunman's eyes tunneled on Sam and Kaz, X-Man reached across, grabbed the man's gun arm, and slammed it down onto the tailgate. The gunman screamed. The revolver went skittering across the truck bed.

X-Man leveraged himself out of his kneeling position and, without letting go the terrorist's arm, took him by the hair and yanked the man inside the truck.

"Don't let the bomb fall," Sam screamed. He let go of the crate and dove for the gun.

X-Man and the terrorist were struggling, arms and legs thrashing. Sam thought he saw the pistol on the truck bed. Then the two men rolled on top of the weapon.

"Sam—" Kaz's voice. "Jeezus, the bomb."

Sam launched himself at the nuke.

"*Ungghs.*" X-Man sensed the pistol underneath his kidneys. But there was no way to get his hands on it. He was otherwise engaged. The son of a bitch was strong. Wiry. He stank, too. Urine, feces, sweat, garlic; a whole panoply of Uzbek aromas.

X-Man tried to roll the Uzbek over so he could get on top and strangle the sumbitch. But he couldn't get any traction, couldn't get any leverage. The guy was a natural grappler. That made him dangerous.

Shit—from the way they were moving, X was pretty certain the Uzbek had felt where the pistol was, and he was gonna try for it. Not good.

X-Man broke free and chopped the little bastard upside the head. He heard something crack. He hoped he'd done some damage.

But not enough. The Uzbek's hand slipped away, out of his grip. Slammed up, choked him around his throat. Tried to crush his windpipe. Gasping, X-Man slipped an arm inside and broke the grip. Kneed the sucker in the balls.

Kaz screamed, "X—the knife . . ."

The Uzbek reacted to Kaz's voice—dropped his guard for just a millisecond.

It was all the opening the security man needed. His fingers found the terrorist's eyes and raked them. He slammed the terrorist's ears. He hammered the side of the man's face again, this time audibly breaking the bone at the outside of the eye.

"Knife? *Where?*" X-Man looked around, wild-eyed.

He smashed the guerrilla's head onto the truck bed and then, using every bit of strength he could summon, he drove his forearm into the man's Adam's apple and pressed down with his entire body weight.

The Uzbek fought back. Managed to put his fist in X-Man's face. But the American held on.

Kaz shouted, "Tailgate, Sam. Get the knife!"

Sam saw it. Saw it. He launched himself. Grabbed the

handle. Thought about using it on the Uzbek, but was afraid he'd kill X-Man.

He scrambled toward where X-Man and the guerrilla were still wrapped up.

Sam's boot found the Uzbek's rib cage. "Uhhhh!" Sam thought about Dick Campbell and took a second, more savage shot that caught the Uzbek in the head. The Uzbek thrashed wildly, bucking and screaming.

The gun. The gun. Sam saw the barrel poking out under the Uzbek's rib cage. He forgot about the knife and dropped onto the truck bed, one fist smashing at the terrorist, his other hand probing, until he wrapped his fingers around the muzzle.

He pulled it out, reversed it. Sam screamed, "X—I got the gun. I got the gun."

The Uzbek may not have understood Sam's English, but he must have known what he was saying, because he kicked out wildly, knocking Sam away.

Then X-Man caught the Uzbek with a hammered fist to the face that stunned him. The American struggled free. "Clear," the security man shouted, pulling his arm away and rolling to his left. "Sam," he screamed.

Sam, kneeling, held the pistol in his right hand, frozen. The Uzbek rolled over, pulled himself to his knees. That was when Sam saw Dick Campbell fall backward onto the desert floor. Saw his dead eyes. He shoved the muzzle of the pistol at the guerrilla's chest, shut his eyes, and pulled the trigger until the gun was empty. The noise was deafening. Something fell on him.

"Christ." X-Man dragged Sam, who was still pulling the trigger, from under the corpse. The security man pried the revolver out of Sam's hand.

Kaz screamed, "X—" The spook turned just in time to see the rear flap move again.

Then there was another explosion. X-Man yelled, "Holy shit!" as the MADM teetered. "Sam—get up here." The three of them, now screaming, threw their weight against the nuke to keep it from falling.

Outside, there was more gunfire. And screams. And explosions, rocking the truck.

And then, as if the sounds were coming from some other universe, Sam suddenly realized the screaming he heard from outside was *in English.* Someone was shouting his real name. Somebody out there was calling, "Sam Phillips Sam Phillips."

Sam screamed, "Everybody—shut up!" And then he shouted, "I'm Sam Phillips. I'm in here. In the truck."

He heard his name called again. They all heard it.

"I'm here, I'm here," he screamed at the top of his lungs. "In the truck. We're in the truck. Don't shoot."

And then the canvas flap was ripped aside. The tailgate dropped away with a rude metallic clang. Bright lights flooded the compartment.

Wide-eyed, blinded, Sam shouted, "Over here."

A malevolent wraith—no, a nimble ninja with a blackened face and knit watch cap—vaulted over the transom, short automatic rifle in his gloved hands, muzzle sweeping the truck interior.

The ninja's eyes found the pistol in Sam's hands.

Sam let the gun drop. His hands went high.

A samurai—a huge, wild-eyed Warrior—came quickly behind, stubby automatic rifle slung across his chest.

"Who's Sam?"

"Sam? I am."

"Hiya, Sam I am." The big ninja took Sam's upper arm. "Let's go, you guys—cavalry's here."

Sam held back. Twisted away from the samurai. "*It,*" he said, his freed arm pointing toward the cab.

"I know, I know. Let's go. Let's go, Sam I am—we're not finished yet." The big man wheeled. "Follow me—stay very close. Do not—repeat: do . . . not—go anywhere, do anything, unless I tell you to. We still got unfriendlies."

He turned away and spoke into air. "Back door. Three live ones. Coming to you, Loner." A pause. "Roger that."

0012. Ritzik saw them drop out of the truck and advance up the causeway, Rowdy riding herd, shouting at the spooks to keep their heads down.

"Tuzz, Loner. Do you have anything on the 4×4 and Truck One?"

"Negatory, Loner—they be gone."

Crap. Ritzik advanced. The quicker he got to them the faster he could get 'em away from the firefight, back to the LUP and safety.

But not yet. This wasn't over yet—not by a long shot. Ritzik's AK was mounted in low ready. His eyes moved left-right-left, right-left-right, to help prevent tunnel vision. His breathing was self-consciously even—in/out, in/out— to fight hyperventilation.

Threat—Ritzik saw motion from the left in his peripheral vision. His AK came up; the front sight swung around and held on center mass: teenage kid in turban and PLA tunic. Kid had a handgun. Muzzle rising in his direction.

Instinctively, Ritzik squeezed off a three-round burst that caught the target in the left side of the chest, spun him counterclockwise, and slammed him up against the fender of the 4×4. The weapon flew out of the kid's hand, its hammer struck the concrete lip of the causeway, and the gun went off.

The fore end of Ritzik's AK took the round, rendering the short barrel useless. The fore-end grip disintegrated, sending wood fragments into his hand and a long, sharp sliver right through his cheek. Oh, Christ, it hurt.

Ritzik's training took over: right hand yanked the big splinter out—deal with the blood later. He shed the useless automatic rifle. Transitioned to the Sig Sauer. Five steps— four shots—and the kid went down. Two more quick shots in the kid's head. *That's another who won't come back to bite us on the ass.*

The hostages were ten feet away now. Noise behind him. In his ear Rowdy's voice. "Drop-drop-drop." Ritzik pancaked onto the causeway. A four-shot burst over his head. Rowdy's voice: "Clear."

Ritzik rolled onto his side and saw the corpse sprawled a yard behind him. He waved the spooks on. "C'mon-c'mon-c'mon." He grabbed the first spook by the shirt. Thrust him roughly toward Mickey D. "Haul ass. Follow him. Move it."

1.5 Kilometers West of Yarkant Köl.
0018 Hours Local Time.

IT COULD HAVE BEEN WORSE. But it could have been better. They had the hostages. They had the weapon. And there'd been no friendly casualties—only a few of what Rowdy liked to call dings and dents. Nothing more serious than the splinter wound in Ritzik's cheek. But at least two dozen of the enemy—maybe more—had gotten away. According to Sam Phillips and the others, the IMU leader, whom they called Mustache Man, was among them. Not good. More immediate, a few hostiles had escaped four, perhaps five hundred yards into the marsh and were taking occasional potshots. Without night vision, they weren't having any luck—so far. Ritzik wasn't overly worried: once their muzzle flash gave their positions away, it was relatively easy for Ty and his night-vision optics to tag 'em.

The most essential thing right now, Ritzik understood, was to get away—and fast. Move to a daylight hide, dig in, camouflage themselves, wait for nightfall, then make their dash to safety. He'd tried contacting the TOC to get an intel dump from Dodger and pass a sit-rep to SECDEF Rockman. But the bloody radio was still on the fritz. All he got on the secure frequency was white sound. Without the TOC he was blind. He had no idea what the Chinese were up to. Or how close they were.

0020. Ritzik calmed the spooks down. Doc Masland gave 'em a quick once-over and prescribed food and water, which Ritzik provided. They seemed to be a good-enough group—for spooks. In fact, Ritzik was impressed when Phillips, the team leader, volunteered his people to go with Rowdy, Shep, Doc, and Tuzz to pluck as much intel from the corpses as they could find. Ritzik accepted the offer gratefully. It would save valuable time.

While the bodies were being searched, Curtis, Ty, and Mickey D scavenged for unexploded ordnance and supplies. Within a quarter of an hour, the three had uncovered two dozen RPG rounds and four launchers, a box of Chinese grenades, and half a dozen undamaged AKs and fifty loaded thirty-round magazines. There were also six five-liter cans of drinking water still undamaged, which Ritzik had Curtis stow in the truck.

Ritzik gave each of the spooks a weapon and three magazines. He loaded the rest of the ordnance in the vehicles. Goose and Bill Sandman stripped the corpses of hats and other useful uniform parts. When the Chinese finally spotted them—it was likely they would—Ritzik wanted everyone looking like tangos, not *yanquis*.

The vehicles were the biggest headache. They had only one operational 4×4, with a half-full tank and six six-gallon

jerry cans of gas, and one truck—fuel gauge reading full
and a full fifty-five-gallon drum of diesel fuel secured in the
bed. Ritzik needed speed and range to effect his exfiltration. He wasn't going to get either one.

And then there was Wei-Liu. The firing hadn't entirely
stopped when she'd tugged at Ritzik's web gear and insisted on examining the MADM. He'd tried to explain that
they were vulnerable out in the open.

"Let me secure the area first," he said. A burst of automatic weapons fire came from the rear of the column. Instinctively, Wei-Liu ducked. "Tracy—"

"But we could be dealing with something that's time-
critical," she insisted.

"Your life is time-critical."

"You have things well under control, Major."

"Do I?"

"I think so."

Two shots rang out. "I'm not as sure as you are." He
edged her closer to the chassis of the number two truck,
where she was less of an obvious target. "We'll get the
MADM stabilized, and we'll drive—well away from
here—until it's light. We'll camouflage our position. Then
you can take all day with the damn thing."

Wei-Liu switched on the flashlight she was carrying.
"We may not have all day, Major. That's what I want to ascertain." She pushed around him and headed for the number three truck.

The round knocked the light out of her hand, shattering
the cylindrical metal case before she even heard the sound
of the shot. Wei-Liu screamed and froze. Ritzik sacked her,
knocking her flat. He dropped his body atop hers.

He waited for a second shot. When none came, he rolled
off and pulled her to relative safety under the vehicle. There,

shielded by the rear axle, Ritzik spoke roughly into his mike: "Put out those damn brushfires, Rowdy—do it now."

He took Wei-Liu's hand and examined it. "You're okay," he said. "You're also very lucky."

Wei-Liu nodded. "I know."

"Look," Ritzik continued. "I know how anxious you are to get to work. But we're gonna move to a better location—"

She started to object. Ritzik cut her off. "No argument, no debate, Tracy. Just like Dr. Wirth once said, you don't get a vote here. We operate at night. The terrorists and the Chinese have a harder time in the dark than we do. So we'll go as far and as fast as we can until it's light. We'll hole up during the daylight hours. Once we're secure, you can take all the time you want."

West Executive Drive.
1430 Hours Local Time.

ROBERT ROCKMAN waved offhandedly at the uniformed Secret Service officer as the heavy, wrought-iron southwest gates swung open, his limo bumped over the antiterrorist barriers, and the big, dark blue armored Cadillac eased up the wet macadam to the awning leading to the West Wing's basement entrance. The vehicle pulled even with the white, brass-accented double French doors. Rockman waved off a blue-blazered, umbrella-toting factotum, opened his own door, tucked his leather document case under his right arm, and hustled straight into the building mindless of the sheeting rain.

The Marines saluted, then closed the doors silently behind him. The secretary paused in the foyer, extracted a crisp handkerchief from his left trouser pocket, and wiped raindrops from his gold-rimmed glasses. Rockman was concerned. Concerned, hell: he was damn worried. Ritzik's Tactical Operations Center in Almaty had lost contact with the insertion element hours ago. They were on the ground all right—all the satellite images showed that much. And they'd ambushed the convoy—or at least most of it—and from the look of things, they'd rescued the hostages. But young Ritzik didn't know about the Chinese. Didn't know they were within a few hundred miles of his position . . . and closing.

Rockman stuffed the handkerchief back into his pocket, put the glasses on, and looked up to find Monica Wirth standing in front of him.

"Mr. Secretary."

His lined face brightened at the sight of her. "Madam National Security Adviser." He liked this woman. She was strong. Forthright. She didn't mince words. And she didn't compromise her values either. Little wonder that the apparatchiks at State and her former colleagues at CIA—especially Nick Pappas—spent an inordinate amount of their time leaking unfavorable stories about her to the press. Christ, he wished the president would fire that son of a bitch Pappas and appoint her DCI. That would shake things up. Rockman looked at Wirth's serious manner and said, "What's this about?"

"The president's waiting," she answered vaguely. Abruptly, Wirth turned into the short corridor leading to the stairway. Rockman followed. They marched up the carpeted steps, turned left at the Roosevelt Room, then cut through a short hallway and walked down a narrow passageway that led past the chief of staff's office suite. Just beyond, two Secret Service agents stood outside an unmarked door.

"Mr. Secretary, please . . ." Wirth stood aside. Rockman

twisted the knob, pushed the door open, and entered the president's hideaway.

Pete Forrest looked up from his desk as Rockman entered the room. The president's collar was open. Rockman saw the First Tie and Jacket tossed haphazardly across the back of the sofa. The secretary stopped three feet inside the windowless room. "Mr. President . . ."

"Rocky." Forrest cracked the pinkie knuckle on his left hand. "Pull up a chair."

Rockman waited until Monica Wirth leaned against the heavy door, shutting it. When he heard the bolt click, he crossed the antique Sarouk and settled into a straight-back chair facing the president's desk.

The president put his elbows on the desk and pressed his fingertips together. "I had a telephone call from the president of the People's Republic of China just forty-five minutes ago."

"Oh?" Rockman's eyebrows went up.

"That's why I hustled you over here. President Wu advised me that elements of his armed forces will be taking what he referred to as, quote—firm steps—unquote, to deal with the Islamic separatists in Xinjiang Autonomous Region within twenty-four hours."

"He's going after the terrorists—the bomb," Rockman said.

"Yes," the president said. "And I think he's going to try to deal with the Uighur separatists—decisively—before the summit."

"They've been a thorn in his side for years," Wirth said.

Rockman stroked his chin. "It would be logical for Wu to act now."

The president nodded. "I agree. He knows we're in our own war against terrorism. The summit's coming up. He'd like to be able to demonstrate that he's doing his part."

Rockman fingered his tie. "Do you think Wu's using the terrorists as a pretext for anything else, sir?"

"You mean our people?" The president turned to face the NSC adviser. "I don't think so. But what's the latest, Monica?"

Wirth said, "I've been checking NSA's intake carefully. There's not a whiff of anything untoward. I don't think Wu suspects. And as you say, Mr. President, Beijing has been looking for an excuse to bring the Xinjiang region firmly under control for years."

"Good." Pete Forrest paused. "Now I've saved the best for last. Wu gave me an opening that may actually help us extract our people."

Rockman's eyebrows went up. "Sir?"

"He requested a favor. He asked me to backchannel a message to Delhi. He wants to assure the Indians that although his troops will be moving into the northwestern portion of the autonomous region, they will not approach within two hundred kilometers of the disputed area on the Indian border. He asked me to persuade the Indians not to react negatively."

"Did you agree?"

"Not immediately," Pete Forrest said. "Never give without getting; right, Monica?"

"Amen, Mr. President."

"So I asked him precisely where his troops would be deployed, Rocky. I told him I couldn't go to my good friend the Indian prime minister unless I knew the request could be absolutely explicit, detailed, and precise."

An approving smile spread slowly across Rockman's face. "And what did Wu say?"

"He hemmed and hawed, I guess is the best way to put it. He tried to keep to generalities. But the bottom line, Rocky, is that he's going to concentrate his forces on the northern side of the Taklimakan Desert—between Kashgar and Ürümqi. His worst seepage—" Forrest read the bemused expression on Rockman's face. "That's how the translator interpreted, Rocky—'seepage.' Anyway, it's from Kyrgyzstan."

"Interesting," Rockman said. He turned to the national security adviser. "Has the Agency weighed in on this?"

Wirth grimaced. "Langley—that Margaret Nylos woman—faxed me a one-page boilerplate analysis, without any conclusions. I swear, Mr. Secretary, those people over there have no clue what's going on. They might as well work for the State Department. I'd like to fire the lot of them."

Rockman's eyes flicked in the president's direction. "He's the commander in chief," he said. "According to what I read in the *Washington Compost* this morning, Monica, you have an all-powerful, Svengali-like influence over the man. You have brainwashed him. Turned him into a hard-liner."

"Rocky, don't instigate." The president frowned. "Believe me, after that screwup with the satellite imagery it wouldn't take much right now to can everyone from the DCI on down . . ." He paused.

Rockman coaxed, "And so, Mr. President?"

"I said, don't instigate. Believe me, Rocky, when we're out of the woods on this, I'm going to make changes. But for now, I don't want to hear another word about what Nick Pappas is or isn't doing." Pete Forrest's expression told both Rockman and Wirth the subject was closed.

Rockman pursed his lips. "Back to business," he said. "What did you tell President Wu, sir?"

"I told him it would be at least eight hours before I could get to Prime Minister Chowdhery. The man's seventy-six years old and he goes to bed early—but he gets up about four and is in the office by six. Wu agreed not to initiate any major action until he's heard back from me." Pete Forrest checked his watch. "Now, I'm not sure I believe Wu—or his motives—either. But let's take him at his word for the moment."

Wirth pulled a map of Western China from a credenza and spread it on the president's desk. "Wu spoke about a Kashgar–Ürümqi axis." She drew her finger over the map. "He's worried about the Kyrgyz border."

"That makes sense," Rockman said. "Our intelligence shows much the same thing. So it would clear the way for Ritzik to move his people into Tajikistan."

Monica Wirth said, "Why there as opposed to anywhere else?"

"There's a twenty-man Special Forces training group in Dushanbe," Rockman said. "They have choppers with them. They can be moved up to the Chinese border area under the guise of a joint exercise."

"But not into China," Wirth broke in.

"No," Rockman said. "No border crossings. That would be provocative." He paused, frowning.

The president read his SECDEF's face. "What's up, Rocky?"

"I just thought of something, sir. Wu said he wouldn't initiate any major action, right?"

Pete Forrest checked his notes. "That's what he said."

" 'Major action.' His precise words."

"That's right, Rocky."

"But Wu didn't say he wouldn't initiate small-unit activity, did he?"

Forrest wrinkled his brow. "No, he didn't. He didn't say anything at all about small-unit activity."

"I see where you're going," Wirth said. "He can move against the terrorists who have the bomb, using the Special Operations force in Kashgar."

Rockman said, "Precisely."

"Mr. Secretary, if the Delta people head south, and cross into Tajikistan, they're less likely to run into large numbers of PLA troops."

"That's true, I guess," Rockman said.

"Any developments?"

"Good and bad, Mr. President."

"Give me the good news first."

"The ruse seems to have worked. The plane Ritzik used for his infiltration returned to Almaty safely. I had DIA monitor Chinese air control. No ripples there."

"Good. Now, what's the downside?"

Rockman bit his lip. "Ritzik's communications aren't working properly. I'm in touch with Almaty, but Delta's Tactical Operations Center there hasn't been able to reach Ritzik's element in four, almost five hours. Not since they left the aircraft."

Pete Forrest's eyes went hard. "Fix it, Rocky," he said. "Those people have to know what they're up against. We have to get them out safely."

"I'll do everything I can, Mr. President. I'll—" Rockman jumped, startled, as the cell phone in his pocket chirped loudly. He saw the look of shock on Forrest's face. "It's Katherine, Mr. President," Rockman said, his face flushing in embarrassment. "She's in Bloomfield Hills with our youngest daughter—it's Samantha's first child, and Katherine . . ."

"Been there, done that, Rocky," Pete Forrest said, breaking into a gentle smile. "Take the call."

"Thank you, Mr. President." Rockman flipped the phone open and pressed it to his ear. "Katherine—I'm in the middle of something, so please, dear, make this quick."

20

RITZIK WAS NERVOUS. He hated being out in the open. He felt vulnerable. Naked. Unprotected. He wanted high ground. They'd driven along the smugglers' track for five or six kliks, heading almost due west. But then Ritzik had the two vehicles abruptly turn south, onto a washed-out streambed. Straight ahead lay Kashgar, the dusty Silk Road trading town. Which was probably crawling with PLA troops. Ritzik's instincts told him to steer clear.

His GPS unit indicated foothills perhaps forty kilometers to the southwest. The topography would afford them some protection and cover. Once they'd gotten off the desert floor, he'd figure out what the hell he'd do next. He scanned the horizon through his night-vision goggles. His cheek throbbed. There were three of them crammed into the two bucket seats of the 4×4: Gene Shepard, who was driving, Sam the Spook in the middle, and Ritzik. Two other spooks—a kid named Kaz and another, who called himself X-Man—rode in the back with Doc Masland. The rest of the crew, and Wei-Liu, were in the truck with the MADM. Ritzik hoped they weren't glowing yet.

Sam Phillips tapped Ritzik's shoulder. "Can I have a look?"

"Sure." Ritzik pulled the device off his forehead and handed it over.

The spook fitted the NV, focused, and peered through the dirty windshield. He whistled, impressed. "Great resolution."

"State-of-the-art."

Sam fiddled with the NV set. He said, "So, what's the plan, Major?"

"I want to get clear of the desert floor. Once we're in the foothills and the bomb is disabled, we'll see which way is best."

Sam said, "For what it's worth, you might consider heading for Tajikistan."

"I was told you're familiar with the region."

"I did two Central Asia tours. Almaty and Dushanbe."

"How'd you like them?"

"Living conditions were kind of primitive, but business was great. I was one of the pioneers—arrived in Almaty about six months after they'd declared independence. It was like living in a frontier town."

"Dodge City before Wyatt Earp."

"A lot closer to Hole-in-the-Wall than Dodge." Sam cracked a smile. "They called it *dikiy-dikiy vostok* in Russian. The Wild, Wild East."

"I didn't go until ninety-eight," Ritzik said. "It was pretty tame by then. There was even a knockoff Mickey D's about three blocks from Panfilov Park."

"No kidding."

"Burger *Khut,* they called it. The French fries tasted like they cooked them in motor oil."

"They probably did," Sam said. "In ninety-eight the

army was selling its supplies to make money. Motor oil was probably a lot cheaper than cooking fat. So, what were you doing?"

"JCET program." Ritzik saw Sam's blank expression. "Joint Combined Exchange Training."

Sam said, "You guys are big on acronyms, aren't you? What does it mean in English?"

"Cross-training. Working with their Special Forces."

"The Kazakhs needed training when I was in Almaty," Sam said. "Big time. I saw them in action once—Chechen terrorists took half a dozen hostages in the lobby of the old Lenin Hotel. The Kazakhs tossed twenty or so grenades through the windows—started a hell of a fire. Burned the place down. All that was left was body parts."

"That's known as the 'Egyptian Technique,'" Ritzik said. In November 1985, an EgyptAir flight from Athens to Cairo was hijacked by three Arabic-speaking gunmen and diverted to Malta. Two Israeli women hostages and three Americans were shot by the hijackers. Egyptian Special Forces then assaulted the plane by breaching the cargo hold with explosive charges. But the Egyptians botched the entry: in the ensuing explosion, fire, and gun battle the rescuers managed to kill all the terrorists, as well as fifty-nine of the seventy-two passengers.

"I'll remember that," Sam said. He handed the NV back to Ritzik. "You guys like Kazakhstan?"

"We love it," Ritzik said. "Hell, they've been good to us. They're a lot more pro-American than I expected."

"Some are," Sam said. "You ever run into a young officer named Umarov?"

"Talgat Umarov?"

"Yup."

"He's a colonel these days. Plugged in with the chief of

staff. He's my main contact," Ritzik said. "We brought him to the U.S. for training—twice." He looked at Sam. "Where on earth did you meet him?"

"Almaty. He was a lieutenant in ninety-three," Sam said. "One of the new generation of officers—the ones interested in all things Western. I got to know him pretty well. Did he ever marry his girlfriend?" Sam fought for the name. "Kadisha."

"They finally married—last year. Just had their first child." Ritzik shook his head. "Small world."

"She's the president's second cousin, y'know."

"No shit." Ritzik hadn't known. Talgat had never told him.

"The connection should do wonders for his career."

"He's already doing pretty well on his own."

"Maybe." Sam grinned. "But I see a general's stars in his future—and a Swiss bank account."

Ritzik frowned. "Talgat's not that kind."

"No disrespect intended," Sam said. "But believe me, friend, in this part of the world, they're all that kind. Even the good guys."

That sort of cold, jaded cynicism was typical for case officers. It was evidence of a degree of existential callousness that had always put Ritzik off. You never really knew where you stood with spooks. They were manipulative; role-players; control freaks.

In some ways, those traits were understandable. Their job, after all, was to play on vulnerabilities. To identify and recruit foreign national spies—traitors—to work on behalf of the United States. And so, a case officer's life—his entire existence—was compartmentalized. Had to be. And out of self-preservation, they "cleared" very few outsiders for entry. So Ritzik chose not to gnaw that particular bone. He let things go silent for about a minute. Then he said, "Tajikistan, huh?"

"There are a series of old smugglers' routes through the

mountain passes," Sam said. "Generally unpatrolled. I always had the impression the Chinese tacitly encouraged the smuggling because it brought certain consumer goods across the border."

The case officer paused. "Of course, that was three years ago. Now they've got Islamic separatists to worry about. And after Afghanistan . . ."

"So you weren't planning to use Tajikistan as your exfil."

Sam shook his head. "Nope," he said. "Hell, Major, we had all the right documents. We were going to spend a night in Kashgar, buy souvenirs, and then drive straight across the Kazakh border like proper tourists."

"Sounds like a plan."

"All we need is the right docs."

Ritzik reached into his cargo pocket for the GPS. His hand settled around the cell phone he'd taken from Mr. Oblivious. He brandished it at Sam Phillips. "Maybe I should just call the embassy and ask for visas," he said.

Sam said, "The IMU headman made cell-phone calls all the time. So maybe you should."

"Oh, yeah," Ritzik said. "Right. Sure."

Sam said, "Why not try?"

Ritzik snorted. But then again, there was nothing to lose. Maybe he could get hold of the TOC—which was more than he could do on the radio. He pressed the phone's on button. The readout was in Cyrillic. But it didn't matter— all he needed was the keypad. The signal-strength indicator told him he'd be able to get out. "What's the international code from here?"

"For where?"

"Almaty."

Sam's fingers drummed on the 4×4's dashboard. "Zero-zero-one, and then seven, then three-two-seven-two."

"Gotcha." Ritzik started pressing keys. And then he said,

"Damn." He stopped pressing keys, pressed the end button to cancel the call, and started over again.

He waited as the circuits completed. "It's ringing," he said. He pressed the phone tight against his ear. "Uh, no, sir, this isn't Katherine. It's Mike—Michael. Remember me?"

51 Kilometers Southwest of Yarkant Köl.
0242 Hours Local Time.

"OH, YES, SIR," Ritzik said. "Gotta keep it short." He paused. "Got it. Okay." He listened intently. "Sure. Yes, we're all fine. Could you call our friends in the other place? The place we came from. Just update them—tell them we'll be in touch sooner or later." Ritzik screwed the phone into his ear. "You're starting to break up." He reached across Sam Phillips and slammed Gene Shepard on the shoulder, signaling him to stop the 4×4. The vehicle screeched to a halt and Ritzik's thumb went up. "Yes. Good. Got it. Absolutely. Okay. Bye-bye, bye-bye. And thanks." He pressed the end button and then shut the phone off. The damn things could be triangulated. He turned to the case officer. "Great idea, Sam."

Sam said, "Thanks. Who was that on the other end?"

"The SECDEF. Robert Rockman," Ritzik said matter of factly. He pressed his radio transmit button. "Rowdy, Loner. Pull over. We gotta head-shed."

0246. Sam Phillips didn't like being cut out of the planning process, and he made his feelings known. But Ritzik was intractable. From the cryptic exchange he'd had with SECDEF, he understood that while the Chinese concentrated their efforts to the north, he had a brief window in which to move quickly.

The unknown variable in this equation was Major General Zhou Yi. From what Rockman had hinted, Ritzik understood that Zhou's Special Forces hunter-killer group was now in Kashgar. But whether it would search by air, or set up static roadblocks, was something Ritzik hadn't been able to decipher from Rockman's enigmatic words. God, how he would have liked the luxury of overhead surveillance.

Sam Phillips was convinced Zhou would use his air assets. Ritzik wasn't. "The Chinese haven't integrated their Special Forces into air ops yet," he said. "They have nothing like the SOAR."

"Common sense tells me they'll use what they have," Sam said. "They have aircraft—therefore they'll use them."

"Their choppers have no infrared capability," Ritzik said. "They're blind at night. Besides, they have no way of identifying nuclear devices from the air."

"How do you know that?"

"I know it," Tracy Wei-Liu interjected. "It's my job to know those things. The Russians have two helicopters in their inventory, the MI-8MTS and the MI-8MTT, which are radiation-reconnaissance-capable. The Chinese are still negotiating with Moscow to get the MTS and MTT enhancements on their aircraft."

"They're an ingenious people," Sam said. "They improvise—and they learn fast."

Ritzik switched his GPS unit on. "Look," he said. "Zhou is two hundred miles north of here. If they believe the IMU is heading northwest, they'll be concentrating here—" He tapped the screen. "We go here—hide ourselves during the daylight hours. Even if Mr. Murphy shows, we'll be able to get that far at least. Miss Wei-Liu will have all the time she needs to deal with the nuke." He tapped again. "And then, after dark, we head straight up there—into the mountains."

Sam threw up his hands. "You're running this, Major Ritzik," he said. "You do what you will."

Ritzik took Rowdy Yates aside. The two men studied the GPS screen and spoke quietly.

Sam Phillips walked over to where Wei-Liu stood. "He's wrong, you know. So're you."

"How can you be so sure?"

"Because both of you are making decisions based on nothing more than assumptions."

Wei-Liu said, "We are doing nothing of the sort. We're making empirical judgments."

She watched as Sam's right index finger pulled at the skin below his right eye—French body language denoting skepticism. "You're mocking me."

"Christ, the two of you sounded like our analysts at Langley. 'According to our most current economic statistical models, we can confidently predict that the Soviet economy will be fundamentally sound and perhaps even resilient for the next fifteen to twenty years, despite the considerable fiscal pressures of maintaining military and scientific parity with the West.' I have a copy of that particular assessment framed on my wall at home. Guess what? It was date-stamped and circulated the day before Mikhail Gorbachev formally dissolved the Soviet Union."

"But—"

"Look," Sam said. "I don't dispute that you know all about nuclear weapons. And that when it comes to hostage rescue or counterterrorism, the major is damn proficient. And I agree that we're much better off moving at night and hiding during daylight hours. Where I disagree is in underestimating the Chinese—and assuming their tactics will be rigid. These guys are good—and they're flexible."

Wei-Liu said, "I guess we'll see who's right in the next few hours, Mr. Phillips."

"I think we will, Miss Wei-Liu."

The Third Forty Hours
FUBAR

21

THEY COULD HEAR the choppers before they actually saw them, a slow crescendo of loud, reverberating *whomp-whomp-whomping* that echoed ominously off the rocky hills and deep ravines. The hair on the back of Ritzik's neck stood up. The sound made him feel vulnerable because it was impossible to figure out which direction the aircraft were actually coming from, or how many of them there were. The only thing he knew for certain was that they were closing in more and more with every passing second. It was, Ritzik decided, a hell of a way to start the day.

They'd halted just after zero six hundred, as the sky was going from midnight blue to dark purple. It seemed to take forever for the sun to come up, and the air was noticeably chilly—only in the high forties. As it grew light, shortly after seven, Ritzik saw why. Fifteen, perhaps twenty kilometers to the north and east, a line of awesome, jagged snow-covered peaks towered thousands of feet above the sparsely forested foothills. Beyond the range they could see, there was a second series of peaks. Beyond those lay Tajikistan, and safety. But they were still a long way off.

The party had left the desert floor behind shortly after

zero four-thirty. The transition had been abrupt. They'd gone from the lunarlike surface of sand and rock, then traversed a ten-klik swath of windswept, sixty-foot dunes, which in turn quickly gave way to steep, precipitous rocky hillocks. From the dunes on, it had all been uphill. The road along which they were currently bumping cut in S-curves between a series of ridges dotted with thorny scrub and clumps of dwarf evergreens bent like hunchbacks by wind and weather. It was rough, desolate, unforgiving terrain.

"Afghanistan without the charm," was how Rowdy'd put it just after first light.

"I see we're given to characteristic understatement this morning," Ritzik had answered.

AT ZERO SIX-TWENTY Rowdy called a halt—it was getting too light to go any farther. He detailed Goose and Tuzz to scout ahead, while Curtis and Shep grabbed one of the captured RPG launchers and four rockets and dropped back atop the ridgeline to make sure their six was clean. The rest of the party was detailed to cut boughs and brush to camouflage the vehicles. Which wasn't going to be easy. The big boxy truck would stand out—unless they buried the bloody thing, which wasn't an option. And so, while they could soften its lines and make it harder to spot from the air, anybody who was flying low and slow and wasn't blind couldn't help but see it.

The rear guard brought the first piece of news at zero seven-sixteen. "There's movement behind us," Curtis reported by radio. "One vehicle—maybe two. I'd say about twenty miles, coming west. More or less along the same track we were on. They're still on the desert floor, moving slowly. But they're raising dust."

Ritzik frowned. "How many people we talking about?"

"No way to tell that, Loner."

"Army?"

"Dunno. Could be. Could also be civilians on the move."
There was static in Ritzik's ear. Then: "Want us to set an
ambush?"

"No," Rowdy broke in. "You guys get your butts back
here. Let's not waste people or time. I don't want to expend
anything we don't have to. We'll keep an eye out. See how
the situation develops."

"Wilco."

Ritzik turned and looked around, searching. "Tracy?"

He finally spotted her clambering over the ridgeline.
"Where the hell—"

She picked her way through the scrub, blushing. "We
girls need some privacy, y'know."

"Sorry." He pointed toward the truck. "It's all yours."

"And about time." Wei-Liu patted the small canvas sack
she carried. "I was able to make some preliminary studies
overnight."

"How does it look?"

"Old. Fragile. The batteries are in terrible shape—you
can smell the acid. Obviously, I wasn't about to touch anything while we were bouncing around."

"Good idea."

She waited for him to say something else. When he
didn't, she said, "Okay, I'll get to work."

0728. She'd just laid out her tools and secured the rear flap
open to give herself some light when she thought she heard
the low rumble of distant thunder. Within seconds, Rowdy
appeared above the tailgate. She thought he and the rest of
them all looked somewhat ridiculous with their faces
striped with black, green, and brown camouflage cream.
She hadn't noticed in the dark. But in daylight, they simply
looked foolish.

"We got aircraft approaching, ma'am," he said. "You gotta clear out—take cover."

Wei-Liu stood her ground. "I'm perfectly all right where I am, Rowdy."

"The major wants you outside with him in case there's gunfire," Rowdy insisted. He vaulted into the truck, followed by Doc Masland. The pair of them rummaged through the crates until they came up with four RPG launchers and two haversacks each holding four of the 85mm rocket-propelled grenades. Rowdy handed a launcher and one of the haversacks to Ty Weaver, who was standing below the truck bed. The sniper pulled the rockets from their pouches, screwed the RDX-explosive warheads and sustainer motors into the tail-finned booster-charge units, slipped one of the assembled rockets into the mouth of the launcher, and held on to the other.

"Get that set to Mickey D," Rowdy said.

"Roger."

The sergeant major threw another pair of launchers over his shoulder and dropped his legs over the transom. "Doc—" Rowdy handed the remaining two armed rockets and one launcher to Masland. Then he reached for the remaining launcher and the haversack of projectiles and jumped off the truck. He looked back. "Ma'am . . ."

Wei-Liu stared at Yates until his expression told her she'd better move. "It would be nice . . ." She began to gather her tools.

"Ma'am," he said, "leave 'em right where they are. You're wasting precious seconds." He pointed through the truck cab. "The major's straight up the hill—sixty, sixty-five yards."

FROM JUST BELOW the ridgeline, Ritzik pressed his transmit button. "Goose, Loner. Sit-rep."

"Nada."

"What's your position?"

"A klik and a half out, to your northeast."

"Where the hell are they?"

Then Tuzz's voice: "I have a visual. Loner, they're coming from the south. Repeat, the south."

"How many?"

"Two." There was a pause. "HIPs, I think."

Goose broke in. "Confirm two HIPs, Loner."

Attack transports. That meant troops—HIPs could carry as many as twenty-four. Ritzik had war-gamed against HIPs in Israel, during joint exercises with *Sayeret Matkal,* the country's lead counterterrorist army unit. The choppers were agile, despite their size and weight. The Israelis had great respect for the big, boxy Special Operations aircraft, too: during the 1973 October War, the Egyptians had used one hundred of them to insert commandos behind Israeli lines in Sinai. Anwar Sadat's bold move had almost broken Israel's life-or-death counterattack.

The whine of the twin turboshafts grew louder, sound slapping off the landscape. "Here." Ty Weaver dropped the armed launcher and a second rocket into Mickey D's arms. The pilot swung the launcher around to make sure he had clearance, propped himself up so the backblast wouldn't do anybody any harm. Then he pulled scrub over himself.

The sniper dropped into a small revetment half a dozen yards from Ritzik. He uncapped the telescopic sight on the big HK, sighted through it, then dropped out of sight. Doc came up the ridge, rockets slung over his shoulder. He settled in fifteen yards from where Ty was concealed.

Wei-Liu followed—lagging behind.

"Tracy, get the hell up here now," Ritzik yelled. "Jeezus H."

She looked confused. She saw Mickey D, then finally spied Ritzik.

Who grabbed her by the arm roughly. "Get . . . down."

She settled next to him, irate. He reached into his pocket and brought out a small container. "C'mere."

Wei-Liu turned her face toward him. Before she knew what was happening, he'd daubed dark paste on her forehead, cheeks, and neck. She tried to pull away, but he held her firm.

"What the hell do you think—"

"Your skin reflects light," he said matter-of-factly. He peered at her face and applied more of the greasy cream. "They can see exposed skin from above." He smeared the backs of her hands and the exposed parts of her wrists. He turned her face left, then right, examining his work. Then he smudged more goop under her eyes and behind her ears.

She'd been self-conscious like this earlier. The forced intimacy of the parachute jump had made her uneasy. And yet there was something comforting about being close to Ritzik that had made Wei-Liu feel good; feel safe. And yet he was always distant; removed; disinterested. She'd never met anyone so intensely single-minded before.

Ritzik pointed toward a stunted conifer about ten yards away. The evergreen was partially obscured by a small rock outcropping. "See that tree? Get under it—squeeze as close to the trunk as you can. Then lie down—and stay down until I tell you otherwise."

The echoes from the chopper's big blades were more pronounced now—which meant they were getting close. He looked at Wei-Liu, his face dead serious. "Tracy . . ."

"Yes?"

"Do not move. Do not look up. Do not shift your position, or squirm." His face was severe. "Got it?"

"Yes, I got it." She was pissed at being told what to do. But his tone had conveyed the absolute gravity of the situation. She saluted. "Yes, sir, Major, sir."

He thrust her toward the tree, oblivious to sarcasm. "Go."

She'd no sooner settled under the little tree than the *whomp-whomp-whomping* grew unbearably loud—and then suddenly eased off, the rotor sound replaced by the high-pitched whine of the HIP's twin turboshaft engines.

And then Ritzik saw the first chopper as its bulbous, glass-enclosed snout rose above the south ridge, three hundred yards away, roughly two hundred feet above the ground. It was a troop transport all right—painted in the Beijing Military District camouflage colors: mottled blotches of gray, blue green, and tan. The flight deck was completely glass-enclosed. He could look past the windshield wipers and see the pilots in their khaki flight suits, their hands on the collective and cyclic controls, even the flight manuals stowed next to the seats and their legs running down to the pedals that controlled the tail rotor pitch.

He pressed his transmit button. "If we're spotted, take 'em out." When he realized what he'd just said, the enormity of it smacked him like a gut punch. He'd just single-handedly told his people to wage war against the duly constituted armed forces of the People's Republic of China. But there'd been no other option. They were cornered and they'd have to come out fighting.

The big bird shifted its attitude slightly, providing a broadside as it dropped its nose over the ridgeline and moved north. The port-side hatch was open—the door slid aft in its track and secured. A machine gun on an elbowed, free-floating gimbal mount protruded aggressively from the doorway. The gunner, in headphones and goggles, craned his head through the hatch.

As the chopper turned, Ritzik could make out the identification on the side of the fuselage and was surprised to see that the lettering was Western, not Chinese. He hunkered, hidden—he prayed—by the branches and the ground. But knowing in his heart that unless the chopper was being flown by Ray Charles and the machine gun was manned by Stevie Wonder, there was no way on God's earth that the truck and the 4×4 would go unseen. Face it: he was screwed.

Ritzik pressed his transmit button. "Ty—"

"Loner, Ty."

"The pilots. Shoot the pilots."

"Roger that."

From where Wei-Liu lay, she couldn't see the aircraft. But she could see Ty Weaver as he brought his long gun up over the edge of the rocks where he lay. The heavy black weapon was draped in cloth. The sniper had shredded one of the Russian anoraks and wound the green-, gray-, and brown-flecked camouflage fabric around the stock, barrel, and telescopic sight.

Weaver's voice in Ritzik's ear: "Got them." The muzzle of Weaver's rifle followed the chopper as it hovered for perhaps fifteen seconds above the ridgeline. Then the bird moved slowly to the north, carefully mimicking the S-curve of the road.

Weaver's voice again: "Lost the pilots—have the gunner."

Now a second HIP hove slowly into view. It flew two hundred yards behind and three hundred yards to the east of the first craft, engines screaming, rotors *thud-thud-thudding*. The second HIP lay back as the first chopper flew a slow and deliberate pass over the road, then disappeared over the northern end of the ridge where the Americans lay concealed.

Ritzik could see the machine gunner in the second chopper. He was hanging out the hatchway, scanning the ravine through field glasses. The goddamn aircraft was virtually on top of the truck before the asshole saw anything.

But he did see it. Ritzik could even see as the man's lips moved excitedly.

He watched, transfixed, as Chopper Two banked in a tight arc and the pilots confirmed visual contact.

The door gunner disappeared, then reappeared in the doorway. He kicked a rope ladder out of the second chopper. Now the first chopper eased back into view.

Mickey D's voice in Ritzik's ear: "Everybody hold until the first troops are on the ground and there's somebody on the ladder—the pilots will be concentrating on keeping the aircraft stable. Air currents in these ravines are treacherous."

Ty's voice: "Roger. I'm back on Aircraft One—got the pilots."

Rowdy's voice: "Doc, Mick, Bill: Chopper One; I got number two—me and the spooks."

Ritzik's voice: "Rowdy—Loner. What about me?"

Yates's voice came back fast. "Loner, you watch and pick up the pieces if we leave anything alive."

Rowdy shifted on the ground, checking his six to make sure that the backblast from the RPGs wouldn't smack the ground behind him and send pieces of rock into his back. There were no optical sights on these weapons, only the KISS[21] flip-up iron tangent sights favored by guerrillas and terrorists.

He looked over to where Sam Phillips and his two comrades lay concealed, some eight yards abreast of him. "I'm going for the aircraft—the door gunner," he called to them, his voice masked by the choppers. "You get the troops. You fire short bursts until they're all down."

Rowdy shifted focus. The door gunner was back at his post. He was dressed in Chinese Special Ops BDUs: olive-drab shirt over dappled, camouflage trousers. Unlike the

---

21. Keep-It-Simple-Stupid.

Delta shooters, he wore no body armor. In his peripheral vision, Rowdy caught the door gunner in Chopper One dropping a ladder as the big craft hovered five yards above the ravine floor. But his focus remained steady on the second aircraft. He chewed the droopy corner of his mustache, happy with the way he'd positioned his people. The choppers had to descend below the ridgeline, which made it harder for them to take evasive action because they were walled in by Mother Nature. Meanwhile, Rowdy and his people held the high ground.

Rowdy checked the spooks and saw that they were ready. "Sun-Tzu says there are six terrains to be considered when setting the location of battle," he said, looking in Kaz's direction. "On steep terrain, the first to claim the high positions and the sunny side will be victorious." He watched as the HIPs eased into the kill zone and then nodded at X-Man. "We've got the sunny side up today."

The Chinese troops—those who actually made it onto the ground alive—would be forced to move uphill toward them, with very little cover and no concealment. Rowdy looked toward Sam Phillips. "The contour of the land is of great help to the victorious army if the general knows how to use it to his advantage. Remember that, Sam I am."

Rowdy's right hand settled around the trigger grip; his left hand held the front-heavy launcher steady. He followed the target as it approached. Rowdy liked the RPG. It was lightweight—the launcher and four rockets weighed less than forty pounds. Much more man-portable than a Carl Gustav or the old Italian Folgore. Sure, it wasn't as accurate as either one. But at close quarters, which is all Rowdy worried about, it was deadly. Most of all, it was simple. And there were so many of them floating around that there was virtually nowhere on earth you went that you couldn't obtain one. More to the point, since your adversaries almost certainly carried RPGs just like you did, you could kill them and come away with extra rounds. That, certainly, had been his experience in Mogadishu and Kosovo, Colombia, the Philippines, Lebanon, and northern Iraq.

He fixed the big exhaust of the chopper's turbo engine in his sight. The bird was dropping slowly, slowly, now just fifteen feet off the road. The bottom of the ladder began to drag. A Chinese trooper, weapon slung over his back, swung out and clambered down, fighting the prop wash, the ground-effect vibration, and the ladder itself.

The son of a bitch almost fell as he caught a leg. Then he recovered, pulled himself up, got his leg free, and continued down two dozen rungs onto the road. He waved at the hatchway, then grabbed the ladder to stabilize it.

Rowdy waited until there were two men on the ladder. He saw the copilot's face, looking down and back, anxiously, as the soldiers descended. His eyes shifted to the door gunner. And then he lowered the sight picture slightly, and squeezed the RPG's trigger.

That action ignited a powder charge, which ejected the grenade from the launcher with a loud explosive *ka-boom* at 84 meters per second. Rowdy was careful to watch as the round flew away, to make sure that all four of the stabilizing fins had deployed. If one of them hadn't, the damn thing could cartwheel, reverse course, and come back to bite him on the ass. He knew that 5 meters—six one-hundredths of a second—after it left the muzzle, the grenade warhead had armed itself. After 11 meters—thirteen one-hundredths of a second—the sustainer rocket fired with a loud *shrieeek*. There was a huge flash, and the rocket accelerated to its full velocity: 294 meters a second.

Chopper Two was less than eighty meters from where Rowdy lay. It took less than a third of a second—.2721 of a second to be precise—for the rocket's Piezo-electric fuse to crush against the interior of the choppers starboard-side interior wall, igniting the 94 percent RDX high-explosive warhead.

The explosion blew the minigunner clear out of the aircraft. Rowdy could see wounded Chinese tossing themselves about inside the fuselage. The aircraft stuttered—maybe shrapnel had hit the hydraulics or guidance systems. It didn't matter. Either way, the pilots had to fight like hell to bring the chopper under control.

But Rowdy wasn't watching anymore. His attention had moved on to the second threat—the soldiers on the ground. He screamed, "C'mon, assholes—get the sons of bitches," at the spooks, who shook themselves out of whatever Langley-influenced stupor they were in and began to lay down a stream of suppressive fire at the Chinese troops.

And then Rowdy was reloading, quickly but firmly jabbing a second rocket into the blunderbuss muzzle of the launcher, bringing the weapon up onto his shoulder, and aligning his sight picture. The process took him less than seven seconds.

He fired again. The round cleared the RPG cleanly. But the chopper dropped precipitously as the pilot tried to keep his aircraft from spinning into the ground.

The HIP began to buffet. The rocket flew over the top of the bird and exploded against the far ravine wall.

Rowdy cursed. Quickly, he stuffed a third rocket—an OG-7 high-explosive fragmentation grenade—into the launcher's muzzle.

Now the chopper careened to the right, arcing away from him like a clay bird coming out of a skeet house. Teeth clenched, Rowdy swung the grenade launcher around, following the HIP's trajectory. He forgot about the iron sights. Instead, he let the wide RPG warhead overtake the center of the cockpit, almost as if he were swinging a big, lethal paintbrush. And just as he "painted" the leading side of the chopper's glassed-in nose with a smooth, even stroke, he pulled the trigger and *"Hoo-ah!"* remembered to follow through the swing.

22

FROM EIGHTY YARDS AWAY, Ty Weaver's 168-grain boat-tail bullet caught HIP One's pilot in the philtrum—that small indentation between the bottom of the nose and the top of the lip. The shot was catastrophic: the target's central nervous system was destroyed and he was brain-dead before he even realized he'd been shot. The chopper lurched vertically ten yards. The HIP's sudden movement shook three Chinese off the rope ladder. They fell hard, twenty-five feet onto the road below. One scrambled away. The other two lay stunned.

The sniper moved the crosshairs of his sight to his left, found his secondary target—the copilot's throat—and squeezed the trigger. Weaver saw the man's head snap sideways. Then the HIP corkscrewed to the right and dropped stonelike forty feet, smacking hard onto the roadbed and shearing its port-side tire off.

The chopper bounced once, then twice, crushing the two soldiers who'd fallen from the ladder. Ty squinted through the ten-power scope, and wasn't happy with what he saw: the copilot in profile, blood oozing from his neck, still alive, working frantically to operate the controls and save his aircraft. The sniper focused again, his pulse steady, his breathing even, his right index finger easing tighter on the trigger.

The HIP dragged itself to clockwise, blades kicking up dust and stones, rotating on its broken landing-gear strut. Ty cursed silently. Now—when he could see at all—what he saw was the profile of the pilot, head thrown back, strapped dead into his seat.

The pitch of the HIP's rotor blades changed audibly, and their velocity slowed. But the big bird still scraped across the ground. As it came around, Ty's scope picked up the minigunner. The poor bastard was fighting centrifugal force, trying to hold on but still vainly searching for a target. The sniper tracked the hatchway, led the target slightly, then squeezed the trigger, the rifle muzzle actually following through the shot. The door gunner pitched backward into the cabin and disappeared.

The HIP's nose smacked up against a boulder. The wounded bird finally came to rest. Ty's crosshairs settled on the cockpit. He saw the copilot's hand move on the collective handle. He raised the crosshairs until they found the zygomatic bone, the thin plate covering the brain between the eye and the ear. He eased the sight back, lifting the crosshairs until they touched the tip of the helix—the curled, upper edge of the target's ear. And then he squeezed the trigger, watching as the copilot's head disintegrated with the shot.

Ritzik blinked as the HIP ground itself to a halt. He raised himself out of his concealed position. "Mickey—" The pilot had the RPG leveled at the chopper. Why the hell wasn't he shooting? "Cream the goddamn thing," he ordered.

But Mickey D obviously had other ideas. "C'mon—" He dropped the RPG. "Ty—give us cover." He grabbed his AK and charged down the ravine toward the chopper, followed by Doc Masland and Bill Sandman.

Ritzik scrambled after the trio, pistol in hand. He was eight, maybe ten yards behind the other three, still crabbing down the ravine, when a bullet kicked up rock splinters six inches from his right foot. He spun, rolled to his left, and brought the pistol muzzle up.

A Chinese Special Forces soldier, helmet askew, was coming up the hill, firing his rifle from the hip. He shot wildly in Ritzik's direction, his eyes wide in double-take shock as he spotted Ritzik's camouflaged but unmistakably Occidental face. The rifle jammed.

The soldier dropped the weapon, reached into a pouch on his chest, and pulled out a grenade. Ritzik head-shot him—*tap-tap*—just as he was yanking the pin.

But not quickly enough. The spoon still flew. Time stood still. Ritzik watched as the small sliver of metal arced toward him. His eyes followed its trajectory, and saw behind it how beautiful and clear the morning sky was; how the high white clouds actually intensified the blueness. Ritzik threw his arms over his face and neck and tried to find cover behind the low rocks.

The Chinese crumpled. And he took the brunt of the blast. But not all of it. Something hot and sharp smacked into Ritzik's flak jacket, knocking the breath out of him. He rolled over, checked himself quickly. He was okay. He half crawled, half walked to the dead Chinese. The man had been cut in two. Ritzik rolled away, looking down the hill. Mickey D was already clambering toward the HIP, AK in hand.

The warrant officer ducked under the still-spinning rotor blades. He came upon a Chinese soldier lying crushed under the fuselage, weapon still in his hands. The warrant officer shot him once in the head, then moved forward, crouched, until he reached the hatchway. He reached in, his gloved hand caught the door gunner's harness, and he pulled the dead man out of the aircraft, drawing fire. The warrant officer dropped flat. Crawling, Mickey D made his way below the hatch, moving to the tail. Once he was safely beyond the opening, he slowly, slowly, raised himself until he could see the forward portion of the chopper, looking into the cockpit area.

He hand-signaled that the cockpit, at least, was clear. Doc Masland eased up to the opposite side of the open hatch, scanning as much of the tail portion of the fuselage as he could. Bill Sandman came up behind him. He put his left hand on Masland's shoulder to let him know he was in position.

Slowly, Masland "cut the pie," sliding closer and closer to the open hatchway to allow himself an ever-increasing slice of vision into the rear section of the fuselage. He could see most of the right side of the cargo cabin. The canvas troop benches were flush against the bulkheads. Masland's vision was obscured by a pile of what appeared to be cargo netting in the rear of the cabin.

Ritzik came up behind Mickey D. Sandman pointed groundward. Ritzik tapped the warrant officer, who dropped onto hands and knees. The Doc put a booted foot on Mickey D's back. Weapon at the low ready, he stepped quickly into the fuselage and moved directly to his rear, scanning as he went. Immediately, there was gunfire— three three-round bursts—from Masland's AK. Without hesitation, Bill Sandman stepped into the chopper cabin and moved in the opposite direction, edging toward the chopper's cockpit, his back to the fuselage bulkhead.

Most Special Operations units practice room-clearing with four- or six-man teams. Ritzik's Sword Squadron was different. His unit was capable of clearing rooms with two, four, six, eight, even ten men at a time, depending on the size of the space and the level of the threat. Moreover, Doc Masland and Bill Sandman had trained together for years, the pair of them clearing spaces that ran the gamut from trinity tenements to town houses, to apartments of all shapes and sizes. They'd taken down double-wides, center-hall colonials, ramblers, and eight-thousand-square-foot McMansions; they'd rehearsed on embassies, office suites, schools, barracks, even jails. They scenarioed ways of dealing with stairwells, hallways, and corridors with eccentric configurations. They'd practiced assaulting warehouses stacked with cargo containers, pallets, or floor-to-ceiling shelving. They'd learned how to clamber up icy North Sea oil rigs and board cruise ships in port or on the high seas; they'd worked on successful tactics to use for taking down buses, clearing trailer trucks, and attacking aircraft of every size and shape. And they'd even rehearsed dealing with hostage-taking no-goodniks who'd commandeered a transport chopper—a scenario, incidentally, more than thirty years old, dating from the Black September terrorists who'd killed Israeli athletes at the 1972 Munich Olympics.

And so, the two Delta shooters worked like the proverbial well oiled machine, flowing into the area without hesitation, the first man taking the long side of whatever space they were attacking, the second following to cover his teammate's weakest side.

Sandman understood exactly where Doc Masland was going to be. So when he sensed movement at his ten o'clock he knew it wasn't his brother-in-arms. Sandman's AK came up and his finger moved from its indexed position on the receiver to the trigger. His peripheral vision caught the movement again. He moved forward toward the threat, releasing one and then another three-shot burst as he advanced.

"My twelve—" Ritzik heard Sandman's voice in his earpiece. It was followed by one-two-three three-shot bursts. Now he stepped up and entered the chopper cavity. Moved quickly but smoothly heel-toe, heel-toe over the greasy decking, easing to his right along the bulkhead following in Doc Masland's trail, his pistol's field of fire centered on the far-side rear corner of the fuselage.

Doc shouted, "My two—" and fired two three-shot bursts.

There was movement at Ritzik's ten o'clock. His pistol came up and he put one-two-three-four shots into the target. It wasn't clean shooting but it was effective.

And then Ritzik's weapon locked back. He'd forgotten to count rounds. He was empty. Like some damn greenhorn on his first day in the shoot house. He was a freaking overpaid RTO. He shouted, "Cover!"

Without removing his gaze from possible threats, Ritzik dropped the magazine out of the well, slipped to one knee, retrieved a fresh fifteen-rounder from his thigh and smacked it into place with the flat of his hand, then released the slide with his right thumb. He shouted, "Okay!" and stood.

Just in time to catch movement at his twelve. Ritzik and Masland shot simultaneously and a Chinese soldier went down. Masland was moving now, using his foot to kick weapons away from dead hands. Quickly, he checked the bodies for signs of life. He found none. He shouted, "Clear!"

Mickey D vaulted into the chopper and made for the cockpit. He reached over the bodies for the power switches and shut the engines down. "Bill, gimme a hand." The pair of them pulled the dead pilot and his number two out of their shoulder harnesses and seat belts. They dragged the corpses aft and rolled them out of the hatch. The pilot slapped the HIP's airframe. "I'm going to see if it's still fly-able," he said to his partner.

Ritzik helped Doc Masland pull six Chinese soldiers out of the HIP's cargo cabin. With the door gunner, the two pilots, and the other three from the ladder, there were ten in all. Ritzik pressed the transmit button on his radio. "Rowdy, Loner—sit-rep me."

Rowdy's voice came back strong. "We got fourteen hostile DOAs and one aircraft down, Loner. No friendly casualties."

That was good news. And there was more: Bill Sandman reported that HIP One's machine gun was operational, with two seven-hundred-round ammo containers secured adjacent to the doorway. Rowdy discovered a third box undamaged in HIP Two.

0751. Ritzik detailed a six-man crew to hide the corpses. He didn't want them visible from the air. He was pleased to see his Soldiers handle the Chinese dead with respect. An hour ago they'd been fathers, sons, brothers. Now they were unwitting casualties of a shadow war, and their remains didn't deserve to be mistreated. War, Mike Ritzik thought, is full of paradoxes, some far more difficult to grasp than others.

He watched for a few seconds more, then struggled back up to the crest of the ravine to find Wei-Liu. She was still where he'd left her. She sat, hunkered, her arms tucked around her knees, her face and neck still smeared with cammo cream, although it was obvious to Ritzik that she'd tried to remove it. She didn't look happy.

"What's up?"

"You just . . . killed them all . . ." she said.

Ritzik was not in the mood for clichés. "What's your point?"

Wei-Liu started to say something. But Ritzik cut in first. "People like you think war is sterile," he said, "because that's the way you've seen it, on television. Oh, you see wounded kids. You see the casualties of suicide bombers. You see victims. God, how good television is at showing victims. But that's not war. War is chaos. War is nasty stuff. It's about killing people. Killing people and breaking things. War is not nice, Tracy. It's not a computer game, or a movie. It's horrific. It's blood and pain and violence and confusion, and mistakes that cost lives and idiots issuing orders that get people killed. But when it comes down to the real nitty-gritty, war is about killing other human beings, before other human beings kill you."

He looked down at her. "So, yes, we killed them all. What would you have me do? Declare a time-out? Ask them to leave us alone? Make 'em promise not to tell anybody we were here and send 'em on their way? For chrissakes, Tracy, we're violating China's sovereignty. That's a bloody act of war. Can you imagine the consequences if one of us was captured?"

"I hadn't thought about it in that way."

Why the hell hadn't she? She was a freaking high government official. She should have "thought about it that way." Ritzik bore down on her. "Why not? After all, you had a hand in designing the sensors—and they're the reason we're here."

"But that's different."

"Is it?"

"Of course it is. The sensors are technical tools. They're no different from a satellite, or the kind of SIGINT or TECHINT the National Security Agency gathers."

"Except for one element," Ritzik said.

"Which is?"

"Four people had to put their lives on the line to plant

your so-called technical tools," he said. "And in order to position them they had to violate China's sovereignty. They had to infiltrate covertly." He paused. "Just like we did."

"But *they* didn't come to kill—anybody. You did."

"We didn't come to kill," Ritzik said. "We came to do whatever it took to get the job done," Ritzik said. "We did what we had to."

"But—"

"But what?"

"I don't see how you can live with yourself."

Oh, Christ. "The problem with people like you—"

Her eyes flashed. "What do you mean, 'like me'?"

"I mean," Ritzik said, "like you. Smarter-than-thous. Piled-higher-and-deepers. Diplomats. Scientists. Technocrats. Thumb-suckers. Head-shedders. Think-tankers. Pundits. Know-it-all journalists. Lobbyists. Political appointees. Congressmen. Senators. Highfalutin moral hypocrites, my father used to call 'em. That's what I mean. People like you. When there's a crisis, people like you scream and yell and beg folks like me to fix it. Go after Usama bin Laden and wax his butt. Break into Saddam Hussein's palace at Tikrīt and blow him into the well-known smithereens. Sneak into Bosnia, neutralize a dozen or so goons, and bring a Navy pilot back. Drop into the Bekáa Valley and dispatch Imad Mugniyah and the Hizballah high command. Track down Pablo Escobar and shoot the sucker dead. But no collateral damage, please. And no mistakes. Oh—and you can kill them, but don't tell us about it, okay? None of that nasty stuff—because hearing about blood and death and pain might make us uncomfortable. And then, when it's all over, and you've done your dirty jobs, please leave. Go back to your cage, or crawl under whatever rock it is that you headquarter."

"That's neither fair nor the truth."

"The truth? The truth is exactly what you just said: 'I don't see how you can live with yourself.' The answer is, I live with myself very well. I like what I see in the mirror when I shave. The problem isn't me, Tracy. It's that people like you consider what I do to be uncivilized. Unseemly. Antisocial. Trust me: it makes people like you hugely uncomfortable to be in the same room as people like me."

"That hasn't been my experience."

"Oh, really. How many soldiers do you know, Tracy?"

"How many piled-high-and-deepers do you know, Major?"

He really didn't have time for this BS. Not now. He turned on his heel and started toward the crest of the ridge. "Currently? One. Which is a sufficient statistical model to substantiate my case, so far as I'm concerned." He turned and pointed toward the truck. "We have carved you out a little time now. Maybe you should start work."

23

**125 Kilometers East-Northeast of Tokhtamysh.
0758 Hours Local Time.**

RITZIK WATCHED, so infuriated he was shaking, as Wei-Liu picked her way around the vegetation, descending carefully toward the ravine floor. "Workmanlike attitude, Mike. Workmanlike attitude." He repeated the mantra half a dozen times aloud, hoping it would calm him down.

Sure, perhaps he'd overstated the case. But not by much. The core of what he'd said was sadly true. Between the demands for politically correct, zero-defect missions and the realities of the twenty-four-hour Internet and television news cycle, there was very little a Special Operations unit could accomplish without being scrutinized, second-guessed, and micromanaged by a laundry list of individuals, organizations, government agencies, and chain-of-command factotums.

Christ, in Afghanistan some IWS—idiot wearing stars—from Tampa had seen a digital picture in a postaction report and was so outraged by how native the Special Forces operators had gone that he ordered all the SF troops in Afghanistan to shave their beards and cut their hair so they'd look more "military." The asshole didn't care that his order caused hundreds of shooters, who'd worked like hell to blend in with their Afghan surroundings, to become Obvious American Targets. But that was par for the course. In fact, these days, the formal postaction mission analyses that were invariably conducted by SOCOM's by-the-numbers staff to ensure that "proper doctrine" had been followed were closer in gestalt to colonoscopies than they were to any sort of previously established military procedures.

Which was why the current acronym around the Combat Applications Group for a SOCOM staff review was BO-HICA, which stood for Bend Over, Here It Comes Again. And you didn't want them finding any polyps, either. Polyps—even benign ones—could prove terminal to your career.

During the Second World War, they hadn't second-guessed Henry Mucci and his Sixth Ranger Battalion. Mucci's bosses had simply turned him loose and told him to get the job done any way he could. An order put like that, Ritzik knew, gave a commander flexibility, the freedom to lead from the front, and the luxury of occasional failure on the way to victory. It allowed an officer to employ individualism, initiative, and audacity. Today, those character traits were likely to get you a letter of reprimand. Of course, Mucci didn't have CNN war tarts, Fox News Scud studs, Sunday-talk-show second-guessers, or al-Jazeera to worry about either. Or for that matter, an Army chief of staff who thought buying new berets was more important than buying bullets.

But then, this was the new Army. The Army of One (although precisely one *what* was manifestly unclear). This was the Army in which three soldiers who were lured across the Macedonian border, and who surrendered to Serb irregulars without firing a shot, were actually awarded three medals each—citations for giving up without a fight. Colonel Mucci must have been spinning in his grave over that one.

And a few years later, Johnny Vandervoort, CENT-COM's commander, had led—if you could actually call it leading—the campaign in Afghanistan from the manicured safety and four-star comfort of MacDill Air Force Base, half a world away. It was another sorry military first for the Army of Washington, Grant, Patton, Merrill, and Beckwith: war by speakerphone.

While Ritzik and his people had been freezing their asses off in the mountains, COMCENT and his staff worked regular hours. Somehow, the guys with stars on their collars managed to get in their eighteen holes on MacDill's PGA-grade golf course. Somehow, their aides always roused them in time for an early set of tennis before the daily conference call to Bagram Air Base. And while Ritzik and the rest of his team ate roasted horse anus and grilled sheep's brain, the generals went off to dinner at Bern's steak house, where the wine list ran thirty or so pages of fine print.

Ritzik wasn't resentful about the disparity of lifestyle. Rank, after all, has its privileges. And he'd actually grown perversely fond of roasted horse anus after the first month or so. What he took exception to was the vacuum of leadership and loyalty demonstrated by his Florida hibernation. COMCENT was remote, aloof, and distant—both literally and figuratively. To those who actually prosecuted the war he was far more an abstract concept than a flesh-and-blood combatant commander.

The problem was compounded further because Johnny Vandervoort was not in his heart or soul a man o' warsman, but a manager of war's men. Oh, he was a talented manager; a decent if stiff and standoffish peacetime general well versed in flowcharts, PowerPoint presentations, and systems analysis. He even had a master's degree in public administration from the University of Pennsylvania. But he was absolutely the wrong man in the job of war fighter. Because this new kind of warfare, Ritzik understood, needed a Grant—a doer—motivated to succeed by private demons, not a McClellan—a ponderer—who preferred even-keel, slow-paced stability to the uncomfortable, rushed tumult of warfare.

0801. "Workmanlike attitude, Mike. Workmanlike attitude." Ritzik climbed the crest of the ravine, took a few seconds to appreciate the brilliantly blue sky, then faced west. He looked longingly at the mountain range in the distance, frustrated by the way things were going. If there were two choppers in the area, there'd be more. But from where were they coming? And how many?

He pulled the retaining flap from the radio on his vest, reached down, and for the eighth time in two hours switched frequencies to try to contact Almaty. "TOC, Loner."

He was amazed to hear Dodger's voice reverb into his earpiece. "Loner, this is the TOC."

Ritzik excitedly pulled a marker and a notebook out of his cargo pocket. "Sit-rep, TOC. We've been running in circles out here with no eyes, no ears, and a bunch of hostiles chasing our behinds."

Dodger's voice came back five-by-five. "You can think that if you like, Loner, but from what we saw, we suggest you change your call sign."

"To what?"

"Tommy."

"Come again?" Ritzik didn't have time for this nonsense.

"Tommy."

"Come again?"

"Tommy. Because for a bunch of deaf, dumb, and blind guys, you sure play a mean pinball."

"Compliment accepted. Now stop kissing my ass and

give us what the hell we need before the damn comms screw up again."

0802. Sam Phillips climbed into the HIP's cockpit and plunked himself down next to Mickey D. "Hi. I'm Sam. Rowdy Yates says you actually fly these things."

"That's why he's a sergeant major. He's always right."

Sam said, "You ever fly one like this? A HIP?"

"Once," the warrant officer said. "During a training course on former Soviet equipment. About three years ago."

"No kidding."

"Flew an MI-24P gunship, and a HIP. Except it wasn't this model. This is a HIP-H—a hot-and-high. It's a second-generation aircraft, configured for high altitude and hot climate. I flew the C version. First generation. A lot more basic."

"All HIPs look alike to me," Sam said. "How do you tell?"

"First-generation HIPs had their tail rotors on the starboard side," Mickey D said. "These newer ones have theirs to port."

"I'll remember that," Sam said, impressed. "Use it when I play Trivial Pursuit." He toyed with the cyclical handle.

"You ever want to fly choppers?"

"*Moi?* No way. I hate flying. Besides, helicopters are far too complicated. Y'know, kinda like rubbing your stomach and patting your head at the same time. I could never do that. But I drove a T-72 tank, once."

Mickey D turned toward the spook. "Why? Were you in the Russian Army?"

Sam gave the pilot a bemused look until he realized his leg was being pulled. "A guy I knew ran a mechanized infantry battalion," Sam said. He pointed toward the snow-capped mountains to the west. "About a hundred miles that way. In Tajikistan. A lieutenant colonel. He let me drive one of his tanks for a couple of hours."

"Sounds cool."

"It was better than cool. I got to crush two cars driving on the training course. It was like being in a *Die Hard* movie." Sam scratched his chin. "Funny thing: in the late eighties, I spent about eighteen months and about half a million tax dollars trying to convince a certain . . . group of people to let me photograph the inside of a T-72. It never happened. And then, all of a sudden, when I least expected it, I got an invitation to drive one."

"You get your pictures?"

"All I wanted," Sam said. "Of course, when I sent them off to Langley, no one was interested anymore." He paused. "But that didn't matter. Because you know what it cost me? Three bottles of vodka. Ten bucks' worth of booze—and a two-day hangover." He looked at the instrument panel and tapped the radio. "Hey, this thing work?"

"Dunno," Mickey D answered. "I don't do Chinese—neither does anybody on the team. So I didn't bother to check."

"I do a little Chinese," Sam said. He saw the dubious expression on Mickey D's face. "Well, enough to read a menu, anyway."

"Read a menu, huh?" Mickey D examined the instrument console. "Wow—nothing but steam gauges," he said.

"Huh?"

"Everything in this cockpit is analog. The chopper I usually fly is all glass."

Sam tapped the wraparound windshield. "This looks like glass to me."

"I'm talking display," Mickey D said. "At the SOAR, our MH-47Es have TV screens—four of them. Everything is digital—attitude indicators, hover page, radar altitude hold.

You can even upload data from a laptop—flight plan, navigation, comms—and it's all in front of your nose instantaneously."

"You're speaking a language I don't understand," Sam said.

"Not like Chinese, huh?" Mickey D flipped a trio of switches. Sam watched as a series of lights flickered to life on the instrument panel. The pilot took a headset from the deck between the seats, wiped the blood and brain matter off on his anorak, and pointed the big plug at a jack on the console. "R-842 high-freq radio," he said, smacking the plug home. "Two-to-eight megahertz. Range is about a thousand kliks in good weather and no mountains."

"Take a listen." The pilot handed the bulky apparatus to Sam. He pointed. "That's the transmit button. If you understand enough to read a menu maybe you could order us some takeout."

0806. "Rowdy—Loner. Meet me at the truck." Ritzik scampered down to the ravine floor. He saw Sam Phillips through the HIP's windshield and waved at him to join them. He watched as the CIA officer's index finger pointed straight up, indicating "wait a second."

Sam pulled the headset off. "Thanks."

"No prob." Mickey D watched as the spook sidled out of the cockpit. "So, what's on the menu?"

"Trouble." Sam jumped out of the hatch and jogged to where Ritzik stood. He jerked his thumb toward the HIP. "You're about to have company," he said.

"I know."

"How?"

"I finally reached the TOC in Almaty. They have satellite imagery."

Sam nodded. "What's the story?"

"Chinese are coming out of Kashgar. Two aircraft: a HIP and a gunship. According to what Dodger told me, the original flight was three transports and two gunships—run by some Special Forces general out of Beijing. Obviously he's holding one of the gunships back."

"From the chatter, they're making good time," Sam said. "They're not holding anything back."

"You heard them?"

"On the radio. Mick got it working."

"What are they saying?"

"You gotta understand I pick up about every third word," Sam said. "But the gist of it—at least I think so—was they think two of their choppers were attacked by a large terrorist element. They're going to use the first two choppers to draw the enemy out, and use the second HIND to flank the tango position and attack from the rear."

"I think—" Ritzik pressed his right hand against his earpiece. "Come again?" He listened intently. "Roger that, Shep.

"We've got more company than expected," he said. He looked at Sam. "Your IMU pal Mr. Mustache is coming back, too."

All the color drained from Sam's face. For an instant his eyes went dead—the face of a serial killer. And then he looked at Ritzik, smiling as cold a smile as Ritzik had ever seen, and said, "It's my natural charm. He can't stay away."

Ritzik frowned, momentarily knocked off course. Then he fiddled with the radio. "TOC, Loner—" There was a momentary pause. "TOC, we're gonna stay on the air until further notice. I need play-by-play tactical overhead." He paused. "Roger that."

Ritzik saw Rowdy Yates jump off the tailgate of the big truck. He put two fingers to his lips, whistled shrilly to get the sergeant major's attention, and beckoned him over.

"How's she coming?"

"She's got the damn thing opened up." Rowdy stroked his Fu Manchu mustache. "I wish we had an exhaust fan. The battery fumes are pretty damn strong."

Ritzik said, "Why not just pull the canvas off the frame?"

"I asked. Steel grommets. Steel frame. She's worried about static electricity."

"From canvas?"

"From everything," Yates said. "The HE[22] is sweating. That is one nervous woman, boss."

"With reason." Ritzik flicked a pebble with the toe of his boot. "Tell Bill to slice the canvas so she has some light."

"Gotcha." The sergeant major wiped a big hand over his bald head. "I gotta tell you—if it had been me working on that thing, we'd all be vaporized by now."

Abruptly, Ritzik said, "Rowdy, we need to buy her some time. You set an ambush—hit the sons of bitches three, four miles down the road."

Yates blinked. "Who? Where?"

Ritzik pointed east. "Satellite says three trucks, four pickups. The TOC estimates we have about forty minutes— maybe as much as an hour."

"That's not a lot of time." The sergeant major's face grew grim. He jerked his thumb toward the truck. "She needs more than that."

"I understand."

"Not a lot of alternatives either."

"Huh?"

"We used up the claymores, Mike. We have Semtex, and a couple of boxes of grenades, and maybe a dozen RPG rounds—and that's all, except small arms."

---

22. High Explosive.

Ritzik said, "You could rig the Semtex—cook up a land mine."

Rowdy pulled at his mustache. "Maybe," he said. "If I can come up with a way to shape the charges."

Ritzik said: "Just do it."

Sam Phillips blinked. "Take Chris—X-Man—with you. He was first in his class in car-bomb school."

Rowdy looked dubious. "Car-bomb school? Who the hell taught that, Hizballah?"

"Close," Sam said. "Fatah."

Rowdy's eyes widened. "Give me a break."

"No—it's the truth. X led one of the first teams to train the Palestinian National Authority as a part of the state-building security programs CIA ran in the mid-nineties. It was a result of the Oslo Accords. CIA contractors taught them crisis driving and VIP protection down in Lakeland, Florida. CIA employees taught countersurveillance, inter-rogation, secure comms—all the tradecraft they'd need to build a security/intel apparatus once they got their own Palestinian state—at a secure site in North Carolina."

"You can't be serious."

"Serious? This was approved at the highest levels," Sam said. "Of course the Palestinians turned it all around. In-stead of making peace with the Israelis, they used every-thing we'd taught them to wage war against 'em."

"Well," Rowdy said. "It is, after all, the Middle East."

"Precisely. Anyway, X-Man met this guy from Fatah who'd spent ten years in an Israeli jail for making bombs. He was known as the Engineer. He taught X the basics of his craft. In return, X gave him rudimentary edged-weapons training."

Rowdy said, "Throat slicing in exchange for car bomb-ing. I like it. And all in the name of nation building."

"Are we a great country or what?" Sam said. "I mean—"

"Hate to interrupt your history lesson, Sam," Ritzik broke in. "But some of us gotta get to work."

0814. "Boss—" Mickey D loped over to where Ritzik stood listening intently to an update from the TOC. Ritzik's hand went up in the pilot's face like a traffic cop's. "Hold a sec."

Ritzik nodded. "Roger that. Loner out." The news was not good. The Chinese were airborne. Judging from the overhead, they were loaded for bear. He focused on the warrant officer. "What's up?"

Mickey D jerked his thumb in HIP One's direction. "It's flyable, if not quite landable. But if I set it down gently, we might just walk away."

The chopper was an option he hadn't considered until now. Ritzik stared at the chopper, his brain spinning. There was no way they'd outrun the Chinese—not HIND gunships anyway. Mustache Man and the IMU were closing fast. And Wei-Liu had disassembled enough of the MADM to make it nigh on impossible to move it. Three nasty balls in the air. The question was, which one to shoot first.

That wasn't hard. The way Ritzik saw it, the most pressing problem was buying Wei-Liu sufficient time to get her job done. Once she'd rendered the device safe, they could all get the hell out of Dodge and scramble over the Tajik border. That was where SECDEF had told him to go. Rockman had passed the word to the TOC that there was a Special Forces training element in Dushanbe and the president was scrambling them. The SF people would move by chopper to Tokhtamysh. There, they'd be put on backchannel comms to Ritzik's TOC in Almaty. If he could just make it across the border, they'd be waiting for him. But the training group was an overt unit. They couldn't come get him. Their ROEs didn't allow them to violate Chinese sovereignty.

So he had to buy Wei-Liu time. And the best way to do that

was to take the battle to the enemy. From what Sam Phillips had been able to decipher from listening in on the Chinese, the PLA element in Kashgar understood that two of their HIPs had come under fire from a large IMU element. That gave Ritzik a tactical advantage—albeit a slim one.

"What's the fuel situation?"

"External tank is about half full. Internal tanks are virtually topped off."

"How much time does that give us?"

"Fuel's about eighteen hundred liters. That translates into just over two hours of flight time."

Ritzik nodded. "What about the other chopper? Can we bleed fuel out of it?"

"If there's a dry bladder tank in the stowage compartment behind the cockpit. I haven't checked, but if there is one and it wasn't shot up, we could use it to siphon avgas and top off the external on HIP One."

"There's no time for that now," Ritzik said. "But I'll get some people on it." He turned. "Rowdy—"

The burly sergeant major fishhooked. "Yo."

"Check on the fuel situation. I'm going to take the chopper. We'll go after the IMU force. What I'm hoping to do is make enough noise to get the Chinese coming out of Kashgar involved—draw them away from you."

"Gotcha."

"You guys stay here—most important thing is to give the lady time to work on the weapon."

"Roger that." The sergeant major gave the area a quick once-over. "Y'know, Loner, maybe we could make it look like the PLA won this one."

"Great idea. If you go that route, you'll have to move the nuke," Ritzik said. "As soon as she does whatever she has to—bare minimum—get the damn MADM out of the truck. Camouflage it—give her space to work, but keep the damn thing out of sight. Flip the truck if you can. Burn it. And set the chopper off, too—once you drain the avgas."

"Can do. We'll make it look like this was the IMU advance party—and it was decimated."

Ritzik said, "Hide the 4×4. You can't let 'em see it, Rowdy—not a hint." He pointed up the slope. "Set up defensive positions—improvise a couple of shaped charges and set 'em. But don't initiate anything unless they're about to overrun you." He looked at the sergeant major. "Oh, hell, Rowdy, you've forgotten more about this than I'll ever know."

"Roger that, Loner."

"But get everybody home. In case things go south and we don't make it back, you take the 4×4 and get everybody out—Tajikistan."

"You'll come away just fine."

"Maybe. But the bottom line is evade and escape, Rowdy. No tracks, no evidence." Ritzik took in Sam Phillips's skeptical expression. "Look, I figure if Mick and I can shift the Chinese eastward—where Mustache Man is coming from—we can focus the PLA on them, instead of us."

"Since you like long odds I have a real estate proposition you might be interested in," Sam said. "A seaside hotel and health spa in Chechnya—it's a Red Roof Inn, run by real Reds. The saunas are all heated with napalm. I can let you have it for thirty cents on the dollar."

"Okay, so I believe in Santa Claus, too," Ritzik said. "You have a better idea?"

The CIA officer's face grew serious. "No." He shrugged. "Actually I don't." He looked at Ritzik. "Let me come with you. I'd like a crack at Mustache Man."

Mickey D said, "Boss, I'll need a second pair of hands in the cockpit."

Ritzik looked at the spook. Finally, he said, "You could work the radio—translate."

Sam shrugged. "Anything you need."

Ritzik focused on the sergeant major. "I want to take Ty with me. And one more to help crew the chopper."

Yates said, "Take Gino."

"Good." Ritzik scanned the cloudless sky. "Rowdy—"

"Loner?"

Ritzik's face was a mask. "You do what you have to. Whatever it takes."

"Wilco." Yates's expression told Ritzik the message had been received.

Ritzik turned to the pilot. "Mick, let's go hunting. Get the bird ready to fly."

24

MICKEY D STRAPPED HIMSELF into the pilot's seat. Sam Phillips pulled the shoulder straps tight and attached them to the waist belt. Then the spook reached down, plucked the big headset off the console, and clamped it around his ears. Ritzik and Gene Shepard held on to the flight-deck support struts, watching as the pilot's left hand used the collective control to add throttle and increase the pitch of the HIP's rotor blades. The ravine filled with sand and loose brush as the twin turboshafts increased thrust and the six blades began to bite the morning air.

The HIP raised itself, shaking wildly as the broken gear cleared. Mickey D fought the controls. The ravine walls were the problem. The steep incline created unnatural turbulence. The rotors weren't getting enough air, and the HIP didn't want to lift off—and if it did, there was a good chance he'd slam back groundward. He eased the chopper back onto the ground, listing dangerously to port. Dammit, the big chopper was out of balance. There was at least two hundred kilos more weight on the starboard side, where the external fuel tank hung.

Mickey D tried to remember what the side clearance for

a HIP was, and drew a blank. Well, if he had a hundred feet of clearance on either side, he'd be okay. He looked to port and starboard. Not close.

"You guys get your asses aft," Mickey D shouted. "Help me balance this thing out."

"Roger." Ritzik hand-signaled Gene Shepard, and the two of them edged aft, to where Ty Weaver had strapped himself and his big sniper rifle into port-side seats. The aircraft rose once more, lifting jerkily. The first sergeant found one of the crew safety harnesses, shrugged into it, and fastened it securely. Ritzik stopped amidships, holding on to a bulkhead strut with his right hand. His left pointed toward three boxes of machine-gun ammunition, stowed against the starboard bulkhead. "Let's move this."

Ritzik had already started for the opposite side of the cabin when the HIP rolled violently to port, corrected, and shot vertically twenty yards into the air. He was tossed clean off his feet and catapulted toward the open door. Shepard, strapped in, one-handed the shoulder strap on Ritzik's body armor before he pitched out the hatch. The lanky soldier dragged Ritzik aft, found a safety harness, and attached it to him.

Then the three of them got to work. There was one seven-hundred-round ammo box already attached to the machine-gun arm, the belted rounds positioned in the feed tray. Ty secured the weapon, which was swinging freely on its pintle arm, while Ritzik and Gino unstrapped the two additional ammo boxes, dragged them port, and secured them where they'd be easy to reach using webbing attached to the canvas troop seats.

Ritzik saw something strapped down across two of the rearmost seats. He clambered aft and found the RPG launcher and three rockets that the first sergeant had brought aboard. Jeezus H. Kee-rist. Unless it was fired at just the right angle, the backblast would bring the HIP down like a rock. Ritzik started to say something, but Shepard cut him off. "Don't worry, Loner—I got it all figured out."

The big chopper's nose tilted down now. As the aircraft rose into the morning sky, Mickey D increased the cyclic pitch so that as the rotor blades passed over the tail of the aircraft, they chewed more air than they did when they passed over the nose. The chopper flew forward, circling slowly.

Ritzik looked down through the open doorway. He could see his people moving purposefully, stripping the downed HIP, carrying equipment, setting explosives. They were, Ritzik noted, doing what they did best: soldiering. For an instant, it flashed across his mind that he might not see any of them again. But that's the way it was. At the compound, you never knew if the brother-in-arms you had a cup of coffee with at zero six hundred, and who departed for Beirut, Lima, Kinshasa, or Kashgar at thirteen hundred would make it back. Delta operators were consummate warriors; the best-trained, most highly motivated shooters in the world. They were comfortable with themselves, and with their abilities, confident they could prevail in any situation, anywhere. But in the end, you could never really know how events would play out. That existential uncertainty was something people like Ritzik accepted; an integral part of their life's equation. You assumed it like a mantle when you were accepted into the Unit. It was a fundamental part of the equipment—both physical and psychological—that you carried every time you left on an assignment.

Ritzik caught a glimpse of Rowdy clambering over the tailgate of the big truck. They hadn't said good-bye. They wouldn't have. Good-byes weren't a part of their lexicon the way greetings were. And then the chopper banked away, Mick turned east, the HIP flew into the sun, keeping a steady three hundred feet above the ridgeline, and Ritzik lost sight of them all.

132 Kilometers East-Northeast of Tokhtamysh. 0829 Hours Local Time.

THERE WAS NO USE trying to talk—there was far too much engine noise. Ritzik looked to see if there were any headsets in the cabin, but found none. So he tapped Gino's body armor, pointed at the machine gun, and mimed firing it.

The first sergeant nodded in the affirmative. His big gloved hands opened the feed cover to make sure the heavy rounds had been seated in the tray correctly. He slapped the cover closed, dropped the operating handle downward, and pulled it to the rear, then eased it forward. He flipped the machine gun's rear sight up, unstrapped the arm, sighted, flicked the safety downward, and squeezed the trigger, loosing a six-round burst earthward. Shepard stuck out his lower lip as if to say, *Not bad,* and gave Ritzik an upturned thumb.

Ty pulled the rifle out of its case. He crossed the cabin, unlatched the starboard-side door, and slid it aft, ramming it home and securing the safety strap.

Ritzik made his way forward, stuck his head through the flight-deck hatchway, and squeezed Mickey D's shoulder. The pilot turned his head toward Ritzik. "We're stable," he shouted. "Gonna be okay."

"Good." Ritzik pointed through the windshield. "Follow the road," he shouted. "You'll see them soon—they're about twelve miles behind us."

"You got it."

"But don't get close. Stand off a few miles. I want to wait for the Chinese." He leaned toward Sam. "Anything out of Kashgar?"

"Negatory."

"Keep listening. I'm going to check the TOC." He rapped the spook's shoulder. "Headset?"

Mickey D jerked his head sideways. "Sam—it's by my left leg."

The spook reached over and fumbled next to the pilot's calf and came up with one. Ritzik pulled the big muffs on over his radio headset to mask the engine noise. He slipped back into the cabin, pulled a troop seat down, and dropped into it. "TOC, Loner."

"Lo . . . OC."

Ritzik repeated the call sign. But all he got out of the frigging radio was static. He stood up, made his way aft, secured himself close to the open doorway, and tried once, twice, thrice again without result.

And then, after fifteen seconds of ominous, infuriating silence, Dodger's voice blasted into his head. "Loner, TOC."

Ritzik exhaled. He fumbled in his cargo pocket, brought the GPS unit out, switched it on, and read out the HIP's coordinates. "Can you give me a position for the Chinese?"

He listened for a response from the TOC, then asked, "Speed?" Ritzik entered the information in his own unit, waited, then squinted at the small screen. "I get fifty-three minutes," he said. "Please confirm." Ritzik listened to the response. "Roger that." Then he switched frequencies. "Rowdy, Loner. You have a fifty-three-minute countdown. Repeat: five-three-minute countdown. Please confirm."

125 Kilometers East-Northeast of Tokhtamysh. 0829 Hours Local Time.

WEI-LIU WAS not having an easy time of it. And now, on top of everything, Rowdy'd just told her he had to move the damn device within the next couple of minutes and no, he couldn't wait. Yet all she'd managed to do in just over a half hour was to disconnect the battery. And even that hadn't been simple.

The four nuts were corroded by acid, moisture—who knew what. It had taken every bit of her strength to loosen them from the bolts. She wasn't worried about sparks because her tools were nonmagnetic. And she'd had four of the Delta Soldiers elevate the weapon so she could slide the thin, three-foot-square antistatic pad from her kit bag under the bomb. But between the energy field and static charges generated by the chopper as it took off, the sorry condition of the batteries, and the huge amount of energy still stored in the capacitors—with no way to drain them in this outdoor environment—the situation was still far more volatile than she would have liked.

She was sweating, even though it was no more than fifty degrees. At least she wasn't worried about radiation. The core of the device was adequately shielded. Oh, yeah, she'd ascertained that significant factoid immediately. But the Chinese Pentolite was unstable. Over the years it had turned a sickly grayish-greenish yellow, and because of the temperature fluctuations it was weepy with drops of nitroglycerine. She would have liked to pack all two hundred or so pounds of the explosive in ice.

She hadn't seen this kind of timing device before, although it was similar to some of the timers they'd found on the special atomic demolition munitions, or SADMs, that Soviet covert operatives had prepositioned during the Cold War. Which scared her a little bit. Wei-Liu had learned to respect Soviet design, because although it was less complex than U.S. product, it was much more cold-blooded. The Soviets were more concerned with winning a war than they were with preserving the lives of their troops or their scientists. They'd willingly absorbed more than twenty million casualties during the Second World War. Fifty million in a war with the U.S. was not unthinkable. So the lives of a couple of thousand nuclear scientists or Spetsnaz Special Forces troops didn't matter worth a damn.

She examined the bundles of wiring, all of it colored black and all neatly ganged together in bunches of six wires, which she'd sliced out of four pliable rubberized conduits. Not what you saw in Hollywood. All of Hollywood's atomic devices, every one, from James Bond to *The Peacemaker,* had neatly colored wires. Yeah—*right.*

Oh, if the filmgoing public ever knew the truth, Wei-Liu thought, *they'd be scared out of their wits.* Real bombs weren't built with colored wires. All the wires were black. Or white. Or red, green—whatever. You tagged your wires during construction with strips of colored tape so you knew what went where. And then, when it was all finished, you pulled the color strips off and voilà: instant confusion. Not that the tactic would stop a good EOD[23] team. But it would give them pause—and keep them busy for a few hours.

Then there were timing devices. All the timers she'd ever seen in movies either ticked off the seconds analog or blinked them digitally. In real life, it didn't quite work that way. The timers on small and medium-sized U.S. atomic demolition munitions—SADMs and MADMs—had no clocks. You armed the weapon using a highly complicated arming sequence, then set the detonator timer by punching numbers on a keypad that resembled a touch tone telephone. There was no readout.

The Soviets had much more sinister timers on their pocket nukes. They were analog jobbies, which could be set

---

23. Explosives Ordnance Disposal.

at one, three, six, nine, or twelve hours. But in point of fact, it didn't matter. Whichever selection you made, the device was actually designed to detonate the instant you moved the switch itself. The Sovs, after all, didn't trust their people to make individual decisions. And so the state took care of things for them.

She ran a voltmeter over the wire bundles, then gingerly separated each strand and tested them one by one. When she'd examined all thirty-six and was confident about what she'd found, she quickly snipped all but twelve. These she examined once more, using a second device. Then she separated the twelve wires into two groups of six and labeled them with red- and green-colored tape. She moved quickly now, still working carefully so as not to disturb the explosive layer that surrounded the plutonium core of the weapon. When she'd isolated the capacitor wiring and run a new ground wire from the MADM to the antistatic pad, she rose off her knees, walked to the tailgate, swung off the rear end of the truck, and searched until she located the big sergeant major. "Rowdy, I'm ready."

0832. X-Man looked over the inventory. It was pretty sparse. He had four two-and-a-half-kilo blocks of Semtex, a hundred yards of firing wire, three blasting caps, and a single Chinese firing device. Blowing the truck was no problem. The truck had been pulled off the road to camouflage it. It sat slightly askew, its nose and right front wheel elevated. All he and Kaz had to do was fashion a shaped charge. Then they'd set the charge under the uphill side of the truck positioned between the front axle and the motor. The upward force generated by the Semtex—X-Man figured on using more than six pounds of the Czech explosive—would be more than enough to flip the vehicle. Flip it, hell. They'd blow it into next week.

But Ritzik and Yates also wanted shaped charges—which was going to be tough. It wasn't that X-Man couldn't build an improvised charge. Unlike Kaz, a computer-science wonk who'd reluctantly taken the one-week basic dynamite and crimp-the-blasting-cap-without-losing-a-finger course because it was required of all technical personnel, X-Man had requested every one of the explosives programs the Agency offered at ISOLATION TROPIC, which was the code-name designator for the Agency's boom-boom school at Harvey Point, North Carolina, just outside the small town of Hertford. He was fascinated by the subject.

X's first instructor had been a private contractor, a Brooklyn-born, seventysomething World War II veteran who called himself Roy (although it was probably an alias, since just about every instructor at Harvey Point worked under an alias). Whatever his real name might have been, Roy was irrefutably a heavily tattooed, bulldog-faced retired chief boatswain's mate, a former member of the Navy's Underwater Demolition Teams. He had first practiced his craft as a nineteen-year-old, blowing up miles of coral reefs and beach obstacles in the Pacific to create channels for Marine landing craft. He'd refined his abilities during the Korean and Vietnam conflicts. According to the scuttlebutt, he'd left the Navy in the early 1970s and been "sheep-dipped" by the Agency, going to work for Bill Hamilton, Langley's smooth-talking, genteelly diabolical head of maritime services.

Roy's instructional style had been . . . unique. He flapped bent elbows against his rib cage, almost as if he were trying to fly, when he growled at his students. And he swore exactly like the chief petty officer he had once been. But he knew his stuff, and more to the point, he was Old Navy—the Navy of oral, not written, instruction. And so he passed his tradecraft on through vivid example, memorization, and anecdote, not the sort of sterile PowerPoint presentations or dry, pseudo-academic lectures they were used to. X-Man had found it hugely energizing.

Roy had started them out with the basics: two days of blasting-cap crimping. "You people at Christians In Action got friggin' money to burn," Roy told them the first day, tempering his language because of the three women in the course. "And so they'll give you all the friggin' toys money can buy. If its electronic, or cyber, or automated, they'll buy it for you."

The old guy paused, then fired for effect. "But lemme tell ya: that don't mean squat. Because when you're gonna need this stuff, you're gonna be out in the boonies in some friggin' sixth-world country where they ain't got no friggin' electricity, or friggin' satellite-enhanced detonators, or what have you. And all you're gonna be able to friggin' lay your hands on is the same kind of blasting cap I used fifty years ago. Which is why I'm gonna make sure you won't blow your friggin' hands off when you handle your basic Mark One Mod Zero keep-it-simple-stupid blasting cap by crimping it too damn high."

And so, X-Man and the rest of them learned. And after a while they progressed to newer-design electric and non-electric blasting caps, pencil detonators, pressure switches, and radio-controlled detonators. They set off ammonium nitrate bombs. They learned to deploy shaped-chain and cable-cutting charges, and how to position Mk-133 and Mk-135 demolition packs to collapse suspension-bridge towers and highway-overpass abutments. In the second week, Roy taught them about improvised demolitions. They learned to make shaped charges out of number-ten cans and C-4, and cobble together blasting caps out of plumbing pipe, ground tetryl, wire, and pencil lead. They learned (one of the women with some noticeable embarrassment) how to waterproof firing devices using condoms.

By the time X-Man took the three-week advanced explosives course the following year, making the earth move was a sure thing. He could flip a bus, vaporize a limo, or even collapse a bridge. Now he learned how to build car bombs, and wire cell phones so he could blow the target's head off when the son of a bitch answered, but not disturb the hairdo of the person across the table. He made huge bombs out of fertilizer and diesel fuel, powerful enough to bring down a ten-story building. He absorbed the intricacies of platter charges, ribbon charges, breaching charges, and roof-cutters.

But no one at Harvey Point had ever taught X-Man alchemy. Making claymores without some way to contain the plastic explosive and direct its explosive force precisely where he wanted it was going to be tough.

He pulled himself to his feet and wandered over to the charred hull of the chopper. Maybe he'd be able to find something else usable inside. But after three minutes, he came up dry and decided not to waste any more time.

He watched as Rowdy and four others gently slid the MADM into its shipping container then moved it out of the truck bed. He stayed where he was: he'd had enough of *It's* company. But after they muscled the damn thing up the ravine wall into a protected position some two hundred yards away, flanked by rocks and shaded by sparse trees, he and Kaz climbed into the truck and poked around.

Wei-Liu had left the MADM battery unit behind. They examined it. Probably weighed fifty, even sixty pounds. It was seeping a nasty-smelling liquid, too. Not a good sign. The truck bed was empty, so they eased themselves off the rear gate and headed back toward the meager pile of explosive.

Which is when X-Man's eye caught the empty water cans. There were two of them, slightly dinged and painted olive drab, tossed carelessly into the ditch at the side of the road. He'd never worked with rectangular containers before. But as Roy had told them, never be afraid to improvise, and always use what you have at hand. He looked at Kaz. "What do you think?"

The sensor tech pursed his lips. "Could work," he said. "Anything is better than nothing."

"Agreed." X-Man plucked the water cans off the ground, shook them to make sure they were empty, and tucked them under his arm.

25

125 Kilometers East-Northeast of Tokhtamysh.
0837 Hours Local Time.

X-MAN REACHED under his trouser leg, retrieved the composite knife from his boot, and drove the blade through the metal side of the water can. "Ritzik wants shaped charges—Ritzik gets shaped charges."

Kaz said, "You play with the Semtex. I can do the scutwork."

"Great." X-Man passed the paramilitary officer the pierced can. "Cut that whole side away."

"Gotcha." Kaz pulled the water can close and started sawing around the perimeter.

X-Man looked on approvingly, then unwrapped a block of Semtex. "I'm gonna knead some dough." The security officer set a small sheet of metal from the downed chopper on the ground. Then he began to work the plastic with his hands until it was vaguely pliable. "Kaz—"

"Yo?"

"When you're done, I need the knife back."

"Take it." The tech handed the blade to X-Man, who sliced a second Semtex block in two and added the smaller portion to the mix. When he'd gotten the explosive in roughly the shape he wanted, he reached over and took the water can.

Working carefully so as not to cut himself on the jagged edge, X-Man laid the blob of Semtex in the can, manipulating it until it was about three inches thick and pressed securely against all five interior walls. Then he began to shape the explosive. Starting in the middle, he formed the plastic into an inverse cone. The formula was simple: he packed the plastic explosive so that the cone was approximately one-half as deep as it was high, which formed a cone of precisely sixty degrees in angle.

"What do you think?" X-Man displayed his handiwork.

Kaz cocked his head at the explosive-filled can. "You know more than I do about these things, Chris," he said. "But it looks a little skimpy to me."

X-Man pursed his lips. "Roy used to say you can never have too much explosive, only too little."

"Roy was a wise, wise man," Kaz said. "I'm sorry I never took the course when he was teaching it."

"He was so cool," X-Man said. "Told us how he and two other Frogs once blew a mile-and-a-half underwater trench in Barbados as a favor to some local guy."

"C'mon."

"No, I'm serious. A mile and a half." X-Man began to knead the other half of the Semtex block. "God, I would have loved to see that one." He rolled the plastic into a salami-sized sausage, pinched off the ends, and flattened what remained. Then he layered new explosive atop the old, giving the Semtex more bulk, still careful, however, to maintain the sixty-degree angle of the conc. The cone would detonate in what was known as the Monroe effect, and would explode in an arc similar to the fan-shaped pattern of a claymore.

Once the Semtex was properly shaped and packed, he passed the can to Kaz, who used the knife to puncture the water can precisely behind the apex of the cone. Kaz inserted a detonator into the explosive. When the detonator was firmly in place X-Man examined Kaz's handiwork and found it acceptable. Then the two of them repeated the operation with the second water can.

0845. X-Man worked his way up the crest of the ravine and along the ridge until he found where Rowdy had set up one of the two camouflaged positions. He glanced around. All things considered, the Delta men had done a remarkable job—he hadn't seen the MADM until he was virtually on top of the device. And the firing positions were great. Rowdy's people commanded the high ground. That alone would make an infantry assault costly. But just as valuable, he'd found positions that afforded the Delta shooters protection from air attack.

Yates was on his radio. X-Man waited until the sergeant major signed off and turned to face him. "Good news and bad news, Sarge."

"Call me Rowdy." Yates was preoccupied and in no mood for the spook's lighthearted banter. "I don't give a shit which you tell me first."

"The good news is that we won't have a problem flipping the truck. The bad news is that there's only enough plastic for these two improvised devices if you want to do a good job on the truck."

"You're wasting my time," Rowdy said. He held his arms out. "Let me have 'em."

X-Man laid the two shaped charges atop a knee-high flat rock, as reverentially as oblations. He was careful to display the explosive without disturbing the detonators. Rowdy's eyes moved quickly over the plastic-filled cans. Then he looked up and his expression softened. "Thanks," he said. "Good job. You two need a hand setting the truck?"

"Naw." Kaz kicked a stone down the hill. "We can do it. We'll let you know when we're set to blow it."

Yates rubbed a hand across his forehead then checked the digital watch on his left wrist. "Work fast," he said. "We got less than a half hour until the opposition arrives."

"Wilco, Sarge."

Yates put on his War Face. "I said, call me Rowdy."

"Why?"

Yates turned on him, coming up very close, eyes wide, bull neck throbbing, invading X-Man's space. The sergeant major, X-Man realized, could become hugely intimidating when he wanted to—and X-Man wasn't easily intimidated.

"Why?" Rowdy stared down at the younger man wild-eyed for a few seconds. Then he growled, "Because 'Sarge' sounds like a character played by William Bendix in all those World War Two movies."

"So, what's the problem?"

"Bad karma, guy. The William Bendix character always used to die. The negative association could affect my *feng shui*."

X-Man blinked twice. He watched as Rowdy's mustache upturned into a sly grin. He pressed his hands palm to palm in front of his chest and bowed his head in mock reverence to the sergeant major. "I am chastened, Master Rowdy," he said. Then he turned and scurried back down the ravine with Kaz following in his footsteps.

Yates watched them go. They weren't bad kids—for spooks. Rowdy looked down at the IEDs[24] with approval. The kid certainly knew his explosives. Still, Rowdy didn't have much use for spooks. His dealings with CIA had been

---

24. Improvised Explosive Devices.

mostly futile. In Iraq and later Somalia, CIA had been more a part of the problem than the solution. Rowdy was convinced that for all the help the suits at Langley provided Delta, the Agency's initials should really stand for Can't Identify Anything. In Mogadishu, faulty CIA intel caught Rowdy's platoon in an ambush that cost him two of his troopers and a painful gut wound that took him out of action for six months. During the Kosovo campaign, Delta's Agency liaison had been a retired Supergrade who'd been station chief in Belgrade in the mid-seventies. He'd had no contacts and no sources, and provided the Unit with no useful intelligence whatsoever. Still, it wasn't the guys on the ground—the kids like X-Man who had some understanding of the real world—so much as the suits back at Langley who kept things screwed up so badly. Christ, *they* were such dumb-asses; they might as well be generals.

141 Kilometers East-Northeast of Tokhtamysh.
0844 Hours Local Time.

"**HEAR ANYTHING?**" Ritzik shook Sam's shoulder to get his attention, then tapped the spook's headset.

"Negatory." Sam shook his head, shouting to be heard over the swash of the rotors. "I think they're maintaining radio silence."

"Possible." Ritzik thought for a minute. He bent his head to get himself closer to Sam's ear. "How's your Chinese accent?"

"Kind of like Maurice Chevalier's English," Sam shouted back. "I sound like a round-eyes. Why?"

"I was thinking," Ritzik said. "Maybe you could try to

convince them the radio was shot up. You know—a syllable or two, and then silence?"

"I could try something real basic like *wǒ bū-dǒng*."

"What's it mean?"

"*No comprendo*—I don't understand."

"Could you say, 'Can't read you' instead? 'Don't understand' sounds pretty phrase book."

"That's an idiom," Sam shouted. "I'm not fluent enough to do idioms. But I could try one-word directions to get 'em where we want 'em to go—y'know, *dōng, nán, xī, běi*—north, south, east, west. And I could probably add left and right: *zoǔmián* and *yòumián*."

"Up to you," Ritzik said. "You do as much as you feel comfortable doing."

"Got it."

"Good." Ritzik looked up and peered through the windshield. His hand found the radio dial and he switched to the insertion-team net frequency. "Mick—"

He watched Mickey D's head go up and down. "Yo?"

"Your eleven o'clock, about nine, ten miles out."

There was a three-second pause. Then: "Roger that, Loner. I see the dust trail."

"Drop down some. Stay low—where they won't see us or hear us for a while."

The pilot's head went up and down. But by the time he'd said, "Wilco," Ritzik had already switched frequencies. He steadied himself as the big chopper slowed and lost altitude. "TOC, Loner—I need an update on the incoming flight."

Ritzik waited for a reply. "TOC—Loner." He transmitted the call sign a third, fourth, and fifth time. But all he heard in his earpiece was white noise.

125 Kilometers East-Northeast of Tokhtamysh.
0854 Hours Local Time.

"CURTIS, can you and Goose give me a hand?" Tracy Wei-Liu had reached a critical stage of the disassembly. She'd unbolted the capacitor bank from the body of the MADM, then disconnected the fuse wires running from the energy cells into the Pentolite, easing the wires millimeter by millimeter from the capacitors. That had been the most problematic element of the exercise because there was no way of measuring whether or not any of the capacitors' latent energy remained in the wiring. More to the point, the core of the fuse wire was made of copper—and Chinese Pentolite, Wei-Liu knew, reacted adversely to copper, brass, magnesium, and steel. There were two wires buried three inches in the pale grayish-yellow explosive. By the time she exposed the end of the second one from the capacitor unit, she'd sweated clear through her shirt.

Rowdy had put her in the most secure position he could find. She and the bomb were concealed under a ten-foot-long outcropping of rock, some twenty yards below the top of the ridge. Slightly below her position, a ragged cluster of scruffy trees, bent almost forty-five degrees by the wind, helped shield her from view. Rowdy and the rest of them had used whatever they could find to obscure her work site. They'd brought boughs from below, as well as using the tarp from the truck to create a trompe l'oeil effect of light and shadow that masked Wei-Liu and the device.

It was time to remove the capacitors, to get them safely clear of the explosives. For that, she'd need an extra pair of hands or two. The capacitors themselves were banked in an insulated rectangular box that sat atop the MADM's hull. The fifty-five-pound battery pack, which resembled the compressor compartment of a 1930s refrigerator, had been bolted directly behind the capacitors. The battery had been removed. But acid had leaked, fusing the six capacitor-unit bolts to the metal hull. Wei-Liu hadn't been able to budge a single one.

The two Delta shooters ducked into Wei-Liu's hideaway. She showed them the problem.

"Give us a couple of minutes," Goose said. He rolled onto his back and pointed a small flashlight inside the MADM shell. "Got to see the nuts." He squinted, then pulled himself onto his knees. "Twelve millimeter—maybe thirteen," he said. "You have a socket set, ma'am?"

"I don't," Wei-Liu said. "I have a set of wrenches, though—here."

The soldiers examined the tools. Curtis fit one of the wrenches to the top bolt and twisted it. "Too big—use the twelve."

Goose picked through the pile, found the wrench, and worked his arm inside the MADM hull. After a few seconds he said, "Damn," and pulled his arm out. He looked at Wei-Liu. "It's fused. Gonna have to muscle it off. You have any pliers?"

Wei-Liu retrieved a small pair from her tool satchel and displayed them. "Will these work?"

Goose's face fell. "Needle nose," he said. "Useless. I can't get traction."

Wei-Liu said, "What's the problem?"

"The bolt head and nut are the same size," Curtis said. "You have a single twelve-millimeter wrench. I need something to hold the bolt head tight while Goose takes the nut off."

"Got it covered." Goose pulled a dark multipurpose tool from a pouch on his belt. "Try this."

He tossed the tool to Curtis, who flipped it open, revealing a set of snub-nosed pliers. "We'll have these off in a couple of minutes, ma'am."

Wei-Liu's hand covered the bolt head. "Wait—"

Goose looked at her. "What's the problem?"

"Those are steel," Wei-Liu said. "You can't use them—they might cause a spark."

"Your call, ma'am."

Wei-Liu plucked the multitool from the soldier's hand and played with it for a few seconds. And then she extracted a saw-edged knife blade from one of the handles, locked it into place, and cut two small strips of cloth from her shirttail. She wrapped one strip around each of the pliers' jaws. "Now," she said. "Now."

0900. "Fire in the hole." From his position behind a boulder fifty yards upwind, X-Man shifted the safety bail on the firing device to its armed position, depressed the flat handle, and ducked. The six-pound charge of Semtex lifted the uphill side of the truck and flipped it, rolling the big vehicle onto its back in a huge orange fireball and cloud of toxic black smoke.

Kaz poked his head up to admire their handiwork. "Was it good for you, X?"

X-Man brushed debris out of his hair. "Oh, yeah. The earth really moved for me, Kazie-poo." He waved at Yates, who gave the two spooks a smile, an upturned thumb, and then beckoned them up to his position.

"As soon as Bill and Tuzz finish siphoning off the avgas, get to work on the chopper. I want it burning when the Chinese show."

Kaz grinned. "How come you give us all the good jobs?"

Rowdy shooed them away. "Go—play with matches. I have real work to do."

He did, too. He had to position the IEDs where they'd do the most harm. He'd already scanned the area, trying to put himself inside the head of the Chinese commander. The PLA wouldn't make the same mistake again. No—they'd try to drop their force above or behind. So Rowdy'd use them on his flanks. They might not stop the Chinese, but they'd slow them down.

He peered down at the overturned truck and the destroyed shell of the HIP. He knew he'd have to move the Chinese corpses again, scattering them to make it appear that they'd died overcoming the terrorists. It wasn't something Rowdy was especially anxious to do. But it was essential if the ruse was to work. He scanned the horizon to the east, saw nothing, then glanced reflexively at the watch on his left wrist. Not nearly enough time, dammit. Not enough at all.

0906. Six detonator wires. Six detonator wires ran from the capacitors into the explosive. Wei-Liu was certain. She'd painstakingly isolated twelve from the unmarked bundles. But six of those had to be either duplicates, dummies, or redundants, because this MADM's circuitry was engineered for a six-point detonation. She pulled the schematic out of her pocket, checked it for the fifth time in eleven minutes, and confirmed once again that the J-12 device was triggered by a six-point detonation.

But what if she was wrong?

SHE'D MANAGED to remove and then drain the capacitor block using an improvised ground to ensure there was no significant power left. Yes, the explosive was unstable. But she'd kept it from being unduly shocked or disturbed and, more important, protected from any sudden surge from the residual power in the capacitors. So, unless someone smacked it, dropped it, or put a bullet into it, the Pentolite wasn't going to blow. And—as she'd explained so that Rowdy and the rest of them wouldn't worry needlessly—

once she'd disconnected the wires, even if it did blow up, the explosive wouldn't trigger the MADM's nuclear core, because the Pentolite wouldn't be able to detonate in the precise sequence necessary to induce critical mass. There would simply be one hell of an explosion.

"How big?" the sergeant major asked.

"Big enough," she said, "to bring a decent-sized apartment house down." That had obviously impressed him, because he'd moved everybody even farther away from the device than they had been.

SIX-POINT DETONATION. Wei-Liu looked at her handiwork and then glanced at the schematic one last time. Okay: all she had to do was cut twelve wires, and the bomb would be rendered safe. *Snip-snip.* End of story.

She sighed. After everything they'd been through, twelve wires seemed so, well, anticlimactic. *But what if she was wrong . . .*

Wrong? She? *Not.* Wei-Liu took the nonmagnetic needle-nose pliers, double-checked to make sure she had both knees on the antistatic mat, took one deep breath, exhaled, and then clipped the six red-taped wires one after the other. *Nothing.* She took another deep breath and clipped the half-dozen green-flagged ones. She set the needle-nose pliers down on the antistatic mat but remained kneeling. Two immense and totally unexpected tears of relief rolled down her cheeks.

144 Kilometers East-Northeast of Tokhtamysh.
0906 Hours Local Time.

"TOC—LONER." Still nothing. Ritzik went forward. He tapped Mickey D's shoulder. The pilot glanced around for an instant, then returned his attention to keeping the aircraft level. "Mick," Ritzik shouted, "you have to take her up so I can pull a signal from Almaty."

Mickey D didn't acknowledge Ritzik. But his left hand adjusted the collective, his right played the cyclic control, and the chopper's nose dipped about three degrees. Mick's left hand shifted again on the collective and the aircraft began to rise as evenly as an elevator. At one thousand feet, Mick slowed the ascent and the HIP began a gentle sweep to the south. Ritzik pressed the transmit button. "TOC—Loner."

"Loner—TOC."

Thank God. "Dodger—sit-rep." Ritzik listened, tapping coordinates into his handheld and getting them repeated so he knew they were on the money. The Chinese were coming out of Kashgar from the northwest—still only two of them: one HIP and a HIND gunship.

"No sign of the other HIND?"

"Negatory, Loner. It departed Kashgar, but we have no position for it."

Ritzik didn't like that at all. But there was nothing he could do about it. Meanwhile, the imagery showed the remaining two aircraft were making a wide swing over the desert. That made sense: they'd make their attack from the east so they'd be coming out of the sun. "Keep me posted."

Ritzik made his way aft, carefully picking his way around Ty Weaver, who was dry-firing through the open hatch from a sitting position. "How's it going?" he asked the sniper.

Weaver looked up. "A-Okay, boss." He watched as the officer moved past him, then slipped back into his shooter's frame of mind. This sit was A-Okay, all right. It was an A-Okay FUBAR.

Weaver was faced with a sniper's operational nightmare. All sniping is based on a few basic principles. Consistency is the most elemental of these, because consistency equals accuracy. Breathing, sight picture, spot weld, trigger pull, body position, platform stability, rifle, sight, and ammunition—the more these elements of shooting are kept consistent, the more accurate the sniper will become.

He adjusted the sling, then slipped into an open-legged sitting position. In most circumstances, Ty preferred not to use the sling. But there were times—like this one—when he needed every bit of help he could get. He extended his left leg slightly to provide himself a little more stability as the chopper bounced, pressed his cheek against the stock, swung the big rifle right/left, then left/right, found himself an imaginary target, and eased his finger onto the trigger. As he did, the HIP hit an air pocket and he lost his spot weld. The shot would have gone wild. Solution: *Concentrate, schmuck. And hold the damn rifle more securely.*

The rifle, ammo, and scope were no problem. Ty could play this particular 7.62 instrument like a bloody Stradivarius. He'd put thousands of rounds through the MSG90. He knew how it would perform with a cold barrel, and where the rounds would go after two, three, four, five, even ten shots. He'd tuned his own body to the rifle's unique vibrations, and so was able to read and understand even the most minute variation in the tuning fork *sprong* that coursed through the gun and through him every time he pulled the crisp, beautifully unfluctuating three-pound trigger. Those things wouldn't change.

But Ty knew he could forget about platform consistency. The platform was the chopper deck, which was not only vibrating from the engines and rotor blades, but moving left, right, up, and down. Not to mention the ear-shattering noise. Body position? He could shoot offhand—standing up—but only if the chopper remained in a steady hover. Not bloody likely in combat. Shooting from a prone position was out of the question, because the field of fire from the chopper would be way too narrow. That meant he'd be reduced to using a kneeling or a sitting position. Sitting also restricted his field of fire to some degree. But it was a lot more stable than kneeling—especially given the chopper's constant bumpy motion.

Sight picture was another important element of consistency. But it, too, was going to be problematic. Back at the CAG, Ty had worked for hours to maintain the consistency of his sight picture. His spot weld—the placement of his cheek against the rifle's stock—was exactly the same whenever he pulled the trigger. That uniformity produced the exact same eye relief—the distance from his eye to the scope's rear lens—every single time he put the rifle to his shoulder. Consistent eye relief, in turn, resulted in an identical sight picture through the scope. Today, the HIP's motion would make maintaining consistent spot weld and sight picture problematic. Not impossible: Ty had worked to develop sniping proficiency from virtually any kind of platform, including choppers. But the HIP added hugely to the degree of difficulty he'd be attempting.

Follow-through was also going to be a predicament. In normal circumstances—like the ambush at Yarkant Köl— Ty had been able to maintain the consistency of his shooting through the stability of his follow-through, which meant that between the time he fired the shot and the bullet actually left the gun there was no movement of the barrel. Stability ensured that the sight picture never changed, not even by a hairbreadth, in the roughly quarter of a second between the trigger pull, the sear release, the firing pin striking the primer, and the bullet traveling down the MSG90's 23.62-inch barrel and emerging from the harmonic stabilizer or the sound suppressor. Proper follow-through was going to be difficult when, even though the rifle might not move, the platform was guaranteed to shift between trigger pull and bullet departure.

Then there was angle compensation. It is easiest to shoot straight across a flat space—shooting on a target range, for example. The flatter the angle, the less the shooter has to compensate for uphill or downhill trajectory, which has to be figured differently from bullet drop, crosswind, or temperature and humidity fluctuations.

At an uphill angle of forty-five degrees, for example, you can put your crosshairs dead center on the target, pull the trigger—and your shot will miss its mark, going high by about eight inches. The difficulty of shooting from the chopper would be compounded because Ty knew he'd be snap-shooting at extreme angles of thirty, forty, even sixty degrees as Mickey D maneuvered the HIP under battle conditions. It would be kind of like trying to shoot ten out of ten bull's-eyes while riding a roller coaster. No—it would be like trying to shoot from one moving roller-coaster car to a target sitting in a second moving roller-coaster car. All things considered, Ty thought, the situation was nasty enough to make a man take up the "spray and pray" shooting technique, or think about forgetting everything he'd ever learned, and reverting to "Kentucky" windage.

0912. Ty sensed Ritzik moving past him. He was shouting, but the sniper paid the major no mind. He was completely focused on his own situation, working Zen-like to exclude every bit of extraneous stimuli, until only he and the rifle remained. If he could accomplish that much, he'd be able to overcome the physical obstacles and do what he had to.

Suddenly the chopper hiccuped, knocking him out of position. The HIP dropped like a stone, recovered, twisted into the sun at a forty-degree angle, fighting its way into the sky. The sniper was slapped to the deck and rolled aft. He fought to maintain what was left of his balance, cradling the big rifle to keep it from smashing into a bulkhead or seat. Oh, this was not going to be any fun at all.

26

"LONER, TOC. Your bogeys are coming in from the east. Distance is twenty-two miles and closing."

"Roger that, TOC." Ritzik hand-signaled Gene Shepard to hang on. He worked his way forward to the cockpit, stepping around the sniper, who was focused, trancelike, on a spot somewhere outside the aircraft.

"Mick," Ritzik shouted, "let's do it."

"Hoo-ah, boss."

Ritzik's fingers whitened around the cockpit support struts as the HIP dropped. "Mick?"

"Yo?"

Ritzik's knees flexed as if he were shooting a mogul course as the craft twisted violently, recovered, shot upward, and finally veered to its left, turning into the sun. "Get us in position for Ty to take the other pilots out before they discover we're not friendly."

"Roger that. What side is he shooting from?"

"Port side. Port side." Ritzik squinted through the windshield as the chopper regained even flight. Then he turned and staggered aft, holding on to whatever he could find for support.

Sam Phillips's stomach queased as the HIP abruptly lost altitude. He fought the nausea, finally regaining his equilibrium as Mick brought the craft around. Instinctively, he reached up and snugged the shoulder straps that held him against the seat back. Sam had never much liked flying, and choppers made him a lot more nervous than planes. They were, he thought, complicated, hard-to-fly aircraft that required total concentration on the part of their pilots. Indeed, as he'd watched Mickey D familiarize himself with the HIP's responses, he'd been amazed that the pilot could keep the big bird in the air at all, single-handedly. And when Mick hovered the HIP the first time, Sam swore he could smell the tension rolling off the pilot's body and permeating the cockpit.

"Sam, Sam!"

Mick's shout brought Sam back to reality. He pulled off the headset. "Yo?"

"Sun visor."

"Gotcha." The spook reached over, swung the lightweight plastic around, and rotated the visor screen down across the windshield. "Okay?"

"Roger that." Mick glanced down at a screen on the console that sat in the middle of the nose, right between the two seats. "Sam, turn that second switch to your left."

Sam put his hand on a black knurled knob on the console's bottom row. "This one?"

The pilot's chin thrust forward. "One row up."

"This one."

"Yup."

Sam turned the knob. A green radar screen flickered to life. Mick checked it, then shouted, "Right-hand switch, top row. Throw it."

Sam moved the toggle upward. "What did I just do?"

"If I remember correctly, you turned the manual IFF transponder shutoff switch to its off position."

The move made no sense to Sam at all. "Why did I do that?"

"So I can convince the other aircraft we have transmission problems." Mick eased the HIP into a shallow descent, skimming the aircraft no more than a hundred feet above the nap of the land. "When I yell, flip it the other way."

"I'm gonna put the headset back on," Sam shouted, his hands miming earpieces.

Mick's head bobbed up and down. "Roger." He paused as he adjusted the chopper's attitude. "Remember—"

"What?" Sam adjusted the head strap and pulled the bulbous mike close to his lips.

"Double orders of pot stickers and Hunan beef—extra spicy."

0914. Gene Shepard ran a gloved hand over his safety strap, which was turnbuckled to a bulkhead strut. He'd attached the webbing to his belt. It allowed him side-to-side movement, but was short enough to ensure that his body would stay inside the aircraft even if the HIP were to bank at a sixty-degree angle. He adjusted his own communications gear, then swung around and double-checked Ty Weaver's safety straps. The sniper's tether was shorter than Shepard's so that he could use his weight and its natural tension to steady himself.

When he was satisfied, he shook the sniper's shoulder. Ty gave him an upturned thumb, then settled down facing the open port-side doorway, his rifle in the crook of his arm.

Shepard waited until his teammate was in position. Then he stepped to the aft side of the doorway, unsecured the machine gun, and swept the weapon left and right, up and down, to make sure it had full play. He'd be the first one firing at the IMU convoy. But once the PLA aircraft hove into view, he'd have to stay clear of the sniper's field of fire.

Ritzik stood just aft of the cockpit, watching as his men prepared for battle. It was at times like this that he was conscious of how great a blessing God had bestowed on him because He'd allowed him the chance to go to War with men like these not once but dozens of times. At Delta, there were few renegades, few rogues, few prima donnas. They just didn't last. Oh, there were personality conflicts aplenty. And Delta, like other SpecOps units, had seen a small but still unsettling share of domestic-violence cases. And sometimes people just plain pissed one another off—and settled things with their fists. But once they'd passed the Selection for Delta and been through the battery of psychological exams, the men tended to find their own place, then stay with the unit for years. Some, like Rowdy, had been there more than a decade. Which was why, when it came down to times like this, there were no better Soldiers on the face of the earth than these Warriors with whom Ritzik was privileged to serve. And his true gift from God was that he'd been allowed to know and understand that fact.

And then the moment was over. He checked his own web gear, then unstrapped the AK from the seat where he'd stored it, pulled himself aft until he reached the starboard doorway, secured himself in a firing position, patted the chest pouches that held a dozen of the Chinese grenades, slapped a fresh mag into the receiver, and chambered a round.

0919:15. Mickey D banked right, then left, at about seventy knots, guiding the HIP along a series of small ridges. He glanced at the radar screen, raised the chopper's nose, then pulled hard left. "Sam—Sam—throw the switch."

Gene Shepard balanced on the balls of his feet, hands on

the machine gun, as the big airframe rolled up, then down, then hove to. Four heavy trucks popped into his field of view. He flipped the safety off with his right thumb, brought the stock up against his shoulder, found a sight picture, and loosed a six-round burst at the first of the trucks. His rounds kicked up stones six yards beyond the vehicle's squared-off hood. Shepard compensated, swung back, leaned into the weapon, and fired again.

Mickey D's eyes caught something on his radar. "Sam— Sam throw the damn switch."

"Roger." Sam's right hand toggled the IFF control. He watched the pilot in amazement. Mick's arms and legs were flailing independently; his body was actually twitching in the seat. His eyes were buggy. The pilot looked to Sam as if he were receiving electroshock treatment.

0919:30. Mick called, "Contact-contact-contact." The HIP banked, then kicked skyward. Sam grabbed a cockpit strut, his knuckles white. He fought motion sickness. And then, in his earphones, Sam heard Chinese. It was like a slap in the face. He'd missed the transmission. Heard it, but missed it. He'd screwed up. Worse, because he was still at the stage where he had to listen word by word, then produce an English subtitle in his brain before he could make sense of what was being said. Sam forgot about the chopper's motion, shut everything else out, and fought to concentrate on what was coming through his headset.

0919:32. Ritzik saw the IMU truck column as the HIP flashed over it. He tried to get a burst into one of the vehicles, but the chopper rolled to port, and all he saw was sky. Even with the ear-shattering noise, he could make out something in his earpiece. He turned the volume up full.

It was Mick's voice. "Contact-contact-contact."

And then Ritzik was slapped against the deck as the chopper popped three hundred feet straight up, corkscrewed counterclockwise twice, banked hard left, then right, and then dove straight for the convoy.

0919:36. The 62's tall leaf rear sight, Gene Shepard concluded, was going to be useless, except to align with the thick front post. He felt the chopper's violent series of moves under the soles of his Adidas. But he wasn't thrown off his stance because his body was compensating gyroscopically for each twist and turn. He was in a groove now, reacting to every minute nuance of Mick's piloting. Pinball wizard. The HIP rolled slightly, and then the convoy appeared at the left edge of Shepard's peripheral vision. He brought the machine-gun arm around, dropped the muzzle until his front sight was where he wanted it to be, and then stitched the trucks broadside as Mick gave him a seven-second window of opportunity. He could see splinters flying as the fat, 7.62 rounds impacted on target. And then the HIP veered away and nosed into the sky. Shep heard the *slap-slap-slap* of rounds as ground fire chased them.

0919:46. Ritzik saw the Chinese aircraft—both painted with the same distinctive camouflage pattern as the HIP. They were coming from his left—out of the sun. And then Mick banked, turned, and the two PLA aircraft disappeared from view. Ritzik yelled a warning.

0919:49. Ty Weaver had the big HK up. He was sitting open-legged, his rear end planted firmly on the decking, right leg tucked, knee bent almost ninety degrees, his left leg extended so his butt and feet formed a makeshift tripod. He'd wrapped the sling around his left arm to give himself increased stability. The bottom of the triceps muscle on his right arm was supported by the outside of his right knee so that bone didn't rest on bone. That was the rule: soft against hard; hard against soft. His hand held the rifle stock firmly in the hollow of his shoulder; Ty's cheek pressed against the comb, making a solid spot weld.

Except—he couldn't see. The sun's glare was too bright. And then Ty felt Mickey D shift the chopper's attitude, moving slightly to the left. The starboard side of the Chinese HIP floated slowly into his frame of view. The sight picture was perfect. Ty's right hand shifted slightly, moving onto the knurled knob to adjust the parallax. Then he was back on the trigger, concentrating on breathing, on the target, and on the crosshairs, zoning everything else out of his consciousness.

0919:52. "Toggle the switch, Sam. Toggle the switch." Mickey D swung the chopper around smoothly so as to give the sniper the most stable environment possible. He caught the spook's hand in his peripheral vision as Sam worked the IFF switch. The pilot saw the Chinese HIP slow and hover so the HIND gunship could make its first pass.

0919:52. Gene Shepard watched, transfixed, from the corner of the starboard-side doorway as the HIND wheeled, straddled the road, and tore into the convoy with its Gatling gun and rockets. It moved almost lazily over the panicked Uzbeks, its heavily armored fuselage impervious to ground fire.

0919:55. Mick maneuvered the HIP, keeping level with the Chinese transport at a distance of three hundred yards, and as evenly as he could, he slowly rotated the craft counterclockwise. His lips were moving: "C'mon, c'mon, c'mon, Ty—get the job done."

* * *

0920:00. The glassed-in cockpit panned inside Ty's field of view. He compensated for the distance using the Mil-Dots in his reticle, eased the fine crosshairs where they belonged, held steady, and squeezed the trigger, sending the 168-grain boat-tail bullet on its way.

0920:01. The Chinese HIP dropped like a stone. Ty's scope followed the chopper until the aircraft slipped below the HIP's floor line. He knew he'd hit the pilot. But now the HIP had turned, and he didn't have a clear shot at the left-hand seat. He crabbed forward, straining at the safety straps, until he could see the HIP's air intakes three football fields away. No good: they had baffles. The Chinese chopper yawed clockwise, then held steady as the copilot gained control over the craft. Ty caught the confused expression on the door gunner's face. The man was shouting into his microphone. Instantly, Ty's crosshairs quartered the gunner's face and held on the bridge of his nose. He squeezed off a second round. The machine gunner went down. Now he raised the crosshairs until they found the HIP's starboard-side engine exhaust. Ty put three quick rounds into it.

The MSG90's bolt locked back. Ty unslung the heavy gun, released the magazine, and let it drop onto the decking. He felt Mickey D rotate the chopper. But Ty fought off distraction. He reached for a second five-round mag, which he rammed home. Then with his left hand he slapped the cocking bolt forward and reslung the rifle. He shouldered the weapon and made his spot weld. But there was nothing in his sight picture except a wisp of gray-brown smoke.

0920:05. Ritzik, strapped securely to a turnbuckle, dangled his legs out the port-side doorway. He peered out and saw the Chinese HIP, pluming smoke, keel over to its right, then fall away, spin out, nose stonelike, two hundred feet to the ground, and explode in a huge fireball, its rotors shattering into shrapnel. Then he lost sight of the burning craft as Mick put their own HIP into a tight, evasive turn, then flattened the aircraft out to make a strafing run at the convoy.

0920:06. Sam screamed, "They don't know what the hell's going on. They think they're taking ground fire." He swiveled in the copilot's chair and shouted once again so Ritzik would know what was happening. But his voice was lost in the scream of the engines as Mickey D put the chopper into a tight turn and swooped down toward the IMU trucks.

0920:16. Gene Shepard swung the machine-gun muzzle forward. He was leaning out the HIP's doorway, the wind slapping at the high collar of his bulletproof vest, the dead Chinese door gunner's ill-fitting soft helmet jammed on his head, its chin straps flapping wildly in the slipstream. The road was below. Mick had them right where they had to be. Shep strained against his web harness, dropped the muzzle slightly, which put the wide post of the front sight directly in the middle of the road. As soon as his peripheral vision picked up the last boxy truck in the IMU convoy, he flicked the safety up, tightened his finger on the 67's heavy trigger, and watched as the armor-piercing rounds kicked up gravel in the center of the road at the rate of 650 per minute.

0920:21. Mickey D kept the HIP centered above the convoy, watching the chopper's shadow as it moved down the road toward the IMU convoy. He adjusted his airspeed; shifted his cyclic stick and pedals, dropping the HIP to fifty feet, so he could come in flat, at about eighty knots. He sensed the dull chatter of Shep's machine gun, although he had a hard time actually separating it from the other noise.

Besides, there was a more pressing problem to deal with. The HIP was giving him no quarter. It was a cumbersome, awkward helicopter; sluggish, unwieldy, slow to respond—a burro of an aircraft.

Mick thought, *And what's the first step to flying a burro? You use a two-by-four and get its bloody attention.* His left hand fought the collective lever. No sooner did he have it under control than the cyclic shaft in his right hand began to stutter. The pedals felt as if they'd been lubed with molasses. He bullied the controls into submission and finally brought the HIP where he wanted it to be, pulled up, swung around, and readied the aircraft for the next run.

0920:24. Sam Phillips pressed the mike against his lips. *"Wǒ bū-dǒng. Wǒ bū-dǒng."* Holding his hand over the foam he pushed the mike up over his head and shouted at Mickey D. "They were asking how we're doing."

Mick's head went up and down once. But he couldn't answer—he was too effing busy trying to stay out of the HIND's way. The big, hunchbacked gunship had come around behind him and Mick wanted those guns and rockets nowhere near his six. He dropped the HIP's tail, flared left, and pushed the big transport chopper into the sky as the gunship flashed past.

As it did, Mick caught a glimpse into the HIND's tandem cockpits. The gunner/copilot occupied the front position, protected by a thick flat pane of armored glass. Above and behind him, separated by heavy armor and more bulletproof glass, sat the pilot. The fuselage door was shut—no sign of a waist gun—so there was probably no third crewman aboard this morning. Give thanks for small blessings. Mick harassed the controls until he'd slowed the HIP and he could see as the HIND yawed right, swerved, and started its shallow dive toward the convoy.

* * *

0920:29. Sam heard chatter in his headset—the HIND pilot
was talking to him. He flicked the switch on/off, on/off, and
repeated his message, trying like hell to sound authentically
Mandarin, and knowing in his heart that he was nowhere
close.

Mick brought the HIP around so he could watch. The
HIND was an ungainly aircraft for a gunship, way too big
and heavy to be maneuverable on the battlefield the way,
say MH6 Little Birds, Apaches, or even Cobras were able to
pop up, shoot, and dart away. Well, the damn thing weighed
twenty-two-thousand-plus pounds at takeoff—almost three
tons more than the American Apache tank-killer. And its
avionics were no more advanced than the HIP's sluggish
controls. Hell, Mick could outmaneuver a HIND even in
one of SOAR's big double-rotored MH-47E Chinooks. But
he couldn't outrun one. HINDs were fast. And deadly. It
had that four-barrel Gatling-type gun in its nose. And under
its stubby, downswept wings—which provided the craft
with more than a quarter of its lift during forward flight—
were four pods, each holding twenty 80mm rockets. On the
HIND's wingtips, two missile rails each held what looked
like two of the old Soviet AT-3 "Sagger" antiarmor missiles. Mick turned to the spook next to him and shouted,
"Watch."

The HIND lined up on the road again. Sam could see the
IMU guerrillas scattering, running into the scrub grass, trying to find cover. Half a dozen of them were carrying
loaded RPG launchers. But he knew the rocket grenades
would be useless against the gunship unless it was hovering. From about twelve hundred yards, the HIND fired one
of its Saggers. The last truck in the convoy was vaporized in
a bright yellow-red ball of fire.

The HIND kept coming. Eight hundred yards out, the

gunship loosed a barrage of rockets that exploded wide of the road, sending shrapnel into the fleeing Uzbeks. The ugly chopper dropped to a hundred feet, its Gatling gun chewing the roadbed, making furrows, cutting the convoy and the terrorists to pieces.

Its strafing run completed, the HIND veered away to port, pulled up in an unexpectedly gentle climb, and turned into the sun. Sam watched as an Uzbek crawled out from under a truck, pulled himself to his feet, and emptied his AK ineffectively at the HIND's armored belly. Mick eased the HIP over the smoldering convoy and Sam felt the aircraft shudder as Gino opened up with their own machine gun and cut the guerrilla in two.

"Jeezus H—" From nowhere, four rockets bracketed the HIP, streaked past, and exploded on the desert floor. Sam managed to choke out, "Didja see that?" And then he succumbed, turning ad nauseam green as Mickey D threw the HIP into a tight climb, rolled to the left, dropped, twisted, revolved, then climbed, leaving the spook's stomach somewhere far behind.

"Hang on, Sloopy," the pilot screamed. "The sons of bitches just figured out we ain't with them." Mick muscled the big chopper almost ninety degrees onto its right side, throttled full, and twisted the aircraft in the second eardrum-popping, breath-stopping, gravity-defying move in less than fifteen seconds, leaving Sam feeling as if he'd just put in a couple of hours of hard time on one of the ride-and-pukes at King's Dominion.

27

144 Kilometers East-Northeast of Tokhtamysh.
0921 Hours Local Time.

MIKE RITZIK got the hint they'd been unmasked when he found himself suspended completely outside the open doorway, separated from the ground by a worn, two-inch-wide canvas strap and a carabiner that had probably been made by prison labor in Shenyang. The shock of the violent evasive move pulled the AK out of his hands and he watched it disappear between his legs. He looked down and saw the ground directly below his feet. Then the HIP rolled again and he was yo-yo'd back inside the cabin and smacked rudely onto the deck face first.

He took hold of the door-frame support to keep himself inside just in case Mickey D decided to try crazy eights again, then craned his neck to make sure Ty and Gino were still among the living. The sniper was walking on his knees, his arms wrapped protectively around the HK, heading for someplace he could strap the weapon down. Gene Shepard was working frantically to secure the machine gun's pintle arm.

Ritzik's eyes scanned the cabin. He saw the RPG rockets tied down aft, pulled himself more or less upright, detached from the bulkhead, quickly secured the safety harness to

the overhead rail with the carabiner, and lurched aft toward
the grenade launcher, only to be swept off his feet as
Mickey D dropped the HIP's nose and began to slalom the
chopper wildly toward the ground. Ritzik slid forward a
yard and a half, finally coming to rest against the cockpit
bulkhead.

0921:21. "Help me find him, Sam—help me find him."
Mick had lost the HIND somewhere behind them. He was
vulnerable. No place to be. He gave the HIP all the throttle
it could stand and started an evasive sequence that took
them in a clockwise corkscrew at about a sixty-eight-degree
angle, followed by a rapid climb and an outward turn, followed by a series of quick, veering, downward maneuvers
that brought him back over the IMU convoy at a height of
about thirty feet.

As they flashed by, Mick heard the ping of rounds on the
airframe. He jogged the HIP left, then right. As he pulled
past the burning truck that had led the decimated convoy,
and swerved violently to his right, a rocket streaked from
somewhere behind him on the desert floor.

Damn convoy hadn't been decimated enough, Mick decided.

Five hundred yards behind Mickey D the HIND
wrenched itself out of its attack trajectory, twisted away, released chaff, and pulled hard to starboard at a dangerous
angle, flying east, away from the chaff.

The rocket seemed to waver, then veered toward the
HIND's countermeasures and headed west, its trail visible
as it cut through the floating, shiny chaff cloud and vanish-
ing into the morning sky.

0921:27. "What the hell was that?" Ritzik pulled himself
into the cockpit area.

"Dunno, boss." Mick jogged the HIP slightly to the south. "SA-7 of some kind. Maybe a Strela. Maybe a Chinese HN-5. Who the hell knows? It was moving too fast."

"Damn." That was all they needed. "We're vulnerable," Ritzik said. The HIP didn't carry countermeasures.

"You guys strap in," Mick said. "Lemme deal with this."

0921:39. Mick pulled the HIP's nose up slightly and careened westward, fifteen yards off the desert floor, chest heaving, his eyes scanning for the gunship. He finally caught a glimpse of it at his four o'clock, turning into him, running flat-out balls to the wall, altitude about six hundred feet.

Where the hell had the gunship been hiding? He'd done a frigging three-sixty and still he hadn't seen the goddamn thing.

0921:43. Mick let the son of a bitch come on. He knew the HIND's rockets wouldn't do him any good—not at such an oblique angle. It was the Gatling he had to worry about. The frigging HIND could fire thirty degrees left or right of center. Mick gave himself more throttle and increased the collective pitch, pulling the HIP up vertically, keeping his own craft out of the fatal sixty-degree funnel. The HIND followed.

"C'mon, c'mon, you asshole—try this." Mick's eyes narrowed. Suddenly he decelerated, bringing the HIP into a hover. As the HIND flashed past, Mick popped the HIP straight up, fifteen, sixteen, seventeen hundred feet. If the gunship was fully loaded—and it appeared to be—it was virtually incapable of quick stops and hovering.

0921:50. Ritzik, Ty, and Gene Shepard rolled onto their hands and knees as the HIP slowed to a hover just above two thousand feet. Ritzik reached for the troop seat just forward of the port-side doorway and pulled it from its storage position. "You guys better do a Bette Davis," he croaked.

"Betty who?" Gino Shepard's words were lost in the chopper noise, but Ritzik understood the first sergeant's raised shoulders. Ritzik dropped onto the seat and secured the harness.

He shouted, "She's the one who said, 'Fasten your seat belts, it's gonna be a bumpy night.'"

0922:11. Mickey D watched as the HIND arced into a wide turn, then fought for altitude, flying an intercept route that would cut them off from escape. Mick's eyes scanned the horizon. They were sitting above the road as it came off the desert basin and curved into the foothills. The burning convoy sat to the HIP's north and west by about two kliks—just over a mile. The nose of the front truck was less than a kilometer from where the desert plain's lunarlike surface gave way to the sixty-foot dunes and S-curved ravines leading to the two mountain ranges that marked the Chinese-Tajik border. Mick rotated the HIP once in a three-sixty to make sure the second HIND was nowhere in sight. And then he popped the HIP another three thousand feet into the sky. "Your move, asshole."

The gunship climbed steadily toward the HIP. At eight hundred yards or less, the Gatling was deadly. The rockets had three times that range.

Mick watched as the HIND's profile grew larger and larger. And then, as it drew within two kilometers, maybe a little more, the gunship loosed two quick quartets of rockets.

Mick dropped the nose of the HIP toward the desert floor, rotated so he faced the HIND, then dropped the chopper in a vertical plunge, as sudden and violent as an elevator whose cable has been sheared off.

The HIP's airframe protested by buffeting violently. Hell, the damn thing hadn't been built for aerobatics. Mick literally stood on the pedals to maintain control as the HIP dropped below the eight rockets. His left arm fought to decrease the collective while his right somehow managed to maintain the cyclic pitch in a neutral attitude.

At less than a hundred feet above the deck he adjusted the cyclic pitch and added throttle, dropping the nose slightly and putting the HIP into forward flight. He skimmed above the desert, heading straight for the burning convoy. Above and behind him, the HIND loosed another rocket barrage.

Mick yanked the collective and the HIP jumped skyward, accelerating to two thousand feet. When he saw the rockets strike, he dropped the HIP and skimmed the ground once more. "I can't see him, Sam—where the hell is he?"

Sam Phillips twisted in the left-hand seat, but all he saw was empty sky. "Can't see him, Mick."

The pilot yawed left, then right. "Damn—" He yanked the HIP skyward and to the left. A hundred yards in front of the chopper's nose, an RPG rocket flashed into the sky. "Sorry." Mick regained control, eased the HIP back toward the deck, and flashed over the convoy, shouting into his throat mike: "Loner, Loner, can you see him?"

Ritzik heard Mickey D's voice in his earpiece. But the noise in the cabin was too loud to make out what the hell the man was asking. "Come again, come again," he shouted, and then clapped his hand over his ear, trying like hell to shut the din out.

Message received. "Hold on—" Ritzik reached up then slid the carabiner onto the port-side safety rail, ratcheted the web strap as tight as he could, then released the seat harness and stood up, his right hand tight on the door frame. He pulled himself into the doorway, then stuck his head outside.

The suction of the slipstream almost pulled Ritzik out of the aircraft. He braced himself with his right hand. And then, using the safety strap to steady himself, he pulled himself aft, grabbed the rear door frame with both hands, and stuck his upper body out the doorway.

The HIND was directly on their six, perhaps a hundred and fifty or two hundred yards above the HIP, and less than a mile away. It was closing fast. Ritzik could see the flashes from the rocket pods as the gunship fired another burst. Instinctively, he ducked his head back into the cabin and shouted, "Rockets!" into his mike.

The HIP shot into the sky again, knocking Ritzik off his feet, slamming the back of his head into the door frame.

Everything went black and white. Ritzik saw big white spots in a black universe. And then he was on his butt, his back against the folded troop seat. Gino's gloved hand was on his neck, and the first sergeant was drizzling water in his face. He struggled to his knees. "I'm okay, I'm okay." Gino released him. Ritzik wiped his face, raised his goggles and swabbed the water out of his eyes, crawled back into the doorway, and stuck his head outside.

The HIND had gained on them. It was still directly behind the HIP, less than a mile out, and four, maybe five hundred feet above them, high enough to be able to block Mick's evasive maneuvering—a fast-reacting cornerback angling on a wide receiver. Ritzik watched the ground blur as the HIP veered north and dropped to within twenty feet of the ground. The narrow ribbon of road came into his field of vision as Mick pushed the HIP westward, balls to the wall.

Ritzik caught the flash of the Gatling, but couldn't see the rounds. Now the IMU convoy flashed by directly beneath the HIP's wide body and disappeared behind them.

Something dangerous tore into the HIP's belly, shaking

the aircraft. And then Mick slammed the HIP into a flat, ninety-degree right-hand turn, pointing the transport's nose north. Ritzik lost sight of the HIND.

In the cockpit, Mick's hands felt as if they'd sweated clear through his Nomex flying gloves. Maybe they had: the leather finger pads were slightly sticky on the controls. It didn't matter. Nothing mattered except keeping the HIP steady, running at full throttle mere feet above the burning convoy, giving whoever on the ground had the missile—if they did have another missile—a tough target. It was human nature: give somebody a choice between a hard target and an easy one and they'll take the easier shot.

The HIP burst through the ground smoke—but took no ground fire. Just beyond the western side of the convoy Mick used the smoke as cover, rotated the HIP six, seven, eight hundred yards to the south, then literally slid behind the first line of dunes and dropped into a hover, putting the convoy and the line of dunes between the HIP and the gunship.

Mickey D popped the HIP above the sixty-foot dune and watched as the HIND pilot took notice and abruptly changed course. Mick grinned at Sam. "Greedy, greedy," he said, watching as the Chinese adjusted his angle of descent then accelerated and careened to the south at about six hundred feet to begin his strafing run.

Which is when the IMU guerrillas fired their second SA-7. Sam was transfixed as the HIND jogged violently left, then right, then pivoted to climb away from the convoy, releasing bunches of chaff.

Except this time Mickey D had suckered the HIND broadside to the IMU missile launcher. Broadside meant that the gunship's jet exhausts, located amidships, just forward and above the chopper's stubby wings, were now exposed to the missile's sensors. And just like scissors cut paper but rock breaks scissors, the fat, round, hotter-than-hot exhaust from twin Isotov TV-3-117 turbines trumps chaff every single time in the missile-sensor playbook.

Frankly, Mick didn't give a rusty F-word whether the IMU was firing an ancient Soviet SA-7, or a newer Strela-2, or a stolen Chinese HN-5. All he knew was that every one of those missiles was an old-fashioned heat-seeker. To work properly, they required a heat source—the exhaust—to lock on to, and a minimum range of five hundred meters for the fired missile to arm itself. Which, Mick noted with satisfaction, was just about what the HIND pilot had allowed, intent as he was on blowing the crap out of the HIP.

Because the HIND was so low, the missile's flight time was less than one-two-three seconds. Which was when the contact fuse of the kilo-and-a-half high-explosive warhead grazed the exhaust vent and the rocket detonated just inside. There was a brief, explosive hiccup as the engines disintegrated. A violent blast jerked the HIND onto its side. A millisecond later there was another flash, which broke the chopper in two. Rotors shattering, the gunship's front end cartwheeled, then dropped stonelike onto the desert floor, bursting into a huge fireball that was immediately enveloped in a funnel-shaped cloud of thick, black smoke.

From the starboard doorway, Ritzik saw the dark plume and then a series of vivid white-and-orange explosions as the chopper's rockets blew up.

Then it was all wiped from his field of vision as Mick rotated the HIP clockwise and accelerated, flying low to keep the dunes between them and the IMU as the pilot headed due west. The Chinese were still out there—prowling and growling. Ritzik had to get his people out before the PLA chopped them all to bits.

28

TEN HUNDRED FIFTEEN HOURS. That was the cutoff
Rowdy Yates had set for himself. If Ritzik wasn't back,
they'd get the hell out of Dodge and head for the Tajik border. But now there was a chopper in the area. He heard the
thud-thud-thudding as rotor sound bounced off the rocky
terrain. Friend or foe? It didn't matter. They'd stay under
cover until he knew for sure. If things had been perfect,
he'd have received an intel dump from Dodger or Marko at
the TOC. But Almaty was off the air. The frigging radios
were still fried. He couldn't reach Ritzik. There was even
static when he broadcast to Doc, Goose, Curtis, and the rest
of the Delta element, who lay no more than a hundred and
fifty yards away, direct line of sight, on the opposite ridge.

The radios, Rowdy thought, were indicative of the problems faced by people like him, who risked their lives using
equipment designed and built by idiots. Just once, Rowdy
thought, it would be nice to go into battle with gear that had
been designed by people who'd actually put their hides on
the line with it, instead of engineers who test everything in
a vacuum. His hand brushed the pommel of the ten-inch
bowie knife suspended on his combat harness. Rowdy's

bowie had never failed him. But then, it hadn't been designed by some shirtwaist marketing expert or a self-styled expert with a Ph.D. in edged-weapons design, but by actual Warriors—the Bowie brothers—who knew what a fighting knife should be because they'd had ample opportunity to field-test the design under the full range of combat conditions back in the early days of the nineteenth century.

0944. Rowdy looked down from his perch on the ridge and prayed the God of War was looking down upon him and his troops with favor, and would bless their violence of action. The work had been done. He'd siphoned all the fuel he could out of the HIP before they'd blown the chopper up. He'd secreted the fuel bladder where it wouldn't be hit if they were attacked. He, Doc Masland, and Bill Sandman had muscled the plutonium core out of the MADM after Wei-Liu had gizmo'd it and pronounced it safe to move. Then they'd carried the nuclear material six hundred yards east and cached it where it would be safe from stray fire. When plutonium burns it can emit deadly alpha rays—and Rowdy wanted the damn stuff nowhere close by. Then he'd packed water, fuel, and some ammo in the 4×4 so they could make their run for it if Ritzik and the rest of them didn't make it back.

Rowdy had lost enough of his comrades-in-arms over the years so that he didn't dwell on the possibility that Ritzik, Gino, Ty, Mick, and Sam-I-Am the spook man weren't making a round-trip. The youngest Ranger at Desert One during the abortive attempt to rescue the American hostages in Tehran in the spring of 1980, nineteen-year-old Fred Yates, had been given the nasty job of blowing up the damaged RH-53D Sea Stallion choppers to ensure the destruction of the bundles of cash and caches of intelligence materials that had inadvertently been left aboard the damaged aircraft. It hadn't bothered him to vaporize the money, maps, intelligence materials, or cipher keys.

But the fact that dead Americans could have been inside the aircraft when he destroyed them had bothered the hell out of him—and still did. In the operational Bible Rowdy Yates carried in his head, the First Commandment was never ever to leave a comrade behind—even on a black op.

And Rowdy'd done his share of black ops. In the 1980s he'd slipped into Lebanon to hunt Islamic Jihad car bombers. He'd worked in El Salvador, where he stalked and killed one FMLN *comandante* who had ordered the assassination of Albert Schaufelberger, a Navy SEAL lieutenant commander, and another whose unit had murdered four Marines and two American civilians at a sidewalk café in San Salvador's Zona Rosa. In the nineties he'd been detailed to Sarajevo, where he worked covert countersurveillance against the Sepah-ē Pasdaran—Iran's terrorist-supporting IRGC, or Islamic Revolutionary Guard Corps—which targeted Western peacekeepers. In February 1999, he'd rendezvoused with six case officers from MIT[25] and a twenty-man element of Turkish Special Forces when they slipped into Kenya to capture Abdullah Ocalan, the head of the violent Kurdistan Workers Party, or PKK. And he'd been in the neighborhood, as they say, when p-p-p porky Pablo Escobar, the *jefe* of the Medellín cartel, had played the title role in *Bullet Sponge on a Hot Tin Roof*.

But this little jaunt was way beyond black. This really was *Mission: Impossible*. They were operating ultra-covertly. Capture was not an option—and neither was leaving anyone to be . . . identified. Rowdy understood the political implications of the mission all too well. Ritzik had

---

25. Milli Istihbarat Teskilati, Turkey's intelligence service.

even put it into words. Or hadn't. "You do whatever you have to do," he'd said. Rowdy had supreme confidence in his abilities. The mission was to get these people safely over the Tajik border. And he'd accomplish it, whatever it would take. Rowdy had a survival mind-set and it would carry them all through.

But there was always the unexpected to prepare for. Not to mention the arrival of Mr. Murphy just when you didn't need him. More to the point, two-plus decades of operating in the real world had shown Rowdy that you've always got to anticipate a worst-case scenario, and have something in your back pocket just in case it develops. Which was why while the rest of the party was otherwise engaged, Rowdy wired one of the shaped charges just forward of the 4×4's gas tank. The detonator was where he could reach it easily from behind the wheel. The end would be quick and pain-less. And identification? Let the forensic pathologists in Beijing try to figure it all out. The sons of bitches would have their work cut out for them, too: there were two spooks, six Delta shooters, and Wei-Liu. That bloody 4×4 was going to be more crowded than one of those little cars at the circus, the ones where a thousand clowns come pour-ing out. Body Partz "R" Us.

0956. "Kaz, keep your head down, goddammit." Rowdy chewed the end of his mustache, noting for the record that it was a very feeble substitute for his habitual cheekful of Copenhagen. Would these spooks ever learn? Movement gave you away. It didn't take much, either. Pilots were trained observers—like experienced hunters in the field. And when you hunted, you never tried to find a whole deer. You looked for an anomaly; something that wasn't sup-posed to be there. The flash of white when the buck flicked its tail. The sudden shift of light and shadow as a boar moved through a thicket toward water. The momentary glint of sun reflecting off the lens of a telescopic sight. Or the callow, upturned face of a dumb-as-rocks spook who'd heard the chopper but still wanted to see the frigging thing so his eyes could corroborate what his ears had just told him.

He'd positioned them well clear of the burning truck and smoldering chopper. They'd moved the MADM back down into the ravine and slid the damn thing into its crate, which they positioned ostentatiously at the rear of the truck. Rowdy made sure they tilted the damn thing so the heavy wooden box transporter sat with its yellow-and-black universal symbol for NUKE pointing skyward. No way the Chinese would miss that.

The 4×4 was a quarter mile to the west, on the far side of a narrow S-curve, sixty yards off the road and camouflaged so well that even Rowdy'd had a hard time spotting it from the ridge high above. The group was split in two. Rowdy, Wei-Liu, and the spooks were concealed on the northern ridge under a jagged outcropping, shielded by a small stand of knobby, wind-sheared evergreens and irregular clusters of nasty, thorned, dark green bushes that stood waist-high, crowned by reddish new growth. The rest of the Delta people were spread along the southern ridge. Their fields of fire would mesh right in the area some eighty yards away where the truck, the chopper, and the Chinese bodies lay. Rowdy'd kept one RPG launcher and four rockets. Doc and Goose had the other pair and all the remaining rockets.

The *whomp-whomp-whomping* of the chopper grew closer. And then the sound altered as Rowdy picked up the high-pitched whine of big twin turbine engines. And then, as the ground began to shake beneath him, he saw the big bird crest a hundred and fifty feet above the southern ridge, veer east, then slow as the pilot spied the battleground below.

He saw the flat, armored, humpbacked dual cockpits.

The stubby wings. The nose-mounted Gatling traversing side to side. The rocket pods. Christ, it was a HIND, a hunter-killer gunship.

The chopper rotated to give the pilot a better view of the scene. He descended to fifty feet above the ravine floor, edged closer to the burning HIP, rotated counterclockwise above the bodies of the Chinese soldiers, then maneuvered over the nose of the upended truck, passing not a hundred feet to the north of the MADM—although there was no outward indication that the pilot or gunner saw the nuke. What the hell did these guys need—flares? Then the pilot dropped the chopper's nose slightly, and proceeded to follow the road westward, its rotor wash creating a 360-degree tsunami of dust, stone, and loose brush.

"Everybody stay down . . . stay down . . . he's trying to pick up a scent." Rowdy released the transmit button, hoping he'd been heard over the chopper's screaming engines, watching as the HIND picked up speed, climbed a few hundred feet into the air, flew off to the east, then reversed course and backtracked, its armored-glass nose lowered to give the pilot and gunner the widest possible angle of vision.

Rowdy had a sudden urge to smile because this guy wasn't playing by the rules. Obviously, the Chinese pilot hadn't been made privy to this particular scenario, which was known in the Joint Forces Command war-game scenario list as "Special Situation Ambush No. 12," or "SSA-12." In "SSA-12," a "Red Force" chopper-borne hostile insertion element sees the bait set out by the "Blue Force" ambushers, lands, and is decimated. And guess what? In ten out of ten SSA-12 war-game simulations, the Red Force chopper always settles right where the Blue Force commander plans the ambush site. That is because at the Joint Forces Command, the outcome of war games is always decided in advance. The red team, known as OPFOR, or Opposing Force, always loses. Which, Rowdy knew, is why JFC war games were totally useless—except as résumé builders for dumb-ass generals.

In real life, as Rowdy knew from bitter experience, the enemy is seldom cooperative. In real life, the situation is always fluid and unpredictable. More to the point, it is always Murphy-rich. The one time Rowdy had been allowed to play the OPFOR bad guy in an SSA-12 scenario, he'd held a pair of chopper gunships back, out of sight of the LZ. When his landing force had been attacked, he'd unleashed the Cobras and decimated the ambushers. Which is when the generals running the exercise had stopped the war game and ordered him to replay the segment so their Blue Force ambushers would win.

The same principle applied here. Once they'd fired on the HIND, the Chinese gunner would know exactly where their positions were—and he could lay down a deadly rain of machine-gun and rocket fire on them from above.

So Rowdy had to hold fire, hoping the HIND would land once the pilot saw the MADM. The HIND's armor was virtually impervious to RPG and small-arms rounds. Only when it was on the ground—its wide twin exhausts and air intakes vulnerable to intensive RPG and rifle fire—could they immobilize the big gunship.

But Rowdy already knew the HIND wouldn't land—no more than a tank crew would abandon the safety of its armored cocoon in hostile territory to go examine something. It just wouldn't happen. No: once the Chinese pilot spotted the MADM, he would do what he had no doubt just done: radio for backup. Send for additional troops and EOD specialists.

Reinforcements were precisely what Rowdy didn't need. The sergeant major sighed. Another tidy war-game scenario shattered by messy real life. He pressed his transmit button. "He's gonna make another pass. When he does, if he hovers—or even if he slows down—shoot his exhausts out and take the sucker out so we can get the hell out of here."

1003. The HIND flew overhead on an easterly course. But it didn't descend, hover, or decelerate. Instead, it maintained a steady altitude of three hundred feet, flying parallel to the road—and well out of RPG range. After a quarter of a minute, it was out of sight. The engine scream diminished, and soon all Rowdy heard was the thumping of rotors. In less than a minute they, too, faded into the distance. But that didn't mean the son of a bitch wasn't coming back.

Rowdy eased himself out from cover and surveyed the scene below. What would Sun-Tzu do? Rowdy knelt, chewing on his mustache. And then he remembered exactly what the Master taught—and knew exactly what to do. "Force is like water: it has no consistent shape. Military genius is the ability to adapt force to your opponent during the fluidity of battle, even as water flows around the obstacles in its way."

"I have been an idiot," Rowdy said aloud, causing Wei-Liu and X-Man to look at him strangely and Kaz to snicker.

Rowdy looked in the tech's direction. "The Master says, 'Wisdom is not obvious. Those who can see subtlety will achieve victory.'"

The spook inclined his head in mock reverence: "I am an unworthy grasshopper."

Rowdy's hand moved in a Zen-like wave. "I forgive you your sins." And then he eased back under cover, lifted the RPG launcher onto his shoulder, aimed it in an easterly direction, and pressed the transmit button on his radio. "Loner, Loner, do you copy?"

THEY WERE LOW on fuel—Mick estimated twenty-five minutes' flight time left. Ritzik tried calling Rowdy to see if he'd managed to siphon the avgas out of the downed HIP. They'd need every bit to make it as far as the Tajik border, given the fact that they'd be carrying fifteen people and flying higher than the aircraft's safe operational ceiling. But the radios weren't working. Mick, pissed, said, "Sam?"

"Yo?"

"Pull my earpiece, will ya?"

"Sure." The spook reached across the console, yanked the soft foam plug, and draped the wire over the pilot's shoulder.

"Oh, that feels better." Mickey D swiveled his head. "Y'know, boss, these damn radios are no better than Polish suppositories."

Mick was a strange one. Ritzik understood that. But this was bizarre, even for him. "Huh?"

"This guy in Warsaw," Mick continued, "he's all plugged up. Y'know, whatchamacallit—constipated. So he goes to the doctor, who prescribes suppositories. The doc says, 'Use one of these twice a day for two days, then come back and see me.' The guy leaves. Three days later he's back, worse than ever. He says, 'Doc, those suppository things don't work worth a damn.'

"The doctor's shocked. 'Whaddya mean they don't work? I prescribed the most powerful suppositories available.' The patient says, 'Oh, yeah? Well, first of all they're hell to take—they're the size of horse pills. Swallowing 'em is just about impossible. Second, for all the good they did me, I could have shoved 'em up my ass.' "

"And your point is?"

Mick's eyebrows wriggled. "Problem with you blanket-heads is you have no sense of humor. You—"

"Mick—chopper. Ten o'clock." Sam pointed southeast.

Ritzik followed the spook's arm. It was the second HIND. It was closing. He didn't need this. "Mick—can you give us some altitude here?" He turned, on the verge of going aft to free up the machine gun, when he heard Rowdy's voice in his earpiece.

Pray long enough, Ritzik thought, *and every once in a while your prayers will actually be answered.* "Rowdy—Loner." Ritzik clapped his hands over his ears so he could make out what the sergeant major was saying. "Repeat-repeat." He listened intently for about twenty seconds. Then said, "Roger. I copy. Wilco. Loner out."

1005. Ritzik leaned forward so he could shout in Mickey D's ear. "He wants us to come in hot—strafe the ravine, then the southern ridge. Then he wants you to hover on the south ridge. I'll drop the ladder and we'll go out—look like an assault team. Sam will retrieve and stow the ladder once we're down. Then you drop behind the ridge—settle on the deck." He squeezed the pilot's shoulder. "Can do?"

"Coming in hot's no prob," Mick shouted back. He looked at the HIND. "The hovering may be a little rough, though." He wiggled his head back and forth. "Hey—somebody stick that Polish suppository back in my ear so I can hear the crap that son of a bitch is transmitting, okay?"

29

125 Kilometers East-Northeast of Tokhtamysh.
1008 Hours Local Time.

ROWDY YATES heard the HIP before he saw it. He'd scrambled the five Delta shooters off the southern ridge, ordering them to leave enough detritus behind so their positions still appeared to be manned. Then they'd all taken up counterambush positions on the north ridge. Doc Masland held down the left flank with one of the RPGs. Goose had the second launcher on the right. Rowdy, who kept Wei-Liu and the spooks close to him, commanded the center field of fire.

The HIP came in fast and low. It skimmed the north ridge, wheeled sharply, then laid suppressive fire fifty feet below the Americans. Rowdy could see Gene Shepard in the doorway, Chinese helmet on his head, working the machine gun, shell casings flying past his feet as he sprayed the ground. As the HIP had careened a hundred yards east of the truck, he detonated the shaped charge, which he'd run down into the ravine.

Even two hundred yards off, Rowdy still felt the heat and concussion. He peered through the thick black smoke. The explosion brought down two good-sized trees. Rowdy shot a quick, approving look at X-Man—the kid obviously knew his stuff.

Mick took the HIP through a series of evasive moves, swinging the chopper up and around and running southeast to northwest. Then he swung back for another strafing run. This time Gene worked the road, just south of the explosion. The rocky base of the southern ridge was shattered by withering machine-gun fire.

Rowdy scanned the horizon. "Loner—Rowdy. Where's the HIND?" He waited, but received no answer. Ritzik probably hadn't heard him—there was too much noise.

1010. The HIND's crew wanted to know what the hell was going on. That much was clear from the urgent tone of the transmissions. But Sam Phillips couldn't make out what was being asked. Nor could he answer. He'd done everything he'd been instructed to do: the IFF was transmitting, and he'd tried mouthing a few garbled words of Mandarin. But military jargon was military jargon, and he just didn't have any of it in his head. Jeezus H. Kee-rist. He was going to get them all killed.

1011. Mick rotated the HIP, then hovered fifty feet below the crest of the southern ridge. When the chopper had been stable for ten seconds, Ty Weaver tossed the assault ladder out of the port-side doorway. Gene Shepard was first man out. The tall, lanky Soldier lowered himself onto the rope ladder and started down rung by rung, fighting the stuttering hover of the chopper, the blast of rotor wash, and the swaying, unstable rungs. Ty followed. He'd left the heavy sniper's rifle behind. Instead, he carried the RPG launcher strapped across his back, the haversack of four rockets bumping up against it.

Ritzik held the top of the ladder to try to steady it. He

glanced up to see Sam Phillips clamber from the cockpit, then turned his attention back to the ladder. Ritzik grappled with the ropes, trying to steady them as Ty fought to keep his balance. The sniper was struggling under forty pounds of launcher and rockets that pulled him backward off the pendulous ladder.

1011:27. Mick caught a glimpse of the HIND. It had circled behind them and was approaching from the south. *How the hell long had it been there? Had they taken the bait, or were they lining up for a missile shot?*

In that instant he lost control of the big chopper for a second and a half. The HIP pivoted abruptly, rose six feet, then dropped a yard.

1011:28. The sudden movement bounced the sniper off the ladder. Ty fell backward. He landed atop Gene Shepard and knocked the lanky first sergeant loose. The two men dropped three yards, then landed in a heap. Ritzik watched as Shepard rolled off the sniper's inert body. Shepard looked up at Ritzik, who was frozen in the doorway.

1011:31. Ritzik screamed, "Sam—you pull the ladder up." Then he swung out of the door, grabbed the two heavy rails of the assault ladder, brought them together so he could get both his hands around them, then dropped like a stone, fast-roping the twenty feet to the ground without using his feet. By the time he'd landed there was smoke coming off the thick leather palms of his gloves.

1011:33. Ritzik looked down. Ty was breathing—so the fall hadn't killed him. But he'd landed hard on the weapons. Maybe knocked the breath clean out of him. Maybe worse. But no time to deal with it now. Quickly, Ritzik cut the launcher's sling in two and sliced through the right-hand shoulder harness of the rocket sack. Shepard gingerly rolled the sniper onto his side and eased the canvas strap off the inert man's shoulder.

1011:41. Ritzik looked up as he unslung the AK. The dark belly of the HIP pivoted, then swung away, revealing a shockingly blue sky. Shepard put his arm through the rocket sack, flipped it onto his back, and snatched up the launcher. Ritzik took Ty by the shoulder straps of his body armor and dragged him to cover.

The sniper's eyes opened and he tried to speak. But nothing came out but a gasp. Ritzik said, "We'll be back for you."

1011:52. Ritzik and Gino ran a jagged pattern just below the ridgeline until they reached the cover of trees. The two men threw themselves down and crawled until they had a clear view of the road below. Shepard reached back, plucked a rocket from the bag, jammed the rocket into the muzzle of the launcher, and hefted the assembly onto his shoulder. Then, careful to make sure that Ritzik was hunkered clear of the RPG's backblast area, he aimed the rocket halfway down the southern ridge and pulled the trigger.

1011:52. "X-Man—keep your glasses on the pilot. Give me a running commentary. I want to know every time he takes a breath." Rowdy's focus was on his RPG, but his peripheral vision picked up the HIND as the gunship reacted to Mick's maneuvering.

"Gotcha." The CIA man squinted into compact field glasses. "Pilot's looking down at his instruments, concentrating on something," X-Man said. "Can't see behind his visor, but his mouth is moving like hell."

The HIND slowly crested the southern ridge, not three

hundred yards from where Ritzik and Shepard lay. X-Man panned away from the gunship, catching Shepard as he fired the RPG. The spook followed the rocket's path with the binoculars.

1011:59. "Didja see that?" X-Man's voice was excited. "It was almost like he stuttered the goddamn chopper when the RPG blasted into the hillside." And then the spook ducked instinctively as the HIND's Gatling began to chew up the south ridge where the RPG had exploded.

"C'mon, c'mon, X. Sit-rep." Rowdy watched as the rounds walked down the ravine, debris flying. Suddenly the HIND yawed, then recovered. "X, goddammit, what's happening in the frigging cockpit?"

"Pilot just flipped up his visor. He's looking down into the ravine."

Rowdy found the gunship and settled the RPG's iron sights on the HIND as it rocked, then steadied itself. The big ship, he noted with some satisfaction, was cumbersome at slow speed. "C'mon, X—where's the John Madden?"

"He's scanning the ravine," X-Man said. "Coming down slightly. Oh, wait—he just shouted something into his mike. His lips are moving a mile a minute."

Rowdy settled the sights on the HIND's baffled air intakes, the muzzle of the RPG dropping evenly with the chopper.

"He's dropping some more. Talking. Oh, oh, oh—his eyes went wide. He sees the bomb now. He's—"

Rowdy shouted, "Execute! Execute! Execute!" into his mike.

There was about a three-quarter-second lag. And then all three RPGs fired in rapid sequence into the ravine, shrieking away from the launchers, trailing white smoke.

Masland's shot missed. The rocket struck the armored

glass of the HIND's forward cockpit. The impact shook the gunship but never penetrated the gunner's thick protective cocoon.

Through his field glasses, X-Man followed the smoke trail as the second round went wide, detonating against the shell of the burning truck. He watched, frozen, screaming, "Oh, shit," as the HIND's gunner manipulated the Gatling's muzzles up, up, up, and left, trying to swivel the gun in the direction the RPG rounds had come from.

And then Rowdy's big forearm smacked the spook's head from behind, the binoculars went flying, and X-Man was knocked to the ground.

Because Rowdy's rocket had found its mark: the big crate holding the MADM, and the Chinese Pentolite detonated with an even bigger explosion than Rowdy had dared to hope for.

The blast caught the belly of the HIND, blowing the gunship's stubby wing off. The chopper yawed right as the pilot reacted. Then a huge pressure wave hit the aircraft, and almost immediately, the HIND began to drop. Rowdy watched as the HIND's pilot fought with the controls, trying to stabilize his aircraft. But he couldn't. The Pentolite created a huge vortex of negative pressure, and the rotors couldn't bite air because there was literally no air to bite.

The HIND bucked, then dropped rocklike onto the ravine floor. The rotor tips hit the ground, disintegrating as they cut themselves into shrapnel.

Rowdy loaded another round into the launcher's muzzle, took aim, and fired at the chopper's exhaust vent. The round went wide. But it hit the aft portion of the aircraft squarely, exploding in a great bright flash, knocking the tail rotor off. The HIND spun once, centrifugally. And then the chopper sideswiped the smoldering truck and exploded in a huge, orange ball of fire.

The ordnance detonated, sending rockets and ammo spewing into the sky, trailing white smoke like so many fireworks. Rowdy could feel the intensity of the heat from where he lay. He rolled onto his side, looked over at Wei-Liu, and cracked a grin. "Nice work, Madam Deputy Assistant Secretary," Rowdy said. "Glad to see we're all still here—and ready to exfil."

Wei-Liu wiped dust from her face. She looked at Rowdy Yates. His eyes, for the briefest of instants, displayed a look of such utter relief that it shocked her. And then, like a curtain drawn, the vulnerability faded. She started to say something, but remained silent; drained. Incapable of words or emotions. She was exhausted. She barely had the energy to blink. She shook her head vacantly and monotoned, vaguely in the sergeant major's direction, "I'd really like a good night's sleep."

1013. Ritzik clambered to his feet, ducking involuntarily as half a dozen Gatling rounds popped like cherry bombs. He ran to the ridgeline and looked south, about four hundred yards, to where the HIP, resting precariously on its broken landing gear, idled. He raised both arms high above his head, fists clenched, thumbs extended. Then he turned, waved at the opposite ridge, and pressed his transmit button. "Rowdy, Loner. Get everybody over here so we can exfil ASAP."

Ritzik listened as the sergeant major growled something. Then he said, "Roger that, Rowdy. We have to refuel."

He turned toward the HIP. "Mick—did you copy that?" Ritzik watched as the big transport's rotors gained speed, and then the aircraft levitated gingerly, rose into the sky, and nosed eastward, crossing the ridge to where Rowdy had prepositioned the fuel bladder.

Ritzik clapped his hand to his ear so he could hear the

sergeant major's transmission. "Roger that," Ritzik said. "I'll bring Ty with me."

Ritzik scrambled back along the ridge to where he'd left the sniper. Ty was conscious. But it was obvious he was in tremendous pain. Ritzik looked down. "What's the prob, Ty?"

The sniper blinked. "Broken ribs, I think," he said between gritted teeth. "Oh, God, it hurts to breathe."

"Pain's good for you," Ritzik said. "Tells you you're still alive."

"Then I must be alive," Weaver said, "because I hurt like hell."

"You'll feel better when we get you to Dushanbe."

"Is there beer in Dushanbe?"

"Affirmative."

"Then you're right: I'll feel better in Dushanbe."

"Time to move out." Ritzik reached down. "Can you stand?"

The sniper grimaced. He took Ritzik's hand. His grip was strong. "We'll see, won't we, Loner?"

Epilogue

Six Weeks Later. The Great Hall of the People,
Beijing, People's Republic of China.
1540 Hours Local Time.

THE TREATY SIGNING was a bona fide media event, with
600 reporters and TV crews from all over the world. The
White House downplayed the summit, bringing less than a
hundred White House, State Department, and DOD
staffers. Despite a last-minute plea from the president, a
150-person CODEL[26] flew in on four of the Air Force's
most luxurious transports to represent the House and Sen-
ate leadership—a shameless publicity stunt according to
SECDEF Rockman, who did not accompany the president.
In marked contrast, the Chinese made sure that more than
9,500 of its officials were present in Beijing's Great Hall of
the People to witness the signing ceremony.

The American and Chinese presidents, the secretary of
state, and the foreign minister of the People's Republic sat
behind a simple rosewood table that had been positioned in
front of the speaker's dais in the main auditorium. Behind
them, six factotums hovered, ready to move the leather-

---

26. Congressional Delegation.

bound copies of the treaty, printed on thick vellum, as they were signed and the seals were affixed.

Mike Ritzik, Tracy Wei-Liu, and Sam Phillips, wearing credentials identifying them as White House staff, sat in the rear echelon of the American delegation, on the right-hand side of the auditorium. Their inclusion in the official party had been Pete Forrest's idea—a small but tangible reward for jobs well done. The sensors were working perfectly. And within days after SIE-1 had inserted them, the devices revealed that the Chinese were indeed testing ultra-low-yield nuclear weapons in the tunnels that ran thousands of feet below Lop Nur.

The summit and subsequent treaty signing was a one-day event. The president, wary of providing the Chinese with more than a limited diplomatic success, had insisted that his visit be brief. And so, Air Force One landed at Beijing's international airport at precisely eight in the morning. The big plane would depart at six for New Delhi, and a two-day summit with Naresh Chowdhery, the Indian prime minister. By ten past eight, Pete Forrest, accompanied by the first lady and the secretary of state and his wife, had begun the forty-five-minute motorcade into the city through the acrid, yellow-tinged air that gave most first-time visitors a mild case of bronchitis.

Sam Phillips, Ritzik, and Wei-Liu touched down nineteen minutes after the president along with the rest of the White House and State Department staff on the big silver-and-blue 747 that served as a backup plane for Air Force One. Once they'd run a gauntlet of Chinese officials and received their summit credentials (which were laminated inside in bright red plastic sleeves emblazoned with gold and intertwined with U.S. and PRC flags), they—and the traveling press corps—were herded onto a half-dozen boxy diesel buses. It took more than an hour and a half to creep through the morning rush-hour traffic into the gridlocked center of the Chinese capital, despite the fact that the convoy had a motorcycle escort of Chinese national police outriders shepherding them to the west side of the hundred-acre Tiennanmen Square, where the Great Hall of the People was located.

Pulling up just beyond the wide portico, the three were struck by the sheer, incredible, gargantuan scale of the place. The Great Hall—*Renmin Dahiutang* in Chinese—was designed in the Soviet neoclassical monumental style. According to Sam Phillips, who'd done the most homework, the Great Hall had been built in only ten months, from October 1958 to the end of August 1959, during the time known as Mao Zedong's Great Leap Forward. The building and its immediate grounds covered thirty-seven acres. The main auditorium, where Wei-Liu, Ritzik, and Sam Phillips would watch the signing ceremony, could hold just over ten thousand people on the vast floor and tiered balconies. The huge, domed ceiling with its immense red Communist star soared more than a hundred feet. Below the star, row upon row of curved wooden desks held earphones for simultaneous translation of speeches.

On either side of the main entrance were hung huge red-and-white banners, pledging, according to Sam, eternal friendship and an endless supply of cross-training footgear from the slave labor of China, to benefit the proletarian masses of the United States. Wei-Liu, highly dubious, checked with one of their Chinese minders, who explained that the banners were five-year-old exhortations to increase domestic production and exports. Sam insisted the minders had been brainwashed and were not to be trusted.

The Americans made their way inside through an oversized polished brass revolving door. The wide, shallow staircase leading to the first floor was carpeted with Ming-

dynasty antique rugs and lined with eight-foot-high cloi-
sonné vases dating from the mid-nineteenth century. Above
them hung a series of intricate crystal chandeliers two
yards across. At the top of the stairs, the delegation was led
into a lounge slightly smaller than the Rotunda of the U.S.
Capitol, where they were served a late breakfast while Pete
Forrest and Wu Min, the Chinese leader, held the first of
their two one-on-one meetings.

1547. The senior American delegates were ushered into the
Great Hall's main auditorium to the polite applause of the
nine thousand Chinese government apparatchiks recruited
as window dressing for the treaty signing. Ritzik scanned
the rows of men in olive green and the big uniform hats
reminiscent of Rittenhouse Square doormen for Major
General Zhou Yi, whose face he'd memorized from a DIA
briefing book. Zhou Yi was nowhere to be found. But his rival, Yin Zhong Liang, the commander of the Beijing Military District, was prominently positioned among the
Chinese dignitaries. Ritzik spent a few minutes watching
Yin. The general was obviously in a jovial mood, reflected
by his animated expression, smiling and laughing as he sat
with his Politburo colleagues waiting for the ceremony to
begin.

And then, the murmuring stopped and there were perhaps five or six seconds of absolute silence as the Chinese
and American presidents began the long march across the
patterned beige-and-green carpet onto the wide platform.
Before they'd gone three paces the ten thousand spectators
in the big auditorium erupted into applause.

1556. Pete Forrest pulled his chair up to the rosewood table,
turned his head to the left, and smiled warmly at Wu, who

returned the gesture. But behind the crinkly-eyed smiles and the deferential manner, Pete Forrest knew the Chinese leader was tough as woodpecker lips. A survivor. As an economics student he'd been thrown out of a second-story window by rampaging Red Guards in the late 1960s during Mao's so-called Cultural Revolution. Wu still walked with a noticeable limp. Initially he'd been denied medical treatment because as a graduate student he was deemed an elitist and sent, compound fracture and all, to a reeducation camp in Hunan Province. In the late seventies, after the death of Mao Zedong, he was recruited by Deng Xiaoping's son, with whom he had been in reeducation, to join the Ministry of State Security, China's vast intelligence apparatus. Under Deng's protection, he advanced quickly. He'd been ruthless during the 1989 Tiennanmen demonstrations. By the early nineties, Wu had become the MSS's powerful vice-chairman.

Pete Forrest had seen a copy of Wu Min's secret twenty-five-year plan for the PRC, so he knew the Chinese leader was committed to building the People's Republic into a twenty-first-century military and economic superpower. That single-mindedness explained why Wu was already cheating on the treaty that was being put in front of them right now.

Wu's rapid Chinese interrupted Pete Forrest's thoughts. The American interpreter leaned into the president's right ear. "President Wu says he is overcome with happiness that this historic day has finally arrived. It is a great leap forward between our two peoples."

Pete Forrest noted the symbolism of the language, looked into the Chinese president's opaque eyes, and said, "I, too, am delighted that this ceremony could finally take place after such long and ultimately fruitful negotiations."

He waited until the translation had finished, then rose and solemnly offered Wu his hand. The Chinese stood. Wu enveloped President Forrest's hand between his own two. There was a flurry of shutters and a crescendo of applause as the two men, eye to eye, shook hands and smiled professionally for the cameras. Then, to a second rousing ovation, they were joined on the platform by the American secretary of state and the Chinese foreign minister.

At precisely four o'clock the leaders were presented with four copies of the treaty for signature. There were two in Chinese and two in English. Each nation would keep one copy in each language. The documents were secured in leather folders, stamped in gold with the Great Seals of the United States and the People's Republic of China.

Pete Forrest laid two dozen pens, each bearing the presidential seal, on the table before him. He would use all of them to sign these worthless pieces of paper. A couple would be given to the senators who'd help to scuttle the treaty during the upcoming hearings. One would go to Rocky Rockman; another to Monica Wirth. One or two others would be slipped to big political contributors. But the majority would go to those covert warriors who'd returned safely from Tajikistan, having put their lives and their careers on the line in defense of the United States. It was the least he could do to demonstrate his gratitude—the nation's gratitude.

Behind him, the factotums began to pass the documents out for signature. Pete Forrest looked out at the sea of faces. He glanced at Monica Wirth, prominent in the front row, her body language a cheerful, animated counterpoint to that of the glum, rumpled director of central intelligence sitting next to her. And then he scanned the crowd until he located Ritzik, Wei-Liu, and Sam Phillips. They sat at the very rear of the American delegation, directly in front of a cluster of taciturn, olive-clad Chinese military officers.

The president gazed for some seconds as the trio, in oblivious, animated conversation, peered around the cavernous auditorium like tourists. And then he experienced a sudden and decidedly unpresidential lump in his throat. Watching those youngsters overwhelmed Pete Forrest, nearly made him tear up, because he understood how clearly they represented the best America had to offer, and how much he respected their character and their integrity, qualities recently demonstrated with initiative, courage, and persistence.

Sam Phillips glanced in the president's direction and caught him staring. The spook nudged Wei-Liu, who elbowed Ritzik. The three of them waved at him, all smiles. Impetuously, the president winked back. Ritzik threw him a thumbs-up. A split second later he was joined by Phillips and Wei-Liu.

A wide, spontaneous grin lit up Pete Forrest's face. Then he raised his right arm and returned the gesture to a barrage of strobe lights.

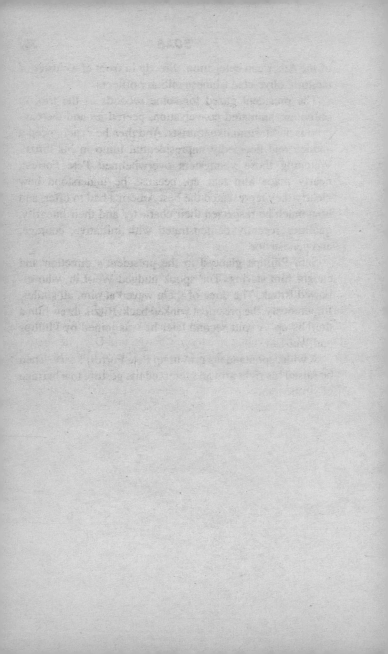

From the *New York Times* bestselling author who "takes the reader into the very heart of CIA and Special Operations" (Robert Baer) comes

JACK IN THE BOX,

a knife-edge tale of international intrigue and covert spy craft and the chilling follow-up to *SOAR*.

Edward Lee Howard, the only CIA officer to defect to the KGB, redefects with incredible charges against the President of the United States. But, before the traitor's stunning allegations can be verified, Howard disappears. Then he turns up dead. Are Howard's accusations real? That's the enigma former CIA Moscow station chief Sam Waterman must solve. Traveling to Moscow, Paris, and D.C., he struggles to unravel a conspiracy involving a mole in the highest reaches of government while friends and enemies die around him. Filled with cutting edge tradecraft, *Jack in the Box* uses actual CIA operations and gets deep inside the Amercian intelligence community as few novels ever have.

1

FRIDAY, OCTOBER 23, 1998*

Sam Waterman spent the morning of his forty-fifth birthday a hostage to his profession, stuffed rudely onto the rear floorboard of one of the consulate's 1985-vintage four-door Zil sedans, the driveshaft hump wedged uncomfortably against his kidneys, his long legs tucked fetal, his body hidden under a damp blanket. Even though he knew he couldn't be seen through the dark-tinted windows, he still held his breath as the car clunked over the antiterrorist barriers just prior to passing the Russian police checkpoint outside the garage gate. He exhaled slowly when the driveshaft under his side whined as the car merged into the late morning traffic.

"Keep going, keep going," Sam instructed tersely from under musty cover. "Don't check your mirrors. Just drive. Nice and easy."

"Don't have a cow, man." That was Consular Officer Tom Kennedy, imitating Bart Simpson. Tom, who'd been recruited to do the driving, could impersonate Bart perfectly. He was still working on his Homer, though, running and rerunning the videotapes his sister sent him through the mail pouch, night after night after night. Which kind of told you what Moscow's social life had to offer a reasonably good-looking African-American junior-grade diplomat, even in these post-Soviet days.

Sam grunted and shifted his position slightly, trying to reduce the pressure on his kidneys as the car turned left, heading west.

"We're on Kutuzovsky Prospekt," Homer told him. "*Doh.* Crossroads of the world."

"Tom, put a cork in it." Christ, he'd warned the kid this was serious business, and the youngster still wanted to talk. Not good. Because they weren't safe. Not by a long shot. FSB,[1] the Russian internal security agency, had inherited the KGB's elaborate passive surveillance system. *Vizirs* they were called—long-range, high-power telescopes mounted on sturdy tripods, positioned in buildings along Moscow's major thoroughfares. The watchers would scan for diplomatic plates, and peer inside the cars. If they saw your lips moving, they'd take note. Were you talking to someone hidden in the car? Were you operating a burst transmitter in the open briefcase on the passenger seat? Were you broadcasting? If they thought you were up to no good, they'd dispatch one of the static counterintelligence teams that were all over the city to do a traffic stop—dip plates or no.

And Sam couldn't afford a traffic stop. Not today.

Today he had to meet General Pavel Baranov at precisely five past one, and failure wasn't a viable option. The rendezvous was critical. Baranov had used his emergency call-out signal, an inconspicuous broken chalk line on a weatherworn lamppost sixty yards from the entrance to the Arbatskaya metro stop. Sam had seen the *long-short-short* Morse code signal last night on his regular evening jog—a five-mile run that began outside the embassy's faded

[1] *Federal'naya Sluzhba Bezopasnosti*

mustard-colored walls and took a long, meandering, but un-
failingly consistent route that brought him all the way to the
western boundary of the Kremlin, and thence back toward
the embassy.

The Arbatskaya signal site and the letter D were to be
used by Baranov only under crisis conditions. Still in his
running gear, Sam sent Langley a code-word-secret "criti-
com," an urgent cable alerting his division chief to Baranov's emergency signal (in the cable Sam referred to
Baranov not by his true name, but by his CIA cryptonym,
GTLADLE; Sam's CIA in-house pseudonym, which he
used to sign the cable, was Cyrus N. PRINGLE).[2] In it, he
enumerated all the operational details for the emergency
PMP[3] and requested comment. Today he was awake by five,
running and rerunning the operation in his mind. By six he
was in the office, checking for response from Langley—there
was none, which was typical—and removing gear from the
duffel he kept in ▮▮▮▮▮▮▮▮▮ walk-in safe.

The next step was to shanghai young Tom Kennedy, one
of three greenhorn consular officers Sam had identified as
potential decoys. The decoy factor was critical. As CIA's
Moscow chief, Sam was "declared" to the Russians. He
even held regular meetings with his counterparts at SVR,
the Russian foreign intelligence service. And thanks to an
American defector, a CIA turncoat named Edward Lee
Howard who'd been transferred into FSB, Russia's internal
security and counterintelligence service by Vladimir Putin,
the Kremlin's aggressive new director of counterintelligence, FSB pretty much knew who was Agency and who
wasn't.

---

[2]CIA in-house pseudonyms are invariably three-part names: first name,
middle initial, and last name. The last name is always spelled entirely in
capital letters.
[3]Personal Meeting Plan.

Ed Howard and Sam Waterman had history. In fact, sometimes Sam felt as if the traitor was shadowing him. He and Howard had been members of the same basic Russian-language studies class at Georgetown University. Subsequently, Howard sat next to Sam at the CIA's language institute in Rosslyn during the two-year, advanced Russian course. They'd even shared a room at ▮▮▮▮▮▮▮▮, the Agency's case-officer training facility near Williamsburg also known as the Farm, for the six-week class in advanced tradecraft procedures required of all case officers assigned behind the Iron Curtain.

But that's where the relationship stopped. As he readied himself for his first Warsaw Pact tour, Sam was already an experienced case officer with a successful tour in Germany. He'd run an agent network and worked against a KGB *Rezident*. Howard was a greenhorn trainee who had never handled an agent or worked in the pressure cooker atmosphere of a real-world op.

Despite that lack of experience, Howard had been selected to go to Moscow under deep State Department cover. But then, in the spring of 1983, Ed Howard flunked four separate polygraph tests—and his career was abruptly terminated.

On May 2, 1983, Howard was told to report to the personnel office. Sam had even seen him in the corridor. The distraught young case officer was flanked by two armed CIA security agents. Later, Sam heard that when Howard got to personnel, he was given papers to sign, fired on the spot, and escorted from the building. Although Howard and his wife Mary moved back to their home in New Mexico almost immediately, he was kept on CIA payroll through the end of June. Sam never saw him again.

Then Howard started acting strangely. From New Mexico, a distraught-sounding Howard made open-line telephone calls to the U.S. embassy in Moscow that let KGB eavesdroppers know that he was a disgruntled CIA employee who'd just been fired. After half a dozen similar provocations, including two trips to Vienna, where CIA countersurveillance teams had spotted the former case officer meeting with known KGB officers, the FBI was called in. Howard was interrogated half a dozen times but denied any collusion with the Soviets. The FBI didn't believe him and assigned twenty-four-hour surveillance to the fired CIA operative. His arrest seemed imminent.

But the FBI blew the case. The surveillance crew assigned to Howard were New Mexico locals who never factored into their operations that Howard had been trained to evade KGB surveillance. It didn't take the former CIA trainee long to note their below-average performance. And so, Ed Howard used basic CIA tradecraft to evade the G-men. Late in September 1985, he and his then-wife fabricated a jack-in-the-box device for their car, then went for a drive along a route he had carefully worked out. Once she'd put sufficient distance between their vehicle and the FBI agents to open a GAP, she slowed down. Howard jumped out and hid in some bushes. His wife activated the JIB, sped away, returned home, drove straight into the garage, and dropped the door. It took the FBI almost twenty-four hours to realize Howard had skipped.

In the meanwhile, Howard flew from Albuquerque through Tucson to New York, where caught a plane for London. At Heathrow, he connected to a flight for Copenhagen, and thence to Helsinki, where he went straight to the Soviet embassy and asked for political asylum. Six days later, using reports from an MI6 source in Helsinki, British counterintelligence cabled Langley's CI[4] gumshoes that Howard had handed the KGB a foot-thick pile of documents. The

---

[4]Counterintelligence

double-crossing son of a bitch even betrayed (among many other jewels) all the Agency tradecraft he'd learned during the "Denied Area Operations" course required of all case officers assigned to Moscow, Prague, Warsaw, Paris, Bonn, Delhi, and other stations where local counterintelligence capabilities were exceptional and the opposition was active.

Howard presented the DAO course syllabus to his new masters at Moscow Center as evidence of his bonafides. He'd immediately been put to work at the KGB's Second Chief Directorate—counterintelligence, followed by a long tour in the First Chief Directorate, where he trolled much of Western Europe for American agents. And now the rotten son of a bitch spent his days working for Vlad Putin at the FSB, using everything he'd learned at Langley against his former colleagues.

Which meant whenever one of Sam's people drove, surveillance was virtually guaranteed. So Sam went outside the box and used an outsider, a junior consular officer Vlad Putin's FSB understood to be totally uninvolved in intelligence gathering.

At 9:06 A.M., Sam strode unannounced into the expansive office of Sandra Wheeler, the consul general. At 9:12 he returned to his own secure ▇▇▇▇▇▇▇. Seven minutes after that, there was a tentative knock on Sam's thick door. *Enter Thomas Jefferson Kennedy, Foreign Service Officer Grade Four, stage left.* Twelve minutes later, a wide-eyed Thomas J. Kennedy headed for the garage, having received his first inculcation into the shadowy Wilderness of Mirrors in which Samuel Elbridge Waterman had lived and worked for almost nineteen years.

10:38 A.M. The drivetrain had developed a nasty vibration. Sam could feel it shudder through the floorboard. He was sweating even though the Zil's heater didn't work. He lay silent, eyes closed, counting the seconds off, timing the route he'd painstakingly devised, as Tom drove in blessed silence. They'd be heading northwest now, less than a kilometer from the Ring Road that encircled the city. At the Volokolamskoe on-ramp they'd turn north, toward the M10 and Moscow's Sheremetevo airport.

But they wouldn't go to Sheremetevo. Instead, the youngster would exit south, onto Leningradskoe, and divert to a narrow, deserted strip of parkland where Sam would roll out. Then Tom would drive like hell to the airport, where he'd wait in the no-parking zone —in vain—for a consular official scheduled to arrive from Berlin. And, yes, tickets had been bought. There was even a Russian visa stamped in the nonarrival's diplomatic passport just in case the Russians ever checked. Sam had thought of everything, right down to the smallest detail. "Plausible" and "denial," after all, were the two foremost watchwords of his particular faith.

Sam squinted at the dim luminous dial on his cheap Bulgarian wristwatch. Thirty-nine minutes had elapsed since the car passed through the embassy gates. The Zil banked hard right. In his head, Sam saw the exit and the industrial zone. He felt Tom brake, accelerate, then brake again. *Showtime.* Sam pulled the blanket off, reached up, opened the rear door, and scrambled out next to the pockmarked brick wall of a narrow alley. He rapped the Zil's door. "Go-go-go!"

Alone, he made his way southwest toward a narrow swath of green parkland. He checked the watch. He was two minutes behind schedule.

10:52 AM. Sam caught the sparsely passengered ferry with seventy-five seconds to spare, paid his ticket, and found a hardwood bench in the rear of the smoky passenger cabin for the six-minute voyage to Zaharkovo. Halfway

across, he went to the men's toilet. Even unheated, the
cramped compartment stank of urine. He stepped across a
puddle under the tin trough that served as a pissoir, entered
the single stall, shut the door, and quickly shed his long
black nylon overcoat. Underneath, he wore a thigh-length
brown patchwork leather jacket. He stuffed the coat behind
the toilet. He extracted a false mustache from its envelope,
exposed the adhesive, and affixed the disguise to his upper
lip. He ripped up the envelope and flushed it. Finally, he
pulled a short-brimmed, green wool cap from the jacket
pocket and jammed it on his head.

He left the men's room just in time to feel the engines reverse as the boat pulled alongside the quay. Without reen-
tering the cabin, he elbowed his way to the rail, nudged up
the gangway, walked up the dock and across the street.
There he climbed aboard a waiting No. 96 bus, which he
rode to the Tušinskaja metro stop. Sixty-nine minutes and
three train changes later he emerged from Textilshchiki station, crossed the road, and stepped gingerly over a single,
rusting set of railroad tracks into a huge, deserted industrial
park where, in the old days, they'd assembled Moskvich
automobiles as part of Joe Stalin's workers' paradise.

What Sam had performed since leaving the Zil was an
SDR, or Surveillance Detection Route. It was a planned,
timed course during which he'd had half a dozen opportu-
nities to spot a hostile tail. Not to shake it, however, simply
to identify it. Only in Hollywood did CIA officers *shake* a
tail. In real life, you *spotted* the opposition. Under normal
circumstances you did nothing to alert them, because if the
other side realized they'd been tagged, they'd change surveillance methods, and the cycle would have to begin all
over. Today's SDR was different. If he'd been spotted, he'd
have had to go provocative—escape surveillance by using
aggressive, evasive tradecraft. That was why Sam had spent

six weeks crafting each segment of this particular SDR, even though he'd use it only once.

Six weeks, because he had to provide himself a number of rabbit holes in case he had to disappear. Six weeks, because he had to make sure that no matter where he might be pinged, he could still go black—vanish in plain sight— without alerting the opposition. Most important, six weeks, because Vlad Putin's counterintelligence people were good. They didn't have the fourth-generation infrared sensors used by American CI gumshoes, or the state-of-the-art, ambient-noise filtering directional microphones built for CIA's countersurveillance teams by National Security Agency audioespionage specialists; instruments that could pick up a whisper across a busy intersection at distances of up to ■ meters. But what the Russians lacked in technical means they more than made up for in human resources. The FSB could put a hundred and fifty people on one American case officer. Putin liked to use multiple teams and sophisticated methods, like the Дохдъ,[5] or rainfall technique, in which scores of watchers were monsooned against a target from all directions. But not today. Today Sam was clean. His finely tuned sonar hadn't picked up even the hint of a ping.

Sam walked until he reached an alley containing a row of corrugated, sheet-metal gated sheds where Muscovites bribed the watchmen in hard currency so they could keep their autos under roof. The deserted streets leading to these shanties resembled a ghost town. But even if they had been crowded, no one would have paid Sam any mind, because the tall, gray-eyed man looked like any other local.

Careful to avoid getting mud on his scuffed shoes, he stepped around a rusted Latta with a tarp spread under the

[5]*Dosht'.*

rear of its chassis. There were two blue-jeaned legs poking out. Sam's knuckles rapped the Latta's hood. "Yuri Gregorovich, is that you under there, or should I call the police?"

Yuri G. Semerov rented the shed next to his. Yuri, Sam knew (the Russian had been checked out by Langley to ensure he wasn't a provocateur), owned a store near the Arbat, where he sold everything from fake czarist antiques to Soviet Army uniforms.

The legs crabbed from under the vehicle, followed by a torso, then a thick arm holding a big crescent wrench, and finally a broad, flat, mustached Tartar face that peered warmly up at Sam. "Hello, Sergei Anatolyvich."

So far as Yuri Gregorovich Semerov knew, Sergei Anatolyvich Kozlov was an up-and-coming businessman with an unhappy marriage in Moscow and a mistress in a dacha near Podol'sk. And if he'd checked—something Sam knew he hadn't—Sam's cover would have been confirmed. "Long time no see. How's it going?"

"Any better I couldn't stand it," Sam answered effortlessly in Moscow-accented Russian. It was a gift. Some people have a natural aptitude for mathematics, or science. Others are innate painters, or musicians. Sam had an ear for languages. He learned them quickly and retained them. He spoke Russian at a five-plus level, in addition to four-plus French, and workable German, Polish, and Czech. To get any better rating in Russian he'd have had to be born in the Soviet Union. Sam focused on Yuri Semerov and smiled mischievously. "Anytime I escape to Podol'sk for a few hours, life is great."

"I can imagine," Yuri said wistfully. He pulled himself into a sitting position and brandished the wrench. "Hey, have you got a number thirteen socket in there? This piece of shit won't catch on what's left of my tailpipe bracket bolt."

"I'll look." Sam withdrew a bunch of keys attached to a chain clipped to his belt. He squinted until he selected the right three, then unlocked a trio of padlocks the size of paperback books. The locks were carefully placed back on their hasps, then he scraped the battered door across the wet ground and disappeared inside.

There was silence for about forty seconds. What Yuri couldn't see was Sam retrieve a small electronic device from his jacket and quickly check the car for listening devices or locator beacons. The Russian heard only the sounds of an ignition stammering, followed by the hiccupping ca-ca-ca-coughs of an engine starting up, followed by half a dozen puffs of gray-black smoke emanating from the shed. Finally, Yuri watched as a beat-up Zhiguli coupe with local plates backed out onto the uneven dirt, sputtering and backfiring as it jerked clear of the shed.

Sam opened the car door and eased his big frame out from behind the wheel, his hand still playing with the choke. "I'll look for the socket for your Bentley while my Ferrari warms up."

Thirty seconds later he was back. "Nothing," Sam said. "I must have taken them home." He wrestled with the shed door, slapped the hasps closed, and replaced the padlocks. "Sorry, Yuri Gregorovich."

"No problem." Yuri watched as Sam compressed himself into the car. *Lucky bastard*, he thought, *to have a piece of ass on the side*. Then Yuri G. Semerov rolled onto his back and pulled himself under the Latta, cursing the cheap Georgian wrench as he heard the Zhiguli's engine grind off into the distance.